About the Author

Chris Bailey-Green was born in Suffolk in 1973. He spent almost twenty years in the police, both as a civilian member of staff and a police officer, before leaving to become a full time writer. He has a degree in philosophy and lives in the middle of the Norfolk countryside with his wife and assorted animals. *The Write Stuff* is his second novel. He can be followed on Twitter @CBGreen9

The Write Stuff

Chris Bailey-Green

The Write Stuff

Olympia Publishers
London

www.olympiapublishers.com
OLYMPIA PAPERBACK EDITION

Copyright © Chris Bailey-Green 2019

The right of Chris Bailey-Green to be identified as author of
this work has been asserted in accordance with sections 77 and 78 of the
Copyright, Designs and Patents Act 1988.

All Rights Reserved

No reproduction, copy or transmission of this publication
may be made without written permission.
No paragraph of this publication may be reproduced,
copied or transmitted save with the written permission of the publisher, or in
accordance with the provisions
of the Copyright Act 1956 (as amended).

Any person who commits any unauthorised act in relation to
this publication may be liable to criminal
prosecution and civil claims for damage.

A CIP catalogue record for this title is
available from the British Library.

ISBN: 978-1-78830-445-0

This is a work of fiction.
Names, characters, places and incidents originate from the writer's imagination.
Any resemblance to actual persons, living or dead, is purely coincidental.

First Published in 2019

**Olympia Publishers
60 Cannon Street
London
EC4N 6NP**
Printed in Great Britain

Dedication

For Debbi who continues to make it all possible and without whom there would be nothing.

One
Midge

My father was killed in a car crash before I was born, so I was told; naturally I didn't know anything about it as I was far too preoccupied at the time with being born. It is best to say that my relationship with my father was somewhat distant.

'I'm sure he didn't mean to do it,' my mother had said to me when I was older, as if it was something that he had really had all that much of a choice in. I hadn't considered the possibility that it might have been a suicide mission up until that point.

I always felt that I had a strained relationship with my mother. She was a little busy doing her own thing for most of her life and primarily took most of her time in denying that the ages were marching on and taking her with it. Each day it seemed that she had discovered some new fad that was designed to make her appear twenty years younger, or some such fallacy. She never liked to introduce me as her son because the older I got the older it made her seem. We were distant somewhat and our relationship was a little tense, but at the end of the day she was still my mother.

I was all the more surprised, therefore, that when I came home from university one day, I found that my mother had moved house without telling me. I am not entirely sure who was the most shocked by this, myself, the new occupiers that I had stumbled upon when I had made my way to the bathroom; or the police that they had called when they thought that I was a burglar intent on sexual deviance.

This all comes much later though. I suppose I ought to put things into a more chronological order so that it's easier for you to understand as well as for myself to remember.

***

I was born in 1980 at the same time as the musical genius of John Lennon was shot down on a cold winter's street in New York. In many ways my mother who was something of a hippy and a great Lennon fan seemed to connect my entrance into the world with John's exit, and she never appeared to forgive me for it for as long as I knew her.

She never said anything directly to me about this, of course, but it was just an impression that I got when she would play Lennon albums loudly and weep into her lager whilst looking at me with darting looks.

This may seem a little irrational, but I always assumed that at the time she was labouring with me she was also labouring with the grief of the death of my father, who around the same time, had seen fit to drive his Ford Capri into a tree. He might easily have survived this accident were it not for the fact that this was before compulsory seatbelt laws, so I am told he carried on with the journey at the time that the car decided to abruptly stop. If nothing else he was a good advertisement for road safety.

I suppose that it makes it sound like he chose to drive the car into the tree in the first place. The truth of the matter is that I don't know if he intended to do it, or whether it was an accident; nobody knows what his intentions were on that night. I have no idea what went through his mind at the time of the collision; other than the obvious bits of windscreen, I suppose.

I suppose that it is possible that it was a deliberate thing. Perhaps finding out that his girlfriend was pregnant was too much for him to take. Facing a life with my mother might have proven to be too difficult for him and so he had decided that it would be better if he became close friends with a tree. I don't know.

You might think that is all rather callous of me, and you would be right. It's part of my defence mechanism of dealing with the fact that I never knew who my father was and he never played a part in my life due to being, well dead for it. If he had decided to stay around then there is a chance that I would have developed a completely different relationship with him than the one that I was ultimately fated to have. I often asked my mother about my father in some desperate attempt to understand my roots and where it was that I was coming from and perhaps to understand the events that led him to his death that night. However, getting my mother to be pinned down to anything factual was the equivalent of trying to nail fog to a brick wall. Talking about my father was something that was top of her list of things that she didn't like doing and I assumed she resented his death and blamed him for it a great deal. She might well have blamed me for it as well. She seemed to blame me for a lot of things in her life.

My name is an example of the kind of mistake that has dotted throughout my life. My mother would tell you that my birth was a troublesome occasion. I am sure that it was a great inconvenience to her to have to go through such a painful experience following the pleasure of having sex. She never outwardly said as much, but I always suspected that this was the case. I was premature and heavily underweight and frail with skin that was transparent. I was probably premature because I had either had enough of being trapped in the womb for as long as I had been, or more likely my mother had decided that she had all that she could take of carrying this tumour around inside of her and it was time that it ended. She probably willed me to be born.

I was taken away from her as swiftly as possible (which probably pleased her) and was whisked straight into an incubator where various doctors and nurses tried to do their best to ensure that I would grow up to continue to benefit from the services offered by the National Health Service. Being a time when religion seemed to matter more than it does today the medical staff were of the unanimous opinion that I was just not going to survive as I lacked the determination and perseverance that is most associated with living. They therefore approached my mother with a view to asking her if she would consent to me being baptised and if so, did she have a name in mind for me?

My mother with her typical attitude to life had still been slightly medicated and tripping off with the fairies, probably entirely unaware that she had a son to her name. She apparently took one look at her recently deflated body and muttered:

'Gym!'

And so it was that I was called Jim; a name arisen from the desire to keep fit and regain your former form.

When my mother eventually came to her senses (if that can be referred to as an accurate assessment) she discovered two things. Firstly, that she had for the first time in her life something, or someone that she had to be responsible for. Responsibility was not the biggest word in her vocabulary. Having come to some degree of acceptance of the situation as it presented itself to her she objected strongly to the fact that I was named 'Jim'. She could not equate that any child of hers would have such a name that was, well so ordinary. She immediately decided that she would reverse the situation and name me something else. All the authorities informed her that it was a little too late to be able to reverse the situation and like me, the name was something that she was stuck with. Never believing that she couldn't reverse things she took the step of reversing my name of 'Jim' to that of 'Mij.' She took this phonetically, and from that day to this I was referred to as 'Midge.' I suppose that this was not as bad as it could have been as given my mother's hippy tendencies she could just as easily have named me 'Moonbeam' or 'Sunflower' or a whole host of other names that I dread and shudder to think about even now.

I never really liked my name though and did toy with the idea of changing it when I became old enough to do so. The problem with that was up until then everyone had known me as Midge, or Jim if they were being formal, and I couldn't imagine being called anything else and I couldn't really be arsed to go through the hassle of telling everyone that I had changed my name and they would have to get used to calling me something else from now on. I suppose a third point was that I also couldn't think of another name that I would like to be called. Names are like tattoos, in my opinion, you have to be very careful of your choices because you will then be stuck with them for a very long time indeed. This is chiefly the reason why I don't have any tattoos, I could never actually make up my mind about what I would have that I wasn't entirely convinced that I wouldn't regret having five years, or more, down the line.

Sometimes we are just stuck with the choices that are made for us in life; sometimes they are choices that we make ourselves that we have to live with and at other times we just have to live with the choices that other people make on our behalf.

So, there I was in an incubator spending the first part of my life looking at the world out of a plastic box. Thankfully, I can't remember all that much about this time in my life, but it is probably around this time that I developed my fear of Tupperware. Well, who am I kidding? I can't remember anything about this period of my life. Who does? If I did remember anything from this period in my life, then I would be nothing short of a genius really.

This sets me thinking about first memories. I have always been amazed by people who can tell you the first thing that they remember. They talk about being in a cot, perhaps playing with a toy; or maybe some traumatic incident that effects the course of the rest of their life. I remember nothing at all. I have absolutely no idea what my first true memory is. The thing about memory is that it has a habit of playing tricks on you. Sometimes we can become absolutely convinced of the truth of a memory that is entirely fabricated and we will never believe anyone who tries to tell us anything to the contrary.

What's my point? I will tell you.

It is that if I did have a first memory then I couldn't in all honesty be sure of the accuracy of it. That's my cautionary warning when it comes to autobiographies – don't believe a word of it. There are, in my opinion two types of autobiography; the first is the one which is a blazon lie where the writer paints themselves the way that they would prefer to remember things and the way that they would prefer you to see them and remember them.

The second type is the one where they think they are being genuine and honest when in reality they have no idea if what they are telling is an accurate memory, or a false one. It is not their intention to mislead, but it is the result that is inescapable.

I suppose there is also the third type of autobiography which is the so-called 'celebrity' autobiography, namely the one that they have not so much as read, let alone written.

At any rate despite the prognosis from the medical team that were looking after me though I began to gain in strength and build up my energy. Outside of my mother I began to thrive and flourish. I was not entirely ready to give up matters now that I had finally arrived. It was around about this time that I developed a lifelong interest in being ill.

I came into the world the way that most of us tend to arrive and leave it – screaming. In many regards there are those amongst us who come into the world screaming and then never stop until the moment they die. Some people just demand to be listened to and they are invariably the kind of people that are not worth listening to.

***

Taking all of this into consideration it is rather difficult to put the early pieces of my life together. I suppose this is tainted by the rather extravagant nature of my mother who failed to live life to any degree of what might be referred to as 'normal'.

'What's normal?' she once said when the very topic of normality was brought up. I don't think she was being clever or making a social point, I genuinely don't think she knew what normal was.

Whereas on the one hand I applaud the nature of this sentiment and desire to stand out from the crowd, I do believe that there are limits to most things in life and if nothing else my mother didn't know what her limits were. When it came to normality, if she thought there was even the smidgeon of a suggestion of normality creeping into her life, then she would march steadily in the opposite direction as far as it was possible to go. She thought this gave her individuality and creativity; the majority of everyone else just thought that it made her weird.

It wasn't until later in my life that I came to understand my mother's background and why she was the way that she was. I will explain all that when I get to a more appropriate place in all of this. I am not saying that there is anything particularly wrong with the chosen lifestyle that my mother decided to take on, but there were times throughout my childhood when I really did long for normality.

People like my mother may have seen normality as boring; but when you are growing up in an inner city school then normality was the safety curtain behind which you could hide and blend into the crowd. Standing out from the crowd meant bullying. Nobody ever picks on the one that blends in with the rest and is 'normal'. In many regards it might have been good to stand out from the crowd when you were older and could stand on your own two feet without short trousers and a snotty nose; but it was not something that was desired when you were growing up and your mother was the strangest person that anyone knew.

Those that went to my school were cruel and harsh and the pupils were not much better. Children, it has been said, can be cruel. This is very true and certainly the case when I was growing up. Most people say that you shouldn't blame the kids you should blame the parents. I can see the logic of this and in many cases the parents are certainly the chief cause of blame. However, on saying that there are also some children out there that are just evil, vindictive little bastards; trust me on this, I speak from experience. The amount of times that I have heard people saying:

'Oh no, you can't blame them, they are just innocent little children. They're not to blame.'

They say this with the confidence that children can't be Nazis of their own volition. They can be. I have met some evil little wankers in my life and in some cases, they would grow up to be racists, football hooligans and politicians. In other cases they actually grew out of it all and turned out to be upright citizens as opposed to uptight citizens like the rest of us.

The children were not the only evil ones at the school. Many of the members of staff seemed annoyed that caning had been made illegal; and yet a surprisingly large number of them still had canes on display in their classrooms as if there was a possibility that at any moment they might flaunt the law and allow their vindictive and sadistic side to get the better of them. I always had the sense that it was a very fine line that would be easy for them to cross. It came as little surprise to me when thirty years later a great number of the staff from this time were arrested on accusation of paedophilia. Fortunately, I have no personal knowledge of this from when I was at the school.

I suppose there is something about the position of power that attracts a lot of sadistic people as well as those who genuinely want to give something back to society and serve their country. Authority and power in the wrong hands can allow corruption and sadism to flourish; take the Third Reich. People did what they did during the period of Nazi atrocities because society allowed them to do it. It was a free licence to do what you liked with impunity. I am not saying that my school was something that could be compared upon the level of Nazi Germany; but it was pretty damn close as far as I was concerned from my child eyes. The teachers rarely did anything to discourage the bullies, turning a blind eye to them because they felt that it was 'character building.' I don't know if this was something that was the same for most schools, or if I just went to a particularly poor school that had fallen off the Ofsted radar.

Some of these individuals are now languishing in prison whereas my hopes are that the rest will soon be languishing in Hell if they are not there already. I am not saying that all my teachers were like this, of course, there were some teachers that I actually got on with and that inspired me for the rest of my life. I will get on to them later.

Inspirational is what I think all teachers should be. You are there to inspire future generations and prepare them for the world. Unfortunately, the vast bulk of them are mediocre and are only there for the money, or because they want the security of remaining in the educational system for their entire life. I suppose it is like never coming out of the womb. Personally, I couldn't wait to leave school, I can't imagine choosing to stay there for another forty, or more years than I actually had to.

I don't remember going to nursery school, so perhaps I didn't. I find this rather strange really when I think about it as I am certain that my mother would have taken every opportunity to get me out from under her feet as quickly as she could. If I did go to nursery school then I have, for some reason, completely wiped it from my memory. I dread to think why that might be. I am certain that if my mother could have afforded it then she would have sent me away to boarding school where she would have done her best to forget about me completely. Sadly, we just didn't have the money, but I have always considered that it was probably a good thing as it prevented me from being buggered at an early age; that's not to say that I was buggered at a later age, because I wasn't. Well, not in a sexual sense at any rate.

As I have mentioned already bullying was rife at my school and was seen as an institutional necessity; probably as some means of preparing us to one day have the backbone and stiff upper lip that was required for us to be able to run an empire that was no longer there to be run. The level of this bullying varied. They never did the cliché of stealing my lunch money because my mother never gave me any lunch money. My mother was very good at teaching me independence from an early age. As it turned out this would prove to be particularly useful.

Most of the time the bullying was centred around name calling. I used to dread sports and swimming due to the embarrassment of having to strip off in front of the other boys. When I was of an age to really enjoy it I got heavily into acne with a vengeance and every time I was in a position of sport I earned myself the nickname of 'pizza back' for reasons that I will leave to your imagination; although it will probably not require all that much imagination.

I hated sport because I was never very good at it and I didn't like the idea of being on public display, which is something that I have always shied away from. My main problem with sport is the complete lack of coordination that I have. Not only do I lack the coordination to make my limbs work in unison with each other, but my brain also lacks the coordination to keep me breathing and tell me what it is that I should be doing next. This lack of coordination and limbs flying in a dangerous manner also earned me the nickname of 'spastic.'

They say 'sticks and stones may break my bones, but names will never hurt me.' This is, of course, complete and utter crap. We know more about bullying these days than we did when I was growing up and we know that name calling can just as much lead to someone going over the edge and taking their life as much as if they had been murdered by the bullies in question. The aim of the bully is to make your life hell and I am afraid to say that it is something that they are very good at.

It wasn't always names that was the limit of their plans against me. I was also physically abused. It was minor attempts from just being pushed by someone when walking down the corridor to all out physical assaults that left me entirely battered and bruised. The only notice that my mother really took of this is if I returned home with my uniform dirty or torn which might mean that she would have to spend money on me, more than was absolutely necessary.

The thing that I really hated about school was anything that put me on show to others. It highlighted me to those bullies that had as of yet not identified me as a possible target. Sport and my inability to blend in with team and competitive sports was a major problem under these circumstances.

It will come as absolutely no surprise to anyone that I was always the last person that was picked when it came to games and if they had been given the option then they wouldn't have bothered to pick me at all and would have left me freezing my bollocks off on the playing field. This would have actually suited me down to the ground as taking part in the sport gave the opposition and my own side, for that matter, an opportunity to justifiably beat the shit out of me. I have always maintained that picking sides in this manner has always been a cruel and vindictive way of doing things and it gives me no surprise that the PE teachers would have chosen to do it.

Aside from sport the other exhibitionist activity that I really didn't like was performing arts classes. I hated these probably even more than I hated sport. I despised the fact that at primary school I was forced to take part in the school play. Due to the fact that there were a smaller number of pupils at my primary school everyone had to take part whether they wanted to or not. For the most part the school play was a nativity, where we were all made to worship the baby Jesus and celebrate his birthday. I usually ended up playing a shepherd and was always the shepherd that liked to hang about at the back and was more interested in looking after the non-existent sheep than being ready to praise the saviour of all humanity.

I have discovered over the years though that keeping away from the limelight in situations such as this perversely seems to push you forward and make you even more conspicuous. By trying to remain in the background I only succeeded in giving off the impression that I was a perverted shepherd who liked loitering around the new born. Naturally I was ostracised by the other shepherds before being beaten senseless by the three wise men. I suppose, in a sense, by exhibiting this violence at the nativity they were paving the way for centuries of violence and intolerance that were to follow.

'You really must make more of an effort to be friends with people,' one of my teachers had told me after they had discovered me in a rather battered about state, no doubt crying my eyes out.

'I don't think they want to be friends with me,' I had sniffled.

'You're just not trying hard enough.'

There was only so much that you could do.

When I progressed onto secondary school it was easier to stay away from taking part in school plays but it became impossible to avoid two years of performing arts classes, which included the hated drama classes and music as well which filled me with probably just as much fear. I hated entering the Drama Studio where the floor was carpeted and you had to remove your shoes, before the drama teacher who was completely eccentric and almost certainly gay, would get us all to warm up by pretending to be trees, or an animal, or some such nonsense before subjecting us to whatever painful journey we were required to undertake on that particular day. Every lesson was as painful for me as if I had been tortured by someone in The Tower.

It was a shame about the Nativity plays that still make me shiver each Christmas because I actually responded well to religion. Religion was compulsory when I was at school and was rammed down our throats at regular intervals. Assembly each morning would be time for hymns and prayers, there would be religious instruction and studies throughout the course of the day and if we were really lucky then a local vicar would come and see us and explain to us why it was that we were all better off with the baby Jesus than we were without him.

All of this would have been enough to depress the hell out of the majority of people, but I was probably the only one who took comfort in religion. The main reason for comfort was because of the fact that there was one kid in our school who was a Jehovah's Witness and each time we all decided to talk about God or the baby Jesus and his angels, he was quietly removed from the instruction and taken away to somewhere else. I have no idea where it was that he went, or what he did. I don't know if he was given his own form of religious instruction; had extra lessons in other subjects or was given a big bowl of ice cream.

The reason why I liked this was because for that one brief moment someone else was highlighted as being separate from the crowd and became a target for the bullies who would seek out his difference and diversity. Later on, and with the logic that only children have, taunt him with the nickname 'Jew.'

I suppose to them it didn't make the slightest bit of difference what religion you were if you were different to them. Later on, when they discovered sexuality they would take huge pleasure in calling everyone who was slightly different from them 'benders.'

I think most of the time these people who were barely entitled to be referred to as humans were bullying and name calling to cover up their own insecurities and dark secrets. Perhaps the 'bender' callers were closet gays who were frightened about their own desires. As for the rest of them I am sure that they were all covering up their secrets.

All bullies are hiding something deep within themselves. In many cases they might be the kind of person who is deflecting the bullying away from them and onto someone else. Remember that. It is true of all bullies no matter how old they are.

What's my point? I will tell you.

Religion made me feel part of something. It made me feel that I could belong somewhere. I remember being in the boys' toilets one day mopping up a nose bleed that had been caused by some person twating me. I looked into the mirror above the sink and thought that maybe I should dedicate my life to the service of God. It was an idea that didn't last that long and eventually I abandoned it completely. God and myself began not to see eye to eye and eventually we reached the point where we just couldn't agree on anything at all. After that it was a matter of not returning each other's calls.

I flirted with Christianity for a while though and was most happy at Christmas. Not particularly because of anything that happened in my home life as my mother wasn't a big one for celebrating Christmas, which she saw as a little too capitalist for her hippy tastes. However, at school I was able to sing my heart out with all the Christmas carols and I entirely bought into the myth of a young boy that was born in a stable and died on a cross who seemed to spend a lot of his time in between pissing off a lot of important people.

As I grew older I began to think more along the lines of the fact that the universe is a very big place and we are surely not the only intelligent beings that are in it. Even if God is omnipotent and omnipresent, what is there that is really special about us? Why would the supreme ruler of the entire universe concentrate on such a tiny little corner with such insignificant beings on it; and even if He did look this way would He really want to interest himself in our day to day lives and petty concerns when there are far more global scale things going on that He equally appears to ignore. He certainly didn't appear to take all that much interest in my little problems.

Due to my desire to blend into the background I buried myself into my studies as best as I could. This I learnt was a terrible thing to do as it earned me the reputation of a swot. The kids hated a swot because it obviously painted them in a bad light because they were not able to get the same results that I was getting because they didn't like to study, of course, probably because of the fact that they were too busy torturing other people or masturbating over the hidden desires in their soul.

Strangely enough the teachers didn't like a swot either. For some completely bizarre reason they thought it was somehow "un-English, not quite cricket". For them it made them suspicious of you because you were either expected to be naturally brilliant or completely hopeless. Anything in between and you were just not playing the same game. It does seem a rather bizarre attitude for teachers to have when you would expect them to approve of someone who studied hard. It just goes to show you that you can't always win.

Being a swot though did give me one brief salvation though. It made me want to be a writer.

Two

My desire and interest to become a writer was born of numerous things within my life. Partly it was due to the fact that being bullied so much at school I became very introverted and being thus withdrawn into myself the most logical course of action was to create my own world, which I could then escape into as a substitute for the real world that I was expected to live in for the rest of the time. I think all of us at some time or another in our lives are looking for a degree of escapism.

Partly it was bullying that had pushed me this way and partly it was because my mother couldn't have had less to do with me if I had come from the moon and so I was left to my own devices when at home. I didn't really have a lot of friends so my own world seemed to be a better prospect than anything else that I was being offered.

I am not suggesting that this is the reason why every writer decides that they want to write. Some are compelled to do it and some do it for their own reasons that I can't begin to imagine. It is a solitary profession that by necessity is something that is done on its own, and that is the reason why I moved in that direction. When you are solitary by nature and by circumstance then you seek to have an occupation or activity that takes advantage of that.

I suppose it all started for me with reading. Any writer that doesn't read is not worth anything in my book; if you will excuse the pun. I didn't really have all that much access to books when I was growing up as my mother was not really a big reader, so it wasn't until I went to school that I had a lot of access to the printed word.

I fell in love pretty quickly though and soon found that my best friend was a book; nobody else seemed all that interested in the role and to be honest I was more than pleased with the comfort that I could receive from being lost within the pages of a good book. Obviously when I was at school it wasn't anything more highbrow than *Noddy Goes to the Seaside,* but we all have to start somewhere. I progressed as quickly as I could and read as much as I could get my hands on, working through all the Enid Blyton books and from there moved onto more serious things which were primarily Boys' Own Adventure stories and vast majorities of stories that were centred on acts of derring-do and gallantry in war torn Europe. It probably isn't all that politically correct in this day and age, but I loved it at the time.

I don't actually remember the moment when I turned from reading to writing. I am not sure what motivated me to make the transition. It seems to me that I was always writing from the moment that I was able to hold a pen in my hand. I believe that I started by writing stories in old notebooks and old diaries, basically in anything that I could get my hands on. My other activity that took up so much time was watching television whenever I could and from there I started to write short stories. The genres from screenwriting to prose didn't match but I nevertheless wrote stories on my favourite television shows – *Red Dwarf, Star Trek, Doctor Who* whatever took my fancy really. Pages and pages of childish handwriting scrawled across these books that would ultimately be doomed to be read by nobody other than myself. Probably a good thing when you think about it.

I carried these writing activities on at school. I always carried a notebook with me and it was easy for me to slide off to a corner during breaks and scribble away in my book. I had to hide as best I could as from time to time the bullies would find me and if they caught my book they would rip it to pieces and destroy what I had worked so hard to create. I found that the best place to hide was the school library, as most of the bullies would rather be dead than be seen in such a place. There are people out there who find it easier to destroy than they do to create. It has always been the way of things. I hid away in literature and writing as a means of escaping from the bullies and I think it worked pretty well.

Some people will say that it was a terrible thing because it was an activity that moved me away from acceptance and fitting in and would ultimately make me more introverted. They would say that I should have undertaken something that made me fit in more like the comedians who tell how they told jokes so that people would laugh with them rather than beat them up. Well I went the other way. I fully understand that if someone is laughing at you they are a lot less likely to beat you up, but I still maintained that if you were invisible then it was even better.

There was a further downside in the fact that because I had a reputation as a swat or a bookworm this enhanced the bullying and made me more of a target so I can understand the logic that my actions were making things worse for me, but I didn't care because it did give me the means of escape into a world where I felt considerably better off. Bullies hardly ever have the imagination to be able to read anything.

***

I have spent a lot of time explaining how I didn't like school and associated staff and students that went there, but there was one teacher that I really did get on with. I have talked about how I feel it is the duty of teachers to inspire the next generation. As I have mentioned there seemed to me to be few and far between that actually did this, but one that did was Mr Jones, my English teacher.

Jones was completely genuine and as far as I could see without the sadistic streak that seemed to be shared by so many of his contemporaries. He was an unassuming little man with glasses and a moustache and a faint Welsh accent that under normal circumstances would have made him the butt of all the children's taunts and jokes. It would have been, were it not that he had the ability to turn the bravest of students into a quivering jelly with one myopic stare. His stare was off-putting to a lot of students who quailed under his gaze. The truth of the matter was that he was so short-sighted that he was probably just trying to work out who you were.

He was the kind of person who spotted that a student had an interest and did all that he could to encourage and develop that interest. He saw that I was keen on reading and writing and would push me to read writers that were off the curriculum.

'I have found that the national curriculum is somewhat bland,' Mr Jones stated. 'We must bemoan its lack of imagination.'

Whereas on one hand he could understand that it was an essential guide for someone who lacked imagination to choose the right books for themselves, he found that it was something of a constraint for those who had a little more interest in the subject that they had chosen to dedicate their life to.

He taught the national curriculum because he had to, but he would push extra books in on the side, Ray Bradbury, Doris Lessing, Albert Camus, Daniel Keyes and Hemingway to name but a few. The kind of books that the Department for Education really didn't want you reading. After all these were the people who kept trying to knock Shakespeare off the curriculum.

He saw that I responded well to the literature and so would go the extra mile for me. There were also lessons that he would timetable in the plan where he allowed students to free read or work on projects. Most of the philistines that were in the class took this chance to do as little as they possibly could. I obviously took the chance to write which would earn me even more of a reputation as a swot or a teacher's pet as I was seen beavering away in my own little world. Mr Jones took an interest in my creative writing as well as my reading. He held a rather unique opinion on it.

'Up and down the country,' he said 'there are numerous universities that offer the chance for a creative writing course. The number of books about writing and creative writing are so numerous that they are ten a penny; I am sure that as time goes by they will multiply even more.' He scratched his moustache as he sat in his chair thinking about all of this before continuing.

'I am of the opinion that creative writing is something that can't be taught; but it is something that can be learnt.'

Having said this he folded his arms and appeared to be satisfied with it all. It took me some time to understand this fully. Jones believed that you could teach the basics of writing and the so-called rules which most writers will break at any rate, but ultimately you either had it or you didn't and if you didn't have it then it was no good trying to polish a turd. You could learn it though by reading.

'If you want to learn how to write, then you must first learn how to read,' was another one of his maxims that he frequently told me.

This is what he stood by, he believed that reading would give you the ability to pick up on the traits of other writers, structure, and grammar and so on. You could then progress this almost by osmosis into your own work. I have to say that it is something that I agree with. I know that it is a controversial opinion and not one that will be supported by a lot of other writers, but diversity is the spice of life.

Mr Jones lived by the printed word more than by anything else. His entire classroom was smothered in books and they were all his own; one assumed overspill from his own house. Every surface covered with paperbacks of all kinds of genres. It was a paradise for a bibliophile as far as I was concerned.

Mr Jones helped me to develop my individuality and creativity. I think it is fair to say that he kick started me on the road of personal writing that I have been following ever since. I don't think that I have ever thanked him for what he did; but then perhaps he knew without me saying. I hope he did.

***

English classes were my all-time favourite classes in school. It probably wasn't that hard as I wasn't really good at a lot of the others or I lived in perpetual fear of them. Literature became my world, my retreat and the only place that I was happy and that I felt I could be myself. Science classes were just as bad as some of the other classes where I was on show. The reason being that I felt that I was going to blow myself and the school up at some stage during the experiments.

I had been following my own course in the public and school libraries since I was old enough to hold a library card, but it was a directionless path that I was taken with no sense of direction or purpose; just stumbling across different books and using it as a launching pad to find the things that I liked. The English classes with Mr Jones gave me the chance to have someone directing my efforts and showing me the road to go.

I genuinely loved reading, I always have and I still do. It is as natural to me as breathing. I can't understand those that have no interest in it, but then I have never really understood that many people at any rate. My biggest understanding of people comes from the pages of books where you can explore the human character without having to get your hands dirty. That wasn't the only thing that I could pick up from books. I would often be trapped in my little room at the top of the house where we lived and I would bury myself in books and travel in my mind to places like ancient Egypt and Greece, meet Julius Caesar and Robin Hood. I would fly off into space or travel in time and do all number of wonderful things that most of my contemporaries would just never know about.

Around about this time I graduated at home from writing in notebooks to an old battered typewriter that I had found in a second-hand shop. It was a little difficult to work and some of the keys were stiff and kept getting stuck when I would get into a frenzy of typing, but it was the most perfect of machines that I had ever come across. It was perfect and clattered with creativity.

It was probably around this time that during the quiet periods in my English class I started to write plays. It may seem a very strange thing to do given my fear of drama, but writing plays and performing in them are two very different things. I suppose that I commenced writing plays as it was a natural progression to all the films and television that I was watching at the time. It was a case of copying a format that I was familiar with and trying to emulate. Testing my abilities, you might say.

The other reason that I really liked my English classes was because of Mary.

***

In my school it was a standard practice that in class you sat boy-girl-boy-girl. The idea of this was to prevent you sitting next to your friends, having a good time and in general creating a nuisance. I didn't have any friends, rarely had a good time and never created a nuisance so it never mattered to me in the slightest who I sat next to. Sitting next to a girl was often the better option for me as I tendered to be bullied a lot less by girls than I was by boys.

Mary, as you may have guessed, was the girl that I sat next to in English and was someone that I developed an amazing crush on. I was extremely surprised by this. For someone that kept himself to himself and was as shy and introverted as I was, to suddenly find yourself with a crush on someone was akin to being a spy and walking around Nazi Germany in RAF uniform.

What's my point? I will tell you.

It was the most ludicrous thing that I could ever have imagined doing. You can't help who you fall in love with though can you?

You might think it a little strange for me to say that I was in love with her, but I don't think that having a crush on her is something that really does full justification to the way that I felt. It probably sounds silly and I don't deny that to a certain extent that is exactly how I felt about it. The silliest thing about it all was that we never really exchanged any words together. Talking was rarely something that was encouraged in class and if it had been I don't think I would have been able to find the words that I needed to be able to talk to her. Ironic really that you can be a writer, working with words all the time and then have them fail you at the moment when you need them the most.

The only real contact that I had with Mary was in the English class, but I tried my best to observe her from afar as often as I could. Of course, this makes me sound like some kind of pervert now that was stalking her, but that wasn't really the case. Okay, it was, but not in a really sinister sense. Well, I suppose it might have been a bit sinister. I suppose it depends who you ask.

One of the things that I did to try and stay in Mary's company was to do something that went against every single grain and atom in my body. I joined a local amateur dramatics company that she was a member of. She was a leading light in the company and obviously had a great deal of talent whereas I was someone who, as you can imagine by now, tried his best to stay firmly in the background and not get noticed. By the time though I was getting pretty good at hiding in plain sight so this probably wasn't as difficult to do as you might think it was.

I also had an ulterior motive for joining. At this stage in my life I was heavily into the writing of plays and I thought that by joining the local amateur group I could observe at close hand how a play is constructed and how it works. If I could uncover some of the secrets of the theatre then it would probably help in how I would write my own plays. I had probably decided by this point to be a playwright.

The amateur company that I joined was extremely alien to me and something that I felt very uncomfortable with. I couldn't act, sing or dance and I didn't want to. Fortunately, there was no real audition process. They were frankly so desperate for people that they would let anyone in regardless of how talented or untalented they actually were. This was fine because I just spent all of my time trying not to be noticed.

I observed that there was a lot of politics that went into the make-up of the company. There were little groups within groups and splinter groups within those. It all seemed tremendously energetic to me and I really couldn't see the point of it. I suppose this is where I realised that even in amateur companies there were prima donnas and others who were trying to grab their moment in the limelight – no matter how much of a backwater town hall performance it might actually be. I found it all rather pathetic if I am entirely honest. I have always found these kinds of Machiavellian manoeuvrings to be extremely strange and futile.

I also discovered, not particularly to my surprise, that I suffered from intense stage fright. There were times when I just stood in the wings and felt as if I was standing with my toes on the edge of a cliff waiting to jump off. I really couldn't understand in moments such as this why it was that I was putting myself through it all. They talk about butterflies in your stomach and your legs turning to jelly, all of which sounds like hyperbole, but I can tell you that it is all true and not a word of exaggeration.

'It's all kind of crazy isn't it?' This was from a male who suddenly appeared next to me in one of the rehearsals, I had not noticed him before.

Rehearsals often took place in church halls and similar places that I suppose the company paid a small fee to desecrate for a period of time. The rehearsals always seemed to take place in the winter as far as my memory serves, so the places were always bloody freezing. If we were really lucky then we would have an electric heater to warm us – only one heater mind you for the entire company. The director was obviously of the opinion that we should keep warm by moving about a lot and being energetic in our acting.

'What is?'

I looked sideways at my companion who was a male that I estimated to be somewhere in his mid-twenties, at a guess. He wore glasses and favoured a pockmarked face.

'All of this,' he replied waving in general at all the actor's activities. I nodded in a non-committed way as I was not entirely sure how I was supposed to respond to that.

'The name's Cohen,' he said extending a hand to me. 'Adrian Cohen.' I shook his hand chiefly because it seemed the thing that he wanted me to do. 'This company really pisses me off at times.'

'Oh?' I felt I had to ask as I had greeted this statement with silence for a few seconds and then I realised that without some prompting he wasn't going to say anything else. I probably would have been rather pleased if he didn't say anything else, but I suppose that was just being very impolite.

'All they do is a pantomime in the winter and a musical every other year and a one act play in the summer.' I had heard about the one act plays and had made a mental note to keep away from them. I could hide at the back of the chorus for pantomime and musical performances, but you could not do that in one act plays. My only interest in one act plays was that I might be able to write one for them one day.

I nodded my head to Adrian's comments, but didn't feel that I could say anything at this time as I felt rather out of my depth.

'I find it all so boring. I used to run my own little student company, you know?'

'No, I didn't.' I really didn't see how I was expected to have known this when I had only just met the man. He clearly thought that he must be more locally famous than he was.

'Yes, a little company when I was at Sixth Form, but it had some promising moments. We used to concentrate on Shakespeare and more important things then this dross that this lot chuck out each year.'

I wondered, if he felt like that why it was that he was here, but I didn't think it polite to ask. Nor did I think it was polite to ask him what had happened to his promising little company. I was now fifteen years old and would be going onto the sixth form college, but I was pretty certain that I would not be running my own theatre company whilst I was there.

'I mean would it kill these old farts to try Shakespeare, or maybe a little light Ibsen perhaps?' He shook his head at the clear idiocy that he believed he was seeing in front of him.

I turned my attention back to the stage area and concentrated on Mary who was singing some kind of song about balloons or something; I was not entirely certain as I hadn't really been paying all that much attention to the plot of what it was that we were meant to be performing. I allowed myself to concentrate on her whilst Adrian droned on in my ear and I made the occasional grunt to make him think that I was still listening to him and agreeing with him. He struck me as the kind of person that didn't need someone else to be able to have a conversation.

A short while later Mary left the company to concentrate on her college studies. The company experienced a great sense of loss of a genuine talent, probably the best one that they had and were ever likely to have. They bemoaned her loss greatly. With her loss there was no great sense in me hanging around either. I very much doubted that they would ever have the balls to be able to perform a play of mine assuming that I had been able to write anything in the first place.

As far as I could tell nobody noticed when I left the company as well.

Three

My birth was an accident. I am pretty sure of this. Nobody has told me directly, but I have the suspicion that my mother becoming pregnant with me was nothing more nor less than an accident.

I would have been conceived a couple of months into the 1980s and it was at a time when the era of free sex was just about in its death throes, literally. Condoms were not yet as widely in use as they are today and AIDS was something that was still a couple of years away from being a rumour that didn't even have a name yet. For the first couple of years the rumours about it were really only something that was considered to be a gay cancer; nobody knew what was waiting for them around the corner.

As a consequence my mother and no doubt numerous others like her relied entirely on the pill. Men would often expect the woman to either be on the pill or provide a condom if they really thought it was necessary. For many of them pregnancy was a problem for the female if it happened. I would like to think that we have moved on considerably from those sexist days, but I am not entirely sure that all my female friends would agree with that.

My mother has never spoken to me about it, of course, and I don't really have anyone else to ask; but I have an inkling that from the little I know or have been told about my father they were not in a stable relationship and it wouldn't surprise me if it had even been a one night stand. I really don't know; but either way I imagine that this fleeting affair was something that involved a lot of stumbling, knickers down around the ankles, probably an alcoholic haze and then a lifetime of regrets to follow. A lifetime of regret that for one of them at least didn't turn out to be as long a period of time as you might have thought. It wouldn't have surprised me if she was also smoking drugs at the time. She has had a lifelong interest in cannabis, as well as alcohol. All of which has contributed to me having a lifelong hatred of smoking and alcohol. Another reason why I never seemed to fit in with anyone else, I suppose.

Add it all up and I think you come to the conclusion that I was an accidental pregnancy. I suppose this belief knocking about in the back of my mind for the majority of my life has led me to believe that because I was an accident I didn't really belong here. I didn't have the right stuff to be able to fit in with everyone else in the world.

What's my point? I will tell you.

I have never felt that I had the right to be here. I wasn't part of the cosmic plan. I suppose I should really be lucky that I am here at all and that she didn't terminate me. I have always imagined that the only reason she didn't have an abortion is that she was too far out of her head most of the time to realise what was going on until it was too late.

What evidence do I have for any of this? Well, actually none at all. It is something that I just believe is the way that my existence started. I have no proof for any of it and I know that it wouldn't stand up in court, but I stand by my convictions. I suppose the main reason why I think like this is because of the sheer lack of interest that she seemed to show towards me during the course of my life. It all led to me having a very lonely childhood and the resulting hiding away in books of one description or another.

There are some, myself probably included, who would state that whilst I was growing up my mother showed a complete lack of interest or involvement in my life and development. She would argue that she was actually giving me freedom and independence whilst at the same time respecting my privacy. I suppose that it is just possible to see this from both points of view. I have stated that my mother was something of a hippy, but she was born in 1958 and I always associated the hippy movement with something that she should really have been too young to appreciate. By the time she was a teenager I would have more expected her to be either into glam rock or punk. However, there was something that attracted her to the hippy lifestyle and it was something that she stuck with for the rest of her life. She even went as far as buying a Volkswagen Micro Bus which was covered in psychedelic flowers and symbols which frankly just looked ridiculous as the century drew to a conclusion. She was once removed from a generation that had been lost and felt that she had in some way been cheated out of her rightful inheritance by not being born earlier.

Yes the hippy counter culture movement still existed in the seventies and eighties, but its heyday had been the sixties when she had been far too young to really appreciate it. My mother seemed to hold irrational beliefs about certain aspects of life. In some sense she still held me responsible for the death of John Lennon and she almost certainly held her own parents responsible for not conceiving her early enough to be able to fully appreciate the hippy movement.

For most of her life she also shared in her belief of communal living, which was about as horrendous as it could get as far as I was concerned, and was a motivation for pushing me further into my bedroom-loft with a pile of books. There is a school of thought about the fact that as this was the reality that I was presented with whilst growing up then I should have been used to the way that we lived and not thought of it as anything other than normal. However, I must have had some degree of maturity within my soul which had made me strand opposed to the situation that my mother presented as living. She was rebelling against society and culture with her hippy beliefs and I countered against her counter culture and rebelled in the favour of normality. It was all starting to get rather complicated. I suppose in many regards I must have been a big disappointment for her.

I hated the strangers that used to wander in and out of the house that we stayed in and the vaguely transient nature of our home life at this stage in my development. My mother also saw furniture as an unnecessary extravagance and for most of the time she and her 'friends' would spend their time listening to vinyl records whilst all seated in a circle on the floor surrounded by smoke from the joints that they passed around to each other. My self-imposed exile to the attic was something that I was rigorous about. I had not really been banished there, it was my own devising to keep to myself in that way. It was my self-imposed exile to the furthest room in the house away from the living room.

It probably does sound harsh living in an attic, but I loved it. It was a peaceful part of the house. The floorboards and general barren nature of the place made it seem like it was something out of the 1950s or C S

Lewis, although there was not a wardrobe up there. It did get rather cold in the winter, but I didn't mind all that much as I would put the duvet over my head and read my books underneath it by the light of a small battery-operated torch.

Sometimes I would sit on the wide window ledge and read whilst looking out of the window. If I craned my neck I could just about see the people walking in the street below. Otherwise I would look out over the rooftops to the distant industrial chimney smoke and rounded metal gas stations that appeared so alien and futuristic to me, and held a deep fascination like some alien creatures waiting to take over the world. In the winter I would watch the weather beating against the rooftops as nature tried to eradicate humanities puny efforts at memorial.

For reasons that I never fully understood this period of communal living did not last as long as I had expected that it would. Shortly after I had reached my tenth birthday we moved away from, what I can only really describe as a hippy slum, and into a tiny two-bedroom house that was dangerously close to normality as far as my mother was concerned. I don't to this day know what it was that prompted this move, whether it was a visit from Social Services, or a quiet word from the headmaster of the school, or what it was. Perhaps it was a sudden crisis of conscience over the way that she had been. I simply don't know, but for a period of time life settled down and became almost normal.

I had my own bedroom rather than an attic space and this is where I managed to get my hands on a television set for the first time and launch myself on my story writing around television programmes. I didn't have all that many toys but that was because I favoured books more than toys, and it was at this stage in my life that I started to accumulate the library that I would continue to buy until today. All in all though there were aspects of me that really missed the attic.

My mother underwent a slight change as well and started to dress less like a hippy and more like someone who was on the cruise for a new partner. This was a rather strange activity to undertake as my mother was never someone that I associated with the ideas of long term relationships. She was discreet about the people that she did bring home (assuming that she did), I was not aware of a line of strange men coming to the house and I was never introduced to any of them as a perspective step-father, but then maybe she did all of this under the radar; which was entirely possible given my immersion in books for the greater part of my life.

I am pretty certain that she was still keeping the hippy interest in recreational drugs up. I have always found that the term 'recreational' is both misleading and dangerous. In some way it seems to suggest that this is a perfectly acceptable activity for people to take part in. Perhaps the term is used to differentiate it from medicinal drugs; in which case I think a better term could have been used than recreational; I would suggest Russian roulette drugs would be a more appropriate term to highlight the risk that you are taking. I am sorry if this sounds like it makes me something of a prude, but that's just the way that it is.

It was around about this time that my mother decided to take more of an active part in my life which seemed to involve taking me to school and then waiting for me at the gates at home time. I very quickly realised that this was because she had taken to flirting with the younger fathers and staff who were around at the time. I might have known it was not because of any other reason. This caused a great deal of embarrassment for me; largely because of the way that she was dressed. Her activities also caused a great deal of further bullying from the other children who naturally blamed me for the actions and appearance of my mother. Perhaps it filled them with a deep sense of worry that one day I could end up as their step-brother. If they were worried about it that was nothing compared to what I felt about it.

Well as someone once said, "you can choose your friends, but you can't choose your parents."

***

I was sixteen and I went to continue my studies at the local college at A level. You might think it strange that I decided to continue my studies given how much I hated school and the educational system in general. I could have exited quietly at sixteen and found myself a job to do which would have seen me plodding along at a pace until it was time for my retirement. I was aware though that if I was even remotely serious in my intention of becoming a writer then I needed to gain at least some degree of education. It is possible to be a writer without any extended formal education, of course, but I figured that with my apparent genetics I needed all the help that I could get.

Sixth form was something that was a little different to how things had been at school. It was supposed to be more adult in the way that staff were treating us. We didn't have to wear uniform any longer so we were encouraged to celebrate our individuality at least as far as what we chose to wear. As this was the first time for a lot of us that this happened a number of students chose to go as far as they could and dress in all kinds of outfits. I tended to stick to wearing black which was the style that I favoured as it was reasonably neutral and allowed me to blend into the background the way that I liked.

'Goth!'

This was one of the shouted comments that was made to me early on in my career at the college. Bullying had almost died out, but there were those who still liked to cling to tradition. Calling me a Goth merely because I was dressed in black was unimaginative to say the least. I may have favoured black, but I was not a Goth by any stretch of the imagination. Dressed in black with my shockingly blond mess of hair that I had I looked more like a pint of Guinness, but I would imagine that was too sophisticated for them to pick up on.

I think that my problems that had surrounded me with bullying throughout school drifted off at sixth form; aside from the early Goth comment, of course, but compared to what I was used to I could live with that. Part of the reason why was because of the fact that in many regards the students had matured a fair amount by the time that we reached this stage. That is the story that most people would like to hear, but the main reason was because a lot of the bullies just weren't intelligent enough to hang around in education and couldn't see the point when they could go out into the real world and start working hard to claim their unemployment benefits. It was good news as far as I was concerned.

I decided to study for English Literature and English Language which was inevitable really when you thought about it. Unfortunately, that was not really enough to study on its own so after much debate I took History as well; not because I particularly liked it, but it was the only other subject that I felt reasonably confident of getting on with.

There was a common room in the college where students were supposed to hang out. I didn't spend all that much time in there myself.

The room was dotted about with old armchairs and sofas that came from God knows where, but looked like they were at least thirty years old. The walls were covered in Nirvana posters and numerous other bands that I had never heard of. Music wasn't really something that I had ever had the chance to get too far into. I suppose that I might have been a little put off by music by my mother and her hippy friends who played unconventional music that would have put most people off.

It won't come as much of a surprise that I spent most of my time in the college library making use of their extensive collection of books. I would imagine that the literature section, at least, had been ordered by someone who really knew their stuff because there was a fantastic range of books there on the shelves to browse through from bumper editions of Chaucer to McEwan. I enjoyed spending my time in there reading around my subject whilst other students ran around on the field playing football and getting cold and muddy.

It is at this point that I should probably come up with a guilty confession. I have kept it a secret all of my life because I suppose I am partly ashamed of it and because I don't want the police knocking on my door even all these years later, but I suppose it doesn't really matter now. I went through the library at college and I was sure that I was the only one reading half of the books that were in there. It is my confession that I liberated some of these books. You would probably prefer to use the term 'stole' but I liked to think about it as a liberation from where they imprisoned to my own shelves where they would at least be loved and read.

You may look very badly on me for this as it would mean that future generations were deprived of the same reading material that I had access to. Most of the people that went to my college never entered the library though and to be honest after all the years of bullying with no intervention from the staff I felt that it was about time that I was owed something. It probably doesn't make things any better, but at least you know I am being honest with you.

My studies of literature were increasing in further education. We were now really getting into the study of Shakespeare with *King Lear* being one of our set texts, a play that I came to love as my favourite of all Shakespeare. There is so much richness in the play and I love how the familial relationships connect and collide with each other. Parents turning against their children and children betraying their parents. I suppose to an extent it made sense to me.

I made a series of discoveries during this period; the aforementioned Chaucer, Kafka, Harper Lee, Lawrence and Dickens. Some of these were set texts and others were just ones that I went off and read of my own freewill. I didn't see all that much of Mary although she was in my Literature class, but that was the only time that we really ever had anything to do with each other. I was still hovering on the outer limits of her sphere; well of everyone's sphere if I was entirely honest.

Mary was someone that I would describe as staggeringly beautiful, she really took my breath away. I know that beauty is something that is in the eye of the beholder, so I have no doubt that she may not have seemed to be so special to someone else, but that is their problem not mine. She had long dark hair that seemed to glisten as it cascaded down to her shoulders. She used to wear glasses every now and then when she was reading which she was very self-conscious of, but was a look that I found all the more attractive. I wasn't close to her all that often, but from the times that I used to sit next to her in Mr Jones' English class I could smell the shampoo that she used in her hair and it made me fall completely in love; I just couldn't help myself. Her voice had a slight rasping sound to it which I also found amazingly sexy. Without me having to go much further it probably doesn't take all that much more for you to work out that I was completely smitten with her with no hope of recovery.

***

I think it was a Wednesday afternoon with the rain splattering against the windows as I sat in the library reading *The Dubliners*. I don't know what it is about James Joyce, but I just can't see the attraction for the life of me although he has a global reputation as a writer. I was finding *The Dubliners* to be a very strange little book at best and at worst a deeply disturbed book from a perverted mind. No doubt the Joyce fan club will be up in arms over this, but I am sorry for my opinion, but it is at least mine.

It must have been the winter because I was huddled at a desk in the corner of the library that was next to the window, but crucially next to the radiator which was producing just about enough heat to prevent me from freezing to death. It was a favourite corner of mine as the bookcases were arranged in such a way that they created a natural labyrinth and kept me hidden from anyone that did actually decide to come in the library, which as previously stated they were not queuing up to do.

'You never talk to me.'

Despite my reservations I was engrossed in Joyce so it took me by surprise that someone had spoken, that they appeared to be speaking to me and that they were close enough to speak to me without me having heard them approach. I looked up and almost died when I saw Mary in front of me clutching a ring binder and a couple of text books across her bosom and looking down at me over the top of her glasses. I had not planned for a moment such as this so I didn't know what I should do or how I should act without looking like a complete idiot. Without the planning in place I opted for looking like a complete idiot.

'What?'

'I said you never talk to me.'

'Don't I?'

'No.'

'Oh.'

'We sat together in Mr Jones' class for four years and we are in the same English class now, and yet you never talk to me.'

'I'm sorry.'

'Are you shy?'

'A bit.'

'Or is it that you don't like me?'

'Oh, no not at all.'

'You like me too much?'

'I don't know what to say.' It was true, I didn't, the last few exchanges had happened quicker than machine gun fire and it didn't take a genius to work out that I had not come off the better of the pair.

'Can I sit down?' She didn't wait for an answer, but sat down opposite me and span my copy of *The Dubliners* round so that she could look at it. 'Urgh, Joyce! Tell me are you finding this as disturbingly perverted as I did?'

I nodded my head not trusting myself to speak. I was in awe. Firstly, because of the fact that the girl that I had admired for probably the last five years was sitting opposite me and talking to me and secondly because *The Dubliners* was not a set text. Mary read more than she had to do! She was a fellow reader like myself and not someone who was just taking subjects at college to delay actually having to go out and work for a living. I was deeply impressed. She tossed Joyce back across the table to me.

'Why do they call you Midge?'

'It's my name.'

'But it isn't though is it?'

'No, not really.'

'So why do they call you it?'

'It's a long story.'

'I'm not going anywhere.'

And so it was that Mary and myself had our very first conversation after so many years of knowing each other but never exchanging a social word at all. We talked and I explained my life and how I had come by my name and she listened to everything I had to say which at first started at a stumble, but grew with confidence as I got into my story.

'Midge,' she said in a contemplative tone when I had finished telling her about myself. She spoke the name as if for the first time and rolled it around her mouth as if trying it out to see what she thought of it. 'I like it.'

And so it was that from that second onwards I learned to love the name that I had hated for all of my life and had contemplated taking out somewhere to kill when I was old enough. It can be rather funny how things change in the blink of an eye.

This faulting start was not perhaps something that you would consider to be the start of a blossoming relationship and you would probably have been right. We did commence a friendship and Mary became the closest friend that I have ever had; to be entirely honest at this point in my life she was the only friend that I had really.

I probably wasn't very socially adept at friendship and was not entirely sure if I was always doing the right thing. It may sound ludicrous to you that I should be seventeen years old and still be such a child when it came to social interactions, but there it was. I would like to think that I was a quick learner though and we both seemed to get along really well.

I never learned to drive a car, but Mary was someone who had passed her test at the first opportunity and had purchased a rather clapped out old Mini which she used to drive in a frantic manner, which with my limited knowledge sounded like it was always in the wrong gear. Driving was something that always seemed too much of a fuss for me. I have said before about how I could not coordinate myself at all when it came to things like sport and for me driving was an extension of this lack of coordination. I couldn't even begin to get my head round the fact that my brain would be doing one thing, whilst my eyes were doing something else, whilst hands and feet were moving on other things. It all seemed so complicated to me.

Mary would pick me up and we would go out and have lunch together, the occasional meal and whatever else took our fancy really. We weren't dating though; as much as I would have liked to have dated her we were friends and I think I was happy with that. We discovered that we had a lot in common and we got on well. Sometimes we would sit and talk for hours and at other times we would sit together and read without either of us saying a thing. There probably aren't that many people that you can just be silent with, but if you do find that there is someone in your life that you do not have to fill the silence with speech then you are probably onto a good thing – no matter what the relationship is. We do seem to live in a society that feels that it is necessary to fill silence with mundane speech that doesn't mean all that much. Aside from when you are on an Underground train when I have noticed that you can be trapped together like sardines and yet not say a word to anyone. We humans are a funny species when you think about it.

There were lots of things that were taking place at that time. Bill Clinton was inaugurated for his second term as President of the United States; British Hong Kong was handed over to China; Tony Blair was elected as the first Labour Prime Minister for eighteen years and Princess Diana was killed in a car crash in Paris whilst being driven by a drunk Frenchman.

None of it really mattered all that much to me though. Whilst all these events were going on I was distracted by the developing friendship that was taking place with Mary. When you are in love, even if it is unrequited, there are a lot of other events that can take place without you really being aware of it all. I vaguely remember the triumphant feeling that gripped the country when Blair came to power. It was like a breath of fresh air that swept the country after the staleness that had been left following John Major's greyness and the surrounding sex scandals that had ultimately been the downfall of their Government. I don't think that anyone who watched the jubilation on that May morning would have imagined the way that Blair and then the Labour Government would have ended all those years later. I look on it with a degree of realism though and think that a great deal of things that start so promisingly can end in such ignominy. It seems to be the way that things often are in life. So much can turn out in the end to be a disappointment.

I remember waking up one Sunday morning to be told that Diana had died. I was never really much of a fan so the news didn't grip me the way that it seemed to take hold of the nation.

'This is incredible,' Mary said when a few days later we sat and watched the funeral together.

'I suppose so.'

'Where has this outpouring of grief come from? When did we ever act like this as a nation?'

'I suppose she meant a lot of things to a lot of people.'

'But, they never knew her. Half of these people wouldn't react like that if one of their relatives died and yet they are going hysterical over the death of someone they never met, who in all reality couldn't have given a toss about them if she had of met them.'

It seemed a fair point to me. I had seen interviews with Diana and she had seemed to be someone who knew how to manipulate the media as far as I was concerned and I certainly didn't think that she was in any way as innocent as she tried to make out that she was to everyone else.

'Do you believe some of these theories that have sprung up about Diana's death?' Mary asked me some time later.

'You mean conspiracy theories, don't you?'

'Yes, I suppose so. Theories that she was killed by MI6 or Prince Philip.'

'I don't, as a rule, tend to give much credence to conspiracy theories.'

'A lot of people believe in them.'

'That doesn't make them true. People tend to hang on to conspiracies because they don't want to accept things for the way that they are.'

'So, you don't believe any?'

'I believe that they did put a man on a moon, and I don't believe that there was some fantastic plot to kill Diana. I think she was the victim of circumstance. Being driven madly by a drink driver in an area famous for car crashes.'

'Well, I suppose when you put it like that.'

'I understand that she meant so much to so many people that they just can't accept the fact that she was killed in an accident.'

'I suppose there has to be some significance to her death.'

'Being driven much too fast, by someone who was heavily over the drink drive limit in a tunnel that is famous for accidents. There really isn't all that much of a mystery about it.'

'Viewed like that I suppose people just can't believe that this extraordinary person was killed in such a mundane way. People feel that there has to be more to it than that.'

Invariably there isn't more to it than there appears to be at first glance.

Four

Mary had as normal a family life as anyone could hope to have. I, therefore took great pains to ensure that whilst she knew about my mother they didn't actually meet. This wasn't because of the fact that I was worried what she might think about my mother, but more to do with the fact that I was worried the way that my mother would react to her. After having experienced so many of my mother's 'scenes' throughout my life I had no particular desire to experience one against what was in all reality the only person that I really cared about in the entire world.

She had a normal mother and father and stable family life that involved doing all the things that I would have dreamt of being able to do, if I had only been given a chance in life. The only downside that I could see was that she had an idiot younger brother. He might have been an actual idiot as far as I knew, but he was an idiot in every sense of the word that I could see. It was like all the intelligence had gone to Mary leaving nothing left for him. That seemed a pretty reasonable explanation of the difference between them.

I envied the fact that she came from a home that liked books and I started to spend a great deal of my time visiting her at her home. Normally we would go off into her room and talk or read, perhaps we would watch a film or listen to some music, but from time to time we had to spend time with her family as her father was of the opinion that it was dangerous for two teenagers of the opposite sex to spend time alone in a room together where the sexual tension was something that you could almost see. Well that's how I imagined it. I very much doubt that Mary thought there was much sexual tension between us, probably just tension.

Mary had clearly developed her love of books from her parents. She had been surrounded by books from birth and no doubt her mother or her father, maybe both, read to her bedtime stories and encouraged her in her developing interest in literature. My love of literature came from isolation as it was really the only thing that I got up to. My mother certainly never read me bedtime stories; that was just something that was far out of her remit of what she thought of as parenthood. I am not entirely sure what it was that she thought was in the remit of parenthood. Probably as far as she was concerned it began and ended with birth, which was presumably a step further than she wanted to go.

I remember being in Mary's living room at some point, and for the life of me I can't remember when this was, but I think we were both irritated by the noise that was coming from the television whilst her brother, mainly, but I suppose her parents as well watched some dross of a reality television programme that were starting to become popular at that point. Television that as far as I could see was dumbing down an entire generation of those that not only would lack intelligence but would also make the talentless feel that they are in some way talented and entitled to their portion of fame. I remember a time when fame was something that was earned, whereas now it was something that could be pretty much given to anyone for no apparent logical reason that I could make any sense of.

I asked her dad why he watched this rubbish or at least tolerated having it on all the time.

'Chewing gum for the mind.' It was an enigmatic answer which he clarified. 'You can't keep pushing high art intellectual matter into your brain without giving your brain a chance to relax and chew over something that is insubstantial.'

For some reason I remember this scene vividly, the curtains drawn tight shut to keep out the night; the Chinese style table lamp that stood in one corner reflecting on reproductions of famous paintings that were all over the walls. The latticed bookcase that was compacted with books that Mary's brother would almost certainly never read and would get rid of if he had half the chance. Her brother, who was probably about twelve years old at this time, was sitting on the floor (I don't think that I ever saw him sitting in an actual chair in all the time that I knew him), he was shaking his head for no apparent reason that I could work out and was rocking backwards and forwards and for all the world giving the impression of someone who had recently escaped from a mental institution. Perhaps he had. We never really saw eye-to-eye and I always hoped that his strange behaviour would be something that he would grow out of; but then perhaps like me he had just decided to disappear into his own mind as a means of escaping the reality around him.

By this time, I had developed a deep friendship with Mary and we were virtually inseparable. I briefly wondered why it was that she had chosen me as a friend; as I got to know her I discovered that she was not as popular as I had believed that she was and whereas she had friends, unlike myself, she was not as staggeringly popular as I would have thought someone who was as wonderful as she was would have been. Because we were close friends I imparted to her a secret that I had not told another living soul in my entire life. I told her about my desires to be a writer.

'Why do you want to be a writer?' she asked as we lay in the grass watching the clouds floating lazily by in an otherwise bright blue day.

'It's something that I think I can do, I suppose.' It wasn't perhaps the greatest answer that I could have given, but I didn't want to go into the matter of talking to her about hiding away in my own mind and creating a reality that was better than what real life had to offer.

'Is it because you want to be famous?'

'I don't think anyone sets out to be a writer because they want to be famous.' This is something that I maintain to this day.

Of all the creative jobs that you can do, writing is the most anonymous of all of them. For every Stephen King and J K Rowling that exists there are a hundred or more writers that are published that you have never heard of. For each of these published authors that you have never heard of there are a thousand that want to be published that probably never will be.

What's my point? I will tell you.

Would you recognise a million-copy selling writer if you bumped into them in your local supermarket? Unless you pay attention to author photographs on the fly leaves of books would you notice any of them at all if you bumped into one of them in the pub? Take screenwriters for example. If I randomly picked a film you might think of it as a Steven Spielberg directed film or a Tom Hanks film because he plays the main role, but how many of you would be able to say who wrote the screenplay of that film? I explained this to Mary.

'So, like *Jurassic Park* then?'

'Yes. Most people would probably tell you it was a Spielberg film.'

'Probably.'

'Another smaller section of the population would tell you that it was from a novel written by Michael Crichton.'

'I know; I've read it.'

'So have I; but would you be able to pick Crichton out in a crowd though?'

'Probably not.'

'Exactly and we can probably be considered to be better read than a lot of other people.'

'Slightly arrogant, but also slightly true, I suppose.'

'Now take it one step further and tell me who it was who actually wrote the screenplay for the film?'

She thought about this for a few seconds. 'I couldn't tell you.'

'No. Neither could I.'

'So, your point is?'

'My point is that writers don't get the fame. Not in the way that other creative peoples do and yet for a film for instance none of them would be employed if it were not for the person who sat down and put pen to paper or fingers to a keyboard. They owe their jobs and all the money that the film makes to the imagination and the skill of a writer, but they are probably the least respected in the industry and the least known by the public.'

'So, no one becomes a writer for fame?'

'Completely. Most people would probably become writers because of the fact that they not only have something that they want to say, but because they have something that demands to be said.'

'Most people would recognise a picture of Shakespeare though even if they have never read or seen any of his plays.'

'Well there are exceptions to every rule and most of the time it's Shakespeare who is the exception.'

In many ways Shakespeare did bugger up a lot of things for the rest of us that were to follow all these years later.

***

My friendship with Mary was not doing anything to take away my feeling of love for her, which if anything was growing even stronger now that I was in closer proximity to her than I had been before when I had admired her from afar. I was doing my best at concealing this from her though so that she didn't completely freak out with the knowledge.

I loved every little eccentricity that she had from the way that she wrinkled her nose when she was reading something that she didn't agree with to the way that she had the intense superstition that you should never open a crisp packet upside down or you would face years of bad luck.

Around this time, I turned my hand to writing poetry. I don't believe that I am alone in being someone who has decided to write verse when they are young and in love. Invariably it is a dismal result that should never be made public. I had no talent at all to write poetry, but for a couple of years I nevertheless insisted on doing so. I wrote in iambic pentameter for no other reason than it was pretentious. I believed that by writing in this way it constrained the verse and made me have to think carefully about what I was writing rather than having the freedom to just write anything I liked with no restrictions. It didn't make it any better.

It will come as no surprise at all that the majority of my poems were about Mary in some form or other. There were poems about how her hair smelt and how I felt being around her and how she made me feel; real sickening stuff when you look back on it. I also wrote a lot of acrostic poetry because if anything this was even more pretentious. For those of you that sensibly could never be bothered to learn this crap, acrostic is where the first letter, syllable or word of each line or paragraph spells out another word or a message. So, even poems that were essentially on the surface were not about her had hidden messages of love to her down the side. You can also hide messages in each paragraph of a novel or autobiography in this way as well.

Go on. Have a look, you know you want to.

You wasted enough time looking yet? I stopped all that shit years ago. If you have found a hidden message then it was either put there by the government or you are smoking too much weed.

I hadn't entirely given up with plays, but there really didn't seem to be all that much of a chance that I was ever going to get one of them produced, so it was nothing really more than a writing exercise to keep flexing my fingers and my mind. I wonder how much writing a writer consigns to the bin that never sees the light of day? Certainly, when I look back on it I wonder about it all. This was a very prolific writing period of my life. I was churning out all sorts of material, often sitting up into the middle of the night to write. There is not one single word of any of it that has survived to this day. This is probably a good thing.

It will come as little surprise to anyone that I never had any of my plays produced. I think I wrote about eight of them in the end and I can't even now tell you what they were about. I remember having read a book on Noel Coward that said that he wrote some of his plays in a day or less. I took this as a challenge, of course, to see how quickly I could write a play. I would be able to knock out a one act play of about thirty minutes in length in half a day. It wouldn't necessarily be any good, but it was something that I felt smug about. No idea why really.

Mary asked if I had thought about writing novels, but this was something that I had steered away from. I think the reason for this was that novel writing was the Mount Everest of writing. In order to write a novel, you had to have a huge amount of endurance to be able to keep something moving for such a long period of time over so many words. I also worried that it would be too boring. For some reason I assumed that because novels were vast they had to deal with vast subjects on epic proportions. They had to be the action films of their genre.

Eventually over a time I came to realise that they don't have to be about earth shattering events and cataclysmic disasters. They can be about the small, the intense or even about nothing at all. Novels come in all shapes and sizes. I didn't know this at this point, but it was something that I came to realise with time. I was right about one thing though. You do need the right kind of energy to be able to write novels. You have to have the quality of perseverance as well as a great memory to remember everything that you have already said and not keep repeating yourself. In brief, in order to write novels, you need stamina and a lot of it. I didn't have it at this point, I was still in training, but I would eventually turn my hand towards novels; more of which later on.

Around about this time I decided to invest in a computer as my faithful old typewriter had really suffered a battering. I bought myself an Amstrad which was really just a word processor rather than a computer in the sense that we would understand it today. It was something that I loved though. It was second-hand when I got hold of it, and only a little less battered than my typewriter had been. It just made life so much easier though. You make a mistake on a typewriter or by writing by hand and the only choices that are open to you were to start over again or use a lot of correcting fluid or leave huge crossings out. On a word processor the words just appeared and disappeared as you wanted them to. It was incredible. I really felt that for me, at least, this technology revolutionised the writing business and made it so much easier. I have no idea how people write without computers these days where you can cut and paste things and change them with no effort at all.

When this faithful old machine eventually died I replaced it with a more modern computer that could actually be used for getting on the internet and doing all of the things that computers now did that they had never done before. It amused the hell out of me that the monitor was about the size of a small car compared to the way that monitors are these days. Moving the monitor from one end of a room to another was a Herculean effort that left you feeling like you had just been pumping iron in the gym for a week. Technology has progressed a long way in a very short space of time.

This is not necessarily the best thing in the world. I rely on technology to get through my day to day activities and I openly acknowledge that it would be incredibly difficult to write if I didn't use the technology that was now available to me. I admit all of this, but I do not like technology. Maybe it is partly because of the fact that I do not fully understand what it is that I am doing and what is happening. It is more likely the case that I feel that technology has become so complicated now that you can only really understand what is happening if you have a degree in computer science.

Whilst the technology is working it is reasonably straight forward and easy to understand, but the moment that it goes wrong things become unnecessarily complicated. I also don't like the way that the manufacturers make it so that you have to keep upgrading and spending more money; as if they haven't got enough. I fully admit to being something of a techno peasant and whilst I use technology I am also just as happy with a fountain pen.

That you fill up with ink from a bottle.

***

University was the next thing on the list. I had considered the possibility of studying creative writing, but I was not entirely sure that I would enjoy this. I still had the ideas of Mr Jones ringing in my head that creative writing could only be learnt and not taught. I considered that possibly the best thing that I could do is study literature. A continuation with study in that direction would enable me to continue reading and would give me the development and breadth that I felt would be useful for learning how to write and how to find my own individual writing style.

University was a breath of fresh air for me as it meant an entirely new start in a new town. The only downside was that Mary was not going to the same university as I was.

'I am going to miss you,' I said to her on the last night that we spent together before we went off to start our new lives. She looked at me with her head on one side.

'It's not as if we are never going to see each other again.'

'I know; but I've kinda got used to being around you over the last year or so. I think it's going to be a big leap going out into the world without you by my side.'

She was silent for a minute whilst she thought about this.

'Well you know, Midge, university isn't going to last forever. We will still be in contact a lot and see each other during the holidays and who knows when it's all finished we might decide that we want to face the world next to each other.'

It was now my turn to be silent whilst I thought over what she had just said and tried to work out if this was an indication that she was interested in me in a capacity other than as a friend. I don't think I had given her any clue that I was burning with love for her as I believed that such a declaration would only cause pain on each side and was certainly to be something that would be unrequited. Now, it might be that I was imagining it and reading too much into what she was saying, but it sounded to me that there was a possibility that the door which I had always believed was firmly closed was in fact possibly slightly ajar.

I now couldn't wait until after university so that I could find out if she meant anything by what she said. Three years was a long time to wait though and attitudes could change a great deal in that period of time. She could very easily be hitched up with some jock from university who had the brain of Swiss cheese, but muscles that allowed him to sweep her off her feet.

'You are going to keep in touch, aren't you?' she asked as my silence had gone on for longer than I had thought it had.

'You won't be able to keep me away,' I smiled. 'I will be there for you whenever you need me with anything you want.'

She smiled in return and leant into me in an almost hug.

'That's my boy,' she said.

I think I was ready to die at this point. This was the happiest moment in my entire life and I couldn't imagine that there would ever come a better time. I had to go away to university, but I would go with a very happy smile on my face knowing that Mary was in the world.

***

We did stay in touch throughout university. We would write to each other on an almost weekly basis and would discuss the news that was happening with us, which in my case was almost entirely nothing, and then we would discuss the books that we were reading on our respective literature courses and argue over which was the better course. We would often resent the books that the other was reading and would go out and get copies of the books that we were not reading so we could discuss them together and, in some way, we felt as if we were closer together and sitting in the same room reading once again like we used to do around her house all of the time.

I scanned her letter each time for any hint that she had a boyfriend or that there was a love interest that would destroy my world, but either she never had any boyfriends or she was delicate enough to keep the news of them from me. I have no doubt that she knew that I was interested in her. We would see each other in the holidays and exchange books and discuss how things were going and we seemed to spend as much of our holidays together as it was possible to do.

And so, life continued like this. We shared books that we were reading and we read a lot of books. I made new friends at university because it wasn't a place where I was bullied any longer. Probably because they didn't know my bohemian background I was easier to accept into the society of the university; or maybe it was because of the fact that at university there were all sorts of people that they really didn't care if I was from a slightly less than orthodox background. University was the very mixing pot of life. It probably also helped that there was such a large student population that it was easily possible to split off into different groups and find like-minded people that you could mingle with.

It was a happy period of time for me. Everything in my life seemed to be right. It didn't even matter that Mary and myself were not dating. In a sense I didn't mind that she wasn't dating me so long as she wasn't dating anyone else. I could cope with her not being my girlfriend, but to be someone else's girlfriend would have been a disaster for me. What really mattered was that we were still together in friendship, university had not separated us even if the miles had done so. It was a truly happy period of time in my life.

And then one day I came home for one of the usual breaks as I had done loads of times before and found out that, without telling me, my mother had moved and we no longer lived there any longer.

Five

I won't deny that it came as a bit of surprise that we never lived there any longer; I acknowledge that it was more of a surprise to the family who now lived there.

It was a surprise because my key still worked in the lock and I had let myself in and had managed to make it all the way to the bathroom before I had been discovered. When I was discovered it was by a screaming woman who was in the bath when I had walked in to have a pee. Hence why they thought that I was a sexual deviant I should imagine. I can't say that I blame them for thinking this and I would almost certainly have felt the same way if the positions had been reversed. Naturally they had called the police. Well you would really, wouldn't you?

'So, tell me again,' the police officer said to me as we sat back at the police station. I went over the story again. I had told the story a number of times to a number of different people by this time, and each time I told the story I felt that it was more unbelievable than the time that I had last said it.

I wasn't under arrest which had surprised me at the time as I half expected to have been handcuffed and dragged off. I was involved in the euphemism of 'helping the police with their enquiries' or 'having a little chat down at the station' as one of them put it to me.

To their credit they believed me when I told my story, which was amazing because by this time I hardly believed it myself. The family that now lived in my home didn't press any charges, I am not entirely sure that I had broken any laws, as such. The situation was explained to them and the police officer that was interviewing me told me that they were sympathetic if somewhat cautious. I voluntarily handed over my key which was no real use to me any longer, but I am certain that the family changed the locks. I know that I would have done, if the entire experience had not been enough to have put me off living there in the first place.

It was approaching my twentieth birthday, it was soon to be Christmas, and it was an interesting start to the twenty-first century which had been going well up until that point.

'So, she just left?' the police officer asked again as if he was having trouble grasping the point, which was only fair, I suppose.

'My mother is a little scatty,' I replied whilst sipping on the vending machine coffee that he had given me which tasted frankly horrible, but had been a nice gesture. Saying my mother was a little scatty was similar to saying that Hitler was a bit naughty.

'And she didn't tell you that she was going?'

'No.'

'Or where she was going?'

'No.'

'It's very strange.'

'Yes, it is.'

'And you don't know where she is now?'

'No idea.'

'Where's your father?'

'He was killed in a car crash before I was born.'

'That's bad news.'

'I would imagine he thought so.'

'Any other relatives?'

'Not that I was ever introduced to.'

The police officer sighed and looked through his notebook again as if the answer to the solution was to be found somewhere within the pages.

'Well, you are too old for Social Services to care about you and offer any help. Obviously, you are an adult, but then in my experience they wouldn't have anything to do with you if you were a lot younger. They try not to do anything that they can't dump on someone else if they can help it.'

This didn't seem to be all that helpful.

'I suppose I could always get in touch with Mary.'

'Who's Mary?'

'A friend of mine.'

'Girlfriend?'

'I wish.'

He nodded at this as if it was a situation that he was more than familiar with from personal experience.

'Well, the family that you scared the shit out of sent this box along for you. They assume it must belong to you it was the only thing that was left in the house when they moved in.'

He hefted a box onto the table which wasn't all that large. I cautiously opened it as if not entirely sure what I was going to find inside. I found about twenty or so of my books that I had not taken to university. Thankfully I took my favourite books with me. I was pleased to see these old friends again, I didn't really have anything else which is why it was such a small box I suppose.

'Do you want to call this Mary?'

'Yeah.'

'I will get you the phone. You want anything else to eat or drink?'

'I'm fine thanks. And thanks for your understanding. I have always had a negative opinion of the police, probably because of my mother who thought you were all fascists.'

I had been concentrating so much on looking through my old books that I had unexpectedly been reunited with that I hadn't really thought about what it was that I was saying. I suddenly realised that allowing this thought to bypass the brain and head straight to the mouth was perhaps not the most diplomatic thing that I could have said in the circumstances in which I found myself.

The cop sighed and stood up. 'Yeah, well when it comes to the police opinions are like arseholes. Everyone has one and they are usually always full of shit.' He left me to the sickly coloured room and my small box of books which with along with what I had at university was the last thing that I owned in the entire world.

***

'So, she just vanished without a trace?'

'Yeah, I went through all that with the police, Mary.'

'What a freaky woman.'

'You can say that again.'

'What are you going to do?'

Mary had turned up at the police station following my call to her and had come to take me to hers. We were standing on the front steps of the police station as I clutched my small box of books to my chest with my rucksack over my back that had all of my clothing and books that I had brought back from university with me. It was a cold day and I could see my breath forming in the chill as I felt colder than it actually probably was.

I had never been overly close to my mother, but I had always thought that we got along fine. Maybe it was just that I was shocked to realise that even though she was an absentee mother she was still my mother and now she had just wandered off without an apparent thought about me in the world. I supposed I realised that some family was better than no family; no matter how shit they were.

'I don't know what I am going to do,' I answered Mary 'I suppose I will have to go back to my digs.'

'Well, you can do that, but not yet. You're not going to spend the Christmas holiday on your own in an empty house. You're coming home with me.'

'Won't your parents mind?'

'I am sure that when they hear what has happened to you then they will welcome you with open arms. They have always loved you.'

I hoped that they weren't the only ones. It was an attractive proposal and one that I couldn't really have turned down if I had wanted to.

***

I suppose I should have been more shocked by the disappearance of my mother, but then when I think deeply about it there seems to be a certain inevitability that something like this would happen at some stage in the future.

I wasn't surprised that she had vanished just before my twentieth birthday, she had missed a great many of my birthdays in the past for one reason or another. Nor was it a particularly huge surprise that she had disappeared just before Christmas. She had always viewed Christmas as something of a capitalist trap or a religious farce which I think was just her way of getting out of having to buy any presents for anyone. She was the kind of person that around Christmas could make Scrooge look like he was over doing the festivities.

I should still have been angry about it all, but I just found it so difficult to get remotely energetic about such things. In the first two decades of my life I had become resigned to a great number of things about my circumstances. I was curious enough to wonder what the meaning of life was and why we were all here doing what we were doing. I suppose because of my strange circumstances I might have wondered a little more than others what life was all about, but I wasn't any closer to getting the answers yet. As always, I suppose that I expected rather too much from things and from people.

And so, it was that I spent that Christmas and my birthday with Mary and her family. It was rather a remarkable experience for me really as I had never experienced a Christmas like it in my entire life.

To begin with there were copious amounts of Christmas decorations all over the place including a tree in the living room which was literally dripping with decorations. My mother had always been against the idea of Christmas trees, which is rather strange as the Christmas tree is really a left over from pagan times and the worship of nature, so I would have thought that it would have been something that was right up her alley really. My mother was often rather ignorant of the things that she professed to care about.

There were Christmas songs played and lights sparkling all over the place linked in with warmth and smells of Christmas that virtually assaulted my senses as I was so unused to the concept of it all. For the first time in my life I felt that I truly experienced the magic of Christmas. It had been great when I was at primary school, but it had never been something that had carried on afterwards.

I cannot begin to express the delight that I felt to be surrounded by warmth and light. I had never imagined that Christmas could have been like this. Obviously, I was aware of the fact that Christmas as we know it now was really something that I think you can put down to having been invented by the Victorians. A lot of it the responsibility of Charles

Dickens and *A Christmas Carol*, which just goes to show you that novels can change the world.

I slept on the sofa whilst I stayed at Mary's house and was woken on Christmas morning to the smell of Turkey being cooked and carols playing whilst a fire was raging in the fireplace. Opening Christmas presents and feeling for the first time in my life that I was part of a family, a warm and comforting family as well; aside from Mary's brother who was still strange and seemed to enjoy playing with wrapping paper rather than the actual things that were inside the packages.

It was the greatest Christmas that I had ever had in my entire life.

***

'So, you okay then?'

'Yeah,' I told Mary as we sat on the sofa in the cold January before we were due to return to university. 'It's been the best time that I've ever had.'

'Good,' she smiled at me in a way that made my heart flutter and various other stirrings in my loins. She was the most goddamned sexy girl that I had ever seen in my entire life.

'I am really going to miss you when I go back to university.'

'I'm going to miss you as well, I always do.' She reached across and squeezed my hand which did things to my body that she couldn't possibly have imagined; but then maybe she knew exactly what it was that she was doing. I decided that the moment was right to try risking telling her a little about how I felt about her; well at least to hint at it as I didn't think that I had the courage to tell her outright.

'There's something that I have always wanted to ask you.'

'What's that, Midge?'

'How come someone as brilliant as yourself doesn't have a boyfriend?'

She was silent for a moment and looked at me quizzically and I wondered if I had overstepped the mark. It also occurred to me that this might be the moment when she would reveal to me that she actually did have a boyfriend, but that she had been keeping him secret from me.

'Isn't it obvious?'

'No, not really.'

'I really only had one person in mind that I wanted to go out with, but I'm not sure that he is interested.'

'Anyone I know?' I swear I could feel my heart beating faster in my chest, not daring to believe that there was any possibility that it might be me that she was talking about, but at the same time dreading that she was suddenly going to tell me about someone else that she was in love with. I knew that there was a possibility that within the next couple of seconds I could either be the happiest man alive, or I would be completely crushed beyond any hope of recovery; or it is possible that nothing would change at all.

'Yeah, I think you know him pretty well.'

'Oh?'

'It's you stupid.'

'Me?'

'Of course, I always thought that there was something special between us, but I assumed you only wanted it to be friendship and were not interested in anything else.'

'Wow.'

'You should probably say something more than that to be honest. You can't leave a girl dangling.'

'Well, the only thing I can possibly say is that I have felt exactly the same way about you.'

She smiled at me. 'So, all this time we both felt the same way about each other, but neither of us dared to say anything about it?'

'Seems like we have wasted a lot of time.'

'We had better not waste anymore then.' She leant forward and kissed me lightly on the lips. After the Christmas that we had shared together I hadn't believed that things could have gotten any better and yet my world had just changed dramatically.

She broke the kiss and looked at me and I pulled her closer, taking her in my arms and we kissed passionately. I had no idea what I was doing; I had never done anything like this before and I had no idea if she had, but it was something that became instinctive. Sex education was something that had never featured very heavily in my school life nor my home life. However, there are some things which just seem to be a natural part of life.

The kissing became more passionate as we made up for lost time. I couldn't believe that my life could have become any better at that point.

Then there came the separation that existed because we had to return to our different universities to continue with our studies. I didn't think that it would be something that was bearable. It had taken us so long to get together and now after so brief a period of time we were being forced apart once again. It was intolerable really.

As you might imagine we kept in close contact, even more so than we had done before. There were many nights when I stood in the corridor using the communal telephone talking to Mary and shivering against the cold of the hall that I hardly noticed for the lengthy conversations that we were having.

I had been in love with Mary for a number of years now, but although that had been a passion that had consumed me a great deal, it was nothing to how I felt now that my love was requited. For someone that had decided that I would make a career out of writing, I suddenly found that I simply didn't have the words that would justify the way that I felt.

My passion had consumed my life and made me feel like I was a teenager again (although I had never really felt like a teenager when I had been one), I walked with a spring in my step and everything about the world seemed to be perfect.

Life was so glorious that I had quite forgotten the mystery of what had happened to my mother and her strange disappearance. The police were not treating it as an investigation as they didn't really class her as a missing person, but rather as an adult that was free to do her own thing. If her behaviour had been out of character then there is a possibility that they may have done something about it, but I have to admit that her behaviour was exactly in character and therefore something that didn't raise any suspicions with them. It didn't raise any suspicions with me, so I could hardly blame them if they were not looking into the matter with any enthusiasm. I am sure that they had other more important things to be taking up their time with.

There would come a time when I decided that I would try and find out a little more about my mother and the family that I knew nothing about and when I did find this out I would be rather amazed at the revelations that would be revealed. Every family has secrets, but I had no idea how deeply mine ran.

This was all for the distant future though. For the moment I was content to live my life the happiest that I had ever been.

***

I am pleased to say that my relationship with Mary gained in strength and I continued to walk around with a big grin on my face and a feeling like butterflies in my stomach for a long time following that first kiss that we had shared on the sofa in her living room.

At university I had made a number of friends that had been different to the way that I had travelled through the misery of my school years. My main particular friend was a guy called Luke, who had been so called by his parents because they had been massive *Star Wars* fans and I suppose that they had felt that it would be a fitting tribute to their love of this film to name their only son after one of the main characters from the film. I suppose it could have been worse, they could have named him Chewbacca.

'You certainly seem happier now than I have ever known you,' Luke said as we sat in the living room of our shared house one evening.

We had moved out of student accommodation after the first year at university when we were forced into the world of learning how to live in the same way that normal people were meant to. Apparently normal people were meant to live in big houses where we each had a bedroom that was basically our home, with the rest of the house communal and freezing.

It is a cliché to suggest that we lived on baked beans on toast and other student activities, but it is also the truth. Apparently, the universities idea of us learning how to live like normal people meant learning how to live in poverty. It was to be good practice when we were to spend the vast majority of the rest of our lives paying off student loans and the price for our education which had evidently been given to us begrudgingly by the government, who would probably have preferred it if we didn't waste our time trying to be cleverer than they were.

'I am happy,' I told Luke.

'Good, because I was concerned.'

'Concerned? About what?'

'Well, Mary is the first girl that you have ever loved – the only girl that you have ever loved.'

'That's true.'

'So, I was concerned about the fact that as she was the only girl that you've really known – you know, in that way – that you might be restless and wonder what the grass was like on the other side, so to speak.'

'Eloquently put, Luke. No, I have no interests in "sowing my wild oats" as I believe that the expression goes, before I settle down. It's true that Mary has been the only one that I have been interested in, and I have no interest in anyone else. I just want to be happy with her and I want her to be happy with me.'

'Well, here's to you both,' he said and we clinked our beer bottles together as we sat back and enjoyed the student life of not really having to do anything at all.

We were aware of the fact that this was the last time in our lives where there wasn't really going to be anything that was expected of us other than to turn in essays and to attend the odd lecture. It was an idyllic time in my life, made more so by the fact that I was in love with the most gorgeous girl in the world, and against all probabilities, she was in love with me as well.

In my own mind I had planned out a long and happy future for us where we would sit by a roaring fire reading our books into our old age being visited by our grandchildren. It's probably a good idea, therefore, that we can't always see the future that is lying in store for us.

Six

I finished university with an upper second-class degree in Literature. Throughout my time at university I had been told numerous times that the class of degree that I gained would matter greatly later in life. It mattered a great deal if I had received a first or a third. The truth of the matter was that nobody ever asked me to tell them what class my degree was. For some it was good enough that I had a degree, for others they couldn't have cared less whether I had one or not. It just goes to show you.

I briefly considered the possibility of staying on at university to continue my studies, but frankly I was fed up and disillusioned by the entire education system by this point and thought it was about time that I left and went into the real world. Also, if I am entirely honest I had no desire to spend a minute longer than I had to being separated from Mary. We had wasted enough time already that I had no desire to waste so much as a minute longer than was absolutely necessary.

We had no money, but we didn't really need it if the truth were honest. We were happy, happier than I could ever have imagined we would have been. We rented a small house which we would have loved to have bought, but could not afford the mortgage on. It didn't matter.

I say that we didn't need money, but that is not entirely true of course. Love is something that can bind us together and keep us moving along in life. Sadly, the baser matter is the fact that you need money in order to be able to function in a day to day basis and to pay the bills that society demands of us. I would love to say that none of this is necessary, but sadly it is. I dream of a time when money and the desire for greed and wealth doesn't dominate the human race, but I can't see that dream happening at any time in the near future. For the moment society seems to have engineered things in such a way that the moment we move into adulthood we are lumped with financial worries and bills to pay in exchange for money to earn. It is a vicious trap in many regards and not entirely essential for life to be able to function.

I found it difficult to get a job, which was another lie that we had been told. We had been told by teachers through to lecturers that with a degree, prospective employers would be falling over themselves to sign us up. This was a complete myth as far as my experience showed.

'It probably doesn't help matters,' I told Mary, 'that I want to find some kind of job that also enables me to write as well as enjoy my time with you.'

'That may be asking a little too much.'

'I don't think I'm asking for all that much. It's the way that I want my life to be. Too many of us settle for what society expects us to do and we sacrifice the difference between living and existing.'

'I think I know what you mean, but we don't always have a choice in these things.'

'I suppose my slightly rebellious streak in bucking what society expects is something that I get from my mother. It's in the genes.'

'I don't think you are that rebellious. Just clear on what you want.'

'Well, it didn't do her all that much good either.'

I ended up by getting a job in a library which was probably not the esteem that some of my tutors had in store for me, but for the time being at least it suited me down to the ground. For a bibliophile the prospect of working in a library or a bookshop is probably one of the best jobs imaginable, if not one of the best paid jobs that you could imagine. It didn't matter to me at the time though because I fully intended that I would develop a career as a writer on the side and would be earning enough to supplement my income within a very small space of time.

It is amazing how in youth and ignorance these things seem so easy which in reality are so difficult. Perhaps that is why as we get older we forget what it is to dream and to set our ambitions high. This is one of life's most terrible tragedies. It turns out that there are many of them.

***

It was whilst I was working in the local library that I decided that it might be time to turn my hand to the writing of novels. I had thought about the idea of starting with short stories, but I couldn't really think of anything that I could do in this area.

There is a world of difference between the short story and the novel. They both have their difficulties and complexities. A novel requires a great deal of stamina and the ability to maintain a plot and character for a lengthy period of time. A short story is concise and requires a very tight form of writing where you only really write what is absolutely necessary as you can't afford to waste any words.

They require different skills as different as the athlete who trains for the one hundred metre sprint and those that train for a marathon. They are very different disciplines, but there are those who have the ability to excel in both. We call those people, smug.

I discussed the matter with Luke.

'Our American cousins talk about "the Great American Novel" as something to aspire to and that many budding authors and established ones should be aiming to write.'

'What exactly does that entail?' he asked.

'I suppose it's a novel that is considered to be about the spirit of the age in the United States.'

'So naturally, it's taken for granted that it has to be an American writer that writes this great novel.'

'Naturally. I suppose that is fair enough.'

'Has anyone actually written one?'

'Well, I'm no expert, but I suppose there would be a case for arguing that people like Faulkner and Hemingway have had a fair stab at it.'

'What about Harper Lee?'

'Yes, I suppose you could argue that case. I suppose it can only be an American that writes it because only an American author could understand enough to write the Great American Novel.'

'Or it could be that non-American authors are just not that bothered about writing one.'

'It might be a bit of both.'

'Do we have a similar thing in Britain?'

'Not really. I suppose you could argue that Dickens has cornered the market in such things. With great novels by the like of Dickens, there really isn't all that much space for anyone else to write anything like it.'

'I don't think we really care about such things in this country.'

'That's probably because we live in a country that spends half its time pouring scorn on success. Dickens would probably not be as popular as he was if he was writing today.'

'Do we have a modern day popular author as successful as Dickens?'

'J K Rowling probably. Not too sure that anyone else comes close.'

'I'm sure she would be very pleased to be compared to Dickens in popularity.'

'I'm sure she would. This country is strange though, we just don't seem to like people that achieve something.'

'Very strange.'

'That brings me around to critics,' I said.

'What about them?'

'I'm not entirely sure that I see the point of them. They offer some degree of opinion that might help the educated to make a decision about something, but on the whole, they are spiteful little people that have no real knowledge of the subject matter that they are passing judgement on, but are more than happy to do so.'

'Anyone would think that you had bad reviews.'

'These people can make or break a career at the merest tap of their fingers. No one should have that power.'

'You make it sound like you are against criticism.'

'That's not the case. I'm more than happy to accept constructive criticism, but preferably from someone that actually knows what they are talking about. Someone that knows what it is like to slave over a keyboard and a computer screen for hours on end trying to create a world with nothing more than what the imagination will allow.'

'You sound very passionate about all of this.'

'Well I am.'

What's my point? I will tell you.

I am not a sculptor and have no skill in this particular area of art at all. Give me a chisel and a block of rock and by the time I have finished all you will have left is an oddly shaped rock that looks like it has been nibbled on by an elephant.

My point is I wouldn't attempt to criticise a sculptor without having any knowledge of the art myself or having created something at least equal to what I was attempting to judge. It seems to be the way though that we are quick to pass judgement on what we could not do for ourselves.

That doesn't mean that there are not poor writers out there. The worst kind of writer according to my beloved English teacher, Mr Jones was the cheating kind. The ones that had no respect for their reader or viewer.

'Take that episode of whatever dire American soap opera it was,' he intoned once, 'where the character woke up and found out that the person we all thought of as dead was alive and in the shower because it had all been a dream.'

He shook his head at what was obviously for him one of the worst felonies that existed.

'Any writer that has written themselves into a corner where the only thing they can resort to is to end it with "and then they all woke up and it had all been a dream" isn't worth a piss in a sandstorm.'

I had no idea what this last comment meant, but I got the general idea of what it was that he was talking about. If you have written yourself into a hole, then write yourself out of it in a proper manner or screw up the draft and start again from the beginning with something that is not going to tax you too much.

'Tastes have changed in writing though and reading,' I told Luke.

'How so?'

'Imagine you could take a novel by someone, like Dickens, and take it out of time so that no one knew anything about it. Say it was *David Copperfield* for instance.'

'Okay.'

'You then copied it word for word from its original format and submitted it to a publisher today. Would they accept it? Or, as is more likely, would they dismiss is as an archaic style that nobody was interested in, and thus a great novel would be lost to the world forever. I think there has been a great dumbing down and there are so many great works from the past that wouldn't get a look in today.'

'I suppose you could also state though that at the time that Dickens was writing, Chaucer wouldn't have been able to find a publisher, or even Shakespeare.'

'You're probably right. Certainly, they would struggle to find a publisher today. Literature is of its time, and yet at the same time of all time.'

'Well, that doesn't make much sense.'

'It's enough to depress the hell out of would-be writers to see the amount of stuff that is actually published that is nothing but dross. The problem is that a lot of the reading public seem to like a lot of dross and don't want to have to think for themselves.'

'Spoken like a man who is in desperate need to find their own publisher.'

'I would have to write something worthy of publication first.'

'And how is that going?'

'It's a work in progress. The problem is that a lot of the reading public seem to like a lot of dross and don't want to have to think for themselves.'

'Perhaps it is something to do with the fact that everyone believes that they have at least one novel in them.'

'What they tend to forget is that in a lot of occasions, the novel is something that should stay in them.'

It took me an extremely long time to come up with an idea for a novel that I thought worth the time and trouble of committing myself to. The biggest error that I made to start with, as I believe I may have mentioned before, was that I felt that the subject matter has to be big and explosive with lots of action. I probably thought this more because of the films that I watched rather than the books that I read.

In reality books are often of the smallest matter rather than big landscapes to fit a cinema screen. They can be about the smallest matters possible, but at the same time also of the largest matters that have ever existed. Take love for instance. A love story between two people without massive complications and lots of explosions can be a microcosm for the world at large. Sometimes it is best to keep matters simple rather than trying to over complicate matters.

I was a novice, trying desperately to learn my art, so I started too big as can often be the case, imagining that the bigger the better. It is very often the fact that this is not the case when it comes down to it though.

There were a couple of things that I had to work out first. The first was to work out what kind of writer I was. I suppose that this would best be attempted by trying to find my genre. I knew that I was not going to be an exciting thriller writer as I didn't think that I had the brain for that kind of thing. I also knew that it was unlikely that I could move into the extremely lucrative crime genre as that kind of thing just bored the life out of me.

On the other hand, I also knew that I didn't want to be pigeon holed into one particular genre and forced to write in that style for the rest of my career. It is rather a difficult decision to make and can lead to all kinds of obstacles. Naturally, if you had a success with a particular style of book then the publisher would want the same thing again.

The writer can be argued to be working for their art, whereas the publishers and the agents are working for money. Naturally, there are a fair number of writers out there that are also working for the money.

The second thing that had to be decided was the audience that you were writing for. There is a lot of contention on this point.

Some people think that a writer should aim for an audience and always know what that audience was.

'Keep your audience in mind,' Mr Jones used to say during one of his many chats on the creative writing process.

Pick your audience and keep them in mind. Aim for them, know their age, their gender, their intellectual (or lack of it) background.

The other side of the coin is the people who are of the opinion that writers should just write whatever they want and indulge themselves. Once the work is completed it is thrown out into the world and it will either find its own audience or it will sink without a trace.

What is the correct way of writing? It is rather difficult to say and to be honest I can see merits in both arguments. At this early stage of my career though I thought it might be better to just write what I wanted to write. For one thing it would be very good experience and exercise for me. Also, as I didn't have an agent or a publisher I didn't really have an audience at this particular time. I only had myself.

One thing was for certain, nothing was going to happen if I didn't sit down at the keyboard and write something.

Which brings me onto another point about the writing process, and one that I discussed with Luke.

'How do you deal with writer's block?' he asked me, as he had an interest in this kind of thing; I am not entirely sure why, just an inquisitive mind I suppose.

'I don't have to worry about that.'

'Why on earth not?' I suppose it had seemed to be something of an arrogant reply which justified the exclamation from Luke.

'I don't believe in it.'

'You don't believe in it?'

'I do not.'

'But just because you don't believe in something, that doesn't mean it doesn't exist.'

'That's true, but ask yourself this, my friend. Why is it that writers feel that they have an exclusive right to a block on their industry? Have you ever heard of plumber's block or builder's block; or any other kind of block on work for that matter?'

'No.'

'So, what makes writing so special?'

'I don't know.'

'The answer is that it isn't special. We may hit stumbling blocks where we have to spend more time thinking than actually writing, but I hardly see that as writer's block. Part of a writer's work is to think as well as to tap away at a keyboard. Sometimes it might actually be better if we thought more than we typed.'

'But there must be times when you just hit a brick wall?'

'True, but there are a couple of ways around that.'

'And they are?'

'The first is to write each day.'

'But if you are blocked?'

'It doesn't matter what you write, you just have to write. You are a keen fan of football, aren't you?' I had never fully understood the game myself, but this had probably something to do with my extensive bullying at games whilst at school. 'So, let me ask you, why do footballers train so much? Why don't they just turn up and play each time there is a match?'

'Practice makes perfect.'

'Exactly. And by writing each day, no matter what, it practices the art and keeps the brain cells, and the fingers, moving.'

'I see. That makes a certain amount of sense, I suppose.'

'Also, another way that I combat it is to have more than one project on the go at any given time. If I hit a "block" as you call it on one project, I put it to one side and like Hercule Poirot I let the little grey cells do their work in the background, whilst I focus on something else. When I have the answer, I go back to the original project.'

'It all sounds rather confusing really.'

'Not really, how many professions are there where you focus on only one thing at a time?'

'I have no idea.'

I think he took my point.

What's my point? I will tell you.

I do not think that writing is any different from any profession. It is something that you have to work hard at to see any results. I know of no other profession that allows itself to grind to a halt because it has a block on it. No employer would tolerate such behaviour. So why should writing be so different and think itself above it all?

The key thing about being a writer *is to write*. If you don't write then you are not a writer. It's as simple as that. Sit down at your computer, your typewriter, or your pen and paper, or whatever it is you choose to write with and write, each day. Set yourself a target amount of what it is that you want to do. It can be anything, a chapter a day, two thousand words, ten thousand words or whatever; but set yourself that target and do your best to keep to it.

That is what writers should be doing. It is what we love to do and what we all hope that one day we will be paid to do. Some of us are lucky in that regard, but not all.

It's a cut-throat business. Largely because there are so many people that are trying to get into it whether they are talented enough to do so or not. What I have also found to be rather frustrating is the legion of people that exist who feel that they would like to give advice, comment on your work or tell you that they have also written a novel and that they would like you to read what they have written. I cringe from reading other people's unpublished manuscripts. I am not entirely sure why, it is just the way that it is for me.

***

I seem to have imparted a fair amount of my opinion on what it is that I think writers should be doing. I apologise if it is boring. Most people tend to be interested because they think you are going to tell them the secrets of how to publish their own work. Why do you think so many successful novelists have written books on how to write? Why do you think so many people buy them?

There is a thriving industry out there and I am delighted to say that despite the death knell being rung for books for years, it has not happened. People are always waiting to forecast the end of the printed word as if it is something to be proud of.

They thought it would be the end of books when theatre was popular, they thought the pages would curl up and die when the cinema came along, they thought that the paper would turn to dust with television and they think that the end is nigh because of electronic books.

It is true that there are probably less bookshops than their used to be, but those that are in existence don't seem to be doing too badly from what I have seen and there is still a thriving market of people buying books online. I think it will be a very long time before books completely disappear, if indeed they ever do.

I have never been one for reading books electronically. I can understand the arguments that one little device can hold an entire library of books that you can just slip in your pocket and take on holiday with you; but I like to feel the book in my hand, I like to hold it and smell it and I like to see it sitting on the shelves when I am not reading it, where it will wait for the possibility that one day it will be read again.

It would be a sad world that existed without books in it. Just look at the Nazis. If you want to be with the kind of people that think it is acceptable to burn books as a prelude to burning people then I am afraid that I just don't want to know you at all.

I, for one, will never give up on them; no matter what happens. As long as I can find somewhere to buy them from, then I will continue to buy them.

***

Time has a habit of marching on regardless of what we might like to do about it to the contrary. I am aware of the fact that I am skipping over a great many years like a young child skipping through a field, but it's my story and there is still rather a lot of things that I need to tell you about. It is hard to keep it in chronological order without allowing myself to muddle the timeline by stating what I now know that I didn't know at the time that it was happening. If that makes any sense to you at all?

1997 had been a time of hope with the new Government of Tony Blair's although it didn't take all that long for that particular pill to turn sour. One might almost say that with it died the hopes of a generation. It just goes to prove to you that you can't trust any politicians. Come to think of it, I can't remember the last politician that I actually either liked or trusted. Sex scandals amongst the politicians which had in reality been going on for a very long time would manifest themselves into corruption and a series of later prison sentences.

The public lost faith in politics and politicians very quickly; that is assuming that they ever had any faith in them in the first place.

I have passed over the millennium because it didn't really hold any significance to me other than to prove that the nineteen seventies television programme *Space 1999* had been proven to be wildly inaccurate in its prediction of the future. Come to think of it that is the problem of trying to predict what the future will be like in fiction; it is almost always unsuccessful, which is one of the reasons why I have never been tempted to write science fiction.

My story now reaches 2004. The year that I would turn twenty-four and four years since my mother disappeared and since Mary and myself had got together. In those four years there had been no sign of my mother and it was not something that I was particularly all that bothered about by this time. I was rather resigned to the fact of what had happened and there didn't seem to be any point in dwelling on the point.

What I did focus on was the developing relationship with Mary which had grown in strength. Four years on and we were still very much in love and enjoying every minute of living together.

From a current affairs point of view, I don't remember 2004 as being a particularly remarkable year. I can't remember any events that happened in the news that really took my attention and made me sit up. I remember ex-President Ronald Reagan died which was mildly interesting as he had always been viewed with a mixture of comedy and fear that someone who was quite clearly suffering from onset dementia should be the most powerful man in the world with the ability to kill all of us without fully realising or understanding what it was that he was doing.

Mind you this has to be taken into context with the fact that in 2004 George W Bush was President of the United States. In fact, it is rather amazing when you think about it that we have survived until as long as we have given the presidents and prime ministers that we seem intent on electing to office.

There was one remarkable thing about 2004 and that was that it was a leap year. You may not think that this is a particularly remarkable occurrence as they do tend to happen every four years. However, if you know your folklore you will know that leap years are the time when women are supposedly allowed to propose marriage to men. Evidently it is sexist to believe that women can propose at any other point in time.

Mary was a traditionalist though, or at least she was when it suited her. She decided to take the opportunity of the fact that we had been together as a couple for almost four years and that it was a leap year by asking me to marry her.

It will come as no surprise to you that I accepted immediately. You may ask why it was that I waited for her to ask me rather than me asking her when marrying her was something that I had wanted to do since I was at least sixteen years old, if not younger.

I suppose the reason for that was because of the fact that I wanted it so much that I almost dared not risk asking her for the same reason that I had not dared ask her out when we had been friends only; I could not risk losing what I had because of the fact that she might not want everything that I wanted.

I couldn't have been happier that she still felt the same way that I did. We began to plan our wedding day.

Seven

We had managed to put a little money to one side over the years despite having to pay off student debts and so we decided that we would like to get married sooner rather than having a lengthy engagement.

'What sort of wedding would you like?' Mary asked me.

'What sort are there?'

I was really of the opinion that a marriage was something that you turned up on a certain day, stood in front of an official of some description and said 'I do' at the right time. What other kind of wedding was there? It just goes to show you how little I know about such things.

'Well do you want to get married in a church, or in a registry office?'

This was a good point, I hadn't really thought about this. It's true that I had been raised a Christian (chiefly by the school that I went to rather than by my mother who didn't believe in any organised religion,) but I had of late become rather lapsed in my religious beliefs, so now I was not sure what I would prefer.

'Well, what would you prefer?'

This might be seen as the cowardly way out of it by avoiding the question, but my justification for this was that I wanted Mary to have whatever she wanted and I would much rather that she chose to have what she preferred rather than compromising by going along with something that I was not overly fussed about.

'Well, I know we are not overly religious, but perhaps a church wedding would be rather nice,' she mused whilst looking at the water streaking down the window as we sat in our living room. 'The problem is that church weddings are so much more expensive than it would be to have it in a registry office.'

'I think you have to go with what you really want, rather than how much it will cost. So long as we don't go totally nuts we'll find some way to pay for it.'

She leaned forward and kissed me on the nose.

'You are far too good for me, Midge.'

'Oh, I really don't think so. I think it's rather the other way around.'

'Perhaps that's why we are so suited. We both see the best in each other.' She gazed out of the window thinking for a little longer. 'Perhaps we should go for a discreet church wedding.'

'That will be fine.'

'Who's going to be your best man?'

'Luke, I should think.' I hadn't asked him but there wasn't a lot of choice in the matter really. 'Well, at least we will save money on my side of the family.'

'True,' she looked at me with her sad eyes 'but that will unbalance the top table slightly.'

'Make it round.'

'A little unconventional, but I suppose it would be an option.'

'I don't really care that there won't be any of my family there. I don't really care what other people may think about the fact that my side of things is empty. All I care about is that you are happy.'

'I will be. This will hopefully be a once in a life time experience.' There was a pause for a moment whilst she clearly debated whether to continue with her line of thought which she ultimately appeared to do. 'Do you want to try and find your mum?'

'No.'

There really didn't seem to be all that much else to say on that matter as far as I was concerned.

You might think it a little harsh that I wasn't prepared to try and find my mother so that she could know that her only son was getting married. If you do think that then I can only ask where the hell you have been so far? She walked out without a word and I had not seen her for four years. If she didn't care all that much about me then I wasn't going to bust my balls trying to find her.

But family is family, I hear you whine. Yes, it is, but you can't polish a turd. I am doing fine as I am, thanks for asking.

***

'Are you sure you want to do this? Luke asked me when we went out for a pint one lunchtime.

I looked at my pint of lager with a degree of apprehension and wondered what it was that he knew that I didn't.

'Well, I know it kills off brain cells, but as long as you drink in moderation I can't really see it being a massive problem really.'

'Not the alcohol. Getting married.'

'Why wouldn't I want to do it?'

'Well, you know.'

'Not really.'

'Well, it's just that Mary is the only girl you have ever dated and now you are marrying her.'

'This the old sowing the wild oats thing again?'

'Well, not really – well, okay maybe it is. I guess I am just looking out for you.'

I squinted at him slightly. 'How is that exactly?'

'I just want to make sure that you make the right decision that is all.'

'Luke, you have known that I have loved Mary pretty much all of my life, certainly for at least half the time that I have been alive I would say. Do you really think I am making a bad decision?'

'No, I just want you to be certain of it, that's all.'

'I don't think I have ever been more certain of anything in my entire life.'

'Well, that's okay then.'

'What you can do to help is to be my best man.'

'I thought you would never ask.'

'I was just letting the suspense build up.'

***

We planned to get married in February 2005.

This proved to be a pretty disastrous decision given how it turned out that because of St Valentine's Day, February was actually a very popular month for getting married. It would also probably mean that the flowers were more expensive than they would have been at any other time of the year. It is nice to see that there is a month in the year when people can charge you twice as much for the same product that you can buy at any other time at half the price. I suppose everyone is entitled to make a living.

We eventually settled on February 10 which turned out to be the day that Arthur Miller died. I didn't know it at the time as I was rather focused on other matters, I imagine he was as well.

It was reasonably informal even if it did take place in a church. We were lucky enough to be able to convince them to hold the ceremony on a Tuesday, we could have gone for the Saturday, but that would have been Valentine's Day itself and naturally everyone that year decided that they wanted to get married on that date, or so it seemed.

It felt cold on that day and I was pleased that I had chosen to wear a waistcoat as well as the normal suit. There was a distinct belief that although we were in February we were nowhere near being out of the winter yet; and indeed, before too much longer we would be hit by a lot of snow that as usual would bring the country to standstill despite knowing that it is coming each year.

We are pretty crap at the weather in England. This is chiefly because of the fact that we are never happy with it. It is either too cold, too hot, too wet or just too boring. The simple fact of the matter is that we are never satisfied, no matter what is going on. This should make things interesting for us as we never know what we are going to see when we look out of the window each morning, but no the variety that we are given doesn't please us. I imagine what it must be like waking up in Los Angeles each morning, looking out the window and seeing that it is sunny, again. Surely that would be more boring than never knowing what you were going to be faced with?

I waited in the church with Luke whilst Mary enjoyed her prerogative of being late. I don't want to harp on about the weather all the time, but it was actually colder in the church than it was outside. Not for the first time I wondered if the coldness and discomfort was designed in order to keep the worshipers in a state of prayer and concentration without relaxing enough and becoming complacent.

We had gone for the basics as we didn't fancy all the unnecessary add-ons that the Church probably rely on to make the most of their money from. I am pretty sure the vicar was giving us a very disapproving look about this and was probably of the opinion that we were likely to go to hell because we hadn't given enough money to the Church. Well, there are some things that you just have to learn to live with really.

Mary looked stunning. I had always considered her beautiful, of course, but she really excelled herself on that day. She took my breath away, not for the first time. I don't remember all that much of the wedding ceremony itself, it was something that seemed to fly by in the space of a few minutes.

And then with the exchange of a few words it was all over and we were married and the dream that I had spent my entire life on (near enough) had finally come true. It just goes to show you that dreams can come true. Not often perhaps and not always, but they can come true.

It is a cliché that I am sure a number of grooms say at a time like this, but I really was the happiest man alive.

I don't remember all that much about the wedding breakfast and reception either if I am totally honest, not because I was drunk or anything like that, but because I was in so much of a haze about what was going on. I still found it all rather hard to believe that something I had wanted for so long had finally happened.

It was true that there were hardly all that many people from my side present at the wedding. It didn't really bother me all that much as I had become pretty used to this situation by this point in my life. If it was a source of amusement to other people then I couldn't have really cared less. I was happy, and Mary was happy and that was really all that mattered when it came down to it.

Mary's brother who took the word 'moronic' to new and unexpected levels acted in the role of an usher at the church. I had frankly considered the possibility that given his general state of things asking him to take on this simple task was something that might well have been considerably beyond his abilities. As I am sure you are aware ushers are meant to be people that are there to show guests to their seats and in general be on hand to answer any questions that they might have. Mary's brother had difficulty finding his arse with both hands let alone being able to find seats for the guests. Fortunately, we didn't have that many guests so it presented him with a task that I presumed that even he would be unable to screw up.

Mary's father made a slightly drunken speech which was very sincere about his daughter and how happy he was for her. He stated that he was pleased that she was marrying me, but if I ever did anything to harm her then he still had his shotguns. Everyone laughed and whereas he had clearly meant it as a joke there was just the slight suggestion that there was a serious threat behind it. I suppose it is the way that all fathers feel about their daughters and the men that they date; or in this case marry.

I don't remember too much about my speech other than it was probably confused and rambling as I tried to remember who I had to thank before moving onto the easy part which was saying nice things about Mary.

Luke performed his best man duties admirably with the right combination of sincerity and humour that you would expect and hope for. It was a glorious day and as silly and clichéd as it sounds I spent the entire day walking with a bounce in my step as if I was walking on air.

***

Our honeymoon didn't follow straight away as we felt that we needed a little break before going away. We only needed a little space and then we would arrange to go away.

I had left the choice of honeymoon entirely up to Mary and had no idea what she was going to come up with. There was always the possibility of a couple of weeks in Hay-on-Wye which would have suited our literature tastes, or maybe a tour of the literary sights of England.

I left the entire matter up to her so it would be my own fault if she came up with something that I had not been expecting.

Married life didn't turn out to be all that much different from what life had been like before. I didn't feel any different. A piece of paper and a couple of rings can't change your life if you didn't have that magic in existence beforehand. We were in love and just as happy now as we had been before only now it was somehow more official and perhaps more solid. There was a commitment that had been made. I suppose that is what it amounts to when you think about it.

I continued to work in the library which although not very well paid, was satisfying to me. It was a trifle limiting in the fact that the kind of people that went there were at one end of the spectrum or another.

What's my point? I will tell you.

Seemed to me that at one end of the scale there were youngsters who were brought in by eager parents or bored school teachers; desperate to either put their child ahead of their contemporaries or shut them up for a few minutes, or more likely allow them to become someone else's problem, namely mine.

At the other end there were the old aged pensioners who came in from the cold or the rain, because it was the only time that they ever saw anyone to talk to or because they simply had nothing better to do.

There didn't seem to be that many people in the middle ground, presumably because they were either too busy at work, too busy with their children or illiterate. It was difficult to tell really.

Therefore, the most questions that I seemed to be asked were about Harry Potter or Catherine Cookson. I tried to sneak more of the educated Nobel Prize winning writers into the stock, but I quickly found out that if you had won the Nobel Prize for Literature it tended to mean that nobody out of a tight circle of readers had ever heard of you.

I tried to expand reader's horizons though and would pay close attention to what was on television and in the cinema and if there were any adaptations of books then I would immediately put out a display of that book with a selection of other works from that writer, assuming there were any of course. In a similar vein if a writer died I ensured that a tribute table of their works was put on display so that people might be reminded of their work, or newly discover them. I probably put too much thought and effort into it because nobody really seemed to care about any of it accept me.

I suppose it was rewarding to help people with their reading though. My only wish that we had been able to spread out our selection a little more rather than the bog standard run of the mill stuff that everyone seemed to be interested in. The kind of books that worried me because they were too much of the chewing gum for the mind and not enough of anything else. Usually the kind of thing that had a picture of someone running on the front cover which served as a general warning sign to me. Some people might say that was snobbish elitist rubbish, but hey well there you go.

Libraries were under threat. Culture was under threat in general. Libraries closed all the time as did bookshops, art galleries, museums and theatres. It was really the mainstream, well established places that survived and flourished whilst the smaller, independent institutions struggled and eventually died out for want of money.

'It annoys the hell out of me that this country just doesn't seem to bother with the Arts,' I told Luke on one of our regular meets shortly after my wedding.

'Don't they?'

'No. Other countries throw money at the Arts and as a result the culture of that country flourishes and produces magnificent works to be proud of.'

'Do they?'

'Yes, they do. We, the country of Shakespeare, Dickens, Turner, Constable, and loads of others that I can't remember seem to be resting on our laurels.'

'What's your point?'

'I will tell you. My point is that we no longer seem to bother to try and excel in excellence or promote the Arts which seem to fall to pieces each year without a hope of recovery.'

'Well, have you considered that the Government might have better things to spend the money on?'

'Like what?'

'Well, transport, education, the NHS, defence and so on.'

'Well Luke, the transport system is shot to pieces, the education system seems to have given up and is not interested any longer, the NHS is on its knees and as to defence we seem to spend half the time in pointless conflicts that we don't really need to be involved in, or they are slashing the budget so we can't afford to be involved in pointless conflicts that we shouldn't be involved in.'

'I am sure there is a point to what you are saying, Midge, but I just have no idea what the logic of it is.'

'I am trying to make the point,' I patiently stated 'that we should invest more in the Arts.'

Luke sighed and folded up the newspaper that he had been reading before I started to rant at him.

'The thing that has always annoyed me,' he stated after a while, 'is that it seems to be somewhat socially acceptable to not have that much knowledge of science, but you are branded a philistine if you don't have that much knowledge of the Arts.'

'That's because you are a scientist.'

'I have never sought to deny it.'

Luke was indeed a scientist. We were in many regards extremes and under normal circumstances we probably would never have met, but when we entered into our second year at university we were all encouraged to get out of university digs and find somewhere else to live. Under such circumstances it was often necessary to club together with all different kinds of people so that you could jointly afford to pay the rent and the bills. Normally it is all your friends that get together to share a house, but at times it is a friend of a friend that joins in and that is how I came to meet Luke.

Being from the science faculty and me being from the arts faculty we might only have met at student events or in the bar as our paths would not normally have crossed, but he was the friend of one of my other friends. We soon became the firmest friends out of everyone else in the house. We would often enjoy clashing like this over the differences between science and art. It was the same debate that we had undertaken a number of times, but it was never something that we were tired of.

'Science is what makes our lives easier, Luke, but Art is what we live for.'

'I am sure someone very clever once said that,' he sighed.

'Yes, me.'

'Other than you, naturally.'

'Probably. As my old English teacher used to tell me, "there is nothing new under the sun".'

'He was probably right.'

'He normally was.'

We sat in silence for a few minutes and contemplated life in general and our own particular views on it.

'My point is,' I said again 'that if we don't invest in the Arts we are in danger of losing our souls.'

'Perhaps you should write to the Government.'

'Do you really think they are remotely interested in what the public think or have to say about anything?'

'No, I guess you are right there.'

'You know it's true.'

***

It is true, or at least it certainly seems that way to me that no matter what political party is in power there never seems to be any noticeable difference between them. They all seem to act the same way and they all have the same air of hypocrisy and scandal about them. Either they are fiddling their expenses or they are involved in some kind of sex scandal. It doesn't really matter what they are doing, but they are clearly only in power for what they can get out of it rather than what they can give back to the public.

It is a tired old view and something that is very boring, but the simple fact of the matter is that these politicians that are supposed to be representatives of the people are so detached from the public that they really have no idea what is going on. It makes me very mad and I get angry with the news to the point where Mary has banned me from watching it for fear that I will end up throwing something through the television.

The reason for the anger is that I don't think I have seen a single politician who is not arrogant, stuck up or just obnoxious and full of themselves. It has reached a point now where it is almost impossible to decide who to vote for. You look at the contenders on ballot day and you just see a list of useless egomaniacs or fools and think that there is no difference between any of them that makes any of them seem outstanding enough to put your cross in their box.

Problem is that they are so arrogant that they genuinely don't seem to realise that we hate them all so much and consider that they all act the same as each other.

***

'How do you feel about flying?' Mary asked me.

'Why?'

'I'm just curious.'

'I've never done it.'

'Are you afraid of it?'

'I've never done it.'

'But are you afraid of it?'

'It would be difficult to be afraid of something you have never done.' She thought about this for a moment.

'You haven't been shot, but I am sure you wouldn't like it.'

'I wouldn't like it, no; but I can't say I live in fear of being shot.'

'But would you go on a plane?'

'Depends whether the intention of going on it involves jumping out of it.'

'Why would you do that?'

'Exactly,' I stated. 'But there are some people who do just that. They love jumping out of planes which I could never frankly see the point of whilst the engines were still working fine. I would be hard pushed to want to jump out of one if the engines were not working to be honest.'

'Well I can't see the thrill in that either to be honest and you needn't worry on that account I would have no desire for you to jump out of a plane.'

'Well that's all right then.' I went back to reading the novel that I had been reading.

'But would you go on one to go on holiday, or something like that?'

I put my book to one side again and looked at her. 'I suppose so if it was absolutely required. I haven't really thought about it.'

'Perhaps you should.'

It was at this point that I began to suspect that the honeymoon might not be a literary tour of England.

Eight

Mary had clearly decided that it was high time that I was to undertake my first aeroplane trip. It had never previously bothered me in the slightest, but it was clearly something that seemed to matter a great deal to her, so who was I to argue?

When people learnt that I had reached my advanced age of twenty-four without having flown they assumed that it was because I had an absolute fear of flying. Clearly in the twenty-first century we are all expected to have been flying from birth and have pilot licences by the time that we are in our teens. The fact that I didn't, clearly was an indication that I was afraid. What other explanation could there possibly be?

This was not the case. It was just something that I was not terribly bothered about that was all; it had been one of those things that I could take or leave and as I was not actually with anyone before Mary I had no desire to go through the rigmarole of going through an airport and flying to a far-off country just so I could be on my own. I was able to do that much more cheaply by not leaving my bedroom.

I did discover one thing though by going on this trip that I had not known before: I was afraid of flying.

Well, sometimes you don't know about these things until you try them; a bit like Marmite and Brussel Sprouts (although that is a combination I most certainly would not like to try).

Mary had decided, however, that she wanted to go to Egypt; like many things and places it was something that I knew a great deal about purely from the things that I had read about it. I did wonder if actually going to the place might spoil my imagination of what I had previously conjured up from the books I had read. There are genuine times when reality can be a real pain in the arse.

I still thought that flying was something that was unnecessary and really unnatural, but I had learnt that this was not likely be an argument that would cut any ice as far as Mary was concerned. Mary didn't have a problem with flying and I even believe that she actually enjoyed it. It takes all kinds of people to make a world.

So it was that I found myself in the metropolis that was the airport. Trailing a suitcase on wheels behind me that was full of clothing and a rucksack over my back that was primarily full of books I made my way through the alien location to bag check-in where a sour faced woman weighed our bags to ensure that we were not trying to cheat the airline of a few pounds, of money that is, although it would equally apply to weight.

From there we made our way to what I would discover as the joy of customs where my boarding pass was examined by a cynical looking man who clearly believed that everyone was a terrorist. Moving forward I had to empty all personal items into a tray that was then sent on a conveyor belt through an x-ray machine whilst I tried my best not to look guilty.

That is the thing about authority, whether it is customs or being stopped by the police or even some authoritative figure whilst at school, I can't help but look and feel guilty even when I know that I am innocent and have done nothing wrong at all. I would be a terrible smuggler or criminal; one look and I would be breaking down confessing to whatever it was that I had done, or that I was trying to do.

This feeling was only enhanced when I walked through the x-ray machine and the alarm sounded and I was taken to one side by a very patient man who clearly looked like he could become very intolerant at a flick of a switch. I was very conscious of the fact that it seemed like all eyes in the immediate vicinity were on me now waiting for me to be led away in handcuffs by sniffer dogs; or something like that. Possibly they were waiting to see if I would explode.

Now I know that the reason the alarm went off was because I was wearing sturdy walking boots that I thought would be useful to wear for walking out of the desert when the plane inevitably crashed. I was aware that these stout boots had huge chunks of metal on them for the laces. Naturally, there was no pointing this out and being allowed to go on my way. Clearly the metal in my boots could have been a distraction to hide the Kalashnikov and machete that were strapped to each of my legs.

I was then asked to stand in a machine that looked rather like one of those cubicle toilets that you sometimes find on some streets. I was asked to put my arms above my head and a scanner of some description went around my body leaving me wondering if the people looking at the computer screen could see my penis.

Standing with my arms above my head did make it all seem strangely perverted as if I had been caught and frozen in mid-stripper pose. Eventually it was decided that I was not trying to carry a bomb onto the plane and I was allowed to join Mary who was standing on the other side of the barrier giggling to herself. She clearly found the entire situation hilarious.

We then went into the departure lounge which was a slight understatement given the vast size of the place. Having carefully weighed your bags outside they now let you into an area where you could reasonably buy other items to triple your weight limit. I decided that I wouldn't do this as I had probably done enough to bring me to the attention of the nice people from customs.

Looking out of the departure window I saw the aeroplane that Mary had assured me was the one we would be using.

'But, it's tiny,' it actually probably wasn't all that tiny, but I had clearly been expecting something bigger, presumably under the belief that the bigger it was the better chance we had of it staying together. 'It looks so flimsy. So very fragile.'

'It will be fine,' Mary stated with the air of someone who was a seasoned flyer and who was becoming used to my paranoid comments about such things by this time.

I wasn't so convinced and it was with great trepidation that I walked down the gangway and eventually stepped into the small metal tube that I would very shortly be entrusting my life to. When we found our seats, I felt very claustrophobic with the small amount of leg room and proximity to all the other passengers, any one of which could have turned out to be a terrorist any second. I am not, by any stretch of the imagination the tallest person in the world, but I certainly felt that I could probably have benefitted from a little more leg room.

We then began the take-off procedure which was one of the strangest experiences that I could have imagined. We slowly taxied along the runway whilst the stewardess told us in the nicest possible of ways that in the unlikely event of anything happening we were in all probability going to die. Trotting along the runway like that was very much like being in a coach going along a normal road. Mary had offered me the window seat, but I declined on the grounds that I didn't think that there was any way that I could really benefit from seeing what was about to happen.

'Well, this isn't so bad,' I told Mary.

'It will be fine. Trust me.'

All of a sudden the pleasant country drive in the coach which was akin to some mundane old aged pensioner day trip to the seaside changed dramatically as the machine that I was strapped into suddenly flung itself down the tarmac with a vengeance and at a level of speed that I was not really prepared for, but I suppose I should have anticipated given how it was logical to know that there had to be a fair amount of speed going to get the bloody thing into the air in the first place.

Just as suddenly we were in the air and with it came a great feeling of detachment, which was due to the fact that we were. I was suddenly detached from the planet that I had spent my entire life clinging to. I was no longer on planet Earth, I was just very, very near it.

I believe that the most dangerous part about flying is the taking off and the landing. This is the time when things can most go wrong, either from human error or because of some mysterious mechanical thing that I could have no hope of ever really understanding. Nor would I probably want to understand it. It was all a mystery to me. I had no idea how this thing magically stayed up in the air. It just didn't seem possible. What was keeping this huge (I had now decided that it was no longer small), heavy, metal thing in the air? It seemed perfectly unnatural (which it was) so I quickly came to the conclusion that the only way that this machine could stay in the air was by the collective will power of everyone on board. I believed that this would take a lot of concentration so became frustrated by those (including Mary) who wished to engage in idle chit-chat.

I became aware that I was fully in the hands of someone else, and it was not as if I could take over the driving, attempt to slow us down or stop us or even jump out if anything went wrong, like you might be able to in other modes of transportation. I was entirely at the mercy of someone that I would never even get to see.

I found myself praying that the pilot was having a good day and that they had not split up with their partner that morning and couldn't see the point any longer. As we launched into the air it was nice to see out of the window that the airport was surrounded by fields so at least when we crashed we wouldn't be landing on someone's house. Oh yes, I may not have been sitting next to the window, but I was still able to see out of it.

Looking out of the window had been a mistake, but it was something that I really found it impossible not to do from time to time. It was disconcerting to see the unnatural sight of fields and farm houses becoming steadily more distant as we climbed. Eventually as I watched they became almost impossibly remote, like children's toys. It was very off putting particularly as Mary insisted on bringing things to my attention that I would much rather have not seen or known about – specifically the ground.

Fortunately, within a few minutes we were into cloud cover and I could convince myself that I was back on the coach only driving through very thick fog. Thick fog that seemed to be causing a fair amount of turbulence. Each bounce and shudder made me think that something vital was about to fall off the aeroplane – such as a wing or one of the engines. It would then plummet thirty-five thousand feet to the ground, shortly followed by the rest of us.

Mary quickly became bored and restless during the flight, a luxury that I didn't have as I was still too busy keeping the plane in the air with only my will power. My discomfort was not helped all that much by the screen in front of me that told me useful information such as that we were at thirty-eight thousand feet now, that the outside temperature was minus twenty-eight degrees and we were travelling at a land speed of four hundred and twenty miles an hour. All of which was information that I could easily have done without.

After a while we started to approach Egypt. I risked another glance out of the window and was surprised to see that the mountains and desert of what I assumed was the Sinai were almost red in colour. It was not what I expected. As the information screen had now been folded away and with nothing to see other than the mountain range and sand it was impossible to get a perspective of how high we were. I assumed that the answer remained, bloody high.

Eventually we came into land and I was hoping that my palms would stop sweating and I would be able to make it through to touchdown without vomiting. You may have noticed that I was using a lot of terms that might normally be reserved for space flight, but I can assure you that I went into flight feeling much the same as the Apollo astronauts probably felt.

As we came in to land, I found myself hoping that the tyres and the brakes were serviced regularly and in good condition so that we had a fair chance of actually stopping at the end of the runway. I had no idea what speed it was that planes hit the tarmac and I didn't want to know.

Yes, I do use the phrase hitting the tarmac to mean exactly that. I was once told by someone that there was no such thing as landing a plane, it just wasn't something that could be done. The term 'landing' was used to reassure everyone when what was really happening was that the pilot was performing a carefully controlled and very skilful crash.

I hope all of this is reassuring; especially if it is something you are reading on a plane.

Well, now you know how I feel.

***

I hadn't really got on all that well with Her Majesty's Custom officials when I had left Britain, but it was nothing to the shock of what it was like in Egypt.

When the plane landed we were met with some steps that I could walk down feeling like I was the President of the United States. Instead I concentrated on the feeling of heat that struck me the moment I stepped outside; it was the first time that I think the term 'heatwave' had been used to describe exactly what it was. The Egyptian evening was humid rather than hot, I suppose, as if all of the moisture had been sucked out of the air; which for all I know it had.

Arriving in Egypt was a stark contrast to the departure in England. Here we were hurdled like cattle into the airport immigration which seemed to be somehow out of place and yet gave the appearance of not entirely reaching snobbish Western standards. We were shouted at in some Arabic language that I had no hope of understanding by angry looking staff that seemed to lack professional detachment.

Taken through we were eventually released into the still night where we were met by a tour rep who again hurdled us towards a VW Micro Bus which was covered in tassels and would have made my mother proud. We were then driven out into the night whilst the tour guide told us not to drink the water.

'Not even to brush your teeth, you understand?' We all nodded dutifully. 'It is very bad.'

'Bad?' I asked.

'Yes, don't even think about drinking any of it. You will be very ill.'

I decided to place my attention outside of the window. I was surprised to find that whereas there appeared to be no discernible traffic laws there were frequent sentry posts that were occupied by heavily armed soldiers who appeared to be dangerously bored. I tried not to think about it.

We then arrived at the hotel which appeared to have been designed by someone who clearly had a fetish for marble and believed that this was the height of uncouth Western decadence and therefore what we clearly wanted. Either that or it was a last nod in the direction of the Pharaohs. We were booked in and shown to our room where we started a week of tipping.

Tipping and haggling, which were clearly part of the culture here, were largely alien to the majority of English people – or were certainly alien to me. I occasionally used to tip in restaurants and the like, but in general the view of the person who was being tipped was being paid a wage so why add to something that existed.

'They don't get paid as much out here, they probably rely heavily on tips to supplement their income,' Mary told me as she tipped the porter as I had just been looking at him blankly wondering why it was that he was still there. Haggling was something that was entirely alien to me.

'The prices are purposefully high and they don't expect you to pay more than about half of what they are asking,' Mary had explained once again.

'Well why don't they just ask the price that they expect you to pay and cut all the unnecessary crap out?'

'It doesn't work like that.'

'Clearly. I don't imagine I would get very far if I went to the supermarket back home and started to haggle with them over how much I wanted to pay for a tin of beans.'

'Just look at what you want to buy,' Mary sighed 'ask yourself how much you would be prepared to pay for it. Fix that price in your head, start lower than the price and if he wants you to go higher just shake your head and walk away. I promise you that they won't be prepared to let you walk away.'

Mary seemed to know all of this because she had spent previous holidays in Egypt with her family when she had been growing up. Looking around me I was amazed that her idiot brother had managed to survive in the country and leave it still alive. Family holidays were obviously something that didn't exist when I had been growing up so I was at a slight disadvantage, or at least that was how I chose to see it. I thought that there were a lot of things that would take me time to get used to in Egypt. I was not sure if I would succeed in the transition.

Egypt was in the middle of a Middle East conflict so much of what could be done was limited. We were not allowed into the Sinai, we were not allowed into Israel. We could not go north to Cairo due to conflict, so the pyramids, Sphinx, Valley of the Kings and all the normal things that you went to Egypt to see were off of the agenda. We were told that we might be able to visit some places in the Sinai if we went with armed guard and police escort.

Suddenly, whatever it was that we were meant to go and see didn't seem to be worth seeing. I certainly realised that I was not in the UK any longer; or not in Kansas if you like your film references, which I didn't say initially because I thought it might confuse you into thinking I was actually from Kansas, when I am not. Anyway.

Now I realise that this next bit will probably make me sound like a racist which I am really not. However, I do have a problem understanding foreign accents. Well, if I am honest they don't have to be foreign as there are a number of dialects from England that my ears are closed to. I really don't think it is racism it's just that my ears are not built that way. However, the matter on hand was people overseas at this time rather than regional dialects.

Now I fully applaud the fact that they have learnt English when the English are pretty lazy at wanting to learn any other language but our own, which we insist on using increasingly loudly when we encounter a language barrier as if we just can't understand why it is that the other person can't speak English.

I applaud the effort of others to learn our language and one day even the Americans may learn English as well, but I just can't get my ear around heavily accented English. Either it is my ears that are just not made that way, or my brain just turns itself off at the effort or something.

I had great trouble, therefore, understanding what people were saying to me. Waiters would speak to me and I just started smiling gormlessly and nodding my head hoping that he was not telling me that his wife had just died that morning. Eventually it would be clear that a question had been asked which actually demanded more than a smile and a nod as an answer, at which point Mary would step in and try and steer away from the fact that her husband was a bloody idiot.

It was frankly an embarrassment and can best be demonstrated by the following incident, which I recount in the full knowledge that it makes me look like a complete fool.

One day we decided that we would get a taxi from the hotel into the old market town so that we could at least have a look outside of the hotel and see if we could buy ourselves overpriced souvenirs of Tutankhamen. We approached the small desk where the man was sitting who ordered taxis for guests.

'Now look,' Mary said as we approached 'this is a very male orientated society. I think it would be better if you did the talking.'

I found this rather strange as it was unlike Mary to easily give into any form of sexism. I realise now that she was just setting me up for a fall.

'Hello,' I said as we sat down at the desk, 'I would like to order a taxi to the market please.'

'Certainly, would you like a surprise?'

I thought this was a very strange response as I clearly had stated exactly what I had wanted in my best received pronunciation.

'That's very kind of you,' I warily said whilst still trying to be polite and yet worrying what kind of surprise he had in mind. 'I think we will just stick to the taxi, if it is all the same to you.'

Mary sighed and lent sideways towards me. 'He said, "do you want the price?"'

'Ah well that makes much more sense,' I said feeling relieved whilst the man looked at me with a mixture of pity and contempt as if I summed up everything that he had ever come to expect from a race of people that had not gotten over the loss of their empire. From this point on I thought it best if I stuck with the smiling and nodding.

Things were not hugely better when we got into the old market. The taxi drive in had been an experience with the driver seeming to have only a passing knowledge of what the speed limit might be. He also insisted on speaking to us endlessly from the moment we got in until the moment we got out. This would have been fine were it not for the fact that he didn't seem to speak English and we didn't speak whatever language it was that he was speaking.

As soon as we walked passed the soldiers into the market we were assailed from all sides by shop owners and vendors who wanted to sell us everything that they could. We were clearly marked as new fodder as we were without sun tan and clearly easy prey.

I was beginning to feel uncomfortable largely because I had refused to wear shorts. I have always been somewhat shy since my bullying days at school in the swimming baths and changing rooms. Ever since I have refused to expose any flesh that it is not absolutely necessary to expose at the time. The world should be grateful for this as it means that they do not have to suffer the terrible sight of my legs, which should really come with a government health warning.

Strange snippets of English were shouted at us as we walked through the shopping area.

'Come inside and look round, it's no bloody hassle.'

'We give you bloody good Asda price.'

'God, we have screwed the world up,' I muttered as we walked through the market and I heard these shouted friendly greetings. We sat down in a café where I was served coffee that had the texture and taste of tar.

'Where you from?'

This was from a small fat bald man that appeared on the street outside. Mary's attitude to this kind of thing was to just politely ignore said people and eventually they would give up and go away.

She had so far dealt with people trying to sell her water skiing adventures, speed boat trips and someone who appeared to want to sell us a camel which seemed to be called 'evil bastard.' The problem was that I was just too English to be as rude as this, so had no choice but to answer when a question was put to me.

'You from England?' the man said in what appeared to be surprise, despite the fact that I had just told him so. 'I used to live in Leeds.'

'Oh really?'

Somehow, I doubted that he had lived in Leeds and would probably be completely buggered if I now told him that I lived in Leeds and then asked him to name the street that he had lived on and started to talk about local landmarks. This would have been a really good way of getting rid of him, unless he really did come from Leeds at which point he would probably have stuck to me like a kindred soul for the rest of the week. However, as I had never even been to Leeds the opportunity never arose.

'What your name?' he persisted.

I had dreaded that this might come up. My name was hard enough for people in the United Kingdom to understand, virtually impossible for foreigners. The only people who really understood my name and would nod knowingly were those of a certain age who remembered the music group Ultravox. If you don't, then Google it.

'Midge,' I replied slightly apprehensively.

'Meej?' he attempted.

'Midge.'

'Me-adge?'

'Midge.'

'Mige?'

I sighed and decided that it was just best not to try and bother and wondered why it was that I just didn't tell him that my name was Jim, although he may still have had the same level of problems getting his head around this one.

'I –.' he told me his name, which I won't even attempt to recreate as I never caught it at the time and had no intention of engaging in the verbal tennis match that he had just had with trying to understand how to pronounce my name. I just nodded in what I hoped was a wise manner and allowed the sun to roll over my eyes.

Mary sighed, whilst simultaneously trying to cover up the smirk on her face with her hand. The little bald man eventually wandered off when it became clear that we really didn't have anything else to say to each other.

I went back to drinking my coffee and then trying to find out where my eyeballs had rolled back to. I was drinking this because I never really liked the taste of alcohol, although there were times when I still forced myself to take part in drinking it for social reasons. Lager tasted horrible as far as I was concerned, ale tasted like lager that had gone off and stout tasted like ale that had gone off. I never really got the taste of spirits where each one would make me shudder at first sip and then involuntarily I would screw my nose up as if I had just drunk something that was not for human consumption. I pretty much felt the same way about wine as well.

My lack of interest in alcohol may have been that as a teenager I did not have a group of mates with which to go on pub crawls and binge drink with. It may also have had something to do with the fact that I was aware from a very early age that alcohol was a toxin and you might as well just pour poison down your throat for all the good that it was doing you. Why do you think you feel ill and throw up when you have too much? Your body is telling you to stop with the shit. I also didn't like the fact that alcohol would slowly kill off brain cells and that they were never replaced. I don't think any of us have that many brain cells that we can afford to be liberal with them.

You will probably tut and shake your head at this and tell me that life is too short to worry about things like this. I know life is short. You sure as hell don't have to tell me that life is short. It is something that I am very much aware of.

***

We arrived back at the hotel and sat in the bar next to an English couple who had clearly popped up from the next hotel along.

'This hotel is bigger than ours, Brian,' she was saying with a dissatisfied air as we sipped on our drinks, which in my case was a local form of what I suspected would have been 7-up elsewhere.

'Why is that?' she asked Brian who I had already decided in a matter of seconds was her long-suffering husband. Why she should ask Brian this was a mystery to me. Clearly, she felt that he had some control over the building and architecture of these hotels and had made the mistake of not booking her into the biggest. It became clear as to why they were here. She was clearly a snob.

Over the course of the next hour we heard lots of random comments from her, most of which were met in silence by Brian, who could easily have been dead as far as I could tell. I am pretty certain that she would only have noticed that he had died when he started to decompose and make a mess on the floor. Even then she would still berate him for a couple of days for not cleaning up after himself.

Her main choice of conversation appeared to be feminism. I have nothing against feminism myself, I am all for equality and I think in all honesty I have tended to view the sexes as equal. I think I pull my weight and do my share of things and I am not the kind of man who resists the idea of doing a particularly job because it is 'woman's work.'

She started by complaining about the fact that there were not enough toilets for the women and that women had to queue whilst men rarely did. I assumed that she meant in general as I had not noticed this particular problem in the hotel where there seemed to be an ample supply of facilities all over the place. I could sympathise with this general complaint as it was something that I could imagine would become rather frustrating.

'It's just typical that all the men sit in cafes drinking coffee all day and as usual the women are left to do all the work.'

This was probably a fair comment as well. Egypt and Islam in general are not perhaps known for gender equality. This has to be put in context. Most religions aren't progressive.

What's my point? I will tell you.

Religion is something that really develops over time and it changes as it develops and grows accustomed to what is going on. If you take the three main religions of Judaism, Christianity and Islam you can begin to see this. Judaism was violent in its early days with warriors going around cutting off the foreskins of enemies and theoretically forcing them to convert by doing so. Eventually it settled down and became a more peaceful closed community where conquer was in general more frowned upon and conversion made more difficult.

Christianity grew up and went through violent teenage years of the crusades and the inquisition where it adopted the attitude of if you were not going to convert then you were going to have to die by the sword or in the fire. To an extent this eventually morphed into coffee and cake mornings and bring and buy sales before once again being slightly derailed by the suggestion that a lot of the clergy were just a little bit too friendly with the choir boys.

Islam had been a late developer, but by the turn of the twenty-first century had probably reached that teenage stage where Christianity had been on the convert or die mentality. Eventually it would settle down and was already showing stages of doing so where it was only the extremism that was keeping the convert or die mentality alive. It was at a cross roads really where it either had to decide to convert the world or accept its part in it as well as the part that everyone else had to play.

Imagine it like the three religions were each given a lot of wood and told to build a boat to sail from England to America. Judaism, after some false starts and issues, had finally built its boat and was just starting off for the new world. Islam had sold its wood and was now arguing what to do next. Christianity had made its ship and had lost its way and was sailing round and round the Isle of Wight.

What's my point? I will tell you.

The woman next to us had come to a male orientated society which to her may have seemed like it was stuck in the Middle Ages, but she was failing to see and appreciate the context of the development of that society.

Her presumed husband Brian decided to add something to the conversation at this point.

'You know, in Cyprus it's compulsory for the men to do two years of military service.'

'So?' she seemed thrown by this.

'Well, you may remember,' he continued 'that I was stationed in Cyprus myself and they had a debate about the fact that they were going to make it compulsory for women to do military service as well, but such a public debate ensued that it was decided that it would remain compulsory for men to do it but women didn't have to although they could volunteer if they wanted.'

'Compulsory military service for women,' she snorted 'you can take equality too far.'

Before I could respond to this Mary was on the attack.

'Excuse me,' she said 'I couldn't help but overhear your conversation, probably because your voice is so crass and loud, but how can you be so stupid?'

The woman looked as if she had been slapped. Up until that moment she had probably been the only one that existed in the world as far as she was concerned.

'You can't pick and choose what you want with equality,' Mary continued 'it's all or nothing. You can't say I want to be equal to men accept for the dangerous bits or the stuff I don't like. Attitudes like that set feminism back decades. Equality is like circumcision.'

I was interested to see where this line of thought was going to go.

'Either you go the whole way, or you forget it.'

'Do you mind?' the woman said summoning up her reserve. 'We were having a private conversation.'

'Then may I suggest you have it less loudly, or better still go back and have it in your own, smaller hotel.' With that she turned back to her book leaving the woman with her mouth hanging open and her husband with a small smile on his face.

***

That was pretty much Egypt as far as I was concerned. I spent the rest of the week in the hotel. Mary sunbathed and read whilst I just read and tried to do a little writing. Many people would think that this was a great waste of time, but I really was more than happy with a stack of books next to me and doing my best to try and forget that I was going to have to get back on the plane soon and go through the experience of flying once again if I wanted to go home. I was not entirely convinced that Mary would get me into an aeroplane again after that. I now could fully understand why the Pope kissed the tarmac of the airport when he landed anywhere, the poor man must have been crapping himself throughout the flight. This being the case it was a brave decision to wear white.

I would like to say that having had the flight out to Egypt my flight back was something that I knew more about this time so there was less apprehension as I knew what was coming and therefore there was more relaxing and less stress about the flight. Having done it once I was much more relaxed about it this time.

I would like to say this, but I can't as it wasn't true.

Nine

I suppose that isn't really all that I can say about Egypt when you consider that it wasn't just a holiday but was actually our honeymoon.

It was romantic. We had a lot of fun times with candlelit dinner and walks along the beach in the moonlight. There were a few things that made it less romantic. For instance, the consistent amplified music and reps that wanted to encourage you to take part in all their activities like it was some Club 18-30 holiday, which it may well have been for a lot of the people there. I just found it irritating. I don't suppose that I have ever been much of a party animal.

We also quickly discovered that the outdoor swimming pool which snaked its way through the complex whilst looking stunningly beautiful as it sparkled in the sun was actually mind buggeringly freezing cold when you actually got in it which was rather unexpected. I didn't really like swimming all that much either which I classed as about as unnatural as flying was and it meant that I would have to wear trunks of course which would mean exposing a fair amount of flesh, unless I went for one of those Victorian one-piece things. I understand the fashion for these onesie things is coming close to that now, of course. It just goes to show you that there are no really true original ideas.

I suppose, if I am going to be honest then I should talk briefly about sex. Naturally it will come as no surprise to anyone that I was a virgin until I got together with Mary, at least I was a virgin as far as real sex was concerned. I was pretty good as far as the imagination went.

Fortunately, sex was instinctive as I had not received any formal kind of instruction or help from anyone else. Sex is one of the things, unlike swimming and flying, that I did think of as natural and it was pretty much as simple as a jigsaw puzzle where you just had to work out which bit went where.

Of course, it is never as straightforward as that, but like many things sex is something that can improve the more you practice at it. I have to be honest that Mary must have been very tolerant of my fumbling when we first got together, I have no idea how experienced she was, but she certainly put up with me.

Sex was an amazing discovery as far as I was concerned and certainly went and blew the hell out of solo activities that had preoccupied my teenage years. When I come to think about it Mary was the predominant sexual figure throughout my life. I didn't have sex with anyone before Mary and the vast majority if not all of my masturbation fantasies were based around her as well. You might find that rather boring, but it is the way of it.

These are probably things that you don't want to know about despite the fact that as someone who is into writing as much as I am, I am fully aware that nothing shifts a book as much as sex does.

As a race the vast majority of us are obsessed with sex, probably even more than that, perhaps it is fair to say all of us, divided into the different groups.

What's my point? I will tell you.

We are all obsessed with sex. There are those of us who are not getting any and are haunted by when we might be getting some. There are those of us who are getting some but want more, or less; there are those that are obsessed with getting as much as they can and rule their life by having every waking moment dedicated to sex.

These groups are all put together in the capacity of those that are either obsessed with wanting too much sex or wanting to get less sex because they are too knackered to carry on with what they are getting.

Then there is the flip of the coin which are all the people who are not getting any sex or are using it only for procreation, rather than fun and are obsessed with the idea of making sure that the rest of us are stopped from having sex as well. Such people are the likes of Mary Whitehouse and most straight-laced Christians who feel that they have to watch everything about sex that they can so that they can complain about it in graphic detail and demand that the everlasting display of arses, penises, tits and pussies are not shown again.

These people, by definition of their moral crusade paradoxically watch more smut than the rest of us. They then try and prevent us from watching what they spend all their lives dedicated to watching.

I am not fully sure that I can see the point of all of this. Sex is natural and as long as it doesn't involve anything illegal then people should really just be allowed to get on with it. Live and let live I say.

It wasn't always about sex though, although it was pretty good. What I really liked about being part of a couple was the companionship and my chance to finally put into practice my romantic side which had previously only been theoretical.

Lots of romantic dinners by candlelight. Soft music playing in the background and general gestures of a loving nature. Some people reserve this kind of thing for only Valentine's Day, some of them didn't even bother with that day. Personally, I thought you just had to make Valentine's Day an everyday occurrence. Treat every day as if it is your first as well as your last together and you couldn't really go all that wrong as far as I was concerned.

It was never much fun being a hopeless romantic when you didn't have anyone to share the romance with. It tended to make the entire thing something that was rather flat and unprofitable.

I suppose that there are people out there who like being on their own and hate having the company of others that they have to bend their life around. There are some people who would perhaps prefer their independence rather than companionship.

I have never worked out if these people genuinely feel like this or whether it is a case of a front that they put up to the rest of the world so that they don't have pity taken on them. I don't know. I can only speak for myself and that is to say that I would prefer not to live a life alone if I was given the choice. Sometimes, of course, we are not given the choice of whether to be alone or with someone. There are other times when it is better to be alone rather than with someone. It all rather depends on who it is that you are with.

***

We had a relaxing time in Egypt which will certainly be something that I will remember for a variety of reasons. It had been my intention to possibly do some writing whilst I was out there as it was a preoccupation that took up a great deal of my time at this stage. However, it was something that I didn't get around to and so I spent the majority of my time with reading instead, working at pretty much the rate of one book a day, which was pretty standard for me when I am at my height.

I returned to normality and pondered about where I was going to go from here. Getting established as a writer would appear to have been something that required as much luck as it did talent. It also involved a lot of work, of course.

'Genius, remember,' Mr Jones stated to me on one of the moments that we spent talking together when most of the other students had gone off to play football or wank, 'is one per cent inspiration and ninety-nine percent perspiration.'

I nodded my head in what I hoped had been an intellectual way.

'Something else you must do,' he continued after a moment, 'is to start collecting rejection slips.'

'Really?'

'Yes. It would be an incredible stroke of luck if your first manuscript was accepted by the first publisher that you sent it to. Almost impossible, but there are those who happen to have the right product at the right time for the right publisher.'

I nodded once again acknowledging the wisdom of what he was saying.

'Most of the writers we now look upon as established have collected their share of rejection slips and been passed over by people.'

'Could be a bit like passing up on The Beatles.'

'It could, but it frequently isn't. Besides, when a publisher rejects a manuscript they do so because of the fact that it isn't the right thing for them at that time. It could be the greatest book in the world, but if they have already published several like it already they may be looking for something that's different.' He took a sip of his tea and was thoughtful once again. 'Or it could mean that it's just total shit.'

'Not always possible to tell.'

'No, it isn't. We become too close to our work to be able to judge it without emotion and from a distance. The renowned Thomas Hardy,' (he loved Hardy with a passion, thinking that he should have a more prestigious place than Dickens had,) 'destroyed his own first manuscript that was never published because it was something inferior in his eyes.

Even when he became published it took a couple of novels to get into the swing of things.'

I remained quiet once again and allowed him to stare wistfully into the middle distance.

'What I wouldn't give to read that first manuscript, no matter how shit it might be,' he muttered.

'Then take Kafka,' he exclaimed changing track slightly. 'He never published in his lifetime and gave instructions that all his manuscripts were to be destroyed after his death. It's a good job that he never got around to doing it himself or we would have lost some classics. Such a shame that he never reaped the rewards in his own lifetime.' He looked thoughtfully out of the window and not for the first time I wondered why it was that he had never sought to publish anything himself. But then perhaps he was not a writer and was more of a reader.

What was his point? I will tell you.

Start collecting rejection slips, collect enough to re-wallpaper your house if need be and then start over again. If you believe in your work, then keep at it. Keep writing and keep sending it off time and time again. It doesn't matter if others think it is shit. As long as you believe then you just keep on going.

Chase your dreams, no matter what they might be or how long they may take to achieve. Chase them whilst you still can so that you have no regrets and when the end does finally come you will be able to look back and say 'well at least I tried.' There is no better epitaph. When you are gone people may forget you, they may remember you, but either way they will never remember you for things that you have not done.

***

That last comment makes me think about death. Have you ever thought that much about your own mortality? Do you wonder when it is that you will die; or how it will happen when the time comes?

Many of us perhaps prefer not to think about such things and put our own mortality firmly in the back of our minds and try not to think about it. For others it is perhaps too predominant and we may end up becoming obsessed, perhaps even running to meet that end before it is really time.

As a writer I believe that it is our job to think about the things that most of us don't want to talk about, and to say the things that most of us don't want to state. It is our job to be the social conscience of the world. It is our task to show you what you look like; what we all look like. For some people this is too much to stomach and they prefer instead to immerse themselves into escapism. The problem with this is that escapism is showing you a way of life and a reflection as well.

Is it the job of a writer to change the world? Perhaps it is. Have we been very successful in it so far? Probably not. There have been some books that have changed the world, of course, *The Communist Manifesto, The Bible, Torah, Koran, Monty Python's Big Red Book* and so on have all changed the world in their own ways. Then there is the huge body of science fiction work which has shown us how we are screwing up the planet and what the future could be like if we are not careful.

Writers have been warning us about the future for years, ever since H G Wells from a science fiction point of view at least, and we have not paid the slightest bit of attention to it. You have to ask yourself if it is worth the effort.

Perhaps one day a writer will come along that will unite the world in seeing the mistakes that we have all made and will help to change everything and bring us all together to make a better path for the future.

It is a dream and would require a level of genius that is far above what I am capable of, but perhaps there is someone who will read these words one day and be able to take up the challenge that I did not have the energy, time or talent to attempt.

The question of mortality came from Luke.

'I don't know when, or how I will die.' I replied.

'Would you want to?'

I thought about this for a while. Would it be better to know and prepare yourself to face eternity, or would it be better to go quickly?

'I don't believe that I would like to know,' I replied after a moment of thought.

'No, I don't think I'd like to know either. It does make you wonder what it's all about though doesn't it?'

'What what's all about, Luke?'

'Life, the universe, you know, everything.'

'I have been wondering about the meaning of life for a very long time. I thought about studying metaphysics, but it's something that I've never really had the time for. Too many other things to read, I suppose. I have tried to wonder what the meaning of life is and from time to time I have tried to write about it in some of my stories. Exploring the nature of it all.'

'Did you get very far with it?' Luke asked leaning forward attentively as if I was some kind of guru about to impart wisdom.

'No. Nowhere at all really.'

I have no idea where, when or how my end will come. I am not sure that it is a good idea to know such things, but what I do know is that I hope that when the time does come I am not on my own. I have spent far too much of my life on my own to end it that way.

***

Being back in the United Kingdom I threw myself into my work with a passion, and by my work I refer to my writing which I had started to see as my real work rather than what I did in the library which was fast becoming something that I viewed only as something that I did when I was unable to do my real work. It was something that I was viewing as something that was increasingly getting in the way of this real work, but what can you do?

As time progressed, and I wrote more with each opportunity that came my way, I would like to think that I was getting better at what I was doing and much of my early work could be safely consigned to the shredder. That is where most of it ends up. That is probably where most of it deserves to end up as well.

Mr Jones had advice on this as well.

'There will be things that you write which you will know is not up to the mark,' he had stated whilst stroking his moustache. 'There will be things you write that you are uncertain of and will have your doubts of the value of. There will be other things that you're convinced are good and they probably will be good. Anything that gets you up out of your bed in the middle of the night to write down is always bound to be good though.'

I had a number of doubts about the things that I wrote. At times I would write something that I was proud of which is why it is all the more painful when critics are so prepared to shoot it casually down. I have always thought though that it is better to have doubts about what you write rather than to have arrogance into thinking that everything you write is pure genius. Even if you were a genius, which you are probably not, then even geniuses have off days. Even Mozart must have written stuff that he ended up throwing in the bin.

Whilst all this was going on I still worked in the library, of course, directing people to where I thought they needed to go, which was not always where they wanted to go. Sometimes people needed a little push in the right direction as they were not always able of finding their way on their own. Mr Jones had been the one who had been instrumental in pushing me on the right path. I have no idea how many others he had pushed on the journey over the years. I can only speak for myself and be thankful for that.

Mary and myself had been living together for some time 'in sin' as some people who considered themselves to be more moral than others would have said. Because we had been living together for some time there was less of a change with getting married where in the older, more moral days, getting married would not only have been the first time that you lived together, but the first time that you engaged in sexual intercourse.

Engaged in sexual intercourse. What a curious expression. Engaged. Such a polite way of putting it. Well this was the twenty-first century so we had been 'engaging' for rather a long time now, sometimes we engaged very hard and engaged our brains out. We both liked 'engaging' rather a lot if the truth were known, but you probably don't want to hear about that.

I celebrated my twenty-fifth birthday and struggled with the emotion of feeling old.

I know that twenty-five is not old, but when you are twenty-five it seems an amazing age to reach. For the first time you become aware of the fact that you have reached the landmark quarter of a century which sounds so incredibly old even if your brain is telling you that it isn't. I am sure that there were some aching bones that were nature's present to me as well.

There are other landmark birthdays, of course. Turning ten and making double figures. Thirteen and becoming a teenager. Eighteen and being legal to do almost anything that was banned beforehand. Twenty-one which seems more redundant now that the age of maturity is seen more as eighteen these days than twenty-one; but none of these compete with the turn of a quarter of a century.

There would be other landmarks as time went on. These usually timed with each new decade. The thought of turning thirty to most people in their early to mid-twenties is a disastrous thought. I can only hope that by the time you start hitting forty and fifty you get used to it and don't care so much any longer. I fear that this might not be the case though.

I still felt old and I still couldn't get used to the idea of the year being 2005 which still to my mind seemed a futuristically impossible date from something out of science fiction. It just seemed to be impossible having been used to the twentieth century for as long as I had anything else seemed strangely alien.

I suppose there was a part of me that was just feeling nostalgic for the 1900s and I wondered if the people in 1905 had considered that to be such a futuristic date and thought fondly of the 1800s.

History is as strange a thing as time. I was probably the only one who lay awake at night thinking that when we reached 2014 and beyond the First World War, which to us is in living memory, would be as distant from us as the battle of Waterloo was to those that fought in the First World War.

I know, my brain works strangely, but there is nothing that I can do about which is why I write. I don't think normal thinking people are driven to be creative. They just accept life.

***

I was extremely happy with my life. I had married the woman that I had always desired. I had a home that I was happy in, even if it was something that some people would describe as humble. My paid work was not something that was particularly taxing or challenging, but that was probably the way that I liked it if I am being honest for it gave me the means and the time to work on my writing, which after Mary was the great passion of my life. Life just couldn't get any better.

'Are you happy?' Mary had asked me one evening in early 2006 when we were huddled near our log fire trying to get warm with the small amount of heat that it gave off against the freezing cold temperature that was outside.

I looked up from the book that I was reading by the firelight across to Mary who was sitting on the other side reading her own book.

'Yes, of course I am.'

'Are you sure?'

'I couldn't be happier. I have everything I want in life.'

'Everything?'

'Everything that matters.'

'Is there nothing else that you want?'

'Did you have anything in mind?' I looked at her quizzically. She seemed to be acting very strangely. She seemed to ignore my question and looked into the fire for a moment. I decided that it was time to bring up something that had been worrying me lately.

'Are you ill?'

'Why do you say that?' she asked looking at me again.

'Well, it's just that I noticed you seemed to have a lot of stomach cramps lately and I thought I heard you being sick the other day.'

'Yes.'

'What's the matter?'

She looked at me with an expression that I couldn't really describe.

'You're an intelligent man, Midge. As a writer your powers of observation are uncanny, but there are times when you just miss the bigger picture, don't you?'

'I'm not sure what you mean.' I said on account of the fact that I didn't. 'If you're ill then we should get you to a doctor. We need to get you checked out.'

I was worried about her. I absolutely despised being sick, as in vomiting. It was one of the worst things that I could ever imagine having to go through and not for the first time I was pleased that I didn't drink sufficient alcohol to mean that I was throwing up all of the time. I cannot understand people who drink so much so that they can end up on their knees throwing up all of that money that they had spent. I can think of better ways of spending your money. It seems a complete waste of time and money for some people to take up as a hobby.

'I'm being sick rather regularly. Pretty much every morning.'

'Well, if you're throwing up every morning then there really ought to be something that we should do about it.'

'When am I sick, Midge?' she sighed at me in that resigned way that she did from time to time.

'Well, you said in the morning.'

'Ye-es.'

Silence overtook us for a moment whilst she waited for me to catch up. That's the problem with being married to a writer, I suppose. They have always got their head somewhere else and never in the moment.

'Oh.' I said.

'I think he's got it.' She said.

'You mean you're. . .?'

'Yes.'

'Are you sure?'

'Pretty sure.'

'Are you okay?'

'I am. I'm more concerned about you at the moment. I'm not sure that it's news that you want to hear.'

I threw my book to one side and went up and threw my arms around her.

'Mary, I couldn't be happier.'

It just goes to show you that when you think you are at your happiest there is always something that can come along and show you what you have been missing and how you can be happier. Sadly, it also has a habit of pulling the rug from under your feet as well.

Ten

Mary was pregnant.

I am not sure my reaction was what she had expected. I was shocked and didn't know what to say and I suppose upon reflection that might be interpreted as being horror at the prospect of what lay ahead. Genuinely though I was delighted when the thought was eventually allowed to find its way into my brain and make itself known.

I had never imagined being a parent. I suppose my own disastrous relationship with my own parents had made me feel somewhat cautious about the prospect of being a father myself. I suppose that does seem a little harsh on my father as it was not really his fault that he was not around when I was growing up, or at any other point in my life, I suppose.

I think that there are two schools of thought on parenthood after absentee parents of your own. The first is that if you are a child from abusive or neglectful parents then you might turn out to copy that behaviour towards your own children. This is the excuse that many of them will use once they are caught for their own crimes, of course. I am sure that being a child of such shameful parents does not give any justification to act like it yourself.

Nevertheless, it doesn't seem to stop people from clasping their hands together and tut-tutting whilst they state 'well, I blame it all on the parents, you know.'

The second school of thought is that if you have been a child of such parents then you have learnt the lessons the hard way and are determined that there is no way that you will act in the same manner towards your own children.

I may not really be able to blame my father for his absentee nature as a parent, but I didn't really have all that many excuses for my mother who had seemed to act in such a detached way throughout her life before she had finally vanished out of my life completely without an explanation.

I don't think at this stage in my journey towards parenthood I could say with any degree of authority what kind of parent I was going to turn out to be. I was certain that it wouldn't be the kind that took his own neglect out on his children, but I had no idea what kind of character I would have for the rest of it. I was pretty determined though that no matter what else I certainly was not going to be neglectful in the way that my mother had been.

Mind you, just being there a couple of times a week would be more than my mother had ever done. It was never all that hard to beat my mother in accomplishments.

I was determined to do everything that I could. I went to the pre-natal classes and I practiced my breathing with the vigour of someone who was planning on some deep-sea diving expedition. I went to the hospital and collected all the scans (which to be honest with you I couldn't make all that much sense of, but which one of the nurses – who was at least as round as she was tall – stated in a rather sickly tone 'baby's first little photo snappy'), I went and looked at baby clothing and toys. I was determined to be there at the moment of birth, holding Mary's hand and watching a new life enter the world.

I found that expecting a baby became similar to thinking about buying a new car.

What's my point? I will tell you.

You know how when you are thinking of buying a new car, say a Ford Mondeo, and once you have thought about that, all you see everywhere you look are Ford Mondeos. That was what it was like with a baby on the way. Everywhere I looked I saw babies in push chairs, or pregnant women. Uncanny how you have to tune your brain into noticing the things that are around you all of the time anyway. I suppose it goes to prove that each of us sees whatever it is that we want to in life.

Another thing that I noticed was the fact that when a woman is pregnant people think that they have a given right to touch her belly. This would include strangers who seemed to think that pregnancy was a ticket to allow you to touch other people up. No one in their right mind would go around touching non-pregnant women's stomachs and not expect to be arrested for it, so why the hell do you think you can do it when someone is pregnant? I don't mind saying that I came close to laying a few people out who thought that they could feel my wife up.

There are men out there who do their best to hide whenever their partners are pregnant. They don't want to know about it. My father for instance went to the extreme to avoid matters when my mother was pregnant. I think he took matters a little too far if I am honest.

There are some men out there, I know, who are of the opinion that their contribution begins and ends with the moment that they ejaculate into their partner. The rest of the time they just want to get on with their lives and forget all about their pregnant other half and the spawn that is about to enter into the world. Some will desert their partners leaving a string of illegitimate children in their wake, others will stick around, but contribute so little that they might as well piss off as all they are is a mouth to feed.

These are usually the kind of men who don't know anything about cooking, cleaning, washing or ironing. All the things around the house that are essential, but that they are convinced is the work of a woman. They spend their time watching football and drinking cans of lager whilst their partner runs everything. They don't see anything wrong in this, and the really worrying thing about it is the fact that their partner seems to go along with it as well. Men who act like this have a special name: wankers.

It seems hard for me to grasp the fact that in the twenty-first century there are still men out there with this kind of attitude and that there are still women out there who are prepared to let them get away with it without attempting to cut off their testicles. It is all very strange, if you ask me.

I have always had an equal partnership with Mary. We share the work and we share the joy. I personally feel guilty about the fact that Mary might be doing some housework, or whatever, and I might be sitting down not doing all that much. I find it very difficult to sit down and not do all that much. I tend to need to keep moving as much as possible. I find it very difficult to relax in what most people would think of as a conventional way.

My brain is something that never seems to stop. It is always buzzing off in different directions, thinking up new ideas and never allowing me peace to be able to rest. I might settle down to sleep and then bang, something pops into my head and that is it, game over. I have to get up and write it down. You have to exorcise whatever it is that has gripped you or it will plague you.

Sleep is something that can be very difficult. I keep a notepad by my bed so that if I get hit by a really good idea I can write it down without having to wander off too far, which is something that wakes you up and makes it even more difficult to get to sleep. By staying in bed and scribbling on the notepad through half closed eyes and I can try and convince myself that I haven't actually woken up.

It is something that is entirely unsuccessful.

At any rate, I was not talking about my sleeping habits I was talking about Mary's pregnancy. To be honest I have no idea how you women go through all that. If men had to give birth it would be the end of the world. It is truly staggering that you do it. What is really staggering is that having been through it once there are those of you out there who are prepared to go through it all *again*. I can't imagine anyone else volunteering to go through all that again after knowing what it was like the first time. The first time I suppose you don't really know what is coming, but you sure as hell do the second time around.

***

'I've been thinking,' Mary said as she patted her enlarged stomach.

'It's a bit late for that, dear,' I replied.

'Now that the little one is on their way, do you give any thought to your own family?' She ignored my comment you will notice which was a wise thing to do. She also had taken to calling the baby 'the little one' which if nothing else was accurate, I suppose.

'What do you mean? You guys are my family.'

'Yes, but I was thinking about your parents.'

'What about them?'

I always started to feel anxious when people started talking about my parents. Their absence was something of a blessing. I could claim to strangers that my parents were anyone that I wanted them to be. Over the course of my life they had both been doctors working to cure AIDS by travelling up the Amazon. They had been royalty that could not openly acknowledge me as their offspring, but they sent me a very nice Christmas card from Sandringham each year; and they had also been astronauts that had come together on the International Space Station. All of this seemed better than admitting that my father was dead and my mother might as well have been for the good that she had done me.

'Well, now that you are about to start your own family I wondered if you gave any thought to what happened to your parents and if you had any other family out there?'

'Can't say that I have.'

'I have.'

'Why?'

'It's a mystery and I love a mystery.'

'It's not that much of a mystery. My father died in a car crash before I was born and my mother sodded off to probably live on a hippy commune somewhere and be at one with nature and all the recreational drugs she can cram into her system.'

'But what about grandparents and the like?'

'Well, they never showed any interest in me so I don't really see why I should show all that much of an interest in them.'

'You're assuming, of course, that they even know about you.'

That was a very good point. I had always felt rejected by my extended family, but then I had never actually heard anything about them so there was always the possibility that they had never heard anything about me. I was aware that other children had grandparents, but they only really existed for me in Roald Dahl novels. Perhaps my mother had kept me secret from the world.

'If that is the case,' I said, thinking it over 'do you really think that they would be all that happy if I suddenly turned up unannounced on their doorstep at the age of twenty-five? Particularly with no proof of who I was.'

'I suppose it depends on who they are and what they are like.'

'It's a nice idea, but I can't see it happening.'

'Why not?'

'Well, for one thing how would we find out who they are?'

'Public records. There is always a paper trial to follow if you just know where to look for it.'

I thought about this for a moment.

'It's possible. I suppose.' I begrudgingly admitted. 'But if I am honest I don't know if it's something that I can really be all that arsed with.'

'Well, if you are happy for me to do it then I thought it might be something that I could look into.'

Mary did actually love a mystery, that is true. She was addicted to the likes of Agatha Christie and Conan Doyle. She liked nothing better than trying to solve the mystery before the great detective did. If I am honest researching my family history was also something that would probably be right up her street.

'Don't you think that you have rather enough to preoccupy yourself at the moment,' I pointedly stated looking at the obvious.

'Yes, but it will also be nice to have something non-related to work on in the background.'

'I would be amazed if you had the time. I don't want you over doing things, you know that.'

'Well, you let me worry about that. After all it might all come to nothing anyway.'

And so the seeds of revelation were set.

***

I have heard tell of some men who have had their doubts about how they will take to fatherhood. They worry about whether they will make a connection to their child, or whether there will be an unbridgeable gap that exists. They worry that the bond will be more difficult to make than it is for the mother who has the natural bond. Then they tell about the time that they first see their child and how they immediate have all doubts fall away and know that they will love their child for the rest of their life. That wasn't the case with me.

I knew from the moment that Mary told me that she was pregnant that I would have no such worries about my child. I knew that I would love them from the beginning, from before the beginning. I never had any doubts in my head at all.

I have no idea if it was a myth or just a complete load of bollocks, but I also insisted on playing Mozart to my child whilst they were in the womb. I know that it is probably a load of crap that it is said to make them more intelligent as they are developing in the womb. Logically it makes no sense at all, but would you really risk missing the chance if there was the slightest possibility of doing such a thing for your child?

We hadn't really spoken all that much about names for the baby. We had a few ideas, but we kept them very much to ourselves. I understand there is some superstition about not revealing the gender of your child and the name before your child is born. I am not entirely sure why this is, but then if it is superstition then there doesn't have to be any particular reason why. Nobody ever said that these things were meant to be in any way logical.

It was three o'clock in the morning when Mary's waters broke and she announced to the world that 'the time had come'. We had prepared for this moment with the same attention as we would have prepared for an air raid warning if we had been of that generation.

I very quickly realised as I hopped around the bedroom trying to get my pants on that no amount of preparation and rehearsal could have prepared me for the real event when it came. I remember thinking why the hell did it have to happen in the middle of the night. Why can't these things happen at a more convenient time? If there is such a thing as a more convenient time.

Now, I had never learnt to drive as it was not something that had really come up for me. It was a vague pain in the arse from time to time that I couldn't drive, but as Mary could drive it wasn't an insurmountable problem. However, in circumstances such as these it proved to be a bit of an issue that I had not previously thought about. In a sense it made me feel that I had failed as a husband in some way.

I called for an ambulance, which is what I had been advised to do by the medical personnel and what Mary now screamed for me to do. I rang them up and hoped that there were not an inordinately large amount of car crashes and stabbings that they were dealing with at the moment that they would place as more life threatening and urgent then attending to my soon to be not so pregnant wife.

Fortunately, that didn't seem to be the case and the ambulance was with us reasonably swiftly despite how the Government always seems to moan about their response times and how they don't meet their targets. To side track here for a moment I have always found it very strange that the government of the time has a habit of always moaning about the fact that this institute or that emergency service (usually the police or medical professions) are failing to meet their targets and are therefore bloody useless and should be punished whilst at the same time they never seem to realise that they as politicians fail consistently to keep their election promises and meet any form of target that isn't of benefit to them. I am just pointing it out, that's all.

I had never been for a ride in an ambulance before so it was quite an experience. I think it is always an experience when you are not the one who is stretched out on the trolley whilst they try and find out what is wrong with you. I think it was pretty self-evident why it was that Mary was there though so they probably didn't have to do too much working out in her case.

After that things moved rather quickly once we had arrived at the hospital. We were whisked through to maternity and all sorts of exciting things were going on that I couldn't really follow. I felt that I was being treated as a spare part by a lot of the staff which to be honest, I suppose I was at that point. My part had been done and now I was left on the sidelines.

I don't approve of sexism, hopefully from what you have noticed so far you will see that I pull my own weight and do not treat women as inferior. I deplore men that do. What is often forgotten is the sexism that comes from women who are disgusted by men. These super feminists are the kind of people who do not think that society needs any men in order to survive, which is, of course, something that presents a slight problem. How they expect to continue the human race without men is something of a mystery. To make matters even worse they seem to think that all men should have their penises cut off as punishment for being born with one.

I mention all of this because one of the nurses in the maternity suite appeared to be of this opinion. She kept flashing me looks of evil that seemed to suggest that because I had taken action that had resulted in my wife ending up in hospital then I was clearly a domestic violence perpetrator and if she hadn't have been so busy taking care of my wife then she would have been on the telephone to the police immediately; or judging by the look of her she might have bypassed the police completely and just beaten the crap out of me.

Clearly the most offence that I had caused her was being born in the first place. There is no pleasing some people though, you just have to let them get on with it.

Mary was in labour for ten hours which I am told is not all that long considering how long these things can go on for, but as far as I was concerned it was an eternity. I have no idea how it was that she coped with it for as long as she did.

I spoke to her about it afterwards as she was rather preoccupied at the time.

'It was the most intense pain that I have ever experienced,' she told me when she was back to talking to me again. 'I just wanted it to end, but it kept on going with no end in sight. I can't describe how painful it was. Anyone who claims to have had more pain is lying. I think you could chop a limb off and it wouldn't hurt as much. And then all of a sudden it was gone. The pain goes away and you can't remember what it was like. Most pain dies slowly until a distant echo, but this just goes off like a light switch. Freaky.'

I had no words that could help to describe my sympathy for all the pain and suffering that she had gone through. Not just the labour pain, but the nine months of carrying a baby around, feeling fat and useless.

Perhaps it was the evil glances of the nurse who clearly had it in for me that made me think that there was no way that I could make Mary go through all of this again.

And then the most marvellous thing happened and after all the pain that she had gone through, Mary gave birth to our beautiful baby daughter, who weighed in at 7 lbs 9.

It was hard to believe that I had become a father. It was the most marvellous thing that I have ever witnessed in my entire life.

Eleven

In that cold, windy day in October I became the father to a wonderful baby girl. I immediately became all gushy and all of the things that I tend to hate in other parents. I suppose it is just one of those things that you can't escape from.

I introduced Mary to the new member of the family.

'This is your daughter,' I said as I placed her in her arms.

'Our daughter,' she corrected me as she took her and looked into her eyes. 'She's beautiful.'

'Well, she takes after her mother, that's why.'

She smiled up at me. I took a photograph of the two of them together which was something that I cherished although in truth I wouldn't need a physical copy to remember the image of the two of them together. Nevertheless, it still sits on my desk to this day as I write.

'We have to think of a name for her,' I said once I had finished.

She thought about this for a moment.

'Jessica,' she finally stated with a degree of certainty.

'Jessica?'

'Yes, I like the sound of it.'

'Jessica it is then. Hello Jessica, welcome to the world. I'm sorry it isn't a perfect place, but we will try and do our best for you.'

Parenthood changes you. Suddenly you do feel that you should have taken greater care of the world and invested more time in trying to make it a better place for future generations. There is a sense of responsibility that suddenly comes down on you that you may not have felt before. Obviously, this was not something that seemed to bother my mother all that much.

'I think the end product is well worth it,' Mary said, 'but my God that was hard to go through. I really wanted it to end. Several times I felt like jumping out of the window if it would just take the pain away.'

'Well, I am rather glad you didn't.'

'So am I,' she said smiling again.

After all these years of being on my own and being without a family, I now had the most amazing family that I could ever have asked for. It just goes to show you that anything is possible. Take me back ten years and I would never have imagined that I would have been in the situation that I now found myself in. Life has a way of surprising us. Not always in a positive way.

***

'I've been thinking,' Mary said a few weeks later when things were settling down a little and the sleepless nights were starting to creep in.

'What have you been thinking?'

'I have been thinking about your family again.'

'You guys are my family, Mary.'

'I know, but surely you must be slightly curious about the rest of your family?'

'I can't say that I am.'

'It makes me curious.'

'That's because you spend so much time reading detective fiction. You think everything in life is a mystery that has to be solved. Real life isn't like that.'

'I think your family is something of a mystery and looking into it might solve it or it might not, but I can't see a great deal of harm in it.'

'Opening old wounds?'

'What old wounds?'

She had me on that one as I wasn't really all that bothered about anything that my family had said or done. I had moved on and it didn't really worry me.

'I am curious about it all even if you aren't, Midge.'

'It doesn't occupy all my thoughts, no.'

'Not all your thoughts? So, it occupies some of them then?'

Mary had an uncanny way of being able to talk me into a corner like this and trick me into saying things that I perhaps would not have chosen to say if I had been in full command of my ability to speak. I chose to say nothing in response to this and allow her to continue as it was clear that there was no stopping her now.

'Would you have any objections if it was something that I looked into?'

I was rather confused by her desire to dig into this subject, but I suppose that there was truth in what she said about it not causing all that much harm if she did dig about into the family tree. Digging about and finding out what there was to find didn't mean that I had to act on anything that she discovered.

'Are you sure you are not busy with other things, what with Jessica?'

'Well, yes naturally things are rather busy at the moment, but then as I am not working at present it would give me something a little extra to focus on to keep my brain active.'

'Well I can't really say no then, can I? Fill your boots.'

And so it was that Mary went hunting to find my family. I wasn't convinced that it was the best idea that she had ever had. Time would tell.

***

I would like to say that I soon returned to normality once again, but the truth was that with a baby in the family now things were never going to be normal again. At least they were never going to be normal in the sense of what normality had meant before Jessica came along. I said that things were settling down, but then that was a total lie when you think about it as things would never be likely to settle down as they once were ever again. I tend to view this more positively than it perhaps sounds.

Don't get me wrong. I am not complaining that she had come along and changed our lives, far from it. That is the kind of shake up to normality that it is nice to have from time to time in life as oppose to the ones that are shit.

Talking of which, what I was not prepared for was the quantity and smell of the poo that Jessica was able to produce which seemed to be far greater than it would have seemed possible for someone so small to be able to do. So hard to believe that something otherwise so angelic and beautiful could give out what could only be described as pure evil. It seemed to be something that had a half-life longer than radioactive material particularly with regards to the smell which seemed to hang around for days and enabled entire strangers that you meet in the street to know that you have a baby. I have no idea what Jessica would do for a living when she grew up to be old enough to go out to work, but at the moment she seemed to have taken up the occupation of being an expert poo manufacturer.

The other tendency that I have heard about is to put endless pictures and updates on social media. Fortunately, this was not an issue for me as I had not seen the point of being part of any social media network. If I wanted someone to know what I was doing then I would tell them, without the need to post it for everyone and their dog to see. Another reason was that being such a technological phobic person that I was, I had no idea how it all worked. It just seemed to mean that technology was becoming intolerably complicated when it didn't really need to be. I am all for keeping things simplistic.

Life rarely seems to allow things to be so simple. I would love for things to be simple, but then I suppose you just have to look at my parents to see how complicated things are when they really could be simple. There seem to be people out there who are really only happy if things are complicated.

Christmas was always a magical time of the year for us. Christmas is magical anyway, but it was significant for Mary and myself because Christmas was the time of the year when we first got together. We had a double reason for celebrating, therefore.

For Jessica it was of course far too early for her to understand what was going on. She was only two months old at her first Christmas after all. Christmas that year was the time when Saddam Hussein was executed, so I suppose he had other things on his mind as well.

There wasn't all that much Jessica was doing that Christmas. Later on, it would take on more of a significance, but I doubt she knew anything that was going on around her at that point.

It was around the time that Hussein was facing his final hours on Earth and Jessica was getting used to being here, that Mary told me what she had found out about my family.

'I don't know where your mother is,' she had stated.

'Well, that makes two of us. I have no idea where she is and I sometimes wonder if she has any idea where she is either. She certainly never seemed to be in the present when I knew her.'

'But I have done some digging about.'

'And?'

I found that despite my initial reluctance and my air of not being concerned about my family I was intrigued to find out what it was that she had discovered. There are times when I think you have to understand the past to understand the present. You have to know where you have come from to know where you are going and numerous other clichés and to be honest I don't know if they are true or not.

Probably not, because to be frank I had made it to the age of twenty-six without knowing hardly anything about my background and it didn't seem to have stopped me from being able to cope in the present or planning for the future by having my own family. I suppose I could take the view then that the clichés about knowing where you had come from didn't really matter in the slightest as far as I was concerned.

Strangely enough it didn't seem to stop me from being curious though. Perhaps that has got more to do with an enquiring mind. Mind you if that were true, why hadn't I done the enquiring myself? Why had I waited this long and then left it up to Mary to do all the work? I could only come to the conclusion that the reason for all of this was because I was afraid of what I might find out. If Mary had discovered something that she thought might be harmful to me then she was likely to keep it hidden and tell me that she hadn't found anything. If she thought I should know about it then she would tell me.

These were just some of the thoughts that went through my mind at a lightning speed whilst I waited for Mary to tell me what it was that she had managed to uncover.

'I had a dig about in all the public records. It's amazing what you can find out if you know where to look and don't mind putting a bit of time into it.'

'And you found out what?' I felt that my heart was beating a little faster than it should.

'I checked from your birth certificate, taking the names of both your parents and seeing what I could find out.'

'Yes?' Mary certainly knew how to build anticipation.

'I couldn't find anything from your mother's side, but that might mean that I just need to cast the net a little wider. Something that is not impossible, but might be something that could be done if there were more time.'

'And on my father's side?'

'I found his parents.'

'My grandparents?'

'That's usually the way it works.'

'They're still alive?'

'No reason why they shouldn't be. They would probably be in their seventies. I haven't got all the facts, but I managed to find their name and then checked with the electoral roll and they are local.'

'You have an address?'

'I do. Of course, there is the possibility that they have moved away or died. The roll must be a good few years out of date, well at least the one that I managed to get my hands on was.'

I could think of another potential issue as well.

'There is, of course, the possibility that my mother was lying about who my father was.'

'How do you mean?'

'Well, we only have her word for who he was. She could have plucked any name out of a hat for being my father.'

'I suppose there is only one way to find out.' She handed me a slip of paper on which was written the name and address of the person who might or might not be my grandmother and grandfather.

'I suppose there is,' I said thoughtfully as I twirled the paper between my fingers and tried to answer the question of whether I really wanted to find them. Did I really want the answers that might change my life forever? Or might, I suppose make no difference whatsoever.

What would you do?

***

'What will you do?'

Luke asked me when we met up for coffee to celebrate the New Year. Meeting for coffee because neither of us really cared all that much for alcohol and because we cared even less about celebrating New Year's Eve. Luke had even been known to go to bed just before midnight to deliberately snub the entire occasion.

I had to admit that I could see his point at times. I am not sure that there was any point in celebrating another year with such excess and abandonment, but then I suppose some people will use any excuse that they can for a party. I have to admit that it didn't mean all that much to me either.

'I don't know, what do you think I should do?'

'Can't really answer that one for you. It's up to you.'

'I would value your opinion though.'

He thought about it for a moment whilst sipping his coffee.

'Well, on the one hand you have nothing to lose by contacting them. They may ignore you, perhaps put you down as a freak and you may never hear from them again. They may tell you that they have no idea what you are talking about. Either way you are no worse off than you are now.'

'True.'

'However, they may welcome you with open arms and you may discover that you have a whole new family you knew nothing about and get some answers about the mystery of your parents.'

'Or, it may open a can of worms.'

'That's the downside, you may regret making contact with them and may decide that they are not the kind of people that you really want to know or that they tell you things that you really don't want to hear.'

'That is a worry. And what's on the other hand?'

'On the other hand, you are happy at the moment. You have a beautiful wife and a smelly daughter; both of which you love.'

'Yes.'

'Why upset the balance of a happy life with things that you seem to have managed to make it through to your advanced age without knowing anything about so far?'

'That is a big point.'

'Alternatively, there is always the fact that if you don't contact them although nothing will change in your life you will have to live with the fact that you could possibly have found some of the answers but chose not to do so.'

'That is the only thing that bothers me. Can I live with the knowledge that I could have dug deeper and I didn't?'

'Can you?'

'I don't know.'

We relapsed into drinking our coffee for a moment, thinking about it from different angles. When it came down to it there was really only two choices. Either to contact them, or to throw the paper away and forget all about it.

I could think about it for as long as I wanted to, but really there wasn't that much of a choice in the matter. I had to learn more, one way or the other.

The first thing that I decided to do was to do a little detective work of my own. Mary had supplied me with the address of my supposed grandparents on my father's side so I decided that I would go and have a look at it.

There might be an element of snobbishness about this. If I had discovered that they lived in an undesirable location with windows boarded up and the rusting remains of a Ford Fiesta in the front garden then I might have decided that it was best to leave them uncontacted. To an extent their house would make the decision for me as to whether I contacted them or not.

I know, it was very shallow of me to plan such a thing in this manner, but I won't make any apologies for that. Perhaps you would have taken the view that family was family no matter what it was that they looked like, who they were or how they chose to live; but all I can say is that if you felt like that you hadn't grown up with my mother.

My mother had been a hippy as I have stated and I have no idea what her parents would have been like to have turned out someone like her. Perhaps they were the original sixties hippies.

I had no knowledge at all as to what my father was like. Because I didn't know him and because my mother didn't like to talk about him other than the basics being that he was dead, I had no idea what his family were like. This was a good way of finding out before I got myself into something that I didn't know the answers to.

I then had the issue as to how I was going to 'stake out' the house without making it too obvious. As I have stated before, I did not drive so I couldn't really sit outside the house and pretend to be waiting for someone. It would be far more conspicuous to be loitering under a tree or a lamp post standing out like a paedophile outside a primary school.

The obvious answer was to get Mary to take me, as she did drive, but I decided to keep her out of it at this time. The only other real co-conspirator that I could get involved was Luke.

That is how it came to be that Luke and myself found ourselves a little distance from the house in question one Saturday afternoon. The initial signs were good. The house was located amongst a leafy suburb with a long row of semi-detached houses in an area that looked clean, tidy and prosperous; not a rusting car in sight – other than the one that we were sitting in, of course.

'If you don't like my car, you can bloody well walk home.' Luke muttered when I had made this comment to him.

We had parked a few houses down from the one that we were targeting so that we could observe it without making it obvious by being right outside of it. Of course, I suppose we would have been highly suspicious to the people whose house we had parked outside.

Fortunately, it was during the afternoon so we looked slightly less suspicious than we would have done had it been dark. If it had been at night then this was the kind of neighbourhood where someone would have called the police to say that there was a suspicious looking vehicle outside with two suspicious looking men sitting in it; and this was also the kind of neighbourhood where the police would have turned up as well.

'Now that you have seen the house, how long do you actually want us to sit here for?' Luke asked apprehensively as he was of the opinion that this was the kind of neighbourhood that would call the police regardless of what the time of the day was.

'Not long. Let's give it a few minutes and see what happens.'

'What exactly are you thinking is likely to happen?'

'I don't know.'

Just then it happened. As we had been discussing the matter a woman came walking along the pavement carrying a shopping bag. My guess was that she had been dropped off by the bus that ran along the top of the road. She turned into the driveway of our target house and taking a bunch of keys from her pocket used it to unlock the door before letting herself inside and closing the door on us.

'Well?' asked Luke.

'Well, that's hopeful. She looked like she was in her late sixties or seventies so she would have been about the right age.'

'What does that prove?'

'It proves that it's more likely to be the house of my grandparents. If some teenage mother had come by and opened the door it would have been less likely.'

'So, what are you going to do now? Go and knock?'

In some cases the direct approach was often the best way to go about things, but I couldn't help but think in this circumstance going up and telling someone that was a stranger and in their seventies that you were their long lost grandchild would most likely result in a heart attack or the aforementioned telephone call to the police.

'I don't think that's a good idea. Let's go.'

He started the car. 'What are you going to do then?'

'Write a letter, I suppose. After all writing is what I do.'

***

I wrote a letter.

No, to be truthful I wrote several letters. I didn't post them all, of course, but I wrote several letters because of the fact that it was an extremely difficult letter to write. How was it best to approach the topic? 'You don't know me, but...' hardly seemed to be the best approach imaginable.

Being a writer, I naturally went through several drafts of the letter and when I ended with one that I thought was acceptable I passed it to Mary who read it and then passed it back to me at which stage it went through several revisions once again.

After several drafts we eventually settled on one that we both approved of. I wrote it out again in my best handwriting and placed it in an envelope and stuck a stamp on it.

I then walked down the road to where the local post box was and stood there for a few minutes wondering if it was the right thing to be doing or whether it would be better for me to tear the thing up now and forget all about it.

Eventually I became aware that I was being watched by someone. I turned and saw the postman who was standing there looking at me in a very suspicious manner. Clearly, he thought that my loitering was a plan to rob the Royal Mail of its post. He then saw the letter in my hand.

'Everything okay?' he asked perhaps now wondering if I was about to post a letter bomb.

'Yes, sorry was just lost in thought.'

He moved forward with his bag ready to empty the box.

'Here you go.' I went to hand him the letter.

'Oh no, I can't take that, sir.'

'Why not?' I was confused it was a letter after all.

'More than my job's worth.'

'I'm sorry?' I was mightily confused.

'You have to put it in there,' he said indicating the slit for the post, 'I can't take it from your hand.'

'Why on earth not?'

'Against the rules.'

I realised that I could argue this somewhat pointless point but that if I did I was liable to be here all day with him getting into the intricacies of legislation regarding letters. I decided that it would be easier just to play his game,

With elaborate over emphasis I placed the letter through the slot and then watched him as he opened the little door and then removed my letter along with all the other items of mail that were inside. He then closed the door again.

'Much obliged, sir,' he said whilst actually touching the peak of his hat that he was wearing before turning around and marching off to his little *Postman Pat* van.

'My pleasure,' I muttered after him feeling deeply surreal about everything that had just happened and wondering if it was in some way some sort of omen about what would happen now that the letter was out of my hands.

I imagined that if I changed my mind and now ran after him demanding my letter back that he would possibly have had a heart attack at the outrageous suggestion that he open his sack for anyone to take whatever they wanted from it. (Having read that back it sounds a little sleazier than I had first intended it to be).

I decided not to try this theory out, but instead decided to head home and wait to see if there was a reply to my letter or whether it would be carefully ignored. I wondered what I would have done if the situation had been reversed and someone had written to me out of the blue claiming to be a member of my family.

The answer was that I didn't have the slightest idea.

Twelve

Fate was not in my hands any longer, assuming it had ever been in the first place that is. I had posted the letter and all I could do was now return to my life and do my best to forget all about it.

This I did.

Aside from the fact that I checked the post with regular scrutiny just in case a letter had arrived in an unfamiliar hand. Sometimes we can try and put on an air that we are not bothered about what is happening around us, but then we know deep down that we are hooked on what is going on.

Each day that I checked the post I was disappointed because there was no reply. All I got were bills in disappointing brown envelopes with little windows in them. I suppose I had been expecting rather a lot to think that there might be something else. It was a massive shot in the dark at trying to find out about my past. Eventually I began to forget about the letter and moved onwards with my life.

It wasn't that hard a thing to do. Jessica was more than a handful and took a lot of our time. She was, of course, worth every moment of it.

I had received a small promotion at work which technically put me in a management position at the library, not that you would have noticed for the pay increase, but it was clearly something that the older employees noticed with a degree of spite that a twenty-six-year-old was in a position above them. I have never understood why there should be jealousy. Everyone has the chance to go for promotion, it's hardly my fault if they chose not to. That doesn't seem to stop them from bitching when others do it though.

Alongside all of that I was still trying to crack on with my novel which was growing slightly. I was at about twenty-thousand words at that time and finding my feet with it really.

All in all, it was an extremely busy time and I was often combating an extreme level of tiredness. It was hardly surprising that I was tired with busy days and sleepless nights going on every day.

Show me a new parent who is in any way different and I will show you someone who is clearly shirking their responsibilities.

'Not heard anything then?' Luke asked me one afternoon over coffee.

'About what?' I knew what he was talking about, of course, but I had started to put on the air of someone who was not really all that bothered about what was going on with regards to my grandparents (or possible grandparents). I had decided that this attitude was something that was better for when the inevitable eventually happened, namely nothing.

What's my point? I will tell you.

Act like you don't care about the situation and when you are ultimately disappointed then those around you won't realise that it mattered to you and that you are probably upset by it. Well, it makes sense to me.

'From your grandparents.'

'Well, to be fair, Luke, we don't know for sure that they are my grandparents.'

'True, but there is more chance of them being your grandparents than anyone else that you have met over the years.'

'I grant you that. To answer your question though, no I have not heard from them and if I am entirely honest with myself I don't think I will hear from them.'

'Why do you think that?'

'Well, imagine how you would feel if some strange guy turned up claiming to be your long-lost grandson, what would you think?

'I wouldn't believe them.'

'Exactly.'

'And do you know why I wouldn't believe them?'

'Why?'

'Because I am only twenty-six so I would really have to be going some to have grandchildren at my age.'

'Cock.'

'That would have come into it somewhere along the line, yes. I do, however, take your point. It must be a rather difficult thing to have someone appear out of nowhere claiming to be a relative.'

'I wouldn't blame them if they just ignored it. They probably think that it is some kind of scam or something, that I am after their money. Bit like those emails you get.'

'How's Jessica?'

'She is pretty amazing really. It's hard to believe that I am responsible for her. That she's from me.'

'Partly responsible, Midge, you didn't do it on your own. As a matter of fact, your creative input was the easiest part of the process.'

'Very true. I don't think I could be happier.'

'You are looking a little tired though.'

'God yes. I really don't know how long these sleepless nights will go on for, but I can't wait until they stop. At the moment they seem to have reached a point where no matter what time Jessica wakes up, that is it. We all have to be up. Kinda screws with your brain when you are trying to lead a reasonably normal life at the same time.'

'I bet it does. I am not sure I could ever have children. All that smell. Poo and vomit everywhere.'

'Well, I am rather hoping that is something that she will grow out of. At least until she is in her late teens when she will probably start the vomiting again.'

'Ha! You wait until she starts showing up with boyfriends that you want to kill on first sight.'

'I hadn't really thought about that.'

'A difficult one to live with.'

'Well, if you will excuse me I'm not going to worry about that just yet when she is still only a few months old. A lot can happen between now and then.'

'Ain't that the truth?'

After that I did genuinely put the matter out of my mind for some time and concentrated on being a father, a husband, a librarian and a writer. Four occupations that kept me fully occupied.

It never occurred to me that my letter would have meant some investigation on their part and that they were probably checking me out in the same way that I had checked them out. Seems logical when you think about it, but I wasn't really thinking about it at the time. I had other things to be thinking about.

And then one morning when I least expected it, amongst all the bills and circulars and other useless things that the post office usually saw fit to send me, was a hand-written envelope that stood out from the rest of the pile of things.

I opened it feeling very apprehensive as to what it might contain. I thought logically about it as I was opening it. If there had been bad news or there was a requirement for me to sod off and leave them alone, then surely, they would not have written, but would have just consigned the entire matter to the bin? The fact that they had written presumably meant that they had something that was worth saying, which was probably positive in its own way.

The time for speculation was over though as I unfolded the lavender coloured paper that was inside the envelope.

It was not a long letter, just one sheet of paper that was covered in a neat, old fashioned script that appeared to have been written by fountain pen. I was rather pleased to see that there were still people out there who liked to use fountain pens. I thought that they were a dying art.

The letter was written by the woman that I had come to assume was my grandmother and invited me to visit her to discuss matters relating to family on the following Sunday.

***

The time between receiving the letter and the following Sunday seemed to drag on for an eternity. It was almost impossible to concentrate on my work, both in the library and on my novel. I kept running over potential scenarios in my head as to what would happen when we met up which was a pretty futile activity as the possibilities were somewhat endless.

I tried to concentrate on my work and family, but my treacherous mind kept bringing me back to the Sunday which slowly approached.

'I do hope that we have done the right thing about this,' I told Mary.

'It's a bit late to do anything about it now, to be honest. All you can do is go along on Sunday and see what happens.'

As always there was logic in what Mary had to say. She was probably always the most logical out of all of the people that I had ever met. It probably had to do with the amount that she read which was even more than I read. The difference being that Mary read for pleasure and enjoyed her reading habits without the need to feel that she had to write as well. That was the problem though, some of us just got a little too greedy and wanted too much.

I continued to work on my grand novel. It went forward slowly, but I was now finding that I had less time to work on it than I did before. Parenthood will do that sort of thing. I used to write every day, but now there were days, if not weeks that went by without me picking up my pen or tapping away on the computer.

Now that I have written those words it makes it sound like I resent the fact that I am not able to write as much as I would like. I love writing, it is something that I am deeply committed to, but I love my family more and if it was a choice between the two then I obviously wouldn't write another word for as long as I lived.

Due to the absence of family so early in my life, I began to realise that when Mary and then Jessica did come along that there was nothing that was really as important as family.

Sounds pretty basic as far as I am concerned. Stating the obvious you might think, but clearly there are people who don't take this as a natural thought – my mother would be a chief culprit amongst them I should think.

The day approached when I had been invited over for tea to discuss things, which seemed frightfully civilised as if it was something that had popped out of a Noel Coward play. Mary had offered to come with me and it was an offer that I had accepted. I felt that I might need the moral support. She hadn't been invited as such, but that shouldn't be a massive issue I would have thought. Besides which, as usual, I was relying on her for a lift there and back. I could have got the bus, I know, but public transport is something that I try to avoid at all costs.

When the day arrived, I spent a little more time than usual trying to make sure that I was smart and presentable, something which Mary found hilariously funny, but I thought it was worth making the effort in order to make a good impression. There are some who would probably say that I needed all the help that I could get.

Having finally got myself into a state that I thought might be the best way of visiting my relatives for the first time we set off for the house that I had last secretly spied on and before we knew it we were knocking on the door.

***

The woman that I had come to think of as my grandmother, even if there was slight chance that there was still no hope about this, was called Julia and I suppose that she was in her early seventies or perhaps late sixties. I have never been particularly good at guessing ages and it is obviously not the polite thing to just ask.

I like to run a tidy house, but Julia's house was immaculate. Not a thing was out of place and there was not a speck of dust to be seen anywhere. It was almost like a museum or some National Trust property, only on a much smaller scale, but nevertheless some place that had an army of volunteers that were behind the scene working on keeping the place in neat repair and tidy. It seemed like that, but clearly that couldn't be the case and it must have all been done by Julia unless she had someone who came in and helped her out.

We were shown into the living room which was as neat and tidy as the rest of the place was. You almost felt like it would be offensive to sit anywhere or touch anything that might disturb the place where everything seemed to have a place.

We sat down and Julia bought in a tray that contained a teapot and associated items all in what appeared to be fine bone china. I am no expert in these matters, but it looked pretty expensive as far as I could tell.

'Your letter was something of a surprise,' she eventually said when she had settled down after poring the tea.

'I'm sorry. I can understand it must have been a shock. You probably thought I was a crank as well.'

'The thought had occurred to me, but you do know some details about the people you claim to be your parents. Perhaps you can tell me more.'

'As you know my father was killed in a car crash before I was born so I only know what my mother has told me about him, and I am not sure how accurate that is as it was never a subject that she was particularly keen on talking about. My mother was always distant throughout my life, as if she had something else on her mind and then a few years ago she just upped and vanished without a trace and I have not seen her since.'

I concluded and sipped on my tea whilst Julia nodded and seemed reflective about the things that she had heard me say.

'It sounds like Lucy if I am honest.'

Lucy was my mother. I don't think that I have told you this.

'What do you know about her?' I asked keenly.

She sighed deeply and stirred her tea absent minded as she had already stirred it several times already. She seemed to be at a crossroads whilst she decided what to do.

'The first thing that I should probably tell you is that we had no idea about you at all. I know you thought from your letter that it was some case of long lost family getting back together, but we had no idea that Lucy was pregnant and that she gave birth to you. Up until your letter I had no idea that you were in the world.'

This was something of a shock, but I suppose upon reflection and knowing my mother as she was it shouldn't have been something that took me all that much by surprise.

'That was why your letter was such a shock. It has taken me some time to come to terms with the fact that there are family that exist that I knew nothing about.'

'You do believe me then?' This had been something that I was worried about that she wouldn't believe a word that I said or my story at all. As a matter of fact that I was surprised at how easily she had believed me, but then it wouldn't have surprised me if she had spent a great deal of time and effort looking into just how serious I was and how true the things were that I was stating. I can't imagine that she was the kind of person who would have agreed to meet me if she had not been certain of the things that I had claimed.

'I believe you,' she stated. 'You should also know that your grandfather, Robert, died a few years ago.'

'I'm sorry to hear that.'

'He had a good life. It was a heart attack and over very quickly,' she picked up a silver framed photograph that was on her table which showed a dapper man in uniform which she looked at fondly. 'There is not a day that goes by when I do not think of him in some way or another.'

'I'm sorry that I will not get the opportunity to meet him.'

'Well, I suppose that is life,' she sighed and put the photo frame back down on the table.

'Your mother was a difficult person, at times.' I didn't really need her to tell me that. 'We did not always see eye-to-eye on matters and I suppose it could be argued that there is not a mother alive who does not want the best for her son.'

I could think of one potential exception to that rule, as I am sure could she, but perhaps she was being too polite to point out the obvious. She continued and I let her talk.

'No mother thinks that there is any girl who is suitable for their beloved son, no matter how much of a saint that girl might be, and you will forgive me I hope if I point out that whatever else your mother was, she was no saint.' I couldn't really argue that point. 'Perhaps you will understand if you ever have children.'

'I understand perfectly. We have a daughter – six months old.' I had neglected to tell her this when I wrote to her as I felt that would have been too much information to take in too quickly. Not that it was any easier to take in now. Her hand flew to her mouth.

'My goodness. Not only do I discover that I am a grandmother, but in almost the same breath I find out that I am a great-grandmother as well. I do not believe that I have ever felt so old.'

I could understand her point of view. It must be rather a shock, but I tried to steer matters back on course.

'Was there anything in particular that put you at odds with my mother?'

'At odds,' she nodded her head, 'yes that is as good a turn of phrase as any to describe the nature of things between us. Perhaps I was being too snotty and uptight about it all, but I did feel that my son could have done better. I know that makes me sound like a total snob, and the only defence that I can raise to that is that I was so much younger in those days and I viewed things differently. Perhaps if it were possible to do things differently, then I would have changed matters and perhaps it would not have created the gulf that existed and which kept you a secret from me for a quarter of century. That is a lot of time that needs to be made up.'

I nodded my head but chose not to say anything as I felt that Julia was on a roll and partly seemed to be in the past and only slightly in the same room as me.

'There was no doubt at all that she was very much in love with my son, of course, I will give her that to her credit. She was passionately, one might almost say compulsively in love with him. He was swept off his feet by her, of course.'

I tried to imagine my mother in such a circumstance as she was describing and I failed to do it completely. I just couldn't imagine that she had ever been in a place where she had loved anyone as Julia was describing for me. I couldn't really imagine her being in a place where she felt so passionate about anything at all. I had never equated her with passion.

'She was different to us, of course. To you, the youth of today, such a thing as class and society will seem to you to be very old fashioned, outdated and even ridiculous sentiments to hold, and who am I to say that you are wrong? Things were very different in those days, having gone through the sixties and the seventies and the turbulent eighties there seemed to be a situation which was very "them and us". All those strikes, power cuts, riots, civil unrest. It was almost as if you had to pick a side to be on.'

I nodded my head as if I agreed with her totally, but I couldn't really have cared less if the truth were totally known. In the twenty-first century that I lived in things like that just didn't seem to matter in the slightest.

'You had the government, the armed forces and the police on one side and the long-haired hippies on the other side who were always protesting about something. Striking about pay, protesting about Vietnam, rioting with the police that they felt they had the right to beat up or even murder because they saw them as fascists.'

I thought that there were probably some people who still held true to that philosophy today, so perhaps things had not changed all that much.

'You had to decide if you were for law and order or if you were for rebellion. Well, I ask you, what would those long-haired layabouts have done if they had of overthrown the government and took over power themselves? They could not even hold down a job let alone run a country. I suppose they would have had us all eating flowers and having promiscuous sexual encounters with strangers on top of double decker buses. As they have advanced into age they have achieved nothing, but to remain unemployed and to pump themselves full of narcotics. I blame them for the spread of AIDS.'

I exchanged a glance with Mary and she slightly shrugged. There was always the possibility that there was going to be a racist or xenophobic rant coming out at any moment as she appeared to be of the generation that supported such things.

'Out family were on the side of the establishment, which was a dirty word to the likes of Lucy and her kind. They were opposites, her and my son. There could have been an opportunity to bridge the gap, of course, but she saw us as fascists as well and the entire moment was lost. She never missed an opportunity to throw little digs in at us and imply that we were going to be the first up in front of the firing squad when the time came.'

'How did your son feel about that?' Mary asked as she finished her tea and replaced the cup delicately on the saucer.

'He was so much in love with her that he would have forgiven her if she had stabbed us to death with the fish knife over dinner. He was heavily under her spell. I cannot blame him. Despite what I say, Midge, I am not one to get in the path of true love.'

She pronounced my name in much the same way that I would imagine that she pronounced the word 'socialist'. Not with disgust so much as with unfamiliarity.

'I tried to get on with her, I really did, Robert and I tried, we both did. We tried so very hard to welcome her to the family and then after some time we realised that she was not interested in being part of our family. All that she wanted was to take my son away from his family. Perhaps she felt that she was saving him by doing that.'

'If I ever see her again I could always ask her,' I put in.

'Oh, it really does not matter now what her motives were. It is all in the past.'

I looked around the room which seemed to be full of the past and thought that it was something that she seemed rather comfortable in living in. Each to their own, I suppose. I had noticed an immaculate collection of leather bound books in a bookcase in the corner and I was fighting the urge to go and run my fingers and my eyes across the spines to see what they all were. I vaguely wondered if they were things that were there for show or if they were actually opened and read at any point of their lives.

'You do not really want to sit there listening to me bad mouthing your mother though, do you?' She stated whilst pouring some more tea that we had not asked for from the gigantic pot that was in front of her.

'You haven't really said anything that I have not heard or thought myself at some stage in the past. My mother was a difficult person to get on with to say the least.'

She nodded her head as she finished pouring out the tea.

'You do not seem to be much like her,' she said whilst she leant back in her chair and examined me in much the same way that I would imagine a High Court Judge might examine someone standing in the dock. 'You look slightly like her, but you have traces of your father in you that I can see. I suppose that is why it makes it even easier for me to believe what you told me in your letter, now that I have seen you in the flesh, as it were. Your character I am not sure where you get it from. I am not sure that you are anything like her and you don't seem to follow your father, in some of his traits at any rate.'

I had no idea what this meant and was debating whether to ask her what she was talking about when she carried on.

'The question is what is it that you want now that we have come together?' This is it I thought, this is what it has all been building up to. She wants to know if I am a fortune hunter and I have turned up after twenty-six years in order to try and claim some inheritance or lost years of child support money.

'To be entirely honest I haven't given it much thought.' This was true. Most of my deliberations had been centred on trying to decide whether or not I should make contact and try and meet her, not necessarily what it was that I was going to do afterwards.

'I haven't really come with all that much of a plan,' I admitted. She nodded though as if this had been a satisfactory answer, but then she chose not to say anything else, so I felt it was an invitation to continue talking. 'I suppose, I have really come for answers. For obvious reasons I never knew my father and I could never really get anything sensible out of my mother and now, of course, she has left the scene completely so it isn't possible to get anything from her.'

'Do you think you can get the answers from me?'

'Well, you've given me some already. Certainly, you've filled in a lot of the background for me that I never knew before and never would have done if I'd never met you. There are still a lot of gaps though.'

'I do not imagine that it will be something that we can get through in an afternoon. I also do not really know anything about you. You have your whole life to fill me in on.'

For the next twenty minutes or so I gave her a potted history of my life, what it was like growing up with a single parent that was mainly absent, what it was like at school, how I had met, fallen in love and married Mary, the recent addition of Jessica to our family and my ambitions and current failed attempts to write. If I am entirely honest it amazes me that it took twenty minutes to get through it all.

I took my wallet out and handed her a photograph of Jessica. She put her glasses on and looked at the small photograph for a moment.

'She looks beautiful, she has your eyes,' she said as she went to hand it back to me.

'No please, keep it if you like. As you might imagine we have thousands of them.'

'Thank you,' for a moment she seemed genuinely touched and placed it next to the photograph of her deceased husband. 'I wonder where you get your love of literature from.'

'I had always assumed that as it was so clearly not from my mother that it must have been my father.'

'I don't think so. James was always on the straight and narrow until he met your mother and then he went off the rails to the say the least. He started questioning a number of things, challenging what he had been brought up with. I will admit that we did not speak for a while, but we eventually managed to patch up our differences and come to an understanding of each other.'

'That must have given you some comfort later on.'

She looked at my blankly for a moment and I suspected that she had phased out into the past once again and was having some difficulty in remembering who I was and what I was doing sitting in her living room drinking her tea. She then seemed to come back to the present which was something of a relief.

'Your mother was never always very truthful with you, was she?' It seemed a bizarre question.

'No, I suppose not. I am not entirely sure that she ever lied blatantly to me. Whenever I wanted to discuss things she was either vague or just refused to talk about it, diverting the conversation elsewhere or more likely just not answering or wandering off. Enigmatic is a word I suppose that I would use with regards to her in that sense of things.'

'You have given me a great surprise.' She stood up and I suddenly thought that the meeting had come to an abrupt ending. Perhaps she had decided that she did not want to know me after all. I looked at Mary trying to work out if there was something that I had said that had perhaps, unknown to me, caused offence. We both stood up with her.

'Yes, you have given me a surprise. To find out in such a small space of time that I not only am a grandmother, but also a great-grandmother is perhaps more than enough surprises for one afternoon. Perhaps I can return the favour though.'

She opened the door that led somewhere else into the house, and not the way that we had entered. 'You had better come in now,' she stated and with that a man walked in the room that I had never seen before.

He stood in the centre of the room looking very out of place and awkward. Julia came around him and put her hands on the back of her chair.

'Midge, this is James. My son and your father.'

Thirteen
James

I've been asked to write my own account of my story to go with what my son Midge has written so far. It sounds strange to say 'my son, Midge' when I had no idea that I had a son until recently. I am no writer so I don't suppose it will be anything like what he writes, but I can only do my best.

I was born in 1953 when my parents were twenty years old. People seem to get married and have children later in life then my parents' generation did, and I suppose as my generation did if I think about it. It isn't really something that I have spent a lot of time thinking about, but I have had a lot to think about recently. It's amazing how things can make you change your attitude towards life.

I grew up in a Britain that was still reeling from the Second World War. It was something that my parents would remind me every time that they possibly could. We younger folks could not possibly understand the hardships and the things that they had gone through. Well, that is true. We didn't need reminding of it though at every second that occurred.

I was too young to remember rationing, but I do remember that we didn't have the luxury and selection of food that there is these days. We all now take supermarkets for granted but in those days, they were something that could hardly be imagined. Everything was bought from smaller shops that specialised in things. Nowadays you can walk into any supermarket and pretty much get all of the shopping that you want without having to go from store to store buying all the things that you need. We bought less in those days as well, there is too much waste these days. Buying things that we don't need and that ultimately get thrown away because they go out of date before we can eat them. We never did that when I was growing up. Firstly, because we couldn't afford to and secondly because things didn't go out of date in the sense that they do today. The only way something went out of date back then was if it rotted. These days people throw things in the bin the day after the magical label on it says it is out of date as if something mysterious happened at midnight which made it perfectly edible the night before, but which now will kill you if you were foolish enough to eat it.

Fuck, I sound just like my mother.

I suppose there are some things that you just can't avoid and turning into my mother was probably one of those things that I was always fated to do.

'Waste not want not,' she would say whilst forcing me to eat something that these days I wouldn't even give my dog. 'There are starving children in Africa that would love to have what you are eating and rejecting.'

I felt rather guilty and upset about this so one day when she was occupied elsewhere I took the grisly, greasy mince that I had not wanted to eat and spooned it into an envelope that I wrote 'To the starving children of Africa' on the front and dropped it in the local post box. I have no idea of the fuss that it must have caused later on when the postman found it but I was not old enough to know any different really. It did install in me a lifelong desire not to waste any food though. I suppose there are some other things that probably rubbed off on me as well.

I go on about food rather a lot because of the fact that I have made my career out of it. I rent a small shop, and when I say small I mean really small, you can get about three people in the shop before you reach my counter and there isn't a huge amount of room behind the counter either. I make sandwiches. As simple as that. I have a little deli counter and inside there is a selection of meats, cheeses and fish along with other things that you might decide that you want in a sandwich. Behind my counter is a selection of bread, rolls and baguettes. Come into my little sandwich bar and you can have a sandwich made up of pretty much anything you see.

I grant you it isn't the biggest industry in the world and I have no doubt at all that my parents, my mother in particular, would have preferred me to have done something better with my life, but I make enough to pay the bills and I have little desire for many luxuries and I derive a great deal of satisfaction out of feeding people and sending them on their way with a full stomach to get through their day. I think that there is little more that you can ask than to make other people happy and that is good enough for me as far as I am concerned.

As I say it is probably something that disappoints my mother a great deal, but that wouldn't be the only thing that she is disappointed in when it comes to me, but more of that later. I am getting ahead of myself slightly with regards to my sandwich making business as well. I think if you can make people happy than that is enough in life.

I don't really know what it is that I am expected to write here, I don't know what it is that is expected of me or what it is that they want to know. I am not used to writing things down like this, but I think it is possible to get carried away with yourself and to write the things down on the page here that you will then forget that someone else is going to read at some point. It might well be that you then don't want them to read it. It is all rather confusing really.

I suppose what they really want to know is how I came to meet Lucy. Well that is something that is easily done. I never had much luck with girls when I was growing up. This was chiefly because I went to a school that was not mixed so you never got to see that many girls. As a result, it made me very shy of them and I really didn't know how to approach them. I was not a great one for going out to pubs and clubs and what have you, so I never got to meet girls in that way either. To be honest if I had gone out and met them in this manner I very much doubt that I would have known what to say to them or what to do. They were an alien species as far as I could tell. They probably thought that I was as well.

I didn't meet Lucy until I was twenty-five which would have been in the summer of 1978. Up until that point I had not had any previous girlfriends and in that respect, I was a virgin as well, which I know is something that is probably unthinkable in this day and age where you are pressured to have sex when you are fourteen, but that was the way of things and there was little that I could do about it.

The reason why I had got together with Lucy was because she was the one that made the approach to me. She was like a breath of fresh air that blew in on the wind and made everything seem okay. We started to date because it was something that she wanted to do and because she wanted to do it she made it happen. If it had been left up to me then there would have been nothing happening at all. That, to a certain extent, is the story of my life.

Everything in the relationship between myself and Lucy was something that she directed and took control of whereas I just followed her and did whatever was required of me, completely allowing her to take the lead on everything. I know that is not something that would suit everybody, but it didn't bother me in the slightest. I was happy to have someone in control. I have never been all that good at being in charge of things.

We had grown up through the sixties which were our teenage years, but the decade of free love and sex was something that must have passed me by completely. I have no idea why it was that this might be, but I just carried on in the middle-class suburbs of my parents where sex was something that only took place if it was something that really needed to happen and only then behind closed curtains and with the lights off.

Lucy was not really a hippy, despite what people may say about her, but she was heavy into the music scene which was more than I ever was. I never really liked that much of the modern music as I had been raised on classical music. I tried to like the groups that Lucy was so keen on, but they just didn't do anything for me.

When you meet people now they think you were incredibly lucky to grow up in the time of The Beatles, The Rolling Stones and The Queen, but they are so deflated when you tell them that you know absolutely nothing about these bands and have no personal memories of them at all. In that sense it is fair to say that the decades which are considered so good for modern music, namely the sixties and seventies passed me by completely without so much as a nod in my direction. Personally, I don't feel that I missed all that much.

Whilst we are in the general area of such things I have noticed that Midge talks a lot about reading, writing and the like. It must be a disappointment to him, but I really am not a reader. I can't see the point of sitting in one place and reading a book. I don't have any books and I haven't really missed out on all that much by not having them I don't think. I haven't read a book since I was at school and I didn't read all that many then. I left school when I was fifteen and went out to work in the real world.

For a time, I worked in whatever job I could find. I worked in all kinds of places, mainly shops which was all good preparation for the day when I had my own little sandwich shop. It probably hasn't been a rocket of a life, but it's the only one I have had, so I tried to make the best of it.

At the age of twenty-five I was working in the local branch of the Co-Op which is where I kept bumping into Lucy. She made it very clear that she was interested in me. She was the first girl that ever really had shown an interest, I suppose, and so after a lot of thinking about it, I decided to take her up on her proposal that we should walk out together which was an old term for the age when you consider how modern Lucy was.

I suppose she saw me as something of a challenge. She was amazed at my apparent lack of musical knowledge, aside from what I did know about classical music, of course, which was something that she had absolutely no interest in whatsoever. She was always more clever than me so she probably decided that she was going to try and rub some of her clever nature off on me, which was a completely hopeless case. She tried to teach me about all the modern things that had slipped me by and I tried to pay attention, but it really was something that I couldn't get my head round at all. I gave up after a while and just used to nod my head.

I suppose when you think about it we were completely unsuited and I wonder why it is that she stayed around me for as long as she did. We must have gone out together from about July 1978 until May 1980. She was making the move into something called punk music which I liked even less than I liked the other stuff she went on about. It all meant nothing to me at all, but sadly seemed to mean almost everything to her.

I say almost everything because there was one more thing that she really went for: me.

I feel guilty about this when I think about it now, and I think I felt guilty about it at the time. She was heavily in love with me, and I don't know why it was that she should have felt like that. I was not really in love with her and there were a number of reasons for this.

Firstly, I suppose that it was because at that age I don't think I really knew what love was. I suppose you could argue that I am still not entirely sure what it is, but I have a better idea about it now than I did back then.

Secondly, and I am ashamed to admit it, but Lucy was something of an experiment. I had never been with a woman before as I have said, but that was largely because of the fact that I wasn't sure about my feelings towards women. I was in doubts about my sexuality and this caused a lot of turmoil and worry. I am not the only one to go through this feeling of course, I know that now.

Lucy was a last attempt to prove to myself and the rest of the world that I was straight – as we used to call it. I tried my best, but the simple fact of the matter was that I was deeply unhappy and there was nothing that I could do about it. There was nothing wrong with Lucy other than that she was the wrong sex to the one that I was interested in. We did have sex, which should be obvious, but it was something that I only managed to get through by imagining that she was someone else.

I wrestled with this problem for a long time. I eventually came to the conclusion that it was not fair on her and it was not fair on me for us to carry on like that and so it was that on a cold and windy day in May we met up because we both had news for each other, and that was when I told her that I thought we should split up because there was no future in what we had going.

There was a lot of crying and questioning and I had no choice but to tell her that I found men more attractive than I did women and there was nothing that I could do to change that, it was just the way that I was. She seemed to take it very badly, but then I supposed that she would. It had never been a secret how much she was in love with me and I have little doubt that I broke her heart when I told her that not only was I splitting up with her, but that I could never be interested in her again unless she had a sex change.

When you think about it I probably ended her world that day, but what could I really do? Could I have carried it on making myself intensely unhappy and continuing to live a lie whilst at the same time making her unhappy because I couldn't continue with sex? It wouldn't have lasted. We only had sex a few times when we had split up. It wasn't as if I did it once and then walked away, I gave it a fair old crack before realising that it was just not the thing that I wanted to continue doing. Eventually if we had stayed together she would have realised that there was something wrong and she would have started to worry about what was wrong with her that I didn't have sex. I could hardly tell her that there was nothing wrong with her because obviously from my point of view there was something wrong with her, and it was something that she couldn't do anything about.

And so, we walked away from each other and I never saw her again from that day until this day. I never did find out what it was that she was going to tell me on the same day. It is obvious now though that what she wanted to tell me was that she was pregnant. She didn't tell me then and she didn't tell me at any other point.

I never knew about Midge until he wrote the letter to my mother. I had no idea that I had a son walking around that had grown up until he was in his mid-twenties and I hadn't spent so much as a day with him. She never told me anything about him at all.

I can't blame her for that. You might argue that she should have told me and that I had a right to know, but I didn't have the right stuff that she was looking for in a father or a husband, and I wouldn't have been any use to her in those roles. If she had of told me that she was pregnant then I might have felt obliged to marry her for the sake of decency and that would have been something that would have been just disastrous for the both of us.

I don't know the woman that Midge describes as his mother. She must have changed and become bitter after we separated and if that is the case then it is something that I feel very upset about, particularly as I know that it must at least partly be my fault, perhaps all of it really.

She told Midge that I had been killed in a car crash before he was born, which did hurt a little when he told me about that, but I can understand why it was that she told him that. She didn't want him to know about his gay father and if she told him that I was dead then there wasn't much chance of him deciding to go and look for me; although as it turned out that was something that didn't work and he found me anyway. I would imagine it must have been a bit of a shock for him when he was introduced to his dead father. It was probably more of a shock when he found out that his father liked men. Not as much of a shock as when my mother found out about it though.

I spent a lot of time thinking about how I was going to tell my mother. My mother was - is - very straight-laced and doesn't seem to have entered the same century as the rest of us, which is curious. The concept of same sex relationships and sex would be something that was as alien to her as meeting someone from Mars would have been. In fact, she would probably have thought that Mars was where you came from, or certainly where you deserved to be sent as you didn't deserve to be breathing the same air as she was. Yes, she was that kind of person. She has mellowed slightly over the years.

It seems to me that these days you have people that are 'coming out' as it were all over the place. Celebrities, in particular, in this day and age seem to love rubbing their genitals in your face; in some cases, literally. It seems less of a taboo now than it did when I was growing up. It seems like that, but I am willing to bet that it isn't like that for the normal folk of the world.

I knew that I was gay all of my life, let's be clear on that front. I may not have done anything about it and I may have tried with Lucy to repress these thoughts, but it was always there at the back of my head and there was nothing that could be done about that. I don't think it was a choice because it was a life that I preferred, I ended up like that because that was the way that I was meant to be. I know that people have all sorts of different views on this and people get very angry and jump up and down if you say something that is contrary to their view, but the simple fact of the matter is that this is who I am, if it was a choice I would have chosen the easier heterosexual lifestyle rather than the gay lifestyle with its stigma, its taboo nature and the violence, hatred and aggression that so called normal people have towards you.

It's always been like that, of course, and it took me a long time to work out that if people want to persecute you then you are probably doing something right. Hitler wanted to put all the gays in concentration camps and gas them and he gave it a fair shot and when the choice comes down to deciding if you are on the side of Hitler or the side of the persecuted then I will stand shoulder to shoulder with the communists, the gypsies and the Jews with pride and bollocks to you if you are in the other camp.

My coming out process was lengthy. First of all, remember that when I was born being gay was illegal, well gay sex was illegal at any rate. You could be put in prison for it. Now you can have gay civil partnerships and they say it won't be long before you can have gay marriage – we have come a very long way in a generation.

I first thought I was gay before I even knew what it meant. Back when I was growing up there was no such word as gay, it meant being happy and has since been hijacked to mean being like me. In those days every word associated with it was slagging you off, poof, nancy-boy, queer and so on. I have been called all of these and a lot worse in my time. Sometimes I have to admit that they do come up with some imaginative titles to call you which makes me think that they must spend a lot of time thinking about gay sex in order to come up with all of these names.

I was about seven or eight when I realised that I liked boys rather than girls. I was at school and we all wore shorts and I remember admiring the legs of one of my fellow pupils and wishing that I had legs that were as muscular and as smooth as his. I then realised that I was more interested in his legs then I perhaps should have been. At this time, it was still illegal, not that I would have done anything at that age any way.

I kept my feelings hidden as best I could for many years confining myself instead to a lot of wanking thoughts, sorry if that is too graphic, but I was asked to be as honest as I could.

Things didn't change when it was legalised though. Some people might have done it but the day after it was made legal to have gay sex you suddenly didn't find people rushing into your arms and welcoming you to society. Things don't change that quickly. Put it this way, I mentioned Hitler earlier. Germany was a Nazi nation that supported Hitler and went along with him for the most part. They gloried in entering the war, but when they lost and it was all over do you think in 1946 there weren't any Nazis still there? Do you think that they stopped thinking about killing Jews and queers overnight and thought it would be good to welcome them into their family? Old habits die hard.

Nor was I going to be dancing in the streets the day after it was legal, flaunting my sexuality for all to see. As far as I could see although the law had changed, nothing in practice had actually changed in the slightest. We carried on living our secret lives and the rest of you carried on either trying to persecute us or pretending that we didn't exist. Or I suppose you could have been like my mother. I don't think that she pretended that people like me didn't exist, I think she genuinely didn't have a clue that we existed.

Coming out as such or admitting to the world your sexuality is something that is done in stages. The first stage is the admission of your sexual orientation to yourself. This may sound obvious and you may think it is not that big a deal, but the simple fact of the matter is that it is something that takes some time, years, to get used to in your own head. The period of denial is something that can last a long time, and I suppose that was partly what was going on with Lucy. I denied it to myself more than to anyone else. Being with Lucy eventually gave me the courage to admit in my own head that sex with a woman was something that was just not for me.

After that it was a case of testing the water with other people to see what they thought. Reactions were varied on the announcement. Lucy was the first person that I told and I told her because I felt that she had the right to know the true reason why it was that we were over. I suppose that I also hoped that the information would assist her and me in not having any ugly scenes should she decide to try and have another go with me, or to convince me that I was wrong and we were in fact perfect for each other. As I said though, I never saw or heard from her again, so I suppose I got the message across rather clearer than I had perhaps intended, particularly given the information that she had about the child that she was carrying at the time. Would it have changed anything? No, not really. I might have had some old-fashioned drive to marry her to give the child a proper family, but it would still have been a lie that we were living and a very unhappy time, probably for all of us.

Afterwards I told a few of my friends and if you ever want to test the friendship of those around you then this is the way to do it. Many were fine with the issue, others proved that they had never really been my friends by their disgust and obvious revulsion about what they had learnt about me.

It seems to be the way that when people find that you are gay they think that it means that you are going to try and sleep with them, this is my male friends, of course. Why they should flatter themselves into thinking that because you were gay you were immediately interested in every penis and arse that came your way was one of the most ludicrous things that I have ever heard in my life. I can't believe that heterosexual people behave in this way, but maybe they do. I am not really an authority in that department.

To be honest and once again this is a side issue, I am not really into anal sex. I think it is something that is hugely overrated and painful. As far as I am concerned bottoms were intended to be one-way traffic only.

Naturally if these friends didn't want to ever see me again, or more likely wished me dead or warned me that I was going to spend eternity burning in Hell, then they were really never my friends in the first place. In my time I have had people say and wish all of these things about me, and much more.

After that came the difficulty. Telling my parents. My father was most surprising of all. He was much more laid back and open minded than my mother and when I told him he stated that he had known this to be the case all along and despite the fact that the law had changed he knew that I was still likely to have a lot of difficulties ahead. Whether it was the case that he had always known I couldn't tell you. He might have done or he might have used it as a very convincing way of covering up his shock at the news, but I have to admit that he didn't look all that shocked when I sat in his study and told him the news as he listened whilst puffing away on his pipe. I suppose at the moment of revelation he might have puffed a little harder so that the smoke obscured his face a little more than it had been previously.

I was never more proud of him than I had been at that moment. I had heard so many stories about sons being disowned by their fathers when they told them this news. I had half expected that within half an hour of telling my father this news that I would be homeless and a virtual orphan. Instead he took it in the same manner as if I had told him that I had just bought some cheese. He then went one step further than I had expected and told me to leave the telling of my mother to him as he would probably be able to explain it better.

I assume that he did tell her and didn't just leave her in the dark about it all. She would eventually have figured it out when I ended up living with a man, unless she felt that we were just housemates, of course, which was entirely possible. On the other hand, I don't think all that much did slip passed my mother. She might not admit to what she knew or perhaps even fully understand it, but I still think she was aware of most of it.

It is probably worth me saying that at this point I had never knowingly met or known any gay people. I had not had any relationships with men either. It was entirely possible that I had known gay people of course, in fact it was odds on that I had done. It might well have been that they were living in the same period of denial that I had been or they simply just didn't want to tell anyone else what they felt like in case they were persecuted. I can't blame them for that.

It took me a long time before I eventually found my first boyfriend and I still had to cope with a number of internal issues when I did. Although it was clear that I was attracted to men rather than women I still had to wrestle with whether I wanted this kind of lifestyle and whether I wanted the stigma that was still attached to it. I don't think it matters as much these days, but then I suppose it depends more on the kind of person that you are.

The bottom line was that I was happy though and that was what sold me on it regardless of what I might have thought about it all or what other people thought about it. I didn't really go in for any of the sordid things like hanging around toilets which seems to cause so many issues. It was not the easiest of things to do to meet other like-minded people.

Eventually I met the man who has been my partner for the last ten years and I would like to think that we have been happy together and I suppose we have also now even been accepted by my mother which was an amazing feat when you think about it.

That's enough of all of that though.

Lucy never told me that she was pregnant and I had no idea that I had a son. I will be entirely honest, it surprised the hell out of me when my mother called me to her house one day and showed me the letter that Midge had written introducing himself and saying who he was. I had not thought about Lucy for years. I did think about her from time to time and I did wonder if I could have handled the situation with her differently. I suppose that there was no real way that I could have done this though without committing myself to a life of lies about the entire thing. Not the easiest of things to have done as I have said before.

I have no doubt that I caused her great pain by breaking up with her and telling her what I did, particularly in her pregnant state, but I am sure that I would have caused her a lot more pain if I had stayed with her and continued with the lie. I have asked myself that despite the lie that I would have been living would I have continued with my plan to break up with her and tell her I was gay if she had told me that she was pregnant before I had told her what I had told her. The simple answer to this is that I have absolutely no idea. It would have been sensible if I had of kept to my original plan, for all our sakes, but I just don't know if I could have turned her away in that state. With the upbringing that I had I would have felt compelled to have married her and helped her to raise her child, our child.

None of it really matters now though. I can't turn back time and correct what I did so many years ago. I will have to live with the action that I took and the fact that I left them both alone and a son to be raised never having known his father and thinking him dead. I suppose it might have been better for him if he had continued to believe that his father was dead, rather than have me walk in on him that day. My mother was convinced of the truth of what he was saying though and was also firm in her belief that I should meet him.

The question that remains now is whether or not Midge will want me in his life, or whether he would prefer to continue without me. I admit that I would like to be part of his life, but I think the decision on this has to rest with him. His mother didn't want me to be part of her life and went as far as pretending that I was dead so that she didn't have to think about me or admit that I was walking and breathing around any longer. I should also talk the matter over with my partner, Brian, as I would imagine that this is something that is going to come as a bit of a shock to him as well.

In the end it will all be down to Midge and what it is that he wants to do about it all. It all seems to be something of a bloody mess to me. Just goes to show you what families can be like, even when you don't know that you have them.

Fourteen
Midge

'Well what do we think of that?' Mary asked me as we sat back in the car after our little visit.

'I am not entirely sure what I think about it, if I am honest,' I replied whilst putting my seat belt on.

'Are you disappointed?'

'Disappointed in what?'

'Your dad.'

'No, why should I be?'

'I don't know.'

'I think I'm still trying to process the fact that I have a dad. Seems incredible.'

'I can understand that.' She started the car and we drove home.

I truly didn't know what to think about all of it. It is certainly true that my opinion of my mother had not grown any since the revelations had taken place. It didn't bother me that my father was gay, although I will admit that was something of a surprise. The real surprise, of course, had been the fact that he was alive in the first place. How could my mother add to her list of callous things by lying to me about my father and pretending that he had been killed in a car crash rather than the truth of the matter? Did she really think that I would have preferred a dead father to a gay one? I always thought that my mother was a hippy and embraced free love alongside everything that was associated with it. It would seem that amongst the other bad qualities that my mother had one of them was homophobia as well.

I was still taking it all in to be honest with you and was finding it rather difficult to put my thoughts into any sort of order. My grandmother had certainly gained the upper hand in the launching surprises game. She had been able to spend a little time adjusting to the news that she had a family that she didn't know about between my letter and actually meeting me. I had suddenly gone from having spent my entire life believing my father to have died in a car crash to having him walk in the room and to have realised that it had all been a lie.

The fact that he was gay was really immaterial. Plenty of sons and daughters grow up with one or more gay parents these days. We have moved on a great deal since the days when my father was a young man struggling with his own sexuality. I cannot imagine the conflict that must have gone through his mind whilst he struggled to decide the way that he was going to go in his life. I have to applaud him for making the decision to live his life according to his desires and nature rather than forcing himself to live a lie.

'Are you alright?' Mary asked me when we got home.

'Yeah, why?'

'You look a little tired that's all.'

'I feel tired. I haven't been sleeping all that well lately, I guess. Probably got something to do with the apprehension about meeting members of my family that I didn't know about.'

'Do you have any regrets?'

'No. How could I?'

We had left matters with my new family that we would stay in contact. There was a degree of awkwardness about the entire thing. After so long of being strangers to each other how can you suddenly pick matters up as if you had known each other all your lives and act as a normal family might? It was a rather difficult situation to have been in.

Being truly English we didn't rush into each other's arms and hug at the wonder of what we had gained. We kept a certain amount of distance and circled each other like wary animals unsure if the other was a threat to us or not.

The plan was to try and build some kind of relationship with my long-lost family, tentatively I have no doubt. My grandmother, who really insisted on being called Julia as she couldn't get used to the idea of being a grandmother, was particularly keen on making the acquaintance of Jessica.

I also had to get to know my father and I am not sure how he felt about it all. He had obviously engineered his life to be one where he didn't have any children of his own, unless he had adopted, which was something that I think he didn't consider. Now all of a sudden, he had a son, a daughter-in law and a granddaughter. If all of this was a huge amount for me to take in, I cannot begin to wonder what was going through his mind at the shock of it all.

Mary was right though. I was feeling tired. I obviously wasn't getting any younger, but I really didn't think that I should be feeling so tired in my mid-twenties, but then I had been burning the candle at both ends lately trying to do too much. It was probably time to put my writing ideas on the back burner and concentrate on other matters in life.

The problem with that was that writing was something that often compelled itself on me. I would put my laptop to one side, but then the ideas would bounce around my head until such time as they demanded to be written down. If you didn't give in to it and write these ideas down then you were in danger of going mad with the creativity that built up inside of you. Creativity demands an outlet. I was in a position where I could no more stop writing then I could stop breathing.

***

'So, your dad is gay then?' Luke asked.

'It would certainly seem so,' I had told Luke everything that had happened in the house.

'Bummer.'

'Inappropriate, Luke.'

'Hey,' he said throwing up his hands, 'I have nothing against gays. I just don't want it rammed down my throat.'

'Have you finished?'

'Yes,' he said returning to sipping his coffee. 'There's no need to get up the arse about it.'

'I can go if you want to be politically incorrect for the rest of the day.'

'No, that's cool. I'm done. Just felt that we had to get all that out of the way. So, what's the plan now?'

'I suppose it's time to get to know my new family and see where we go from there.'

I had been thinking about the entire situation for some time now since meeting. I had not seen any member of the family since our original meet. I think we had all withdrawn to think things over and decide what to do about the revelations that had all been announced. A number of years had been missed and there was nothing really that we could do about that.

'What about your mother?' Luke asked bringing me back to the conversation.

'What about her?'

'Well now that you have found a large portion of your family that you didn't know that you had for one reason or another, are you going to try and find your mother and put the family back together again?'

This made it sound like we were a rock band from the seventies that were getting back together again. I thought about this as I was reluctant to appear to dismiss it completely out of hand so quickly.

'No.'

'You seem pretty sure about that.'

'My mother was never really all that much of a mother to me and then she abandoned me. She hasn't shown all that much interest in me throughout my life and now shows none at all by having been gone for years. She lied to me about my father because she was presumably disgusted that he was gay and hid him from me when I could have at least grown up knowing him partly. I don't think she deserves any favours from me. She chose not to be part of this family a long time ago. I see no reason why she should want to come back into it now.'

'Well that seems pretty final then,' Luke commented whilst stirring his coffee. 'If you did see her again, what would you say to her?'

I sighed. I had spent time thinking about this many times over the years since she had vanished out of my life without so much as a word.

'If I had the opportunity then I would want to know why she always kept me at a distance, why it is that she vanished out of my life the way that she did and I suppose I would want to know why she lied to me about my dad. They would be the most pressing questions, but then from experience I have learnt that it is almost impossible to pin my mother down and get answers out of her, so if I were to meet her again I see no reason why it is that she would answer my questions now.'

The conversation lapsed into silence as it seemed that I had been rather forceful in my argument and I am sure that most of the rest of the coffee shop had heard what I had to say as well. It seemed that I had no problem in being outspoken. To be honest I don't think it has ever been that much of an issue throughout my life.

'You are looking a little tired, Midge,' Luke used his diplomatic skills to change the topic of conversation.

'I have a cold,' I said rather primly.

'Ah, well that explains it.'

***

I should point out that I do not like having colds. I suppose it is possible to argue that nobody likes having a cold, but there are some hypochondriacs who probably glory in the attention that it gives them. I am not one of them. I don't actually consider myself to be a hypochondriac at all, but then there is always that moment when you don't feel all that well and you decide to Google your symptoms. This is always a mistake and you can easily convince yourself that you are on the verge of death within minutes of working through the pages. I confess that I have done this, although it is not something that I really make a habit of.

Women will no doubt tell you that men can't handle illness in the way that they can. There is probably some truth in this as well as there can be truth in such generalisations. I have known women to collapse into bed with the slightest malady, these women are few and far between whereas us men don't hesitate for a second in going to bed and summonsing doctors, lawyer, priests and loving family to surround our bed so that we might impart our last words of wisdom onto the world.

I am as much at fault with this as anyone else you probably care to mention. The girls laugh at us and call it 'man-flu'. I think it appears to be human nature that makes us enhance the symptoms. A mild cold becomes a severe cold; a severe cold becomes flu; flu becomes pneumonia; pneumonia is impossible to qualify because you would never make it that far to an actual case.

I had been suffering from a cold for a couple of weeks now, which I had tried my best to get rid of, but it was making no difference at all no matter what I did and I was showing no signs of improvement. I genuinely felt that there was nothing that could be worse as I lay in bed surrounded by extra strength tissues, cold mixtures and cough syrups; none of which seemed to help in the slightest, but which I nevertheless clung to like a rosary.

It was no wonder that I was tired as it was impossible to sleep when just as you had managed to get yourself comfortable one or other nostril would start streaming which would then force you to have to get up once again and stuff tissue up your nose. I could have slept with tissue stuffed up each nostril, but then I feared that I would forget to breathe through my mouth and would suffocate in the night. You may think that I am being unnecessarily paranoid, but that was the way that I was thinking in my illness.

'Things can't possibly get any worse than this,' I informed Mary as she waited on me hand and foot with an infinite patience that I could only marvel at. 'Clearly this is the end, Mary.'

'No, it isn't but it soon will be if you continue to talk utter bollocks like that,' she fixed me with a cold stare whilst taking my temperature. 'There are worse things in the world and there are people who are suffering far worse than you are.'

'It seems hard to believe at the moment.'

'Stop feeling sorry for yourself, Midge, it's singularly unattractive.'

Naturally in my weakened state the lack of sympathy made me feel that I was being kicked whilst I was down rather than seeing the sense in her words.

I could make excuses for why it was that I was so pathetic. It might have had something to do with the fact that I was never comforted and cared for when sick as a child. My mother seemed to be preoccupied with other matters than my health which didn't seem to feature all that high on her list of priorities. I suppose that this had an effect on me later in life and made me feel pretty crap whenever I felt slightly ill. The feminists will tell you that the reason for my pathetic nature was because of the fact that I had been born with a penis.

The cold turned into a sore throat and hacking cough that stayed with me for longer than the cold had ever seemed to have done. If anything, it had made me feel worse than the running nose and the sneezing had done.

The cold, or as I suspected flu, had taken a lot out of me and it naturally left me feeling rather tired, but the truth of the matter was that I had been feeling tired and worn out before I went down with my cold which had left me feeling run down. As before I suspected that I had simply taken on too much. Family life, work life and writing life had combined to leave me with little energy which had naturally then made me susceptible to the virus when it had come along.

Someone once said that old men got up early in the morning to have one longer day which might be their last. I don't know if this is true generally, but specifically the older I got I was finding that I needed more sleep in order to get through the day, rather than the less sleep that was predicted by some people that you would need the older you got. You might argue that I was sleeping my life away but I was so tired at some stages that I was more than happy to crawl into bed at nine o'clock in the evening with a good book which would invariably go unread.

It doesn't sound like the rock and roll lifestyle that some people think that writers have, or should have, but then I was still unpublished and could only be termed a writer in the sense that I wrote. As I have said before though there is very little fame that can be attached to the writing profession. True you might get a knighthood I suppose, that was possible and had happened before. I am not sure that I could have been really Sir Midge or Sir Jim though, what do you think? It would only serve to confuse people after all.

What's my point? I will tell you.

The honours system confuses the hell out of people and not just the Americans, although they are largely confused by it and I would imagine that they can't understand the point of it seeing as how they come from such an untainted republic, where there has never been any corruption or leaders who are serving their own interests as can so easily happen in a monarchy.

People of all countries, but mainly America, always seem to get the title wrong though. I am going to try and explain it to you if you have the same issue. Firstly, if you are knighted you use the person's first name or what quaintly used to be referred to as a Christian name until Christianity fell from favour. Let us use an example in the shape of that great British actor Laurence Olivier. A figure which sadly seems to be much neglected in this day and age as a new generation grows up that has never heard of him.

Anyway, the point is that Laurence Olivier was knighted so he became Sir Laurence, not as some people mistakenly said Sir Olivier. Simple, yeah? The issue came when Olivier was later made a lord, in which case his surname was used so he became Lord Olivier and not Lord Laurence as he could be referred to as well. It was probably very confusing to a lot of people and possibly irritating Olivier at the same time which is why he allowed so many people to just call him Larry.

What's my point? I will tell you.

I didn't think that I would be suited to be addressed as Sir Midge. That's all really.

***

I needed to do some catching up with my father now that I had found out that I had one. I won't pretend that it was the easiest thing to do in the world. I should point out straight away that this had nothing to do with the fact that he was gay, but rather due to the fact that never having seen your father for all of your life there was an inevitable awkwardness in conversation and meeting. The gap of the years had caused a great deal of damage between us and I would imagine that we were both slightly uncomfortable the first time that we met after the initial meeting in Julia's house.

We had agreed to meet in a mutual public place. I stress again, this has nothing to do with the fact that he was gay and that I thought it would be safer to meet that way, but more to do with the fact that we wanted surroundings that were neutral or familiar to try and offset the fact that we might be uncomfortable until we got to know each other a little better. We ended up deciding to meet in a café where we could discuss things and start to make up for the lost time that we couldn't do all that much else about.

'So?' my father said as he stirred his tea.

'So?' I replied whilst I stirred my coffee. We lapsed into silence for a little while noticing that so far, the surroundings that we had chosen had not done much to make us all that comfortable. It also made me realise that as we had not grown up in any form of normal family and had never known each other there was a distinct possibility that we had nothing in common and the bridge between us was just too far to be able to cross.

'You don't see much of your mother then?'

'I don't see anything of my mother, not now.'

'Ah, yes, you said. Damn peculiar if you ask me, can't imagine why she is acting like that. Certainly not the girl that I used to know.'

'Perhaps the years changed her.'

'Well, they have a habit of doing that to all of us.'

We lapsed into silence again.

'You make sandwiches then?' I asked more in desperation than anything else.

'Yes, I find it very rewarding making sure that people are not hungry and can go about their business with a decent sandwich, or something inside of them at lunchtime, or whenever they want it.'

'That's noble then.'

'Yes. And you work in a library?'

'Yes, I do.'

'I am afraid I never really had time for books. I never really spent all that much time since I grew up in reading and I don't perhaps get as much time to read in my private life as I could. I keep long hours you see.'

'Yes, of course.'

'How's your coffee?'

'Very nice thanks. How's your tea?'

'Very good.'

'So, this is what is going on is it?'

This last question was not one that was asked by either of us, but came out of the blue from someone that I suddenly became aware of as standing near out table looking at us with a mixture of disgust and annoyance.

'Oh shit,' my father said.

'Oh yes James. Oh shit, indeed.'

'Is everything okay?' I asked a little confused about what was going on.

'You can keep out of this.' The interloper said looking at me with scorn.

'Brian, it isn't what you think.'

'No? I go around to see you at work only to find that Martin is running the place and he tells me that you have gone off and here I find you meeting with your, your, your floosy.'

'He is not my floosy, Brian and you are making a scene.' My father said trying unsuccessfully to control this man who was evidently called Brian and whom was making a rather spectacularly camp scene for the entire café to see.

'What would you call it then if you slide off secretly from work to have coffee with some young tart?'

'Brian, sit down.'

'I will not sit down to be humiliated.'

'The only humiliation that has been caused so far is the humiliation that you are causing yourself. If you sit down I will try and explain everything.'

I realised that Brian must be my dad's boyfriend or partner or whatever term it was that he chose to use. It was also becoming clear that my father had not yet told him that he had a son.

'You haven't told him about me, have you?'

'No, you little bitch he hasn't, but the cat's out of the bag now.'

'Please Midge. Let me handle this.'

'Yes, *Midge* let the grown-ups handle this.'

'Brian will you shut up. I told you it is not what you think.'

'And what am I supposed to think? You have been acting distracted and strange for weeks and then you sneak away from work to meet up with some young guy. What other possible explanation could there be.'

'How about he's my son.'

To his credit Brian took this like a slap in the face and silence settled over us and the rest of the café which had strangely become quiet and was undoubtedly following the drama that was being played out unexpectedly for it.

'Your *son*?'

'Yes, my son.'

'You don't have a son.'

'Yes, I do.'

'You have kept it from me for all these years that you have…' he seemed to struggle for the word '…offspring?'

'Until a few weeks ago I didn't know that I had any - offspring, as you put it – at all. His mother kept the entire thing secret from me.'

'You had sex with a *woman*?'

'Well how the fuck else do you think I got a son. He didn't come out of a test tube.'

'God, I think I need to sit down.'

'Well that was something I asked you to do before you decided to go into a number from *A Chorus Line*.'

With that Brian turned tail and marched out of the café whilst everyone else tried to pretend that they were not looking at us and had not been listening to what had been going on.

'Well that could have gone better,' my father said as he returned to his tea which had probably gone a bit cold by this time.

'I'm sorry.'

'Oh, it will be fine I will talk to him when he has calmed down from his hissy fit and explain it to him and if he still doesn't believe me then I will set my mother on him.'

'I don't want to cause any problems though.'

'Not really your fault. More your mother who has placed us all in this situation really. I wonder where she is.'

'I don't know, but there would be a few questions that I would like her to answer.'

'You and me both.'

'I hope you get things sorted out with Brian.'

'Oh, I am sure it will. He will settle down and if not, as I say your grandmother is a formidable woman.'

She would have to be to tolerate a family such as ours.

***

My cough and aching throat were not seeming to get any better despite the amount of money that I was spending on cough mixtures and lozenges and the like from my local pharmacy. Feeling ill all of the time I was starting to become concerned that I would end up infecting Jessica and causing her to feel really poorly. At her age getting sore throats and colds was even worse than it was getting them at my age, and that was bad enough I don't mind telling you.

It was with mixed feelings that I decided to go and make an appointment to see my doctor.

Fifteen

I had mixed feelings about going to see my doctor because on the one hand I knew it made sense as the longer I had this sore throat and cough the bigger the chances were of Jessica catching it and turning her life, and ours, into complete misery. On the other hand, I hated going to see doctors as you either felt like you were completely wasting their time, or you might learn something that you would really not want to know about.

I know that there is no sense with regards to this, but there is often not a lot of sense in how I feel about things. It just tends to be one of those things that I am stuck with. I dislike doctor's surgeries for the simple reason that they seem such sickly places which I know is possibly the stupidest thing that you have ever heard anyone say, but do you know what I mean? There is that clinical atmosphere and disinfectant smell that seems to permeate over everything.

I disliked it intently, but it was something that I took in with the observation of a writer, trying to file away things that might be of use later on for some material for something or other. You will find that this is what us writers do. If we are silent and looking around with an unworldly expression on our face it means that we have either seen something or you have said something that we are putting away at the back of our minds to be dragged out at some point in the future.

I sat in the waiting room on the PVC seats and looked at the television screen that was mounted on the wall that seemed to be wasted as instead of showing any television was on an endless cycle loop of adverts for "Get your flu jab this winter," "Check your blood pressure" and most bizarrely of all "Have you considered chlamydia?" as if it was some designer option or accessary that you could get, or maybe a holiday destination.

The advertising television bored me so my attention began to wander to the rest of the room and at the tired old magazines that littered the tables which I imagined that nobody ever paid the slightest attention to. There certainly didn't seem to be anything of any interest that I could see among the worn materials. My attention then wandered to the lime green painted walls that someone seemed to think would be somewhat soothing which to me just looked sickly.

I looked at them, or indeed anything other than my fellow patients that surrounded me who seemed to be suffering from the usual mixture of colds and coughs and other forms of illness that resulted in the silence of the room being punctuated every now and then with the odd sniff or muted cough. It was the ones that looked perfectly fit and healthy who worried me the most as it was impossible to work out why it was that they were there.

I had once been told that if you were ever at the scene of some trauma such as a major car accident it was the ones who were screaming out in pain and hysteria that you should give the least attention and aid to, whereas those who were being silent were the ones who were probably the most seriously injured and needed help. I tried not to think if that equated to the waiting room. It probably meant nothing in this context, but my mind has a habit of working overdrive into things such as this.

One of the patients opposite me, who did not seem to be remotely ill or suffering at all, but almost seemed to be enjoying himself was busy completing a Sudoku book, the type that you can buy in W H Smith. He seemed very intently engaged in the activity and I wondered if it was something he was doing properly or whether he was just writing any old nonsense in to make himself look clever to the onlookers, such as myself. Sudoku was something that had completely passed me by. It had become a craze at a time that I was busy dealing with other things and I had no idea what it was that you were meant to do and there didn't seem to be any explanation that I could fine. It had become such a craze by this time that I didn't feel that I could ask someone how to do it without feeling stupid.

I sat in the uncomfortable chair and watched as one at a time a doctor came out of their room and called their particular patient forward who shuffled off out of sight after their individual doctor down the corridor and disappeared out of sight to re-appear within ten minutes usually clutching a piece of paper in their hands which was either a prescription for something or other, perhaps a referral note for a blood test, or a sick note for their work.

Despite myself I began to find the ballet of movement to be so fascinating that I almost missed it when my own name was called. When it was called I had the usual flush to my cheeks whenever the name 'Midge' is mentioned in public and when I identify myself as being the owner of this name all eyes turn to me with curiosity and wonder why it is that I have such a strange name. I felt very self-conscious as I took my turn as the principal dancer in the ballet that I had been watching and all eyes turned to me as I walked down the corridor after the doctor.

'How are you?' the doctor asked me as we each settled into our designated chairs. I thought this was a rather bizarre question given the circumstances and had to fight back the instinctive English response to say that I was fine which would have surely have caused the doctor to look at me and wonder why I was wasting his time.

Instead I explained about how I had this sore throat and cough that wouldn't go away and that I was feeling increasingly tired and it was all a load of nothing, but if I could be prescribed some behind the counter medication which might have a better chance of shifting it then I would be on my way and get out of the doctor's hair and leave them to the more seriously sick.

The doctor gave me the smile that all professionals give when they are met by some layperson who is trying to tell them how to do their job, no matter how well meaning they might be. He smiled with that well practiced look and commenced to look down my throat with a small light, poked a wooden ice lolly stick down there whilst getting me to make various noises and then commenced to feel my throat with his fingers progressing around the neck whilst making little noises, which I could not always work out if they were of approval or interest at whatever it was that he was feeling. To me it was all impossible to interpret, but to him I suppose it was like Braille that only the trained could work out what it meant. Either that or he might have had some kind of neck fetish.

After some moments of this he went over to the wash basin and washed his hands before drying them on the paper towels that were stacked up by the sink and reminded me, with a shudder, of the towels that were kept in the toilets at school.

The doctor then came over and took my blood pressure which was always a mystery to me as to what it meant, but I sat in silence whilst all this was going on and wondered what blood pressure might have to do with a sore throat, but then I am not a doctor so what do I know; I assumed that he was just being thorough perhaps he had recently had some kind of malpractice case and was determined to stretch the NHS as far as the resources could go in order to save his own arse from any future claims.

'Okay,' he finally said when he had finished prodding and poking at various parts of my anatomy. 'It could be glandular fever or something like that, but I think we will run a couple of blood tests and see where we go from there.'

With that he filled out a blood test request form and handed it to me with a smile and I left the office feeling that some medication would have been nicer than his desire to save his arse.

***

A few days later I had the blood test and returned to the doctor where there was much shaking of the head and apparent disappointment that the test results had not shown up some horrible disease or illness that the doctor could really get his teeth into, metaphorically speaking of course.

I suppose if I was honest I could see things from his point of view. It must be soul destroying being a general practitioner and dealing with similar complaints all of the time. Boring people coming to moan about coughs and sneezes; hypochondriacs that really had nothing wrong with them at all other than an unhealthy knowledge of all of the illnesses and diseases that you could get. From time to time there might be something a little more adventurous such as something that might require a referral to hospital, but then all of the interesting things would be done by someone else at the hospital and you would be like the child who was left out when everyone else had been picked to play football.

He must have sat there day in and day out longing for something to really fire the imagination with and something that would enable him to use the talents that he had worked so hard to learn at medical school for so many years.

'Well everything seems to be in order here,' he said as he sighed and reached for his prescription pad with the air of a man who had been told that he had to write a cheque for a very substantial bill. 'We will give you some antibiotics to take for the coming week and then see how we go from there, but I suspect that you will be just fine.'

I had never heard someone sound so depressed in all of my life and I wondered if he was in need of taking some anti-depressants himself. I also found it highly amusing how he used the royal 'we' implying, presumably that whereas it was only himself that was writing the prescription he did so with the support and weight of the entire medical profession at his back. He was clearly extremely disappointed that I was not seriously ill. He seemed to take this as a personal attack upon himself.

I took the prescription from his hand, thanked him and left him to sadly type up my notes as he waited to see the next uninteresting patient with a mundane complaint.

No doubt to the annoyance of the doctor within a week I was feeling just fine.

***

2007 began to draw towards a close and I was faced with something that I had never really had before, a family Christmas. I had celebrated Christmas as a family with Mary and Jessica of course, but I had never had the opportunity for an extended family Christmas before and so it was with a mixed amount of excitement and apprehension that we decided to invite the family over for Christmas dinner. To my delight they accepted which had been by no means certain as they could easily have had a different idea of how to celebrate Christmas to the one that we had.

Christmas in our house was something that we had grown to celebrate with increasing passion. It will, no doubt, upset the avid Christians among you that we did not celebrate it as the birthday of little baby Jesus, but as a secular celebration of family life together, where we could give each other presents and be thankful for what we had; and then on the other hand as a pagan festival where you huddled together in the coldness of winter and commemorated the fact that you were on the slope towards spring.

Christmas might have started with a small amount of caution as we were not naturally relaxed in each other's company and there was still a lot of distance that needed to be covered before we could act in the way that I imagined a normal family would have.

My father turned up on his own.

'I'm sorry, but Brian couldn't make it. He sends his best wishes though.' He said as he fumbled to take his coat off in the hallway.

I suspected that Brian could have made it but had chosen not to. Clearly, he either thought that there was still something going on that my father had not told him; or he might have been angry that his partner had a secret family that he had not known about; or possibly he was just embarrassed by his outburst in the coffee shop. I decided not to make things any more difficult for my father by pressing the point.

'Why are your curtains drawn?' my grandmother asked as she stood in the living room looking around at the possessions that we had.

'I thought it would show off the Christmas lights better if the curtains were drawn,' replied Mary as she fussed about taking drink orders from everyone. My grandmother sniffed loudly at this as if she was inhaling some kind of vapour rub.

'In my day,' she said, which was curious because as she was still alive I assumed that in some way this was still her day rather than reference to some ancient time that no one else had lived through. 'In my day, if the front curtains of a house were closed during the day it meant that somebody in the house had died. If your curtains were closed you would get neighbours coming to pay their respect and to find out who had passed. Of course, in those days neighbours were friendlier than they are now when you could lay dead in your own bodily fluids for days before anyone would find out.'

Silence greeted this strange proclamation for a moment whilst we all took in what she had said.

'Well, that is a cheering thought for Christmas Day,' my father said as he stood awkwardly in the living room.

'I'll open the curtains,' Mary said.

I had also invited Luke as his parents lived far away and he was too busy working to travel back to see them for only a day or so. Also, he didn't have a girlfriend so Mary and I thought he could join our family for Christmas Day rather than spending it alone.

'Tell me something,' Luke said after we had all had dinner and were sitting around the table feeling stuffed and that we would have moved to go and sit in the living room if it were not for the fact that we didn't feel that we could move all that much at the moment. 'Tell me if you will why it is that I have seen so many gays wearing a pink triangle badge?'

My father looked uncomfortable for a moment but tried to rise to the question.

'They wear it because it is the symbol that the Nazis made homosexuals wear as an identification badge during the Holocaust.'

'Yes, I know that, but isn't it then the symbol of oppression?'

'I suppose they view it as a symbol of defiance.'

'I suppose I can understand that to an extent, but I just can't see Jewish people today wearing a yellow star as a symbol of defiance, it just seems such a strange thing to do.'

'Yes, well I suppose it is.'

'Well, that is quite enough talk of willies,' my grandmother stated with firmness which caused Luke to almost choke to death on the drink that he had just taken, necessitating Mary to thump him rather heavily on the back. 'It is time for the Queen's speech which I suggest we all watch.' It wasn't so much a request, as an order and I had already learnt that there was no going against my grandmother.

***

2008 began very slowly. It was a year that very early on would shock the world with the sudden death of the actor Heath Ledger and by the end of the year would astound the world that America had decided to elect a non-white president. I say astound because there were many who still saw America as being racist, particularly in the south perhaps, and it was not after all that long since the civil rights movement had gone through so much persecution in the sixties. It seemed that he had come a long way in a relatively short space of time. In other regards we still had a very long way to go.

'It wouldn't surprise me if someone tries to assassinate him,' Mary said as we had watched the news of his election.

'Why?'

'I can't imagine that every American will be happy at the idea of having a black president.'

I hoped that her words were wrong and that there would be no issue such as that in the future. There is enough hatred in the world for it not to have been a surprise to me for it to have happened though. All of this was some time in the future though as we were still at the beginning of the year which like most years had started cold and miserable with good intentions which would be lucky to last out the week.

I spent the first few weeks on holiday from work and used it as a writing holiday. I often took a little time off in January when we were not due to go away anywhere as a family and I would use it as time to bury my head in my writing and try to set the year off to a good start with a decent amount of material under my belt.

It was psychological more than anything as I could have committed myself to writing at any point and have made as much progress, but the start of the year would mean that it was somehow a fresh start to move forward with. I know it probably doesn't make a lot of sense, but then it makes about as much sense as starting your diet or your fitness regime on January 1.

I wrestled with the problems that my characters were suffering from and tried to construct their lives in a manner of a God controlling their every move and their every thought. This is what writers end up like, I suppose, God like, controlling characters. Perhaps you might argue that it compensates for some lack of control in our real lives, but I don't really know about that.

2008 started no differently to any other year really.

Sixteen

I started the year off by having a complete blitz on my writing in a desperate attempt to finish the novel that I had been working on, on and off, for the last five years. It was very much like an uphill race at times that I struggled and wrestled with like it was my own private demon that had been sent from hell to torment me. You might wonder why it is that if I felt like that I put myself through such torment when I could surely have had an easier life.

I could have had an easier life, but it was never really an option for me. For those of us that are compelled to be creative we can't just sit back and prevent that creativity from having an outlet. It would be like sticking a cork in a champagne bottle that has been shook up until the pressure can no longer be contained within the bottle and it explodes.

This is what creativity is really like. I had no choice, but to write or otherwise the pressure of creativity would build up to frustration point inside of me and I would go mad if I didn't find a way of getting the creativity out of me. Mary knew all about this. She would see me sitting downstairs of an evening when we were meant to be watching a film and I would start drumming my fingers on the arm of the chair, or we would be in bed at night, perhaps reading before we went to sleep and she would see the glint in my eye which meant that an idea had popped into my head and was dancing about demanding attention. On each of these examples and many more besides she would sigh and tell me to go off and do what I needed to do. She knew that there was no chance of me being in the here and now when I had an idea in my brain and needed to be sat in front of the laptop. My wife had to put up with an awful lot being married to a writer, even a non-published one.

There were also moments of extreme despair that came as part of the package of a writer's life. Despair that what you were writing was not worth anything and that you were banging your head against a brick wall because nobody was ever going to be interested in what you were saying and because the odds were so heavily stacked against you ever getting published. At times you would wonder why it was that you were putting yourself through so much for possibly so little in return.

I continued to read and expand my library until it threatened to take over the entire house, which was probably another cause of mild annoyance for Mary. I read as much as I could get my hands on. It was then that I felt the rivalry of the unpublished writer. I don't suppose I can be too jealous of other novelists as I had not yet even finished writing my novel let alone tried to get it published. Nevertheless, there was something that made me grit my teeth every time I looked at the flyer of the book and read the biography of the writer which might from time to time state that this particular novelist had published their first book at the age of eight and was on course for winning the Nobel Prize for Literature or the Pulitzer before they had breakfast.

It was difficult to feel gracious about someone that had achieved so much more than I had at a younger age than I had. I supposed that it is jealousy and a very unattractive quality, but that was the truth of the matter. It might be that if I ever published I would be able to feel a lot more gracious about the success of others, but for the time being it was difficult enough as it was.

I realise this doesn't paint me in the best light, but it paints me in an honest light. I think there is something about the English that makes us dislike success. We treat it with a degree of suspicion if it is something that you have too much of. Too much success and we think that you must have cheated your way to it or done something dashed underhand to get where you did. As a race we are naturally suspicious of a lot of things. Suspicion is what has kept us alive for all of these years.

***

And then there was the work that they were actually paying me to do rather than the work that I wished that they were paying me to do. I worked five or six days a week in the library, trying to maintain the interest in books that the public might have or not have.

It wasn't the easiest of things to do as a great number of people such as myself who were really into books preferred to buy their own books rather than go to a library and borrow someone else's. We tried to vary the opening times of the library to encourage those that used to work during the day to be able to come and take books out. Most of the workers didn't borrow books because of the fact that they were too busy at work to visit the library which had clung to archaic opening times. I mean, when I had taken over they were still doing a half day closing thing when most shops had given it up as something that belonged in the 1950s.

One of my tasks when I took over as manager or head librarian as they liked to call it was to vary and extend the opening times. I also discarded the early closing day which was an activity that met with a lot of disgruntled muttering around the kettle from the Old Guard. They were even less impressed by the introduction of rental DVDS and CDS. I have to admit that I was not overly happy with this myself. We were a library, not a video club, but it was a multi-media thing that lots of places were setting up now and if we hoped to survive then we had to compete.

We had then introduced computers and had virtually become an internet café only without the coffee and blueberry buns. The idea was that those who did not have internet connection at home could come and use the computers to do some research or whatever it was that they were looking to do. It began to look like the days of doing research by searching through endless dusty tomes was long behind us.

The problem with the computer section of the library was that whereas in principal it was a good idea we were also starting to live in an age where it was pointless.

What's my point? I will tell you.

Internet usage in public spaces were once a good idea, but these days there were so many people who had the internet at home, or at work that the need to go to a library, or somewhere else, to access the internet was becoming as outdated as chivalry. Another problem was one of cost for us. We would buy the computers to use in the library and then within a short space of time they were outdated and useless once again and you would have to buy a new lot. It was an endless stream of renewing.

I suppose also that with the wide use of internet capability in your own home there was less reason to come to the library unless you were looking at something that you didn't want to appear on your own computer history or have traced back to your computer. We had safeguards in place, of course, that would prevent them from looking up things that they really shouldn't be looking up in a public arena, but that didn't stop the computer section from being a magnet to potential terrorists and perverts.

The Old Guard muttered and moaned even more at the changes that were coming in and seemed to completely fail to realise that without keeping our head above the water we would all be out of a job. They seemed to think that we could keep things the way that they were without the need for any changes and the world would bow down to us, rather than the fact that libraries were closing all over the place.

The Old Guard were led by my nemesis at the library which took the form of Mrs Van Hopper who looked a cross between Margaret Rutherford and a sailing ship in full sail. She was a formidable woman and didn't shy away at making her feelings known. She also seemed to resent the fact that I had been promoted above her. She was the kind of woman that if she had of been put in charge then the library would have been ruined within weeks as she tried to drag things back to the 1950s, which seemed to be where she most longed to be. She certainly dressed like it was a decade that she had just stepped out of.

'Mr McKenzie!'

I was working in my office and the sudden exclamation from the door caused me to be quite startled for a moment and made my heart race. I had nothing to fear but it suddenly felt like I was back at school once again and had been caught by one of the teachers doing something that I shouldn't have.

I didn't need to look up to know that it was Mrs Van Hopper who was exclaiming in my doorway. She was near enough the only person that I knew who called me Mr McKenzie.

'Mrs Van Hopper,' I replied looking up from what I had been doing and seeing her with a scowl on her face which made me think that she had been sucking on a lemon.

'Mr McKenzie, I must talk to you.'

'You know you can call me Midge, you know.'

The expression on her face changed to that of someone who was reacting as if I had just asked her if she wanted to go behind the foreign language section of the library and engage in some extra marital activities.

'I really don't think so,' she said instead. 'A most serious matter has arisen that demands your immediate attention.'

I groaned inwardly. I had experience of Mrs Van Hopper's ideas of what a serious matter demanding my immediate attention was and it was almost always something that did not demand my immediate attention at all, but was actually something trivial. The last time had been that she wanted to point out to me that someone had used the coffee spoon in the sugar bowl in the staff canteen area those causing coffee to mix with the sugar. Mrs Van Hopper only took tea so for her this was regarded as a serious matter. The time before that it had been to inform me that someone had removed some of the Blu Tack from some of the posters so that one end was left free.

'But it is theft, Mr McKenzie,' she had moaned at me over the Blu Tack incident. 'Pure and simple it is larceny. I feel that we should contact the police.'

I didn't feel that we should contact the police as I was pretty sure that the police had more important things to be doing rather than looking for some missing Blu Tack. Yes, in the strictest possible terms it was true that a theft had occurred, but I think you have to see these things in perspective. I was not convinced that the local constabulary would have been all that interested in helping us look into this particular mystery. I told Mrs Van Hopper as much.

'I find your complacency alarming, Mr McKenzie,' she said whilst apparently trying to suck her teeth into her throat. 'I must inform you that your lack of action over this theft may result in me having to inform head office.'

I have no idea if she ever did inform on me, but I was never summoned to explain why it was that I was not taking the 1968 Theft Act so seriously. Perhaps it was that head office agreed with me on this. It probably didn't help that Mrs Van Hopper was always telling head office about my inadequacies. She clearly did this because she wanted to point out to them that if she had been promoted rather than me they would have had a far more efficiently run ship.

Mrs Van Hopper was the kind of person who would have told the Nazis where Anne Frank was hiding. I think that's all you really need to know about the woman and her character.

You can imagine that I was not filled with all that much hope, therefore that she was once again standing in my office doorway reporting another serious incident.

'What is it this time, Mrs Van Hopper?' I had tried to use her first name once, which was Maureen and I swear she was prepared to kill me where I stood for the audacity of presumption. It was politically incorrect and I apologise if it causes offence to anyone, but I privately nicknamed her the Poisoned Dwarf.

She looked at me with her famous scowl, probably because of the emphasis on the first part of what I had said as opposed to her name. Nevertheless, she was not about to surrender what I assume she felt was the high ground, so she waved a book at me so fast that it was impossible for my eyes to focus on what it was.

'This was out of place,' she flung the book onto my desk. 'It is an outrage. Is there no respect left in the world?'

I might have pointed out to her that throwing the book on my desk in the manner that she had hardly constituted respect, but I decided to keep quiet about that. Now that the book was not being waved about in the air I could see that it was a copy of the Bible, one of many that we have in the library.

'So?'

This appeared to be one of her little unimportant tantrums that she had about the trivial. Customers, or readers as we were encouraged to think of them, were for ever taking books off the shelf and having a read of them and then putting them back on the first shelf that came to hand without thinking about putting it back where it belonged, that is assuming that they bothered to put it back at all rather than just leaving it where it was that they were reading it. It was one of the jobs of all staff to keep an eye on the shelves and spot any out of place books and remove them to their normal home. We did it every morning before we opened up and kept a constant eye on it during the day.

'So? So? What do you mean so?' She seemed to be on the verge of hysteria, which was not all that unusual a state for her to be in.

'Mrs Van Hopper,' I said with more patience than I was feeling, 'as you know our readers are constantly moving books about and misplacing them. It is hardly a matter that demands my attention like this.'

'Mr McKenzie, I do not think you realise the seriousness of the situation.'

I granted to her that I probably didn't. Certainly, I failed to see what the entire point of it all was so far.

'It is not the fact that the Bible was misplaced, Mr McKenzie, it is where it was placed that is the issue.'

'And where was it, Mrs Van Hopper?' I thought that I would dread asking the question, but she was taking forever to get the point because she loved having her moment on the stage and was dragging things out for as long as she possibly could. She might not have had any work to do, but my desk was full of it.

'It was in the Children's *Fiction* section,' she virtually spat at me with venom in every word.

Now, Mrs Van Hopper was allegedly a very good Christian, but apparently from what I could see a very bad human being. I could on the one hand understand why it was that she was upset that someone had seen fit to place her Holy book in the Children's Fiction section; but then on the other hand I found the fact that someone had the sense of humour to place it there rather funny, the same way that I did when they placed political biographies in the Horror section. I had my suspicion that it was the same person who was probably doing this. Unfortunately for me I laughed out loud.

'As you sow so shall you reap,' she spat at me before picking up the Bible and marching to the door. 'Perhaps you don't realise that it is blasphemy, Mr McKenzie.'

'I am not entirely sure that it is.'

'Head office shall hear of this you can be assured,' she threw back at me before swanning out the door like a hurt diva.

'I have no doubt that they will,' I muttered after her. I was trying to think of a reason why I didn't just fire her, but she was the kind of woman that you couldn't get rid of without a bloody good reason and the annoying thing was that she was actually very good at her job, when she was doing it. If I sacked her purely because she was an evil hearted little bitch, I would never be rid of her through the solicitors and tribunals that would be thrown at me. It might have been a case that it was better to have her inside pissing everywhere then outside pissing in.

Not for the first time I wondered if there was a Mr Van Hopper, or whether she had murdered him years ago. It is possible that she just nagged him to death until he was forced to commit suicide rather than face another day with her. I could entirely sympathise with him if that had been the case. If he was still alive then I imagined him as some meek and mild little creature that was afraid to say anything. On the other hand, he might have been a giant bully of a man and pestering me was the only way that Mrs Van Hopper could get an outlet to her true soul.

It didn't really bother me all that much if I am honest.

***

The year slowly worked its way on and I had never been contacted by head office to moan about the fact that I had not respected Christianity. I suppose in this day and age of extremist reaction to religious intolerance I should have considered myself lucky that Mrs Van Hopper had not arranged for nuns to picket the library demanding more tolerance.

'I still feel so tired,' I moaned at Mary one day over breakfast.

'Really?' she asked with her head on one side whilst she chewed on her bran like breakfast, which just reminded me of the kind of thing you would scrape out of the bottom of a hamster cage.

'Yes, I always seem to be so knackered.'

'Perhaps you are working too hard. Too much time at the library and too much time at the computer tapping away.'

'Well you know I'm trying to do that for a better future for us both.'

'Yes, but you're also doing it because you love to do it.'

'Well, that's true.'

'There is only so much of the burning of the candle that can be done at both ends, darling, and you are approaching thirty now of course.'

'So are you.'

'Yes, but I'm better at managing my time than you are.'

'Of course you are. You're a woman.'

'Perhaps you should join a gym.'

'So I tell you I'm tired, so you want me to join a gym so that I get even more tired. Is there an insurance policy that you have out on me that I don't know about at all?'

'It's well known that if you have no energy and are tired sometimes a little exercise will release the necessary chemicals to give you more energy. It's one of nature's little weird idiosyncrasies.'

'Well I suppose it couldn't really do any harm.'

***

And so it was that I found myself entering the local gym for the first time. It seemed to be such an alien place with so many unfamiliar machines all over the place that seemed to vaguely resemble instruments of torture which I would eventually learn was exactly what they were.

Because I was new to the whole working out culture I was assigned a personal trainer in the form of a young man called Josh who clearly spent a lot of the time in the gym and not only because it was where he worked.

Josh walked me around all the machines introducing me to them and whilst I had practice goes on the machines he would wander off with a bored expression on his face and either eye up the other gym members or would look in one of the mirrors where he would rearrange his hair or generally admire himself.

He wasn't the only one. I could see that there were mirrors all over the place which largely seemed to be there for the only reason that you could admire yourself in some perverse sexual way whilst you sweated. It also occurred to me that some of the people might not have been looking at themselves in the mirrors, but might have been looking at each other in the mirrors. It struck me as nothing more than a soft porn palace.

Going into the changing rooms did nothing to dispel this belief when I saw lots of men walking around having showers where there were no doors so you could see them naked and others were walking around in states of half dress or less. I made my mind up then and there that if I were going to use the gym I would come to the gym in my gym kit and go home in my kit and shower at home and never step foot in the changing rooms again.

It struck me as really strange that most of these guys were probably homophobic in their everyday lives and then would come to the gym and parade around and then compare their muscles with each other and talk about how they were pumping themselves up etc. It was probably one of the strangest things that I had ever seen in my life.

Don't get me wrong I am not making any judgements at all. I did wonder if it was the same in the female changing room as well. I spoke to Mary about it as she had joined the gym at the same time as me as an act of solidarity.

'It's exactly the same,' she replied. 'Some of the women are discreet but others walk around half naked or with nothing on at all with their nipples so hard that you could hang coat hangers from them.'

Nobody was doing this because they were gay, I should point out. They seemed to be doing it because they had put so much work into their bodies that they were in a position where they wanted everyone to see how fit they were so had decided that they were going to show off and strut about so that we could all appreciate all the hard work that they had done.

It might have been something that I could have appreciated more if I had been allowed to use the female changing room. I don't think that Mary would have approved of this idea though.

Seventeen

There is being tired and there is being tired.

What's my point? I will tell you.

All of us during our lives will experience tiredness of varying degrees and levels. Late nights, the odd interrupted sleep and a day where you are rushed off your feet with no time to rest are amongst the many reasons that can cause tiredness to us all. The difference comes when you are feeling tired all of the time and there doesn't seem to be any reason for why you are tired.

People will sometimes put this down to the fact that you are getting older and as you get older you can expect to have aches and pains and to feel more tired than when you are younger and bouncing around with lots of energy with the enthusiasm of life. People argue that the older you get the more these aspects of your life are sapped and you can expect tiredness at the very least.

There may be some truth in this opinion, or it may be that is a complete load of bollocks. However, whatever the truth of the matter I still didn't feel that as I approached my twenty-eighth birthday I should be feeling as tired as I was. I grant you I had spent a lot of time burning the proverbial candle at both ends and that may have contributed to why I was feeling so tired when I should still have been bursting with the energy of youth. Plus, I was a parent and I don't think I know that many parents with young children who do not know what a sleepless night means.

Nevertheless, I was still feeling that it was strange that I should be feeling so tired when although I was busy I did think that I was sleeping well enough. After talking over the matter with Mary I found myself back at the doctor's surgery.

Once again, I found myself sitting opposite my chronically depressed and bored doctor as I explained to him the reason why I had come to him. His eyes lit up as I went through my tiredness and how it seemed to be more extreme than I would perhaps expect from the amount of activity that I was doing. He nodded his head sagely at what I said and told me that he had decided that the best thing to do was to run a series of tests. They would take blood to test for calcium and for vitamin deficiency and for anything else that they could think of.

'We will send you off to the hospital to have some tests done and see what we can find out,' the doctor said and for some reason I imagined that he would have been happier saying this whilst puffing on a pipe and looking at me with the interest of a puzzle that he must crack at all costs. I was wondering if it was a little unnecessary for me to be sent off to the hospital because I was feeling tired, but what do I know?

I have to admit that I have little understanding of medical science and I tend to forget about terminology and what is happening when it comes to medicine. I beg forgiveness now in advance if I become a little lost and make no sense over everything that this ambitious doctor decided to put me through. He seemed genuinely pleased by the fact that I had returned and had presented him with a challenge to try and solve. I imagine I broke his boring routine and it was something that he would be forever grateful for. I suppose if it was something that made him happy then I couldn't really complain.

I have already expressed my dislike for doctor's surgeries with their clinical nature and people being ill all over the place. You can imagine what I felt about hospitals which were ten times worse than going to a doctor, primarily because there was an increased chance of going into hospital and then not coming out again on your own two feet. This may be an irrational belief, but there has always been something of the neurotic about me when it comes to illness, hospitals, well-being and all that kind of thing.

I had not spent any time in hospital since I was born and had spent the early part of my life in a plastic box whilst the medical profession decided whether or not I was likely to live or die. I had kept away from them since then out of a superstitious belief that I might owe them something if I were to return.

My practical knowledge of hospitals was somewhat limited, therefore, and I had some belief in the back of my head that they would be in some way like the kind of hospital that you saw in films like *Carry on Doctor*, this was pretty much my only knowledge of what they were like.

This was not the case. At some point since my birth and today hospitals have changed and had turned into small towns. Hospitals had whole shopping arcades in the centre of them where you could get everything that you wanted at a drop of a hat, even stuff that surely nobody could want whilst they were in hospital. I thought hospitals would have small shops where you might be able to buy grapes and newspapers et cetera, the little things that patients and visitors might actually need whilst they were in hospital. Now I saw that there were virtual supermarkets as well as fast food outlets for all the major companies. It was amazing, and somewhat unnecessary.

The other thing that struck me was the apparent miles and miles of endless corridors that all looked identical. It amazed me that anyone could ever find their way around the place, it must be something that took years to get used to. Along with the shopping area and the endless corridors it was more like a city than a hospital. It was more like a city than some cities were. The hospital seemed so big I imagined that it had its own ecosystem.

It came as no surprise to me that doctors were always tired if they had to traipse from one end of the hospital to the other countless times a day. It was an easy way of maintaining fitness though and I would imagine it was easy to clock up miles of walking each day. As I watched the doctors, nurses, porters, technicians and admin workers running about the place like bees in a hive it occurred to me that the most important thing that you could possibly need in this place was comfortable shoes.

Strangely enough because of the metropolis status of the hospital it seemed less clinical than the doctor's surgery had been. If I had entered through the accident and emergency department then things might have been different. I had never been through A & E, but from what I had seen from the television it could appear to be a chaotic place with lots of running about and bodily fluids arching through the air. Nurses and doctors stressed by the amount of work coming through the doors would desperately try to keep a lid on things in an effort to prevent the chaos from descending into complete Bedlam.

Elsewhere in the hospital things appeared to be kept more tightly under control and indeed in some cases as you aimlessly wandered the never-ending corridors it was almost possible to believe that you were not in a hospital at all. At least it would have been possible were it not for the fact that there were ominous signs on the walls telling you where all the departments were located. Departments that had strange alien names in a language that appeared to be entirely made up of medical jargon designed to confuse the uninitiated.

I suppose they stuck to the medical terminology because to have been frank and honest would have scared the patients. Entering a ward which says 'Cancer Ward' or 'Heart Attack Unit' or even I suppose 'Certain Death Area' might not have been designed to help with the mental recovery, if not the physical.

My doctor had decided that I should get the full measure of what the NHS had to offer and so I was sent for a number of blood tests over a period of weeks where they drew so much blood from me I became convinced that they had Count Dracula somewhere on the ward. These little vials of blood were drawn from my arm in a not altogether easy manner, often leaving me with bruises where the needle had refused to go in. As soon as they had managed to drain what they wanted from me then the little vials were labelled and whisked away to different parts of the hospital where I never saw nor heard from them again. For all I knew they could have been storing my blood in a fridge somewhere so that one day they could clone me and make lots of little Midges, which sounds strange.

Okay, I am not entirely sure why they would want to do that, but it is the sort of thing that they might have chosen to do if they were so inclined to do such things.

With each blood test that was completed I returned to the ambitious doctor who I became convinced was looking for a new disease to discover that he might then attach his name to and thus obtain worldwide fame at the expense of me being his first 'victim'. He looked at the blood test results on his computer screen and clicked his tongue and made strange noises in his throat before sending me off to have further blood tests. So back I went again and we continued in this circular motion for some months as the winter stripped its way into 2009.

We go about our everyday lives with consideration mainly focused on the mundane and ordinary tasks that we choose to centre our time upon and allow all our thoughts to be occupied with. How many of us take the time to stand and look about us and truly see what is going on? To appreciate a good sunset or to stand under the stars and marvel at the limitless possibilities of the universe. Take the time to marvel at nature, the rolling fields or the song of a bird in the morning or wonder at the flight of a bumblebee.

We allow all of these things to go by unnoticed for the main part whilst we concentrate on soap operas and making money. I think that is a great shame because we miss so much of the wonder and beauty that surrounds us as we choose to focus on the baser things that life has to throw at us. The baser things seem to be the things that are man-made whereas the wondrous things are found naturally.

It might sound that I have become all whimsical all of a sudden, but there can be moments in life where everything is shaken up and it is time to review your priorities.

2009 was the year that everything was set to change for me. Sometimes these shake ups in life can be very good and at other times they can be very bad indeed.

***

So, from blood tests it progressed forward to more serious tests as things developed. The strangest test was when I was sent for a CT scan. I was stretched out on the strangely white and clinical machine whilst a nurse fussed about me attaching various tubes.

'Now we are going to flush you through with a special dye,' the nurse told me whilst she continued to hook things up and try and poke needles in my already bruised and punctured arm that was beginning to make me look like I was a heroin addict. 'Once the dye enters into your system we will be able to have a much more detailed look at what is going on inside you.'

I was beginning to wish that I had not bothered to go and see my GP in the first place as it had led me to this strange table whilst I was leant over and fixed to the machine.

'When the procedure commences,' the nurse continued 'you will possibly experience hot flushes and a sensation that will make you feel like you are wetting yourself, but you won't be, I assure you, it is just the way this makes you feel.'

With that she finished what she was doing and vanished out of the room. It did occur to me that if there was nothing to worry about with regards to these tests then why did the nurse feel the need to actually leave the room entirely and monitor things through a reinforced glass window. If it was that safe then they seemed to want to leave as quickly as they could.

The procedure started and I slid into the machine and was asked to hold my breath at periodic moments. The nurse had been entirely right the injection of the fluid into my system did give me a hot flush which reminded me exactly of how I felt when Mary first approached me in the library back at college. The next sensation that she had promised of the feeling of urination did duly follow, which was a most unsettling feeling as it did genuinely feel like you were wetting your pants. What made it more worrying for me was that I had needed to go to the toilet before the procedure began and it now put me in the awkward position of not knowing if I was actually wetting myself or if it was the sensation that the nurse had promised me I would feel.

I tried to forget what was happening below my belt and concentrated instead on laying as still as possible. I had noticed when I had first stretched out on the machine that there was a large picture of a poppy fixed to the ceiling which was not the most exciting of things to look at, but it was better than worrying if I was wetting myself and causing potential damage to a machine that had probably cost the taxpayer millions. I looked for the poppy picture and discovered that it was no longer visible as my position had moved since I had slid into the machine so I was no longer in the same position as I was before. Instead all I could see this time was the machine which was blocking the view of everything. This had clearly not been designed with any thought to what the patient would be experiencing. With little to look at I decided to concentrate instead on not actually pissing myself.

It was a lot harder than you might have thought.

***

Before too long the tests were completed and then it was just a question of waiting for the results which seemed to take an age. On the one hand I was worried that they might have allowed the test results to become lost within the bureaucratic mess of the hospital where they might never be seen again, and on the other hand I thought that if they were that concerned about the results then they would contact me straight away and have me whisked into hospital faster than you could imagine.

I was spending a fair amount of time in the hospital becoming familiar with the corridors and where things were located as I popped in and out for various tests that they still decided to run. I was certainly getting my money's worth out of the NHS. As I was leaving the hospital one day, I was arrested by a familiar figure sitting in a wheel chair in one of the public areas. I was sure that I knew the figure, but decided instead that I would covertly watch from behind a wire metal stand of books that rotated to see if I could confirm my suspicions.

Thus, positioned and feeling as if I was suddenly taking part in a Cold War thriller novel, I watched the figure in the wheel chair with interest as I tried to determine if my assumption was correct or if I was mistaken. Being quintessentially English, one just doesn't march up to potential strangers and demand to know who they are.

I watched the figure in the wheelchair as close as I could whilst pretending to be interested in the latest paperback offering of Dan Brown. I was unsure of my original belief because the wheelchair was positioned slightly so I could not get a clear view, hence the doubt that I was feeling.

'Are you going to buy that?' the crisp woman from the Women's Institute or whoever it was that ran this particular stall asked as she appeared out of nowhere like the ghost of Hamlet's Father.

'Not this time, thanks,' I decided to move away from the stand and approach the figure that I saw. I tried to make a few more passes to double check and see if I was sure of who it was that I thought it was. Eventually I decided to approach the figure.

'Mr Jones?'

The figure didn't look up so maybe I have been wrong, but now that I was so close I was certain that this was my old high school English teacher that I had not seen for about ten years. He must have retired a couple of years after I had left college and gone to university, so I would guess he must have been somewhere in his early seventies now. He was definitely older than I remembered him, of course, but he was still recognizable although the strain of the last ten years was clearly showing on his face. He had aged a great deal in those ten years since I had last sat in his literature class and taken advice on creative writing from him.

'Mr Jones? It's Midge.' I didn't think that I needed to say my surname with a first name as stupid as mine. He still didn't seem to respond to his name, but now looked up at me as if he was responding to the sound of my voice rather than what it was saying. He seemed to have a degree of difficulty focusing on my face and then a look of confusion crossed his own face mixed in with what I can only describe as a look of sheer panic or fright.

'It's okay, dear,' a female voice said as she appeared carrying two steaming paper cups of what I assumed was either tea or coffee that were dished out in this area of the hospital, probably for a very large sum of money. She placed both cups down on the small table that Mr Jones was sat in front of and moved round to make him a little more comfortable. His face seemed to clear as he took her in and he seemed contented once again as if all was well. As if normality had been restored to the chaotic universe.

The woman settled him back down and reassured him that everything was fine and she had only gone to get some tea and then when she was convinced that all was well she turned her attention to me. I stood up.

'Hi, hello, sorry. I'm Midge I used to be in Mr Jones' English class at school.'

She nodded her head as if this made perfect sense to her and was only right and proper that he should be accosted by old pupils several times a day.

'Ah that's nice. He likes to meet his old pupils, don't you Gwyn?' He made no reply to this and she spoke as if she was a primary school teacher addressing a particularly stupid pupil.

'I saw him and I wanted to come over and say how much I really appreciated everything that he had done for me when I was at school. He set me on a path to literature that I am still on and have never regretted for a moment.'

'Oh, that is nice of you to say so, my lovely.'

'He was the best teacher in my entire school. I never told him at the time.'

'Ah he had a lot of successes. He would be very pleased to know about you, Midge'

'Sorry, are you Mrs Jones?'

'Oh, where are my manners, my lovely? Yes, I am Mrs Jones. Mari Jones. I am very pleased to meet you, Midge was it?'

'Yes,' I shook her hand that she offered me which was laden with large amounts of rings and bracelets that made me feel that for a brief moment I was shaking hands with a fortune teller. 'Forgive me, for asking, but Mr Jones, is he okay?'

It was a difficult question to ask as the Englishness slipped in again. Clearly, he was not okay because he was acting like he had just recently come out of having a lobotomy and as he was also in a hospital unless he was visiting someone and given how he was looking the way that he was and was sitting in a wheelchair I suspected that he wasn't visiting. What I really wanted was to just say 'What the hell is wrong with him?' but that kind of thing is just not cricket.

'Okay? No, I am afraid not, my lovely.'

She didn't seem to be about to tell me anymore so I thought I would try and push it a little further. 'What's the erm…?'

'What's wrong with him, dear?'

'Well yes.'

'Dementia I am afraid, the dreaded Alzheimer's disease that we all hear so much about these days. All those years of teaching boys and girls, like you, the written word and now he has almost lost all of his words completely. Can't find the words to say what he wants to half the time, and I think he knows it as well which is why he hardly bothers to speak at all. Wouldn't know what a book was now if it was in front of him, would you, my lovely?'

I suppose she was used to his condition now which had probably been creeping on for some time. She was accustomed to all of this now and took it in her stride whereas for me it was a huge shock. I could not imagine how terrible it must be for this man that had spent his life surrounded by, and commanded by, the written word to now have them completely robbed from him. It was no wonder he didn't recognise me or respond to his own name.

'Is there anything that can be done?'

'No, not really, my dear. I suppose it's just a matter of time, isn't it?' She certainly seemed to have adjusted to the situation that she was in and more precisely he was in. I wrote my name and contact details down on a piece of paper and handed it to her.

'If there is anything that I can do then please don't hesitate to get in contact with me, will you?'

'Well that's very kind of you, my lovely. I will do that, don't you worry.' She bent down to pick up the tea to help her husband drink it. Whilst she was turned away for a brief moment Mr Jones focused on my face and his expression became a little clearer.

'Midge?'

It was very faint and very soft, but I could have sworn that he had looked at me and said my name, but even as I bent down to hear him more clearly his face became clouded over again and he slipped away to whatever world it was that he now spent most of his time in.

I straightened up and leaving the couple together I left them as I walked out of the hospital into the open air, which was clearer.

***

I had been deeply shocked to see how Mr Jones had deteriorated in the ten years since I had last seen him. He was a steady reminder that time moved on. I found it so unbelievably tragic that someone who had spent his life immersed in books should now have lost the world that he had lived by.

I had often wondered if his love of literature was something to do with the fact that he was Welsh. Love of literature seemed to be something that although not unique to the Welsh was a huge part of their culture. Many had written their way out of poverty, in many cases only to write themselves into alcohol. He was very precise in his use of words and his understanding of them. He had once told me that he had an ability to visualise words. He would see them in his own head as you spoke and could therefore very easily deconstruct what you had said, something that probably annoyed a vast amount of his pupils.

His life had been surrounded by words and books and now both of them were completely useless to him. It was a reminder to us all that no matter what our little vanities were in life they would all come to nothing one day. It was a sobering thought.

'It's hard to believe,' Mary said as she shook her head when I had told her about Mr Jones. 'He always seemed to be like a pillar. Something that was always there and always would be there. It's hard to believe that he would fall so low.'

'It has to happen to all of us at some point or another.'

'Most of us tend to spend our lives trying to forget that there will be an end to it, and for the most part we are very successful in this deceit. Perhaps if we didn't put such things from our minds and allow ourselves the deception then we might all end up going insane rather quickly.'

I grunted and returned to my book thinking about the fragile nature of the world that we lived in, or rather the fragile nature of the humans that lived in it.

***

I went back to see my doctor and I was getting pretty fed up now of the round of tests and visits to hospitals and doctors. It was starting to make me feel geriatric. My doctor flicked through some hard copy notes as well as scrolling on his computer and from time to time comparing the two. He reminded me of one of my university lecturers pouring over every detail of the paper that I had submitted to him, desperate to find something that he could jump upon and rip to pieces.

'Well,' he said after some time of silence as he shuffled through the notes. I had never known anyone draw out such a short word for such a long time. 'I think we will refer you to some specialists. Your test results reveal that you have a shadow here.' He pointed at something on his screen that I couldn't make head nor tail of. 'This looks very much like a lump to me which I think we need to look at in more detail. I am going to refer you to the oncology department.'

The silence that had occupied the air whilst the doctor had been looking through the notes now extended as I thought about what he had said. I noticed then and I have noticed since that doctors and the medical profession tend to dress things up and use euphemisms rather than say it to you directly. I heard the words 'shadow', 'lump' and 'oncology' and the only word that I really heard which was not said was 'cancer'.

Eighteen

There is a school of thought that states that cancer is something that is a modern curse and can be entirely blamed on the tobacco industry, which is responsible for killing us all whilst they line their pockets with cash and get fat on the graves of their victims. There is one problem with this opinion and that is that it is something that is extremely narrow minded.

What's my point? I will tell you.

Cancer is not a modern disease. It is something that has been with humanity for thousands of years, probably in all reality for the entire period of human history. We may not have always known what it was, but it has always been there. I dread to think what it would have been like having this terrible disease hundreds of years ago when there was not the pain relief and medical expertise that there is to deal with it these days. Mind you on saying that there will probably be people in hundreds of years' time who will look back at us in the early twenty-first century and wonder if we really did do the barbaric things that we did to people who were ill.

At least that is the hope. It is also just as likely that things will be so bad in the future that they will look back at us with admiration and wonder what went wrong. Either way I don't think it is going to be something that we have to worry about.

They say 'cancer is a word, not a sentence,' and I agree with this sentiment wholeheartedly, but nevertheless I would imagine that there isn't a single person who was diagnosed with cancer who didn't immediately think 'I'm going to die.' It's a natural reaction. I would like to take some time before continuing to talk about the culture of cancer and what has happened over the years about it. There is quite a lot that I would like to say about this, so it is a little difficult to know where the best place to start is.

First of all, I suppose is the fact that having cancer puts a great many things into perspective for you. Many is the time that I would be in bed struggling with a cold that I was convinced was flu, and many is the time that I might be laid up with a bad back, unable to move and I would be convinced in my hypochondria that things could not possibly get any worse than they were. In your feeling sorry for yourself you can't see how things can possibly get any worse. Cancer shows you that things can actually get a lot worse and gives you less tolerance for those that are moaning about things that you would love to be suffering from rather than living with cancer.

The second thing that I have noticed is the language of cancer. I have already mentioned the medical profession's reluctance to use the C word, even using the euphemism 'the C word' rather than saying it outright. I am pretty sure that throughout my experiences not a single professional used the cancer word when talking to me.

This then extends further into the military usage that seems to abound throughout the language. Such things as 'the war on cancer', 'long battle with cancer', 'long fight against cancer' and so on, you get the idea. I am not sure that these military terms are something that really helps. It seems to suggest that those who 'lose the fight' have done so because they somehow didn't put enough commitment into doing battle and they are somehow at fault and blame for their failure. This is, of course, not only completely bollocks, but also rather insulting.

This is a perfect example of why we have to be careful with the language that we use. Most of us go about our everyday lives without much thought into the language that we use. This is a case in point where not thinking creates the wrong impression. Personally, I don't like the idea of using such militaristic terms.

I noticed then that the way people treat you is amazing. There is a massive switch in the way they treat you. It is like there is a stigma about the disease and it is still seen in the language today where obituaries will say things like 'passed away after a long illness' thus getting double the money out of the euphemism jar. It is like they are afraid to say that someone died from cancer as if it is a taboo that must not be mentioned. It upsets the normal folk.

It then raises the question of how you tell people that you have this disease. I found that the direct approach doesn't work.

'Hi, how are you?'

'Oh, I am fine, aside from having cancer.'

This tends to stop the conversation rather quickly, or:

'Hey, have you lost weight?'

'Yes, I have cancer.'

These are the kind of examples which will suddenly have the other person fumbling and mumbling and then trying to do everything they can to get away from you as quickly as they can as if they fear that just being near to you will mean that they are going to catch it.

At no point has anyone said in response: 'Cancer? Oh, that's interesting, tell me about it.'

Nobody wants to really know.

I found that telling people you have cancer or a tumour means that they look at you as if you are already dead. When you say you have cancer people do think you are going to die. When you are told that you have cancer (even if the doctors don't use the term) you think you are going to die as well.

'Aren't you angry?' Mary asked me soon after the diagnosis that I did indeed at the age of twenty-eight have cancer.

'About what?'

'Having cancer?'

'I don't see the point. What would I gain by shaking my fists at the sky and asking "why me?"'.

'Bloody hell, I think I would do.'

'So many of us are going to go through this in some form or another in our lives that to ask "why me" is somewhat redundant. Rather we should ask "why not me?"'.

It's possible that I am remembering this slightly more heroically and calmly than the actual conversation went, but in essence I stand by these points.

Cancer is something that is so common. We will all be touched in one way or another, either by being diagnosed with it ourselves, or by having someone in our family being diagnosed with it. So why all the mystery? Why all the cloak and dagger whispering of the word and not talking openly about something that will touch us all in one way or the other?

I might have sounded unduly optimistic in what I was saying to Mary, or perhaps resigned to it all would be a better phrase. I have always thought that despite the medical advances and the excellent treatment progression that has been made there is no total cure for cancer. Yes, you might go into remission and there might be many years when you are cancer free, but you won't truly be rid of it. It is a tough little bastard and is always waiting in the wings for another entrance. You never beat it, not really, you can just wound it a lot.

On saying that the chances of pushing it back are much extended these days. Years ago, the chances are that the bastard thing would carry you off on the first chance it got. Now you had a pretty good chance of beating it back. I suppose this means that it would have to work a lot harder at trying to win.

There you go with all the military imagery again. I hate it and yet even I don't seem to be able to resist the usage of it. Perhaps it has become too ingrained with the disease.

I did think I was going to die though. When Mary was pregnant I saw pregnant women and babies everywhere that I looked. Since my diagnosis I saw death everywhere I looked. On television, film, books and I never realised how many cemeteries there were. It was like a conspiracy.

When do you tell everyone that you have cancer? Is there any point in holding the news back, or is it better to get it out there in the open immediately? It might seem strange to be thinking about how other people will take the news more than how I had taken it, but I did find that some others seemed more struck by it than I was myself.

I suppose I took a more philosophical view of the entire situation. What causes it? Smoking obviously, but then it seems as if every week there are news items that claim all kinds of things can cause or prevent cancer, they can't all be right as it pretty much seems to cover just about everything you can eat or drink. Perhaps it is best to just live your life and do what you want.

Cancer is something more genetic than dependant on whether you have eaten the wrong food or sat in the sun for ten minutes. I think if it's in your genes you are probably going to get it no matter what you do.

Although before I am killed by the liberal lobby, I should add that smoking is not really going to improve your chances all that much.

Luke seemed to respond well to the news. I mean he was shocked and upset, I know this because he told me so, but he didn't react in a hysterical way and was in many regards very helpful about the entire thing, assisting me in when I wanted to talk about these things in general. That is not to say that Mary wasn't there for me as she was.

'How do you exorcise everything you feel about all this?' Luke asked one day shortly after diagnosis when we were drinking coffee as usual.

'I'm not sure I know what you mean.'

'Well, you're a writer.'

'You mean do I write about it?'

'Yeah.'

'I'm not writing about cancer, no. I don't keep a diary either. I admit that writing has always been therapeutic for me, but I dunno.'

'Perhaps you should write about it. Maybe it will help.'

'Perhaps. Perhaps it will help me to make sense of everything in life.'

'Worth a try.'

'There are some in society who don't like the idea of someone writing about cancer. It's something that you shouldn't talk about let alone write about. If you do that they might have to admit that it is real.'

'Are there really people like that?'

'Some. Perhaps less than there used to be, but like racists and fascists they are very good at hiding in society and not necessarily letting their true feelings always show.'

'Rather a bleak outlook.'

'Such is life.'

***

What's my point? I will tell you.

Cancer has been around for thousands of years. We haven't always called it by the name of cancer, but it nevertheless is something that has always been there. Following humanity and developing and evolving with it. Perhaps it is true that it is more common now than it used to be, but that will only be because of the fact that as we evolve we live longer.

The longer we live the more chance we have of developing some form of cancer or another. It is the way of things.

It may all sound very bleak and depressing and I suppose that I can come across like that, but I have very mixed feelings about it all and to be honest there is hope and there is warmth and compassion in life. Perhaps I do have a habit of viewing things from the worst possible stance, but I don't walk around all day with a frown on my face asking what the point of it all is. I am actually rather happy and contented in my life and there really is no cause for complaint.

***

'You are fucking kidding me,' my father said when I told him my news which exclamation was something that caused more of a snort of disgust from my grandmother than the news had done.

'Please, there are no circumstances that cause for such profanity,' she said whilst screwing her face up with the expression of someone who was watching someone else pour the milk and the tea into a cup in the wrong order.

I could understand the reason for my father's exclamation even if my grandmother couldn't. He had gone throughout most of his life not knowing that he had a son and now after finding out a couple of years ago that he did have a son, his immediate reaction now was that he was about to lose his son again.

'What is the prognosis?' my ever-practical grandmother asked as we all sat in her drawing room sipping tea and acting as if we were in a Noel Coward farce.

'Well a lot of the medical jargon goes over my head and it all becomes rather complicated, but it seems to me that the first course of action is to have some surgery.'

'An operation?' my father, somewhat redundantly asked.

'Of course, an operation, please do be quiet James,' my grandmother appeared to be in control of the situation as usual. 'Continue,' she commanded.

'Yes so, anyway they cut out the tumour and then give it a dose of radiotherapy in the surrounding area to make sure it is all killed off. There is every chance that all of that will be successful and there will be nothing else that needs to be done other than regular monitoring.'

'And if it is not successful?'

'Then there is chemotherapy which is somewhat more problematic.'

'How so?' my father asked which earned him a glare from my grandmother.

'Radiotherapy is like zapping the cells with radiation which will kill or damage healthy cells as well as cancer cells. The healthy ones have a better chance of recovery than the cancerous ones do – up to a point.'

'Go on.'

'Chemotherapy is using chemicals to attack the cancer cells. The chemicals reduce the cancer cells ability to reproduce.'

'Then the issue is?' my grandmother asked whilst continuing to sip her tea as if it was the last days of the Raj happening around her.

'It also interferes with the legitimate activities of normal healthy cells causing the ill side effects that we all tend to associate with cancer, hair loss, weight loss and so on.'

'Rather like using a sledgehammer to crack a walnut,' Mary put in at this stage in what she probably hoped was a helpful analogy.

'Indeed.'

'I'm pretty confident that it will not go that far though,' I said as I put my cup down.

'It is not, however,' my grandmother observed, 'a confident picture that you paint.'

'I think it's as just as well to know all of the consequences and possibilities before setting out on these things.'

Silence prevailed in the room for a few moments whilst we all reflected on our individual thoughts about the situation. It was then that Mary decided to release a bombshell into the room that was not expected by me at all.

'I think Midge's mother should be told.'

If the room had been full of conversation then this would have brought the conversation to a stop, as it was it seemed to me that the silence deepened even further.

'What on earth for?' my father broke the silence.

'She's his mother,' Mary said aware that she was having to justify a position on shaky ground, 'I think she has the right to know what is happening to her only son.'

'I don't think that is a good idea,' my father continued. 'She was a hippy she will probably think that Midge is to blame for having cancer.'

This may sound like my father was overreacting in this regard, but I do happen to know that there is a movement out there that takes the very radical view that cancer sufferers have no one but themselves to blame. They seem to work on the basis of if you have a 'cancer trait' such as depression, self-loathing and the like then this negativity will express itself in the physical form of cancer that you have sub-consciously manifested. Conversely, they believe that if you changed your attitude then you would cure cancer, and if you didn't change your attitude then you quite clearly wanted to have cancer and would not be cured.

There is a problem with this belief that was very popular at one point in the 1970s and beyond. It is a very simple problem and that is that it is complete bollocks. It is not only bollocks, but it is insulting to someone who has cancer to suggest that it is their own fault.

It is just possible that my mother with her strange attitudes and outlooks on life might have fitted into this bracket so I could see that my father was coming from the point of view of wanting to protect me from any further grief.

My grandmother looked at us each in turn with a long-held look before finally passing her judgement.

'I think Mary is right.'

'You can't be serious, mother?'

'I am perfectly serious, James. I would have thought that you would have known that by now. Mary is right because I do believe that a mother has the right to know what is going on with her son.'

'Yes, but this is Lucy we're talking about here.'

'I am well aware of who we are talking, James. I am not yet senile. The Lord knows that I have not always seen eye-to-eye with Lucy in the past, but I do believe that she has the right to know. It is a motherhood thing, James, you would not understand.'

With that she seemed to dismiss any argument to the contrary and adopted the position of final word in the family. For a brief moment I looked between her and Mary and wondered if this had been a put up and planned from the start.

***

'You didn't say all that much back there,' Mary commented when we were driving back home later.

'I don't think that I knew what to say.'

'What do you want to say?'

'I don't know. The entire thing came so far out of the blue that I was not expecting it at all.'

'Sorry about that, but your grandmother is right, it is a motherhood thing. I know that no matter what happens between a mother and her child in life there is always a bind there.'

'Why do people always assume that and that there is no connection between the father and his child?'

'Probably because you don't carry the child around inside of you for nine months.'

'A chance of biology doesn't limit my feelings for my daughter. I didn't carry her around inside of me, true, but that is hardly my fault and it wouldn't stop me from doing anything I could for Jessica.'

'I'm sorry I didn't mean to suggest otherwise.'

'Well, I mean to say this myth of motherhood bonding has hardly stood in good stead with my own mother and me, has it?'

'Well that's true. So what do you think about it all?'

'About finding my mother?'

'Yeah.'

'To be honest I don't know what to think. She clearly doesn't think all that much about me so why should I think all that much about her? I'm not convinced that getting back together after all these years is a good idea.'

'It's possible of course that your father won't be able to find her.'

'Possible, but I don't think my grandmother is the kind of person to accept failure once her mind is made up about something.'

'Well that's certainly true. You must have some idea about how you feel about the possibility of seeing your mother again, or at least knowing where she is.'

'I really don't know. I suppose that there are questions which I would like answered, but I am not sure that finding my mother is likely to provide those answers for me.'

'What answers?'

'Well, two I can immediately think of. One, why did you walk out and vanish out of my life without a word, and two, why didn't you tell me my father was actually alive. Why lie to me all these years?'

I wasn't sure that finding my mother would provide these answers or in any way do the slightest good for me or the situation. She had proven to me that she had an impressive track record for lying, so even if we did find her and get some answers from her, how did we know that she was then telling us the truth and not another lie?

I really was not convinced that finding my mother would do any of us any good at all.

However, for better or for worse, my father had been tasked to find out where my mother was after all the years since he had last seen her and then make contact so that she could be informed about her son.

It was something that if I had been tasked with I might not have put all that much effort into, but then I did have rather a lot of other things on my mind.

Nineteen
James

I don't think that there is any cause for suggesting that my sexuality and character are because I have a domineering mother. I know that there are those out there that would make much of things like that, but as far as I am concerned it is all horse shit. It seems to me that there are people out there that want some excuse for justifying why it is that people are gay. I understand the genetic argument, but ultimately these people just can't seem to accept the fact that it is for many of us a choice.

It has got nothing to do with my mother at all.

I do admit that my mother is somewhat overbearing at times and when she has made up her mind then there really isn't all that much that can be done about it other than to go along with her and hope for the best. I sometimes wonder how it was that my father managed to cope with her. We each are attracted to our own kind of person I suppose.

Which reminds me. Brian had been taking the news of Midge rather harder than I had imagined that he would. It is true that he had first thought that I was having an affair with him and had become insanely jealous for a while. It had taken a huge amount of effort to convince him that Midge was actually my son, but I had no idea that this would make matters worse for him.

He eventually came to realise that Midge was my son, but this alienated him from me. Brian was frankly disgusted by the thought that I had been with a woman and had produced offspring with her, as he would have put it. He didn't want anything to do with Midge or the rest of my family, which was the reason why I had to start making excuses for him at Christmas dos and family celebrations which I am sure that nobody else believed in the slightest.

You see the thing is that I think of myself as gay. So, I admit I was with Lucy, but as I have already said it was not a happy time and we broke up and I settled on the gay sexuality that I believe and still believe defined my tastes. For Brian this meant that I was bisexual, and paradoxically Brian was extremely prejudiced against people that were bisexual.

Chiefly I think this stemmed from the fact that he just couldn't believe that there were those out there that preferred both men and women. He thought that if you termed yourself bisexual then you were really just a heavily repressed homosexual that was refusing to come fully out because of the stigma of society.

In some cases, he might have been right about this. However, I took issue with a couple of points.

Firstly, I do believe that you can be attracted to both sexes and attraction to one doesn't mean that you are not attracted to the other. Secondly, just because I had once had sex with a woman didn't mean that I was bisexual. I was gay!

Brian couldn't see this though and it started to become an issue between us as he somehow felt that I had betrayed him by having sex with a woman almost twenty years before we had met.

I have to admit that I have experienced this prejudice against bisexuality in the gay community a fair amount, a surprising amount actually. I say surprising because a group that have themselves been the victims of extreme prejudice should be illogical to have prejudice against another group of people purely because of their sexuality. Where is the logic in that, I ask you?

Ultimately it will come as no surprise to you to learn that tensions between Brian and myself became more difficult as he became increasingly paranoid at what else he thought I was hiding from him as he still refused to accept that Midge's existence had come as much of a surprise to me as it had to him; more in fact if you think about it. He was convinced that I had known him all along and that I had been meeting him secretly whilst also having secret trysts with Lucy. Nothing I could do or say convinced him otherwise.

No relationship of any kind can survive amidst a lack of trust and so it was inevitable that we would part and the entire thing would fall to pieces. Perhaps in the end we both went our separate ways with a feeling of relief and a belief that we had both been in the right and had been wronged by the other.

Perhaps that is how so many relationships end. A belief that we have been in the right and the other person has been wrong all along.

So after more than a decade I found myself single again. I was fifty-four years old so it was hardly the best state to be in. You could argue that it is never good to come out of a relationship and find yourself back to square one as it were, but to come out of a relationship in your mid-fifties was worse because I just didn't have the energy, or the inclination to start the whole dating thing over again. I was rather resigned to the fact that I would probably just stay single from now on, which would presumably give me a lot less hassle.

I suppose it made things a little easier for me as trying to track down Lucy whilst still being in a relationship with Brian would have been a nightmare. If I told him that I was trying to find her he would never believe anything other than I was intending to get back together with her and if I kept it secret from him and he later found out, how much worse would it be that I had kept it secret from him? There are some situations that I have learnt over the years that it is just impossible to win. Without him being around it certainly made it one less argument that I was going to have about the whole thing.

I can't say that I agreed with my mother and her support for finding Lucy after all of these years. I was pretty much convinced that the best thing to do was to let sleeping dogs lie and that there wasn't anything to be gained by stirring things up now. As always though my mother had made up her mind so there wasn't anything that could be achieved by argument now.

My concern was partially because I didn't want to rake up the past and cause further problems in the present. Obviously, we didn't part on the best of terms and Lucy had demonstrated that she was prepared to lie about the past, she had lied to Midge about what had happened to me and although she hadn't lied about being pregnant she hadn't told me that she was when we had parted. Us all turning up on her doorstop, wherever that now was, making it obvious that we had discovered the truth could result in all sorts of confusion and chaos.

There was also something else that I was worried about though and that was Midge's welfare. I think it is only natural that I should be concerned about my son and his welfare. I may not have been a father for very long, but it was something that I seemed to take to rather naturally, which was probably more of a surprise to me than it was to anyone else.

One of the things that I was really concerned about was that Lucy would turn out to be one of these people who blamed Midge for his cancer. I know that the others had poo-pooed this idea the moment I had mentioned it, but I am aware of the fact that there are others out there who do actually think like this. I know that to an extent, and to a scientific, reasonable person the concept of any physical illness being caused by mental ability is somewhat bizarre, but there are cases.

I am not sure if I believe it all myself, but I suppose that I tend to keep an open mind about these things. Take Voodoo, for instance. I don't think that it actually works that you can put a curse on someone and then have it come true. I don't believe that you can stick pins in a dummy and make someone else feel real pain. However, I do believe that if *you* believe it to be true then it can happen. Let me explain.

Voodoo works because if you are so convinced that you are cursed you could potentially work yourself up to a state of delirium or illness. There is so much that we don't know about how the mind works that it might be possible to even scare yourself to death. If you don't believe in it then it can't work. The power lies in the 'victim's' belief that it is true.

It is the same thing with witchcraft for the hundreds of years that it thrived. People believed in witches, it was part of their culture, upbringing and belief. If they thought that they had been cursed by a witch then they could easily get their brain to convince themselves that they were doomed. You can probably think yourself to death if you wanted to. You just have to have the right mindset to do it.

Bringing it up to a more relevant and modern example I recently heard about a case where a man was told by his doctor that he had inoperable cancer and that it was only a matter of time. Over the period of time that was left to him the man became sicker and eventually, as predicted by his doctor he died. He was given a post mortem examination and to everyone's surprise he was found to not have a single cancerous cell in his body at all. It would appear that he had died because of the fact that he had total faith in his doctors.

I suppose I am saying that the mind is a funny thing and it can do all sorts of things and I thought that Midge was in a difficult enough place as it was without his mother making him think that it was his own thoughts that had given him cancer and it was all his fault. I don't know maybe she wouldn't have done that, but I couldn't really be sure of all that much any longer.

All I could do was try my best to look after my son and I was not entirely convinced that bringing his mother back into his life was something that was going to be the best for him. Perhaps I was jealous. She had been a part of his life for a long time where she had excluded me completely. Perhaps now I felt that it was my chance to be with Midge without her being around.

This probably sounds callous and I would imagine makes it seem like I didn't love her. Love is a very difficult thing to talk about. I certainly didn't love her now as we had not seen or spoken to each other for decades. Did I love her at the time that we briefly dated? I really cannot be sure. My feelings at the time were all shaken up with trying to find my own sexuality that it is difficult to look back now and work out if I was in love or not.

I suppose the difficulty with being with Lucy was I was trying to be with someone that I was just not suited to be with. In that sense I wasn't really like to be in love with her, I suppose. In that sense I was one of the only people who probably understood that when Prince Charles and Lady Diana were engaged and were asked by the press if they were in love and they confirmed that they were and then Charles said: 'Whatever love is.' Do you remember that?

Well I knew what he was talking about. To be honest I can't even put my hand on my heart and say with certainty that I loved Brian either. I might have done at the start of the relationship, but I don't think that I did at the end of it. I was just used to him by that point so I suppose he was better off in getting out when he did. I don't wish him any ill feeling, any more than I do Lucy. I hope he finds what he is looking for. It's all that any of us can hope for in the end.

Anyway, I am not here to try and explain what love is, which is a good thing because I don't think we have the time to try and explain it, or I have the skill to be able to explain it. I sure as hell don't have the energy to even try.

I digress somewhat. I suppose it is true to say that I was also concerned about how Lucy would react to seeing me again after all of these years. People can change a great deal over the years. When I had last seen Lucy, we had been in our twenties, now we were in our fifties and a great deal can change in a person over a quarter of a century. The Lucy that Midge described to me was certainly not the woman that I had once known. I never would have imagined that she was the kind of person who would have abandoned her only son and disappeared; nor would I have imagined that she would have been such a distant mother throughout his life. Perhaps we never really know people, no matter how close we are to them; or how close we think we are to them.

I was also concerned about how she would react to me when I popped back into her life after all these years. After all, she had hid our son's existence from me and had told him that I was dead, which as far as I could see had slammed a fair few doors without leaving much room for negotiation about opening them again in the future let alone walking through them.

By telling Midge that I was dead I suspected that she was showing what she really wanted from me and me reappearing in her life was not a good idea. I was more than a little worried about the entire thing if I am honest.

My mother, as I have stated is a formidable woman who should never be underestimated. I really have no idea at all how I would go about tracing someone that I have not seen for more than a quarter of a century, but such a thing didn't faze her at all. She had lived a long life and in that time she had met many people and made loads of contacts. It is my belief that she already had a notion as to how to find Lucy before she had set the task in hand.

It turned out, therefore that I didn't have to do that much work to try and find where Lucy was as my mother had done it all behind the scenes, but clearly for reasons that only she could know she wanted me to act as the frontman for the investigation into finding her.

I have given up trying to understand my mother. I gave up a long time ago, life is just too short to work out the impossible.

It wasn't all that difficult to find out where Lucy was. Not if you are as formidable and determined as my mother is about these things. I had nurtured a small hope that maybe we wouldn't be able to find out where she was and things would be left at that, but clearly this was not going to happen. The truth about where she was took us all by surprise, however, and was something that I imagined would have made even my mother stop and think about the wisdom of what it was that she was doing.

I don't know what any of us expected to find out. I suppose that given the things that Midge had told us about growing up with Lucy and the way that she was, I half expected to find that she was in India getting in touch with her inner lightness, or maybe in some druid commune somewhere isolated. I don't think that any of us expected to find out that she was in a mental hospital.

Twenty
Midge

I don't believe that physical symptoms can be influenced by the mind. I have to admit that if I had the choice of putting my confidence in medical science, or placing it in the power of prayer, or in the range of alternative medicines that are out there, I would come down on the side of medical science every time.

When people go through such serious illness, or physical trauma and they are worked on by numerous medical staff desperately trying to cure them, or put them together again it demeans all of the efforts when their recovery, or survival is put down to a miracle.

What's my point? I will tell you.

When you are in hospital and you recover from illness or injury, it is the medical staff, medicine and medical science that has achieved the recovery and not by some hidden miracle by someone who is reported to 'move in mysterious ways.' I have no idea what the medical staff think about these people who proclaim their survival as a miracle, but it insults the hell out of me just thinking about it.

It would drive me insane to think that I had studied medicine for all those years, that I had the most expensive machinery and drugs at my disposal and that I worked my arse off to save someone only to have them completely blank me and put their recovery entirely down to some being with a long white beard sitting on a cloud. Do you have any idea how ridiculous that sounds?

On saying all that though I think you have to remain positive. It is possible to just give up and refuse medical help and roll yourself into a corner and just die. That isn't the line for me. I have nothing against you if that is the road that you decide to take, but I won't be coming down it with you.

I have no intention of giving up on life and intend to remain positive and keep on going for as long as I am able to and even longer if I can. It was possible to become overwhelmed with everything. It is almost something that we are conditioned to believe that when we are told that we have cancer that we think we are going to die. It isn't really like that any longer. Now with the advancements that have been made there is a fair chance of recovery and I do truly believe that the day will come when it can be beaten completely without fail.

'The problem with this kind of disease,' my consultant, Doctor Moody told me on one of my early visits to him, 'is that it can be around in the body for a number of years before we get to detect it. It is never really discovered at any early stage, it usually, by definition has to be reasonably advanced before it is noticed.'

'So, you are saying that Midge has had this for some time then?' Mary asked as I noticed that neither of them were using the C word again as if it was as sacrilegious as saying 'fuck' in church.

'Yes, and it is really impossible to know how long for.'

'That doesn't sound particularly optimistic.' I didn't think it sounded optimistic at all, but I was trying to retain a level of outward belief that everything was going to be fine even if I did allow my private thoughts to wander into dark areas from time to time.

'It doesn't have to mean that it is bad. It may be advanced, but that is not a problem, providing that it is not too advanced. Do you see what I mean?'

We thought we did. I wondered how he managed to get through his working day. It must be one of the most depressing jobs imaginable having to tell people each day that they have cancer and that they might die, and then there being the days when you have to tell people that there is no hope that everything that can be done has been done. It made me glad that the worst thing in my job was telling people that the latest Dan Brown novel was not available. I had to admire him for doing this job, it certainly wasn't the kind of job that everyone could do.

'The first step that we have to take is to operate.'

'That seems quick.'

'It is the best way of dealing with these things. We will operate and remove the offending article from your neck and then once we have removed as much of it as we can, which will hopefully be all of it, we will then give you a healthy dose of radiotherapy which will zap the surrounding tissue to prevent the spread of the disease. After that you will hopefully be fine.'

I found that some of Doctor Moody's choice of words were interesting to say the least. It was my usual curse to be able to see words as they were spoken and recall them and it still interested me that I had never heard Doctor Moody say the word 'cancer' yet, I also wondered how worried I should be at the choice of words 'offending article,' 'healthy dose,' 'zap' and 'hopefully.'

'Hopefully' was perhaps the word that worried me the most out of all of them, but then I was also pretty concerned about a professional using the word 'zap' as well. Still I suppose he knew what he was doing; or at least I hoped he did.

My experiences of the hospital were not getting any better. I can't believe that there are people out there who really like hospitals and that kind of thing. I suppose there are some hypochondriacs that might get off on being in hospital, but it really didn't do anything for me. I was much less of a hypochondriac since I had been told that I had a serious illness. All else fell to insignificance. I wish that those who moaned about having minor ailments would be aware of this. We spend too much time focusing on the insignificant and pay too much attention to it when life can be literally slipping away.

'Have you been to the dentist yet?' This was an unexpected question from Doctor Moody.

'No. Should I?'

'Yes. When you are exposed to radiation on your neck and throat area it is advisable to visit a dentist so that if there are any teeth that need pulling they can be pulled before you have the radiation. They won't be able to extract them afterwards, you see?'

'Why?'

'Radiation damages the blood vessels and their ability to carry oxygen. A tooth pulled takes longer to heal and may not heal at all as a result of it, you see? The usual practice is to get rid of any teeth that look like they will be future problems before we start.'

'I see.' You learnt something every day in this world.

'There will be effects of the radiotherapy, of course.'

'Of course.' Well there would be wouldn't there?

'You will possibly find that you have a loss of appetite and when you do eat your taste buds will be effected. Obviously, there will be a soreness to the skin and a sore throat, but these will be hopefully temporary. As you would expect there will be a loss of hair as well and also a loss of your saliva glands, we can give you some fluoride gel to rub in your gums for that.'

They seemed to have thought of most things.

'The process is zapping the cells with radiation, you see? This will kill or damage the healthy cells as well as the . . . the. . . um . . . non-healthy ones. The healthy ones have a better chance of recovery than the . . . um . . . other ones.'

Not for the first time it amused me that radiation was something that caused cancer if you were exposed to it and yet here they were now using radiation to try and cure cancer. When you thought about it that didn't make much sense. It also was fuel to the fire for those who were opposed to medical science and felt that alternative treatments were the only way to survive this disease. If you went down the conventional treatment path and then died they would point to the evil radiotherapy to indicate that putting your faith in such destruction would bring you nothing more than you deserved. If you survived then they would probably say it was because of some divine intervention, or because you had also drunk herbal tea, or something like that. It therefore became impossible to win against these people in an argument.

It will come as no surprise to you that my position is to pour scorn on the philosophy that is held by these people. I can understand the position that radiation is unnatural. Just think of Hiroshima, Nagasaki and Chernobyl and all the fears about it will come to the surface. It's all the same radiation that can kill cancer cells and create them. However, I am still sure that I would rather submit to the radiation than submit to treatment of a crushed dandelion each day, or something as equally as stupid. If this offends you then I am sorry, but that is just the way that it is.

***

After that things moved rather quickly. I had expected there to be lengthy delays whilst they decided what they were going to do next. However, it would appear that even if they don't use the word openly, they take cancer very seriously.

I was in hospital within a couple of weeks and then I was wearing one of those stupid gowns that they make you wear that shows your arse off to the world and caused much amusement to Mary. I waited around on the ward for a little bit of time and tried not to look at the other patients who appeared to be in varying states of health. Some of it was rather frightening because you realised that you could be looking at the future in front of you.

Thankfully, I was soon taken away down to the operating theatre where I was injected with something that soon turned everything into oblivion. When I woke up my neck was bandaged and I felt like there was something lodged in my throat.

As soon as I came back to reality I came back to pain that hadn't been there before I went under the knife. They gave me some liquid morphine which was nice as it certainly helped and strangely was something that seemed to be familiar to me, although I was certain that I had never had it before. Tasted a little like cough mixture, I suppose, and that was probably what it reminded me of.

After that it was reasonably all over. A bit of time spent in the hospital and some help in making sure that I could speak again as everything that I initially said sounded like I was about to hack up a load of mucus at whoever I was trying to speak to.

It was then time for some recuperation. That lasted a little while before my family decided that the time had come to launch another one of those surprises at me.

***

It was a few weeks later that we were summoned to see my grandmother. We normally tended to visit her, she had only really visited us at that Christmas when Luke had caused what was referred to as the "willygate incident." Since then she had not returned to see us, but seemed to prefer that we visit her. At least that way she could be sure that she wouldn't bump into Luke at her own house.

We entered her living room which seemed to be a place that was set for perpetual tea. Perhaps when you reached my grandmother's age and social class time began to stand still and it was always time for tea no matter what the time of day was. Perhaps little else mattered when you got to a certain age and you could fill your days up with what you might have thought of as trivial when you were younger. Priorities change the older you get though.

Once we had settled down with our cups and saucers and had made the idle chit-chat that protocol demanded we got right to the point.

'We have located your mother,' my grandmother announced.

'You have?'

'Indeed.'

I wasn't sure, even at this stage that I wanted to particularly know about where my mother was or what she had been up to since she walked out of my life. Nevertheless, my grandmother seemed to be dragging out the moment for some kind of dramatic effect.

'Lucy is in a mental hospital,' my father stated breaking the tension of the moment and creating a whole new tense atmosphere.

'A what?'

'A mental institute,' my grandmother said with a certain amount of distaste which is a position that I had noticed she often took when talking about anything that she appeared to disapprove of; which seemed to be a lot of things.

I looked at Mary in astonishment. This was news that I had not expected to hear about my mother out of all of the things that I could possibly have imagined I might have heard.

'What are you talking about?'

'Your mother is in a mental institution. It is a place called Crippen Hospital. We have spoken to the staff there and after much deliberation it has been agreed that it would be acceptable to visit your mother.'

'Well how the hell did she end up there?'

'We do not know that at this time. It is hopeful that by visiting her we will get to know the truth behind what has happened to her and how she has ended up there.'

It would seem that the only way that we would find out what had happened to my mother was to go and visit her.

***

I had never visited a psychiatric hospital before and I was not entirely certain of what it was that I was likely to find when I did visit. I had visions of something similar to the historical depictions of Bedlam Hospital, but I hoped that things had moved on since those days.

Visiting a psychiatric hospital is not something that I imagine would figure high on anyone's list of things to do, much less to be committed to one of them. They say that at least a third of us will suffer some form of mental illness in our lives; but you rather hope that the area that I was visiting now was the extreme end of the scale as opposed to a mild form of depression because your local football team had lost.

It had been decided that it was to be my father and myself who visited the hospital. We felt, and so did the staff, that anyone else would be rather too much and something of an overload for my mother. They were still not telling us what was wrong with her, but they seemed keen for us to visit and I gained the impression that she had not had all that many visitors in the time that she had been there, however long that had been.

We arrived at the hospital which from all intents and purposes appeared to be a normal hospital, or at least it certainly looked that way from the outside. We had yet to see what it was like on the inside. We walked into the reception area which again seemed to be like you might have expected in any hospital.

Approaching the desk, we informed the rather morose looking man sitting behind the bank of computer screens and telephones why we were there. He seemed to be someone who didn't believe in talking unless it was absolutely necessary and after clicking his mouse and keyboard for a short while informed us that my mother was on the 'Christie Ward' and he would arrange for someone to escort us to the ward.

This was the first indication that things were not like in a normal hospital. Normally we would be pointed in the right direction and told to make our own way and hope for the best. After a while a man came through the door who introduced himself to us as a psychiatric nurse called Roger. I had never seen a psychiatric nurse before so I was not entirely sure what to expect. I suppose part of me was expecting something along the lines of a traditional nurse in uniform. Instead I was presented with someone who was wearing cords, Hush Puppies, a strange jumper and with a beard and a swipe card on a lanyard around his neck. He appeared to me to be more like a social worker than a nurse. Perhaps that is what he really was.

He walked us through a series of secure doors along a lengthy corridor, pausing at each closed door to use his swipe card and then to quickly punch a number into the keypad which was located next to the door. He took great pains to keep the number from us, hunching his back over the keypad as if he was entering the nuclear code and was frightened that we were spies; or perhaps he felt that we would knock him unconscious steal his swipe card and allow everyone to escape using his key code.

'Are you the person who has been looking after Lucy?' my father asked managing to put a slight emphasis on 'looking after' to suggest that this was the last thing that he suspected that they had been doing with her since she had been in the hospital.

'Yes, I am.'

'Can you tell us what is wrong with her?'

'I think it best that she tell you herself.'

He didn't seem to be all that interested in engaging us in further conversation and continued to walk down the corridor from door to door, working his way through the complex. As he was not that much of a talker I took to looking around me and it was then that I noticed that the place was not only as clinical as you would expect from any hospital – you know white walls and all that disinfectant like smell – but there were also the added extras that you didn't find in normal hospitals. Little things like bars on the windows. Well I say bars but perhaps it was a better description to say a wire mesh. Bars would have kept people from escaping, and the wire mesh had the same effect, but it also prevented you from being able to throw anything at the window and break the glass, which I suspected was probably toughened anyway.

I also noticed that the corridors were rather bare, there were no things like pot plants and paintings on the walls. Anything that was dotted around, such as chairs and tables a second glance showed that they were screwed to the floor. Either someone was really into Feng Shui to such a degree that they *really* didn't want you moving anything around; or, as I admitted was more likely, they were screwed down to prevent them being picked up and thrown at the windows or the staff, or presumably anything else that happened to be around.

We eventually entered a corridor that was populated. In the sense that there were a number of rooms leading off from it and that there were people, who I assumed to be patients, shuffling about from one seemingly pointless direction to another. I was rather afraid to notice that they had a zombie-like expression on their faces and appeared to be medicated up to their eyeballs on something or other. To be honest it scared the living shit out of me.

One of the patients saw us and stopped in the corridor staring at us with a look of surprise and confusion on his face.

'Wow. Reality check,' he said before turning off and shuffling in a different direction with his hand rubbing his forehead. I was not particularly hopeful for anything else that lay waiting for us in the further depths of the building.

Roger, the nurse, took us into a room which opened out into what appeared to be some kind of a day room where a number of people, in what seemed to me to be various states of catatonia, were sitting in large armchairs watching or ignoring a small television that blabbered on in the corner playing some day time rubbish programme, where some arrogant host was trying to sort out some boring people who were sleeping with their sister's boyfriend's aunt, or something.

'This is Lucy,' Roger suddenly announced and I was dragged away from the television that has a habit of catching our attention no matter how shit the programme is and looked on my mother for the first time in almost a decade.

Twenty-One
Lucy

I have been told that it would be a good idea to write down my thoughts. To tell what has happened to me. Doctor Rubesh thinks that this would be a good idea. He thinks it is helpful. He thinks it will help me understand the things that got me here. He thinks it will make me feel better. I think he is a cock.

He won't be happy with me. Not for calling him a cock. Even if he is. Well it's his problem for making me write it.

I am tired. I don't remember not being tired. Maybe it's the pills they make me take. Maybe it's life. I know it's been a long time. I am almost fifty-five years old now. I only know that when I look in the mirror and see this old woman looking back at me. She's a stranger. I have no idea who that woman is. In my own head I am still in my twenties. Before it all went wrong. I don't know who you are in the mirror. It isn't me. Don't make no sense.

I know why things are the way they are. Instead of the way that they should be. I know where it all went wrong for me. It is all because of James.

My mother would say that it is always because of a man when you get to the bottom of it. I have never had that much experience with men though. The experience that I had was not the best experience. At the same time, it was the best. That makes no sense. There is little about life that has made sense to me.

His name was James. I used to call him Jim. He didn't look like a James to me. Nobody else used to call him Jim. I think it was just me. I didn't mind that. It made it something special just between the two of us. I liked that.

Jim worked in the local Co-Op. I liked the look of him from the moment I first saw him. He was a couple of years older than me. He was so sexy. He didn't seem to notice me. He was shy. That made him all the more interesting to me. I tried to make him notice me. He just didn't seem to notice me at all. No matter what I did. That only fuelled me to want him all the more. The fact that he seemed not interested made me all the more interested. Makes little sense. That seems to be the way that love often works. Although it was lust at that stage.

I kept dropping hints about how it would be nice if we got together. He never picked up on it. Jim wasn't the kind of person who responded to hints. I wanted to go to the cinema with him. We eventually did and saw *Jaws 2*. It was an effort to get that far.

The fact that Jim was so shy appealed to me a great deal. I don't know why. I will admit that I hadn't had that much experience with boys or men before Jim. I was twenty-three when I met him. Before he came along there had been the odd boy that I had dated on and off. Nothing serious. Nothing that lasted all that long a time. My parents thought I should have been married and had children by this age. I was in no rush. I was enjoying the freedom of being single. I was an idiot.

Whilst other girls were dropping their knickers to the first cock that came along I was more interested in other things. My big passion in life was music. I miss my music now. All I can do now is replay it in my mind. They took my music away from me. I can't forgive that. I might forgive a lot. Not that.

I can't forgive Paul either. Paul was the first man who ruined my life. I had no idea how upset I could be until Paul changed my world forever. April 10, 1970 it was. I was fifteen years old. He broke my heart. I will remember that day for the rest of my life.

The day that Paul decided that he wasn't going to be a Beatle any longer and the world collapsed. Nobody else could perhaps understand it as much as I did. You had to really love that band to understand how bad it was that they broke up. It put me off men for a long time. I would sit in my room crying over *Sgt Pepper* over and over again. I knew every note. Every chord. Every little bit of that album. It is good that I listened to it so much. I can now replay the entire album over in my own mind. Whenever I want to. Every night.

I dated a few boys as I got older. We never did that much. There was a lot of kissing. A lot of fumbling about by them. They didn't know what they were doing. Neither did I. It showed. We never progressed far above kissing and a hand up a jumper. I was a virgin when I met James.

I suppose now that is rare to be a virgin when you are as old as I was. Maybe there were those then who thought I was an old maid. It was the seventies. Everyone was having sex. Not me though. There are more things in life.

Music didn't seem to be as good since Paul did what he did. There were some good things going on in the seventies. I tried to enjoy it. It seemed that there was a part of me that had died though. I had a hollow inside of me. An emptiness. As if a part of my soul had been taken away and was not being replaced. I tried to overcome it all. I would listen to a lot of Bob Dylan and Leonard Cohen. Which only made me more depressed.

This is when I first came across depression. My parents thought it was stupid to be depressed about a music band. This is because they liked classical music. All of their favourite musicians had been dead for hundreds of years so there wasn't anything to be depressed about. Used to depress the hell out of me though. All that old shit.

Jim had no music knowledge at all. Not that I would call music. It rather amazed me at his lack of musical knowledge. I tried to interest him in the things that I liked. It didn't work. I played him all my best albums. He didn't get it at all. Strangely enough that didn't stop me loving him though. Or playing the records.

I don't know what he thought about my playing my records over and over again until I wore out the needle. I would replace the needle. Then start wearing it out again.

Music doesn't sound as good when it isn't on a turntable. I don't hold with these ways of listening to music now. You can listen to music now without it physically being there. That isn't right.

I don't think Jim thought that much of *Jaws 2* either. Neither did I. That wasn't the point. He hadn't even seen the first one. Hard to believe. Popular culture passed Jim by.

I don't know if I can explain why it was that I was so attracted to him. I just was. He had that unattainable air about him.

My hints of my interest were not working in the slightest. I decided that the direct approach would be better. I asked him out over the meat counter. He seemed shocked by this. Not sure why. He seemed to think it over to the point where he was becoming insulting. Eventually he accepted and we went on a date. That was when we went to see a disaster film. About a fish. Should have been warned by that as to what was to come.

Despite our differences I felt that we were suited to each other. I was wrong. Didn't seem so obvious at the time though. I fell in love with him. Really in love. All the love that the poets talk about. Head over heels and all of that. I suppose you would call it an obsession. Real love is though.

It seems strange when I think about it. We were together a really short space of time. Not all that long. Not when I think about all the years that have gone by. Not that long when I think about the lasting impression that happened.

We were different. He was more straight-laced than I was. That's funny now I think about it. I had followed my idol, John Lennon, and I was really into India and all of that. I had dreams of life in India. New Age stuff some called it. Kind of strange when you think how old it is. I wanted to go and live in India. I loved the culture. Maybe if not India then I could have lived on a kibbutz in Israel. At one with the soil. Looking back, I can't imagine James would have responded well to either life.

It was a dream. I learnt pretty quickly that dreams don't come true. It's just one of those things that you had better get used to in life.

Jim was the first man that I had sex with. I was scared shitless. The longer you leave these things the more nervous you get. Or maybe you would be nervous whatever age it was you had it.

Jim was nervous as well. I wondered if he was a virgin. I asked him. He would never answer. He always changed the subject. I had seen cock before so I knew what to expect. I had never had it in me. One of my previous boyfriends had asked me to rub him off. I had liked him. Not enough to let him put it in me. I thought I had better get used to the idea of it. It felt very funny. It didn't really do anything for me. It was amazing what it did for him though. I was surprised how just touching some skin could cause such an obvious good feeling for him. I wasn't prepared for when he came though. That was unexpected. It was also very messy.

He lost interest in me after that. Clearly me bringing him off ended the mystery for him. Perhaps he wanted something else.

Jim was different though. He respected me and didn't seem to want to get into my knickers the first chance that he got. We had been going out for a couple of months before sex came up. We had done a lot of kissing. I helped him to cum a few times as I had some experience of that. I also tried blow jobs. That was an interesting experience. I found it confusing at first. It seemed to imply that you had to blow. Should be called suck jobs really. There was a bit of confusion over that to begin with.

I suppose when it came to sex I was slightly prepared. I had done myself in a few years before with a hairbrush. So, had a rough idea of what to expect. I thought I did. I was wrong. I am afraid I am not overly experienced in the different sizes of cocks. I am not that experienced. Jim seemed to make me feel aware of his presence though. Enough said.

You liking this Doctor Rubesh? You get off on hearing about this sort of thing? Is that why I am writing this shit story of my life?

Maybe I am being too harsh on the old doctor. I guess he is doing what he has to do. Thinks he has to do. I am not sure that writing all this out will help me purge all this emotion. All these ghosts. He seems to think it will work. I have my doubts. Life has made me have doubt about everything.

We tried sex with a johnnie to start with. I don't think either of us really liked it. I went on the pill. It was a new experience to have sex without a johnnie. I think I liked it better. I was so in love with Jim that I decided to stop taking the pill. I suppose now that would be thought of as a dangerous thing to do. It can kill you now.

I wish it had killed me then.

I wanted to marry Jim. I wanted to have loads of kids with him. I wanted to spend the rest of my life with him. I didn't want anyone else. I had the entire happy future mapped out in front of me. I told you that dreams don't come true.

They tell me that it was wrong of me to come off the pill and not tell Jim. They are probably right. They normally are. Or think they are. I have given up trying to argue. They always win. You can't beat the system.

It was then that I thought my dreams were about to come true. I realised that I was pregnant. I was the happiest person in the world. My future was going to be perfect.

It was May 1980. I decided that it was time to tell him the good news. I was sure that he would marry me. Make an honourable woman of me. As they used to say.

Turned out that he had news to tell me on that cold, miserable day. Of all the things that I might have expected to have happened I was not expecting him to break up with me. That's what he did. I couldn't understand what was going on. It didn't make sense at all. This wasn't the way that it was meant to be.

I was too shocked at the time to tell him I was pregnant. What had gone wrong? Why was he breaking it up? Why was he leaving me?

I demanded to know what I had done wrong. What was wrong with me? Why was he leaving me? He said it wasn't me. It was him. Yeah, that old story. He told me that he was gay.

I don't know if I believed this. I don't know if I believe it now. It made sense. But he also took a long time to say this. So, he could have been using it as an excuse because of something else. I suppose it would have to be one hell of an excuse to pretend that you are a pillow biter.

I was shocked by it all really. No idea what was going on. It was over. That much was clear there was no chance of a change in that. Jim walked off. That was the last that I saw of him. Probably a good thing.

I remember it then started to rain. It would. I was dazed. I went to the train station and sat down to gather my thoughts.

I fucking hate train stations.

They are so busy. So many people. Comings and goings. Lovers meeting. Lovers parting. Families. Friends. Saying goodbye to people. Waiting to say hello to people. All that bustle. The hustle. The fuss. Horrible places really.

Some people collect models of the places. What the hell for? I can't really think of anything worse. Not for me.

I don't know how long I sat in that terminal. Waiting. Thinking. Crying. At least with the way that I was crying nobody sat near me. Nobody asked me if I was alright either. Bastards. Never expect anything from anyone.

My own parents abandoned me as well. As soon as they found out that I was pregnant and not only not married, but unlikely to get married. If I did get married it wouldn't be the baby's father. They didn't want anything else to do with me again. Bastards.

I was on my own. I was still heavily in love with Jim. I don't think that you can just fall out of love with someone. Like a switch being flicked off.

I could have had a termination. I couldn't have had a termination. It just wasn't the kind of thing that I could have done. I couldn't have done that and lived. He could have been adopted. I couldn't see that happening either.

He was the only part of Jim that I had left.

I went through the pregnancy on my own. What other choice did I have? I don't remember that much about the birth. Maybe I don't want to.

I loved Jim so much. He broke my heart. There is no other way of saying it. I was thinking of him more than anything else. They kept telling me to be calm. I was calm. Then they told me that I had a son. They told me he was sickly. I wasn't really taking it in. The grief of losing Jim and being a single mother was too much for me. They told me that I had to name him. All I could do was say the name of my one-time lover.

Not because I wanted them to name him after him. But because he was the only thing that I was thinking about at the time.

When I found out that they had named him Jim I was horrified. It was bad enough that my heart was aching with every second of the day. Now not only did I have a son to remind me of Jim all of the time, but they had also named him the same. I reversed his name to Mij or Midge. Made things a little easier to bare.

Not much though.

I know that I had my son. I couldn't really relate to him though. He reminded me so much of Jim that it hurt. The older he got the more he looked like him. That made things even worse. It was unbearable.

Anyone who dismisses the ache that can come from the heart has never had to experience it. I lay on my bed most of the time wishing my heart would break. Let me die. I never had the balls to take my own life. I was happy to die naturally though. I just wanted it to hurry up. I was not so lucky.

I was facing my future alone. Not with the husband that I had so wanted. My parents had outcast me. What else did I have? What hope did I have? I know I had Midge. I know I was a shit mother. I just couldn't handle it. I couldn't handle how much he looked like Jim. He had the same eyes. Jim had broken my heart. I didn't want the same thing from Midge. You don't get what you wish for in this life.

I know that I created a distance. Between Midge and myself. I couldn't help it. I know that he wasn't to blame. He reminded me of Jim so much that it was painful. There was not a single day that went by without him reminding me of Jim. He never knew. Poor little sod. He never really stood a chance with me as his mum.

I was a distant mother. I was distant from life in general though. The pain was extreme. It never got any better. It only got worse. Each day became a struggle. Harder and harder.

I tried drink to make it better. It didn't. I tried drugs. Bit of cannabis. Nothing too serious. I am not proud. It didn't make me better. It dulled the pain when I was out of it. I always had to come back to real life though. The drugs and booze helped me hide. Helped me to forget who I was. Helped me to forget the past. Helped me to not give a shit about the present. Helped me forget that there was a future.

They tell me that this was a very wrong thing to do. They say I should not rely on drugs to forget or dull the pain. Then they put me in here. And give me drugs. Why is this world so fucked?

I went a bit hippy like. It was an alternative thing. Alternative to having to face the real world. I didn't really know what was going on. It didn't really matter.

There were men who were interested in me. I didn't want to know. After Jim and what had happened I didn't want to be with another man. I didn't have sex again. No sex before Jim. No sex after Jim. Some thought I was at it. I wasn't. It didn't interest me any longer. Never had really. I was only ever interested in the one man.

From time to time I came out of the fog of alcohol and drugs. When that happened I tried to smarten myself up. I would put better clothes on. Make-up. Try to look normal. I remember one time doing that when Midge was at school. I made an effort to talk to the staff and the other parents. Trying to be nice. For some reason Midge just seemed really pissed off with me. I have no idea why. Seems like there is nothing that I can do right.

Live with it.

I am sure nobody would have believed that I wasn't having sex. I don't care. People can think what they want to. My parents thought I was a slut for what I did with Jim. They probably weren't the only ones. People are funny like that. Always quick to make judgements. It's what we do. People can't seem to believe that you can't be having sex. That you are not interested. Some live for sex only.

I know Jim's mother didn't like me. She made it as clear as anything. She didn't think I was good enough for Jim. Nobody would be good enough for her son. His dad was good though. He was understanding. He wasn't a demon. She was a dragon. I bet she loved it when I disappeared from the scene.

It would have been worth turning up on their doorstep in my most pregnant state. Just to see the look on her face. It would have been magic. His dad might have been better at it. Might have helped me out. Maybe I should have gone to him. Too late now.

Too late now for a lot of things.

Either way I didn't go and see them. I didn't tell them about their grandchild. I didn't tell Jim about his son. Should I have done? Some say I should have done. I had no right to keep it a secret from them. I did. If your own blood can cast you out then why should anyone else give a toss?

No one in this world that you can rely on but yourself. I gave Midge his independence. I knew he would be better off without me. He would be better finding his own way. Some of it was because he reminded me so much of Jim. It hurt. Not his fault. Somehow, I started to blame him for the break-up though.

Jim must have known I was pregnant. It freaked him out. He couldn't cope with it. It made him run away. If we could have talked.

Explained it. Come up with some way that we could have dealt with it. Together.

Or maybe if I had not stopped taking the pill. Maybe then none of this pregnancy thing would have happened. We would still have been together. We could then have faced children together. At the right time.

Life is full of lots of big ifs.

It took me a long time to admit that I was ill. But I was. Things started to get on top of me. It was becoming more difficult with each day. I know it started with Jim. I suffered trauma at his loss. It was as if he died. The loss of a partner though break-up can be just as bad as grief from death.

As far as I was concerned Jim was dead. I had no one to share my grief with. I had to bare it alone. At the same time as having to deal with being pregnant. I then had to deal with the fact that I had a son. I didn't have a husband. He didn't have a father.

There are so many lies in life. People lie about everything. People lie all the time. Some big lies. Some little lies. Some lies to hurt people. Some lies to try and not hurt people. We all do it. If we say we don't then we are lying.

Get it?

I told a big lie. I didn't tell it for anyone else but myself. I told Midge that his father was dead. I told him this because it was easier for me. If he knew that his father was still alive he would want to see him. I am sure he would have done at some point. If he saw him that would mean I would see him. I couldn't face that. Not again.

Better he thought him dead. And that being an end to it. I thought it would be easier. I told him that he had been killed in a car crash before he was born. I made up all the details about it. After a while I started to believe it. It made sense. As far as I was concerned his loss had been like death anyway. He might as well be dead for real. I believed it.

The more a lie you tell the more difficult it is to ever go back and tell the truth. Once you go down the path of lies you can't go back to the truth. Not without looking like a twat.

Midge was born the day John Lennon died. Can you believe that? My biggest hero. In some ways I felt that if Midge hadn't have been born then John wouldn't have died. It's like there is only enough room in the world for so many people. If someone comes into it then someone else has to go out of it. One in and one out. That is the way of it. Midge entered so John had to leave.

Simple as that.

This created a distance between Midge and me. More of a distance than there already was. If that were possible. I could have tried to explain all of this to him. I would then have to admit that his father was not dead though, but was very probably a bum bandit. I thought it might be better that he thought he was dead. Hate me for it if you will. I don't care.

My depression because of all this grew. I admit that maybe the alcohol and the cannabis didn't help at all. It might have made things worse. It became more difficult though.

The social services got involved and we were given a nicer house to live in than the commune that we had been in before. I missed the people. They had been a distraction. Even if they had not helped me in any other way.

I am not a fan of the social services. Not for nothing that their initials are SS. I say no more about it.

It was the start of the real decline for me. I had been suffering from depression. I see that now. The drugs made it worse. They added paranoia to the mix. Difference was that it was not an illusion. People really were out to get me. Were talking about me. Hating me. Whispering about me behind my back. They never stopped. They all did it. All the time. It was getting worse.

I didn't have anyone to talk to. That's what I think was worse. I had nobody that would understand. Nobody I could talk to. Get it all out in the air. Stop things from getting out of hand. From all the building up that goes on inside. Like a kettle before it boils over. Or explodes.

That's what happened. I boiled over. Couldn't take no more. Bound to happen. Nothing that could be done to stop it really.

I had what they like to call a breakdown. Wasn't my first. It was the biggest though. Midge was away at university. I made a rod for my own back. We were so distant. If we had been closer he might have noticed when things were wrong with me. He might have seen things were different. He might have been able to do something.

As it was we were so distant he wouldn't have noticed if I had grown another head. I wouldn't have noticed if he had.

I couldn't cope anymore. He was at university. I sold the house and left. Another thing that I shouldn't have done in my life. Can't change it now. I thought it would be better to just make a clean break. For both of us. Cut the ties.

I knew Midge would cope better without me in his life. I knew that I might be able to cope better without him reminding me of Jim every time I saw him. It might not have been the best thing that I have done in my life. It made sense to me. At the time. I ran away. Simple as that really.

You can't expect someone who is thinking irrational thoughts to act rationally. The SS didn't care any longer. Midge was away and old enough now to be an adult. Out of their care. Out of their responsibility. Out of their interest. Fend for yourself.

I have not seen Midge since. I hope he made a better life of it than I did. Wouldn't be hard.

I wish I had made a better life of my own. I know that I don't feel 55 years old. I know it is only the strange old woman in the mirror who reminds me. I still feel like I should be younger. But I know that I am not. Deep down. Where did all the years go? How did I get to be here so fast? What happened?

I have spent so many years of my life. Wasted so much time. Wasted so many years. What do I have to show for it? I had no idea that I was pissing so much of it away. Not at the time. I do now.

What use is that knowledge to me now? I wish I could go back to the beginning. Start again. Get it right this time. Make the right decisions. Live without the arrogance of youth. The arrogance of youth that throws away time with the sure knowledge that there is plenty of it left. Until one day you wake up. And there are less days ahead of you then there are behind you. Where did it all go wrong?

When I can I ask what the meaning of it all is. I can't always remember to ask. Not these days. Why do we do what we do? We run around on the face of this planet. Preoccupied with our petty matters. None of it really matters. It is all a huge waste of time. There must be more to it all than what we do all the time. I don't know what it is.

I didn't run away. Not really. I ended up here. They thought that I needed to have myself looked after. I thought I did as well. I did.

I came here voluntarily, you know. It seemed to be the safest thing to do. I knew that I couldn't cope any longer. The first step towards getting better is to admit that you need help. Right? I needed help. I admit that. The breakdowns were becoming more frequent.

I knew that I couldn't cope on my own any longer. Too much of my life was spent on my own. I made so many mistakes. If only I could go back to the beginning. Do it all over again. Only this time do it right. Not make the mistakes. Live each day for what it is really worth.

Do you ever wish that you could go back to the start? Do it all right this time. Maybe keep the things that you have learnt. Do it all again with the knowledge? Get it right this time.

What if you can't though? What if this is it? Even if you went back and did it all again you still ended up where you are now? You could never learn from the mistakes. You were just destined to live them over. Time and time again.

I ended up in here. With Doctor Rubesh. He looks after me. Apparently. I think they tried to help me. I think they tried to make me better. I don't think it worked. They tried lots of therapy. I think that is what they were doing. I don't remember. It was all kinds of different things.

I don't think any of it worked. I don't feel any better. They don't think I want to be better. Not trying hard enough. I heard them discussing it once. Heard them discussing me. Like I was an experiment. Or something. Not a human being. Maybe I haven't been a human being for some time. They dehumanize you. I am not even sure if that is a word. But that is what they do.

The therapy didn't work. They talked. A lot. Then they talked some more. Not even sure what it was that they were talking about. I switched off. Just let them ramble on after a time. Nod your head and make noises now and then. They seem content with that.

I probably shouldn't have said that. Rubesh will not be happy with that. Some people don't like the truth.

I think they ended up just giving me pills. Give me pills and shove me away in a corner. Forget about me. I am here voluntarily. I can leave any time I want though. Would have to get off the pills though. They make me so tired.

I regret some of the things that I have done. There I have said it. I know I did it to protect myself. I know I was selfish. I know I could have done better by Midge. I just didn't know how. It was too difficult. I tired. I really did. I was a crap mother. But there was no one to give me lessons in how to do it. There was no one to point the way. Tell me what to do. What not to do. I was on my own. And I messed it up.

Maybe it wouldn't have been any different if I had been helped. Maybe I would still have ended up here. Maybe there would still be a son that I didn't know. Who probably hated me. I know I acted like I hated him. I didn't. I know it may sound cruel but I was not entirely sure that I loved him. Not enough. Not because of him. But because I had used up all my love on Jim. I don't think I had an ounce of love left in me. Not after everything he took from me.

He left me a husk. Maybe he didn't mean to. But he did. I had nothing left for myself. Let alone anyone else. I regret that. I regret that my heart was given away. That it was shattered. And it left me with no heart for anyone else. Not even my son.

Is that why I have to suffer? Because I didn't love my son? Like a mother should? Is it cosmic justice?

No. No. No. It's not my fault. I didn't do it wrong. I know where it went wrong. I know where the decay started. I know where the world fucked up. That is where the problem lies. Not with me. Not my fault. What chance did I have? Really? You see I have had lots of time to think about this. Lots of time when I am just sitting here. Nothing else to do. Nothing else you can do. And I have been thinking. It took me a while. But I finally worked out where it went wrong. I know what the start of it all was.

It was when Paul left. That was when the whole thing started. If Paul hadn't of left then John wouldn't have died. None of this would have started. I am sure of it.

You know there are strange people here. Some of them I don't think are all that right. In the head. I think they have other realities. Someone is hiding them from the rest of us. But I know they are there. It isn't easy.

Not easy at all. Not so easy living amongst people who are crazy. They have to be crazy. I know they are. Cos, I got it right. They got it all wrong.

They don't see it. Why would they? They just go about their lives. If you can call it that. Funny thing lives. Not much of a life in here. Most of them live from one meal to the next. Doing nothing in between. You don't have to be in here to be like that. I know enough people who do that. No matter where they are.

At least it's warm though. Most of the time. Somewhere warm to sleep. Don't have anything to worry about in here. Not really. Not above the usual anyway.

Some people in here will never leave. I don't know if they know that. I know that they will never leave. Poor bastards aren't safe to leave. Not safe for themselves. Not safe for others.

I don't suppose that they are criminally insane. That is the term I heard Rubesh use. He doesn't keep people like that here. They have to be taken to real safe places. Some of them that are here are funny.

Ady plays with himself all day. I mean *all* day. He doesn't do anything else. I still think he does it when he is asleep. He has to be drugged. His cock gets inflamed. I heard them talking about it. Laughing at him. He had to end up here. Something went wrong in his brain. He just pulled his cock out one day and started to wank it. At the bus stop. Never stopped since. Didn't even stop when the police got him. He could get a gold medal for it.

Terry likes to dress up. Nothing wrong with that. Each to their own. As they say. He likes to dress as a woman. That's up to him. Trouble is he don't go buying the clothes. He steals it from washing lines. From anywhere he can. Can't stop stealing it.

Sarah is my friend. She is married to the Prime Minister. She writes to him every day. Grieving that they are apart. She also writes threatening letters to the person who thinks that she is his wife. Threatening her for trying to take her place. I don't think the staff here post the letters. She posted them herself when she didn't live here. That's why she now lives here.

Some like me can leave when they want. We are here because we want to be. Others would be arrested if they tried to leave. They have no choice. They have to be. I think they will be here until they die. Then they will probably bury them here.

I am here voluntarily. I can go any time I like. Just tell them that I want to leave. Probably have to sign papers. Saying I won't blame the staff if I go mad again. They would have to let me go. Would be illegal of them to keep me. I could walk out the door. Tomorrow.

But where would I go?

Twenty-Two
Midge

I was rather shocked to see my mother again after so many years. She looked old. I suppose she was. Older than when I last saw her at any rate. I suppose it didn't help all that much that we spent so little time together when I did know her that I probably didn't pay all that much attention to her at any rate.

Her hair was grey now which I am pretty sure that it wasn't ten years ago. The decade had aged her a great deal. She couldn't have been more than in her mid-fifties somewhere by this point.

She sat in a high-backed chair which was vaguely pointed in the direction of the television set which droned on in the corner. The entire room was depressing to be honest. She didn't respond to us at all. We tried to talk to her, but she just sat there starting into space not looking at anything at all. She didn't respond to anything either. It was simply like she was not there. She was an empty shell of the person that she used to be.

It was dispiriting for us. It must have been soul destroying for her, that is assuming that somewhere locked inside her brain she was able to know what was going on and who she was. I could only hope that whatever catatonic state it was that had gripped her had not just frozen the outside, but had also frozen the inside. I dread to think how terrible it must have been to be locked inside a shell. Seeing what is going on around you, but entirely unable to do a thing about it. Unable to interact with anything. Just watching the world go on without you whilst you were stuck behind a pane of glass.

I had been kneeling down beside her chair, trying to get her to respond to us, but there was not so much of a flicker across her face to show that she even knew that I was there.

'What's wrong with her?' I asked as I stood up.

'It's the medication,' Roger replied whilst looking rather bored as if it was a question that he had to answer a lot and found very tedious.

My father turned towards him with a look on his face that made me think for a moment that Roger was going to be needing a real nurse really soon. 'Is it your policy then to pump patients full of medication to the point where they are zombies?'

Roger sighed. Clearly this was a discussion that he had engaged in a number of times and was hoping that he would have been able to avoid once again.

'Lucy is often very agitated and becomes confused. At times she can be fine, reasonable even. Every now and then though she will have an episode where it will be necessary for her own safety and the safety of those around her for her medication to be upped to relax her. Until the episode is over.'

'Relax her? If she was any more relaxed she would be in a coffin.' My father was raising his voice by this point and I had noticed that there were a couple of patients in the background that had covered their ears and were rocking backwards and forwards slightly whilst incanting something. Probably something that they hoped would make my father disappear. To be honest from the noise that he was starting to make I could understand where they were coming from on that front and was starting to wish that he would disappear as well.

'Perhaps if you are not satisfied you should see Doctor Rubesh,' Roger stated with the air of someone who was about to pass the problem people over to someone else in the hope that it would cease to be his problem any longer.

And so it was that we found ourselves in the office of Doctor Rubesh, a man who appeared to be fast advancing towards his retirement. As we sat opposite him I found myself wondering what it must be like to be a mental health practitioner all of your life and then perhaps face dementia or some kind of mental health as you get older. Suddenly to find yourself as a patient rather than the doctor. Helpless to the whims of another doctor and yet at the same time knowing exactly what it is that is going on, well for a time at least.

Doctor Rubesh appeared to have been hasty in his shaving that morning as he had missed several little bits of stubble that were dotted about his cheeks and neck, here and there like small islands. Perhaps it was a style that he opted for rather than an indication of haste.

Strangely enough he seemed to opt for having his head titled to one side as well for the entire duration of the time that we were talking to him. It vaguely reminded me of looking as if someone had cut the string that held his head fully upright and he was semi collapsed. I suppose there was a possibility that he might have been having a stroke, although if he was he didn't seem to be all that bothered by it.

'What's wrong with Lucy?' My father demanded after the pleasantries were out of the way and we had declined a coffee.

'Quintessentially,' he said as he interlocked his fingers and looked at us over the top, 'depression is the problem.'

'Depression?'

'Yes.'

'Is that all?'

'Oh, let me assure you that there is nothing trivial about depression. It is something that comes in many guises. Many shapes and many sizes.'

'Forgive me though,' I said trying to understand the world, 'but there are many people who are suffering from depression in the world and they don't end up in a, in a, well in a…'

'A mental institute?'

'Yeah, a place like this.'

'Well, of course, what you say is true, Mr McKenzie. Not everyone ends up in a place like this, as you call it. That is true. There are cases where it becomes more extreme and it is necessary for the person who suffers from the illness to be placed in an institution such as this one in order to be looked after and treated.'

'Forgive me doctor, but it didn't seem to me out there that Lucy was receiving all that much treatment, nor did she particularly look like she was being looked after all that much.'

'Well, I suppose that it might look like that, but I can assure you that it isn't the case.'

'I hadn't even really considered depression to be a mental illness anyway.'

'Oh, but of course it is. I grant you that there was a time some years back when depression was not considered to be all that much of a mental disease. Not unless you were suffering from severe depression, of course, but times have changed now and we recognise that all forms of depression are something that need help and treatment on.'

'You must be very busy then?'

'Oh, we are. As I said though there are those that don't need to come here. Those that can be treated successfully at home with medication or with outpatient appointments. It is the more extreme cases that come here.'

'You are saying that Lucy's case is extreme?'

'Yes. Some of the people who come here are suffering from all sorts of different ailments, not just depression. You see, some of the people who come here are treated and recover enough to go back into the world and live normal lives.'

'Right.'

'And then there are the others who I am afraid will never be able to return to normality but will remain here for the rest of their lives.'

'Lucy will have to remain here for the rest of her life?'

'It's likely.'

'This is presumably because my mother is more than a little down then?'

'I take it from your questions that you don't know anything about Lucy's condition?'

'No. We have never been close.'

'No that is clear. Well where to start? Where to start?'

'At the beginning?' I was getting a little tired of Rubesh, particularly as he had adopted a tone of self-righteousness, which I really didn't think suited him at all.

'As good as place as any. Lucy was admitted to us after being detained by the police under the Mental Health Act.'

'She was involved with the police.'

'Yes. As I said they detained her under the Mental Health Act.'

'And what does that mean?'

'The police have the power to detain people that they think are acting in an irrational manner or perhaps seem like they may be a harm to themselves or others. They then take them to a hospital where they are assessed by a number of people, a psychiatrist, a social worker and a GP. All three of these people have to agree with the original assessment of the police in order for the individual to become sectioned, as it were.'

'And if they don't agree with the police?'

'There are other options. They might get the person to agree to voluntarily admit themselves for treatment. That does, of course, mean that they are free to leave whenever they want, whereas someone who is sectioned is unable to leave. We have sectioned people here as well as those who are here voluntarily.'

'And Lucy is here as what?'

'Lucy is sectioned. Lucy can't leave at all. If she were to try to leave she would be stopped and if she somehow managed to get out of the hospital then we would inform the police and they would find her, hopefully, detain her and then bring her back.'

'That sounds serious.'

'Oh, it is Mr McKenzie, let me assure you that it is.'

'What did Lucy do to be detained by the police in the first place?'

'Suicide attempt.'

'Suicide?' We both said it at the same time.

'Yes.'

'How?'

'She attempted to jump off of a bridge over a duel carriageway.'

'What?'

'Oh yes. Very popular form of suicide, I am led to believe. In many cases it is just a cry for help as if they really wanted to jump there wouldn't be anyone able to get there quick enough to prevent them from doing it. It does seem though that jumpers do pause at the moment of truth. Partly this is because they might be waiting for someone to talk them down, these are the ones who are there to cry for help, of course. In other cases, I suppose it is a philosophical moment of reflection before the end. Difficult to really know as these are the people that end up on the concrete, of course.'

'Good God.'

'Yes, there are many forms of suicide, of course. Hangings, pills and so on. Trains are the most reliable from what I understand.'

'Trains?'

'Yes, there are few people that survive jumping in front of a train. I have always worried about jumpers, of course. Too much time to change your mind on the way down, I suppose.'

'As fascinating as they may be to you, do you think we could concentrate on Lucy?'

'Of course. It was not the only time that she attempted suicide. She had been brought in by the police a number of times.'

'She wasn't sectioned the first time then?'

'No. It is actually very difficult to section someone. The reason for this is historic.'

'Historic?' I was getting very confused by Rubesh's ability to dart his mind all over the place without seeming to make that much sense.

'Yes, you see the Mental Health Act and associated legislation is there to protect individuals. In the Victorian period, for instance, a husband could section his wife almost entirely on a whim and on his say-so without so much as a care as to whether she was mentally ill or not. Many people who were not suffering from mental illness ended up in the most appalling conditions merely because they were inconvenient to their relatives. Thankfully all of that has changed now.'

'So eventually she was sectioned?'

'Yes. After a period of time it became clear that she was determined, if not efficient at trying to harm herself. Since she has been here she has from time to time attempted suicide again, which is why she has to be watched most closely.'

'And being drugged to the eyeballs?'

'A temporary measure. Lucy is not always like that. Every now and then she has episodes where she falls into really very deep depression and at times she develops her suicidal thoughts again and will do almost anything she can to try and harm herself. She can also move between being lethargically depressed and actively violent. When she becomes violent she has to be sedated. For her own sake as well as the others around her. She will lash out at anyone. The sedation will not last all that long. Just until she has overcome the episode and returned to normal. Well, what passes for her as normal at any rate.'

'Oh Jesus Christ.' It was all very upsetting but was upsetting my father even more than me.

'And there is nothing that can be done?'

'Lucy has sadly not responded to treatment as well as we would have liked. In many ways it is as if she refuses to get better. She is locked within herself and determined to punish herself in some way.'

'What is to be done then? You just going to feed and water her like a pot plant?'

'It is a rather sad if accurate analogy, Mr McKenzie. In many cases there are patients here who are exactly as you say and there is nothing that can be done, but to feed and water them. To try and look after them the best that we can. There is little else that we can do.'

Rubesh then pulled open a drawer in his desk and brought out a sheath of papers, A4 about twenty pages or so. Neat tiny handwriting.

'I tried to get Lucy to write down her thoughts some time ago. I thought that it might help her to understand her feelings better and perhaps by putting her words down on paper she would somehow purge some of the more negative feelings that she had been having. It was not entirely successful, but it might make an interesting document for you to read so that you can perhaps understand things a little from her point of view. I have had it transcribed for you as the handwriting can be a little erratic.'

He peeled away some sheets from the back of the pile and handed them over to us.

'As you are next of kin I don't have a problem with sharing this with you. Normally, of course, such things would be confidential, however in her more lucid moments Lucy said that she would be happy for you to have this if you ever found out where she was and came looking for her.'

'Will we be able to see her, in her more lucid moments?' I asked whilst taking possession of the papers. Rubesh lent back in his chair and laced his fingers again as if he had been asked the most important and the most dangerous question that anyone could have asked him.

'I am not entirely sure that would be a good idea.'

'Why not?'

'Once you have read the document you may understand better. I think that Lucy seeing you in particular,' he said indicating my father, 'might be extremely detrimental to her well-being.'

'Really?'

'She took the break-up with you all those years ago very badly I am afraid. There is no telling what would happen to her if you suddenly appeared in her life again. Either of you really, I suppose.'

'You think we should keep away? Just abandon her here?'

'Lucy abandoned her life. She ran away from it. She tried to run away from it in the ultimate way by killing herself. I don't think we should rush anything or force her into something that she was not ready for.'

'Why did you let us see Lucy today then?'

'Because I knew that in her medicated state at the moment she would not recognise you at all, and I thought it was important for you to see her.'

'Well, we have that.'

'Indeed.'

The conversation seemed to have come to its natural conclusion and despite this Rubesh didn't seem to make a move to usher us out of his office or for anything else to happen. He merely sat there with his head on one side looking at us as if we were a particularly interesting specimen. I began to think that if we were not careful and stayed much longer then there was a chance that Rubesh would seek to section us as well and keep us all in his little nursery of insane people that he waters and feeds like flowers in a greenhouse encouraging us to grow and be less crazy.

It was time to leave. There was nothing else that we were going to gain from being there.

***

My father and myself read what my mother had to say in the car outside of the hospital which was looking more like a prison than it had done when we first went into it.

I think it is fair to say that it entirely devastated my father.

'I had no idea that she was that much in love with me. That obsessed about it all. I can't believe that I was breaking up with her when she had come to tell me that she was pregnant with you.'

'It's not your fault, dad, you weren't to know.'

'What a fuck up.'

'It is that.'

I had no idea the things that were going through my mother's mind. I had always put her down as being useless. I had no idea that she was suffering from mental health issues. I had no idea of the struggle that was going on in her own head.

It just goes to show you that you can never fully understand anyone else. You can only be aware of your own head and what is going on in it, and it seems that there are times when you can't even be sure of what is going on in your own head.

I suppose that it is fair to say that after reading what he had we were both feeling pretty guilty about our own involvements and judgements that we had made about my mother in the past. I had made many judgements in the past about my mother and the things that she had done and the decisions that she had made in life. Seems I was not always entirely correct in my assumptions.

Perhaps there is a lesson in there that we can all learn.

Twenty-Three

Another Christmas came and went followed by a New Year that took us into 2010 which was once again a year which sounded so futuristic that it seemed to be an impossibility. I spent the last few weeks of 2009 having radiotherapy on the area that they had operated on. Having removed the tumour from my neck they then bombarded the area with their special rays to try and treat the surrounding area in the hope that the cancerous cells (which they were still not naming as such) would be destroyed before they had the chance to spread.

You might think that I am passing my treatment and cancer related incidents by rather quickly at this point. I suppose it is because I want to skip over it and talk about other things at the moment. I still haven't really got into the idea of spending a lot of time talking about my illness and the associated things.

I don't think it does me any good to dwell on them all that much. I have always wanted to focus on other things in life. I suppose the chief thing that I tried to focus on was my family life with my beloved wife Mary and the fast-growing Jessica who was soon going to be old enough to go to school. Hardly seemed possible at all really.

I suppose I was also still trying to work on the 'great unfinished novel' as I had started to call it for want of anything else to call it as I had not come up with a title at this time. I hadn't really come up with all that much at all if I am honest. I was having enormous trouble with finding my narrative voice which is one of the first things that I really have to get my head around before I start filling up that dreaded white page which brightly glares at me whilst the cursor button flashes tauntingly, daring me to start filling the page with words.

Like many writers before me and no doubt after me I would also spend a lot of my time finding distractions to divert me from having to start putting the words together. There are times when I think that the main preoccupation of a writer is finding something to help delay you from actually having to get down to the writing. This could be anything at all from surfing the internet to staring out of the window. There are many other degrees of time wasting that the really committed writer can get down to. It takes a lot of time and effort to be able to find things to do to delay the inevitable.

I often found that once I was in the zone and the words had started to flow then I was alright. The difficulty for me was the first word of the first chapter of a new work. You had all the ideas of what it was about and probably you even knew where it was going, but that didn't mean a thing until you put the first words down on the page. They were probably going to be the most important words of the entire novel. What's my point? I will tell you.

The first words you write are the most important because these are the ones that have to grip your reader into wanting to read more. Rather obvious really when you think about it. These are the words that will not only determine whether your reader wants to read more, or will discard your novel, but also whether the casual browser in the bookshop will decide to buy your book when they come across it and flick it open to the first paragraph and have a read. Your first words are your biggest selling point. Get them wrong and the game is over.

It doesn't just begin and end with the casual browser in the bookshop either. That casual browser who wasn't interested in your first paragraph will probably remember it and won't even bother to pick up your second one; assuming you are lucky enough to get a second one after your first screw up.

The thing is there are a lot of bad books out there. Maybe that is a little too harsh. There have been times when I had read a book and wondered how the hell it got published. It is especially annoying if the person is younger than me. That's not the point though. The point is that publishers publish all kinds of books and you are not always going to get on with it. Does that mean that the book is bad or it is just not suited to your taste? Opinion is somewhat divided. However, it is true that someone, somewhere, saw something in it that made them want to publish it. It doesn't necessarily follow that you will agree. If we all agreed then it would make for a very boring world.

The introduction of books being sold in supermarkets at half their cover price or less is a God send to the kind of person like me who likes to experiment. Luke dislikes supermarket books as he feels that they are undercutting the bookshops and will eventually lead to their extinction.

I can see his point, but then it is up to the bookshops to compete. Why would I pay twice as much for a book in a bookshop if I can get it half the cost in a supermarket whilst buying my milk?

At any rate what's my point? I will tell you.

Cheap books in the supermarket give the avid reader like myself a chance to buy books for less than the cover price as an experiment to see what they are like when normally we probably wouldn't have bothered at their full price.

There have been times when I have made some great discoveries by doing this and there have been other times when I have given up on the book that I am reading. I tend to read the first fifty to one hundred pages. If I reach the hundredth page and it is still not gripping me then I give up and push the book on to a charity shop somewhere.

Luke thinks this is an appalling thing to do. He thinks that if you start reading a book then you have to read it through to the end regardless. I totally disagree with this. I am of the opinion that life is short and literature is long. If by one hundred pages into the book I have not got on the same page with it then it is time to put it to one side and move onto something else.

That's what a writer has to face. The ability to grab the reader and then keep them. It isn't as easy as it sounds. You try it.

***

Something else that preoccupied me around this time was my mother. I have to admit that in the past I hadn't spent a lot of time thinking about my mother. I have not had all that great an opinion of her, as I am sure that I have demonstrated by now and I had not forgiven her for apparently abandoning me, leaving me homeless and being distant from me all of my life.

Having read her views on her life I began to understand a little more about my mother and how she hadn't entirely been selfish and vicious all of my life in the manner that I had previously assumed that she had been. You might argue that it didn't change all that much, but it made me feel as guilty as hell.

I suppose that you could argue that the revelations from my mother changed my attitude and relationship towards my own daughter, but I don't think that is really the case. I always think I had a positive attitude towards my lovely Jessica. Unlike some parents though I didn't really feel the need to spread endless pictures of her all over social media, nor did I think that there was a need to update everyone on each little thing that she did from teething to farting every fifteen seconds.

Parents, you must learn that no matter how taken you are with your little child and how over the moon you are with them, nobody else gives a shit and endless pictures and updates just bore the hell out of everyone else. Before we had Jessica, I used to get very irritated by people who paraded their children around like they belonged in a little club and were showing off their offspring as if to prove to everyone else that they had at least had sex once in their lives. It was an attitude that I was very determined to ensure that I kept away from when I became a parent myself. All in all, I think it is something that I have largely achieved and managed to steer myself away from becoming a baby bore.

Many parents say that this is how they will act, but I have to tell you that they almost always fail to achieve it. Why you feel that we should have to be interested in your children is a mystery to me.

Being the kind of person that I am I also read to Jessica every single night a bedtime story. I started this when she was far too young to understand anything that I was saying. I would read her Dickens at that point because the words were not as important as the tone of my voice and getting her used to the rhythm. Some people might think that this was a complete waste of time, but I felt it was something that was essential to her development as well as a defining part of our relationship.

As she became older the stories changed to something that she had more of a chance of understanding. I never had bedtime stories read to me and it is amazing really that I turned out to have the love of reading and books that I now have. I was determined that things would be different between me and my own children.

I think teaching your children to have a love of books and reading is one of the biggest legacies that you can ever pass on to the next generation. Take note of it, people. There are far too many people out there who don't know what a book is. Don't be a lazy parent and think that it is the job of teachers and school to educate your children and that you don't have to play a part in it. From my own experience schools are not enough alone to provide the education that any half decently ambitious child would need.

What's my point? I will tell you.

Get involved. Simple as that. Life is too short to have regrets later in life about what you should have done with your children. Life is too short to mess about with things. I certainly have never wanted to look back at the end of my life and regret that I didn't do some of the things that I would have liked to have done, or that I wished I had done.

There is no telling people though, you really have to make your own mind up about these things. Remember when you were kids and all the adults tried to tell you what to do and how to do it and you thought it a load of old rubbish and that you would do things your own way, and then when you got older you realised that they were right all along and that it would have saved a great deal of time if you had just listened to them in the first place? Nobody ever does though, do they?

I suppose that is what it is all about. You have to go through life and make your own mistakes. Where would be the fun if you got it all right the first time around?

Jessica was now old enough to start school. I mentioned earlier about parents now falling into the trap of leaving everything up to the school when it comes to educating. I know that there are many parents who have done just that. I made sure that when she went off to school she had the knowledge of the alphabet and had some degree of ability to read and write. This may have put her slightly better placed than some of her school friends as I know for a fact that some of them turned up to school with hardly the ability to wipe their own arses.

I suppose I shouldn't moan. Each to their own at the end of the day and if you want to raise your children in a certain way then who am I to argue it over and say that I am right and you are wrong?

Jessica was starting school. I suppose that is the most difficult time for a parent. Up until that time you have a better control of your children and then all of a sudden you have to hand them over to some strangers. You have to let them out of your control for several hours a day and hope and trust that they will look after them in the way that you would want them to.

In many ways it is a nightmare for most parents. For over protective parents it must have been something that was a complete nightmare. I have no idea how they manage to get through their day. Perhaps they spent all of their time some distance away from the school carefully observing it through binoculars in the hope that they would see their child.

I wasn't really as bad as that. My main concern about Jessica being away at school was that the school might not have been educating her to the standard that I would have liked.

I think education has changed a great deal over the years and I think a lot could be achieved by going back to teaching the basics. There seem to be many that don't benefit by old fashioned things such as learning grammar, knowing the history of your own country and knowing about maths.

It seems strange that history is not taught properly any longer. It seems to be as if as a country we have become ashamed of what we are and we are frightened of being patriotic in case we are considered to be racist. We are afraid of our own past, ashamed of who we are and who we were. I think a lot could be gained by learning history from the beginning upwards.

Children used to leave school knowing about grammar and mathematics and who the kings and queens of England were. Did this make them monsters? What do they leave school knowing about now? Buggered if I know. Seems to be unpopular these days to be educated in the good old-fashioned way.

I can't think for you, I will have to let you decide for yourself and make your own mind up about these things, but you decide if we are better off the way that we are now or whether we would now benefit from some good old-fashioned education once again.

At any rate I digress, as I am afraid I seem to do rather a lot of. The point that I was trying to get across was that I was hoping that Jessica would have a better time at school than I had. I suppose I wasn't prepared for school and then when I did get there as I have documented already there were problems and I was bullied and in general had the most miserable time that I could have imagined. I had no desire for Jessica to go through with what I had put up with in those years.

Adults at the time would tell me that it was the best years of my life, which was in my case at least complete bollocks, but I could see that there were possibilities when it could have been the best years of your life in the sense of lacking in financial worries and with no real responsibility. I wanted Jessica to at least have a better chance than I had when I was her age. I at least tried to prepare her for school and what was to come. I wanted her to enjoy school. I wanted her to make friends and enjoy learning. I wanted her to have all the things in life that I had been deprived of in one way or another.

***

'So, how are things going?'

'Things are going well.'

I had told my father time and time again that everything was fine, but it is as if he didn't believe a word I said, or perhaps thought that as a parent that had missed out on most of my life, it was now time to make up for the lost years by asking how I was every few minutes.

That actually sounds a bit harsh. I can't really blame him for worrying. After all he hadn't known about me for most of my life and his. When he did finally get to meet me within a very short space of time he finds out that I have cancer and risks losing me all over again.

'Are they really going well?' We were having a coffee in our favourite coffee shop.

'Yes, Doctor Moody has told me that I am cancer free.'

'He has?'

'Yes, it was the first time that he had ever used the word "cancer". I was rather amazed.'

I was rather amazed. Throughout the whole time from speaking to my GP through to the consultations, operations and radiotherapy the word had not been mentioned at all. Not so much as a hint of it. It was almost as if none of the medical staff wanted to tempt fate by mentioning the word, but now that the all clear had been sounded they felt that it was finally safe to talk about what they had been trying to keep hidden for all the time.

I had been declared free of the dreaded little disease. After my therapy I had returned to the hospital on a weekly basis for further checks, which had then extended to monthly checks. At my last check I had been told that all things being equal I could now move to six monthly checks. If these continued to be fine then they would progress to annual check-ups which could then be downgraded to five yearly. All in all, it was looking rather positive.

'It's good news. How do you feel about it all?'

'I feel good.' It was true. I did.

'Quite a scare that we all had there for a while.'

'Well, there is nothing to worry about. I plan to be around for a very long time to come.'

'I'm pleased to hear it.'

My father was concerned about my health there is no doubt about that in the slightest. The topic that we were really dancing around though was my mother. Our visit to the hospital had shook us up a great deal.

'So then.' I started.

'Yes.'

'Well.'

'Indeed.'

Clearly it wasn't going to progress all that far along those lines.

'I spoke to Doctor Rubesh again,' my father suddenly said surprisingly bringing us directly round to the subject that we had been dancing around.

'Oh?'

'He thinks that it would be a good idea if we didn't try and visit your mother.'

'Yes, he said.'

'He thinks that in her moments of being medicated it would be okay, but when she is lucid enough to know what is going on around her then she would find visits from us rather disturbing.'

There might have been some truth in this when you took time to think about in a rational way, but it wasn't necessarily possible to view it all that rationally when you first encountered the idea.

'Who the hell is he to tell me that I can't see my own mother?'

'I suppose, he thinks that he is the doctor in charge and acting in her best interests.'

'The man is a fool.'

'As true as that might be he is also someone that is in legal charge of her at the moment. His request that we keep away from your mother could just as easily be a demand that he has the power to reinforce.'

'This entire situation has been screwed up from the beginning.' I was aware that my father was looking uncomfortable. 'You really wanted to see her didn't you?' It suddenly occurred to me that there might be someone in the world who had a bigger stake of claim on my mother than myself.

'Yes, I did. It was horrendous seeing her like that, after so many years. She was hardly recognisable. Not the person that I knew all those years ago at all. Either physically or mentally, it would seem. It was something of a worry really. Very distressing.' He sipped his tea and tried not to look too miserable.

'Did you ever wonder what it would have been like if you had stayed together?'

'From time to time. Not all that often, if I am honest with you. I think there comes moments in life when you look back and think about all your past loves and encounters and wonder what it would have been like if you had stayed together, or if things had worked out differently between you.'

'I have never really had that much experience on that front. Mary was my first and only love really.'

'I envy you that. True love is very difficult to find. If it does come along then it comes along once in a lifetime, if you are lucky. If it does come along then you've got to grab it with both hands. You had the sense to do that. Never let it go, Midge.'

'I have no intention of doing so.'

'To answer your question though. I don't think that things would have worked out between us. I am afraid that I just wasn't compatible with your mother. In order for things to have worked out between us then it would have been necessary for a lot of lying, on my behalf at the least.'

'Yes, I suppose so.'

'A life of lies. Some might say that is the basis for most relationships, but I think it would have been a lot worse in our case, don't you?'

'Yes, I suppose so.'

'So, I made the decision to tell her the truth about me so that we wouldn't have to face the lies that would have existed if we had stayed together. Ironically my telling the truth to avoid lies just resulted in a life of lies anyway. Life is funny like that.'

It certainly is.

'I will say one thing though, Midge. If it's for the best that we stay away from your mother then I think it's something that we should do. I, for one, think that I've caused her more than enough pain already without appearing and then stoking it all up again.'

I nodded my head, not feeling that there was really any argument that I could use against it. Perhaps it was for the best after all.

'We're agreed then?'

'Yes. Let's leave her in peace. Whatever peace she can find in the present situation. If she ever comes around to being better than Rubesh will know where to find us, I suppose.'

'Of course he will.'

We had come a great distance and had achieved hardly anything. Or at least that is how it felt. And that seemed about all that you could say on the subject.

'Dad there is something that I need to tell you, well want to tell you, really.'

He looked at me in a slightly worried way as if for a moment he was afraid that his own genes had influenced me and I was about to tell him that I was coming out.

'Oh?'

'Mary's pregnant.'

He looked completely taken aback for a minute. I guess that all of the things that he was likely to think that I was about to say this hadn't been one of them.

'But that's fantastic news.'

'I think so. You're going to be a grandfather. Again. Only this time you can be there from the beginning.'

I honestly don't believe that the smile on his face could have grown any bigger than it was at that point.

Twenty-Four

'Can you believe all of this crap?'

I looked up from the book that I was reading to see Mary becoming very frustrated with the television. It was something that she often did. I would say that it was a fair hobby of Mary's to get her frustration out at the television whenever she could. Most of the time she watched the news and it gave her something to rant at, but at other times I think she deliberately watched soap operas and reality television so she could rip them to pieces. She seemed to enjoy it, which is fair enough.

My own enjoyment of the visual media, which I grant you had never been all that great in recent years, had taken a total dive since I had seriously got into my writing. The problem with working closely on something that you are passionate about is that it can destroy the same medium when seen elsewhere.

What's my point? I will tell you.

Because I spent so much of my time writing and being involved in it all you tended to notice bad writing when you saw it and it was usually on television that you saw it. Bad writing coupled with bad acting was a complete recipe for disaster in my book that covered at least most of the soap operas being aired, if not a great deal else.

I had a few script ideas for some of the soap operas which were unsuccessful in getting accepted. Largely this was because they usually involved most of the cast dying or there being some disaster which would wipe the entire place off the face of the Earth. It worked for me, but I don't think the producers were keen on the idea, which just looks narrow-minded as far as I can see.

The problem was that if writing was good writing then it could be so good that you didn't notice how good it was because it was just natural. Who'd be a writer, huh?

The thing that had got her annoyed this time was politics. I could understand that if I were honest, it is something that gets me annoyed all the time. What had particularly got her annoyed now was the 2010 General Election campaign. Let me put you in the picture in case you are unaware of it, have forgotten about it or couldn't have given a toss about it in the first place.

The Labour Government that had been in power since 1997 was in its final death throes. What had chiefly killed it was the premiership of Gordon Brown who had taken over, or seized power greedily with both hands, depending on your point of view, from his predecessor Tony Blair. Blair had gained a terrible reputation, after starting off well, due to the war on terror when it appeared that Saddam Hussein was not hiding weapons of mass destruction in his kitchen. Blair's reputation was tainted, but began to recover surprisingly quickly when it was revealed exactly how incompetent his replacement really was.

I call him incompetent on at least three counts. The first, the country was in an economic meltdown. The politicians liked to disguise the disaster by calling it a "credit crunch", which in some way made it sound less like a global economic disaster and more like a breakfast cereal. High street shops as famous as Woolworth's had gone under and were never to be seen of again. Brown reacted by trying to blame the Americans and in general not accepting the fact that as someone who had been Chancellor of the Exchequer since 1997, and therefore in charge of the finances for the country, he might just have to accept some degree of responsibility for the fact that we were all financially screwed over now. This was something that didn't seem to have occurred to him though. Instead he just kept stating over and over that when it came to the crisis he was "the right man for the job", which was all very well, but then he just kept saying that and never did anything about it.

The second reason was that he appeared to me to have been someone that had been working behind the scenes to gain power during the decade of Blair's premiership and then the moment that he gained that power and was in charge, it was as if he really didn't know what to do with it and couldn't handle the pressure. He seemed to slowly go to pieces.

Which leads me onto the infamous third reason for why I thought he was no good as Prime Minister. It came less than a month before we all went to the polls. Brown had been on the campaign trail and had forgotten that he was still wearing a microphone when he returned to his car and had a private conversation with a member of his staff where he described one of the Labour voters that he had just met as a 'bigoted woman'.

This was a major cock up and above all else could well have cost him his seat in number 10. We all know that politicians think little of us and are only using us to step on whilst they are on their way to gaining power, but this time we actually had proof of what they thought about us when they thought we couldn't hear them.

He immediately went to the woman's house and apologised to her (well, he did something to her for forty-five minutes behind closed doors) and then emerged with the remains of his career in his hands trying to put a brave face on it all despite the fact that the woman refused to come out and shake hands with him for the cameras. If it had been me that he had spoken to in that way then the cameras would have been treated to me slamming the door in his face and not letting him in at all.

It was a disaster and the final nail in his political coffin. It must have been clear to everyone that from that second onwards they were looking at a Prime Minister who was in the dying weeks of his premiership. You could almost have felt sorry for him were it not for the fact that he had shown the world that he thought he was arrogant and above it all.

And so, it came to the big General Election. Labour were pretty screwed thanks to Brown, but the other parties all suffered as well. This was largely because of the huge expenses scandal that had taken place where it was revealed that the majority of the MPs were all corrupt and had been claiming expenses left, right and centre in an attempt to line their pockets with our money.

As a result, there was a general feeling of antipathy towards the entire thing. People were just losing interest in voting for these people that didn't give a flying bollock about us. The upshot being that no one political party gained a majority that would mean that they could out rightly form a government on their own.

Now this should really have acted as a warning and you would have thought that the politicians would have all thought seriously about the fact that they had lost the faith of the people. Sadly, their arrogance had gone too far though. Despite the fact that Brown had to all intents and purposes lost the election he clung to Downing Street with bloody fingers until he had to have them ripped away. He tried everything he could to cling to power rather than do the honourable thing, which he should be lucky was to walk away and not go around the back of the house and blow his brains out; which would have been an action which would paradoxically have probably won him a few extra votes.

The 'crap' that Mary was referring to was the fight that had taken place between the main parties to try and jump into bed with each other to form a collation government which was the only alternative because no one single party had been put above the rest.

Eventually the Conservatives and the Liberal Democrats had been the ones to join forces together. David Cameron the leader of the Conservatives had joined up with Liberal Democrat leader Nick Clegg. Cameron had probably made the decision because he wouldn't have wanted to join with Brown (who would probably have still wanted to remain PM under any collation agreement), and Clegg had probably agreed because he realised it was as close to real power as he, or his party were ever likely to get.

The particular 'crap' that Mary was talking about was the press conference that the dynamic duo were giving where they couldn't have looked more uncomfortable if they had tried.

'Look at them,' she continued whilst eating pickled onions which was her current pregnancy eating fetish. Didn't make for great kissing. 'Clearly they hate each other; it's sickening. They both hate each other and yet they really want power that much that they are prepared to join forces to get it.'

She had a point. Watching them you could see the resentment literally dripping off Cameron that he was unable to be having this press conference in his own right, rather than having to stand there and share the glory with someone else. I can't remember the details now, but I remember a joke being made and Clegg saying something along the lines of that he would be off then. Cameron, in a rather sickly way, said 'No, come back.' It was said in a rather sickly way because you knew that he hated saying it and that he had really wanted to say, 'Yes, go on fuck off then.' Problem was that he knew that he needed Clegg as his minority government would have only lasted a few months without him. You could just tell how much he hated it.

'I can't see these two lasting,' I said with a mild amount of disgust whilst looking at the screen.

'Just two shits that pass in the night? You'd like to think that this election will be a humbling experience for all of them and they will make some real changes so that in five years we might actually think that some of them are worth voting for.'

'Not very likely though is it?' I returned to my book, preferring to bury myself in the pages of my book rather than listen to another second of the lies and arrogance that was pouring from the television set. It amazed me why it was that Mary put up with it when she so clearly hated them.

When it came to politicians though I think we all hated them.

***

Mary was indeed pregnant as I had stated earlier and we were going to have a second child.

'Do you want to know the sex?' The burly nurse had asked us when Mary was having one of her scans. I could never make sense of those scans. People who were expecting birth would proudly display a scan picture and it would mean absolutely nothing to me, I could make no sense of it at all. Problem is you didn't want to look like you could make no sense of it and end up hurting their feelings so you would coo and ahh over it and in general make it feel like you appreciated what you were seeing. It was not the time to say things like 'Oh he has your eyes,' though that would come later.

I was a parent, but I had still not fallen for the little click that seemed to form around some new parents who seemed to think that they suddenly belonged to a club that non-parents were unable to join. These were the social media pests. I tended to keep well away from it all.

But did we want to know the gender of our child before they were born? It was a difficult one. This seemed to be a reasonably new thing that had come up over the last generation or so. I don't think it was something that my mother would have been asked, but then it might have been something that she wasn't really all that keen on knowing anyway.

I suppose it was a matter of convenience these days. Parents of my own parent's generation would have had to try and cater for either gender appearing. Neutral colours in the nursery and clothing etc, although I really have no idea why it is that we are still so sexist with gender-colour assignment when it comes to children. Hardly sets a good message up for the rest of their lives. Now that you know the gender in advance you can orientate your nursery and clothing etc to the sexist notion that somehow takes your fancy.

We decided that we did not want to know the gender of our child. I think that the reason for this was because it somehow seemed to be tempting fate or unlucky to know what the gender might be before you found out the natural way. You might think that silly, but that was the way that we were thinking.

If I thought that having been through it once already would make it any easier the second time around then I was very quickly proven that I did not know what I was talking about. What amazed me was that having been through all the pain of it all the first time around Mary was prepared to go through it all again. I was buggered if it was something that I would have done a second time. I had to think myself lucky that Mary didn't decide to crush my testicles between two bricks whilst I had been sleeping to ensure that she didn't have to go through it again.

I mean, don't get me wrong I am glad that she didn't and I can't say that I wouldn't have blamed her if she had of done, because of course I would have done. I mean killing your partner's testicles is a few steps above talking things over isn't it.

And then Joseph came into our lives. A small bundle of pink fun. I had the most wonderful daughter that I could ever have wished for and now I had a son. I suppose there are those out there who make fuss over there being a preference in gender, but it isn't something that ever bothered me.

Being the more introverted book reading kind of person I never had any desire to run around kicking footballs. I could see that there were some fathers or would be fathers out there who desired to have a son so that they could impart what it meant to be a lad to them. That is all the world needs; the next generation of thugs and football hooligans raised to be brain dead by their brain-dead fathers. I also think that I wasn't Henry VIII so the requirement for a son was not so pressing for me as it had been for him.

I might be being a little harsh here about this as I am sure that not all fathers act that way to their sons. It is just an impression I got from the many that I bumped into over the years at hospital and schools. I can only speak from my experience, and if that offends you then I am sorry, but write your own book and put your own opinion forward in that.

I can honestly say that with both Jessica and then Joseph I didn't care in the slightest what gender the baby was. I am sure that Mary felt the same. All that you wished for was a healthy baby.

So, I was a father again at the age of thirty. I was there for the birth once again and this time I was joined by my own father who was able to see his first grandson coming into the world. Our family was growing.

Thirty years old! I could hardly believe it. I was no longer in my twenties and it shook me to the core to think how time was flying and how much I had gone through in the last ten years. My twenties had certainly been a busy time. Most of it had been fantastic, but not all of it by any stretch of the imagination. I will be honest that there had been times in my twenties when I really didn't think that I was going to make it to see thirty. There is always hope though. There is always a chance in life.

***

The phone was ringing. It was unusual because the landline almost never rang. The only people who rang the landline were cold callers, business calls or my grandmother who didn't seem to believe in anything as modern as a mobile phone.

I had just got in from the hospital from a visit to see Mary and Joseph. Thankfully now that I had an extended family I had managed to con my grandmother into looking after Jessica whilst I had paid the visit to see them both. Normally I would take Jessica with me as she had developed a very quick bond with her little brother and seemed to want to take care of him. From time to time though it was nice to be able to use the services of an unpaid babysitter. Ask any parent.

As I walked through the door carrying a selection of the cards and toys that we had been sent at the hospital the strange object that I kept in the hallway was ringing. I picked it up before it went to answerphone.

'Hello, is that Midge?' I didn't recognise the voice on the other end and was about to say that I didn't want whatever it was that they were selling. Nevertheless, I confirmed that it was me that was speaking rather than asking who wanted to know or what it had to do with them, which was my usual stock answer over the telephone. I guess I was probably just feeling in a really good mood at the time.

'It's Mari, my love.'

Who the hell was Mari? She must have sensed the lack of understanding from the silence that came from me. 'Mari Jones, you know Gwyn Jones' wife?'

It all clicked into place, of course my old English teacher's wife. I had been confused as it was the last voice that I had expected to hear and the one that I had only heard the once when I had met her at the hospital and given her my number in case there was anything that she wanted from me to help.

'Of course, Mrs Jones. Sorry I was a little flustered there. Mind on other things, took me a little while to place you. What can I do for you?'

'Oh, you can't do anything for me, love.'

I wondered why it was that she was calling me then, but I was polite enough to not say anything and to allow her to get out whatever it was that she wanted to say.

'I just wanted to let you know that Gwyn passed yesterday.'

'Passed?'

'Yes. He died, my sweet. It was a very peaceful end and he didn't suffer as much as he could have done. I thought that you would like to know.'

I thanked her and asked her to let me know about the funeral arrangements as I hung up.

It seems that there are times that whenever you are feeling on top of the world there is always someone who comes along and kicks you in the knackers. Seems to be something about the universe wanting some form of balance, I suppose.

The loss of my old teacher and mentor, the only one who had really believed in me when I was younger hit me like a blow from a sledgehammer. I would never have thought that it would have done, but it did. It quite clearly knocked me sideways.

I thought for a moment about what Mrs Jones had said. The timings were just about right. Mr Jones had died at about the same time that Joseph had been born. I remembered what my mother had said in her scribbled words. She had blamed my birth as a cause for the death of John Lennon. She had made some comment about the fact that as one person came into the world another person left it. That was the true cosmic balance. I wasn't sure that I believed this as people were dying and being born all of the time. In my irrational state though it seemed to make a degree of sense as if that was exactly how the universe was run.

That December evening had never felt so cold to me as I sat in the hallway.

***

I decided that I would go to the funeral on my own. I thought it would be better for Mary to stay at home with the kids so soon after having given birth, but I had not counted on my wife's persistence and determination. She reminded me that it had been her sitting next to me in Mr Jones' English class that had really got us together in the first place; or at least got us moving in the direction that we had ended up in. We had a lot to thank Mr Jones for and Mary was not going to miss out on paying her last respects to him.

I have learnt that it is easier to just give in and agree with my wife when she has made up her mind about something. So it was that we both found ourselves wrapped up in our warmest clothes on that cold December morning. There was a deep frost that had come down overnight and had left a covering over the landscape which under normal circumstances might have been considered beautiful.

The coffin looked so insignificant when it was carried into the church to the strains of 'Men of Harlech'. My mind wandered throughout the service as I remembered all the help that I had been given over the years from Mr Jones. Without his inspiration and support I doubt that I would ever have had the courage to try and become a writer.

I looked around the cold chapel. A cold miserable December morning made even colder by the marble chapel that had undoubtedly been designed to try and make it difficult for the congregation to fall asleep during boring sermons. I looked around the chapel and observed a few of the teachers from the school when I had been there. I had no particular desire to see them as I had little respect for them as the only teacher that I had cared about was the one who was now in the coffin that was before us all.

It occurred to me as I looked around the chapel that funerals were really things that were planned for the living rather than the dead. Most of the time it was the living that planned the funeral rather than the dead who planned it the way that they wanted to before they had died. In most cases it was left for those that were left behind to sort out something that they thought that the deceased would probably like.

The service concluded rather more quickly than I had imagined and I was wondering if I had been daydreaming and had missed most of it. I tended to find that I often drifted away when there was any kind of religious service these days. A price I paid for getting older and not believing as much as I used to.

The coffin was shouldered once again and slowly left the chapel to the sound of 'All Through the Night'. I ambled out with the rest of the congregation and found myself bumping into Mrs Jones.

'Oh, hello my lovely, it was lovely of you to come.'

'I wouldn't have missed it for the world. He meant a great deal to me.'

'I am only just beginning to realise how many lives he touched. It is a very humbling experience.'

'Mr Jones would probably appreciate the quotation from Shakespeare if I were to say "he was a man, take him for all in all, I will not look upon his like again".'

'He would have liked to hear you say that, I am sure. I hear you have had a little boy?' I had no idea where she got her information from, but despite the death of her husband she certainly seemed to have her finger on the pulse of what was going on. 'What's his name?'

'Joseph.'

'Ah, that is a lovely name isn't it?'

'Yes, we went with Joseph. Joseph Gwyn McKenzie.'

For the first time in the brief time that I had known her she seemed to be entirely lost for words at this unexpected development. I am sure that she appeared to be crying slightly as well as she moved away to speak to the other mourners.

Twenty-Five

There is more ignorance in the world than there is intelligence. That was one of the things that I most remember Mr Jones saying to me. If I remember correctly he was making the point during a lesson on free speech; which again was something that I imagined the School Governors would have been horrified if they had known he was teaching us; it was something that was most certainly not on the school curriculum. I would imagine that if news ever reached government then we could expect a visit from John Major at any time during which we could expect a stern talking to and finger wagging.

'More people burnt *The Satanic Verses* than read it,' he stated whilst leaning back in his chair and surveying the entire class with a professional eye of a top-notch teacher in action. 'There are people who always seem quick to attack rather than to use their brains. I do not mean to demean the death threats and life that Mr Rushdie has had to live under since the fatwa after the publication of his book, but as a writer there are several things to be thankful for.'

He had a point here. For the first instance a book that would have received medium coverage in the press and publicity was suddenly catapulted to become a household name. You couldn't pay for such publicity as people desperately tried to get hold of a copy to find out exactly what it was that all the fuss was about.

The fundamentalists, largely being in the camp of ignorance rather than intelligence, also failed to realise that they had to go and buy the book in order to burn it in the streets, thus continuing to pay the wages of the author. As far as I am concerned you can burn millions of my books if it means you have to buy them beforehand.

'We shouldn't ban publications,' Mr Jones had continued. 'Whether they are books or newspapers, we should never ban them. Banning them means we curtail the freedom of speech.'

'Well, what do we do about such publications that are hateful or dangerous?' one of the pupils had ventured.

'Don't buy them.'

This was also true. We risked much in what we might term a civilised society if we were to turn around and start banning things that we didn't agree with. Personally speaking, and this is just my personal opinion, I dislike the *Daily Mail* newspaper. I think that it is a sensation grabbing, fear provoking publication that is designed to stir up the unintelligent masses to fear the differences in society. I feel that in many regards it is a dangerous publication as there were those out there who would religiously buy it and believe everything that they read within its pages, no matter how rubbish it was.

The solution therefore was not to ban it, but to simply not buy it. For the rest of the time it remained opium for the masses, as you might say.

The important lesson to be learnt was not to curtail your activities as a writer because you fear that it might be offensive or might cause trouble. It was the responsibility of the writers of this world to stir up thought and make people think. Without the Salmon Rushdies of this world we would all be doomed to believe the same thing and to go about our lives like drones. We needed people to stand up every now and then and shake our world. We would then either settle back down afterwards feeling more content in what we had believed in that it had survived such a threat; or we would realise that our beliefs were false and we would go off in a different direction, perhaps until such a time as another writer popped up to shake the new beliefs as well.

'However,' he had continued looking sternly at the class as if we had all committed a terrible error that would never be corrected. 'It is important to remember that although we may mock some of these institutions, if Shakespeare were alive today he would probably be writing soap operas.'

'Well I suppose he might be if he were that hard up for money,' responded the same pupil that had stuck his nose in before.

'Possibly, but although we may not consider it High Art there is nothing wrong with writing for a daily rag or for weekly television. There are many unemployed writers out there that would kill for the chance.'

I missed Mr Jones a great deal and it was true that I would never see the like of him again. No matter how long I lived.

***

There are times, I have noticed, in life when everything is going well and then all of a sudden there comes something that will shake you up and kick you in the teeth once again to remind you that you are not meant to be going around having an easy time of things.

'I am afraid that it isn't the greatest news that we could have hoped for.' We were back in Doctor Moody's office following one of my regular check-ups that I was required to have and it had to be said that these were not the words that you wanted to hear from your cancer specialist. We both sat patiently waiting to hear what the news was going to be. 'Your latest test results indicate that the cancer is back.'

I don't know if I was more shocked by the fact that the cancer was back after being free of it for almost two years, or that I was more shocked by the fact that he had used the forbidden word for the first time in the long history of me having this illness.

I supposed the return was something that had been at the back of my mind as something that I always expected. I maintained that I still felt that cancer was something that never truly went away. You could be free of it for years, maybe even decades, but it would always get back to you at some stage and continue where it left off. I was rather hopeful that one day they would develop a cure that would stop it in its tracks and kill it off permanently. For the moment the only thing that medical science could do was throw it off its course and give the sufferer a few more years.

That does sound rather defeatist. Just because of the fact that Doctor Moody was telling me that my cancer was back did not mean that I was ready to go and lay down in a coffin. I had become clean of it once before and I could become clean of it again. I announced this fact to Doctor

Moody who smiled and nodded his head as if I had answered a particularly difficult maths question to his satisfaction.

'So, what is the plan? Another operation? More radiotherapy?' Having been through it all before I can't say that I particularly relished the idea of having to go through it all once again. However, if that is what was required than that is what you did. It was as simple as that.

'It's not as simple as that,' Doctor Moody stated whilst looking through his notes. 'We will need to run some more conclusive tests to be certain and to get a better picture of things, but my own personal opinion is that we are unlikely to be able to gain anything further from what we have done before and we may be required to consider other measures.' For some reason as he said this I felt that what Doctor Moody was really missing was a pipe. He seemed to have been someone that I would have imagined would have been happier with pipe in another era. You might ask why it was that I had time to think about this, given the news that he had just given me. All I can say is that the brain works in mysterious ways.

I won't bore you with the tests and procedures that Doctor Moody had in mind for me. I had done most of them before. It made me feel like I was a guinea pig once again in a laboratory where I was poked and prodded by various different doctors, nurses and technicians who all had their own agenda. It was rather difficult to keep track of everything that was going on and I found that it was often better to simply submit to what was going on and hope for the best.

I had a lot of blood taken from me once again and not for the first time I wondered how much blood you would get if you were able to put together all that they had taken from me over the years. I imagined it would be enough to earn me several blood donor points.

The strangest thing of all was that now that I had been told that I was sick once again I did not feel sick. Before when I had gone to see the doctor, I had been motivated because of unexplained tiredness. I didn't feel any different this time around to how I would normally feel. Yet here I was being told that I had cancer, again. It just goes to show you that you don't have to look sick in order to be sick.

One thing was certain though and that was that I was fed up with hospitals. I had spent a lot of time in them over the last few years, for my own issues and then pacing up and down in maternity wards. I would be pleased to see the back of them entirely, if that were ever possible.

The tests were rushed through rather quickly. I was worried about this as whilst on the one hand I was pleased that I didn't have to spend a lot of time waiting around for appointments to come through, on the other hand it was worrying that they obviously deemed it serious enough to move quickly rather than having me waiting around for months. Difficult to really know how you feel about these sorts of things really.

I was pushed around from department to department as they all had out of me whatever it was that they wanted. I felt like a pin cushion for most of the time. All of the time that this was going on the one thing that kept popping into my mind was Mr Jones.

It wasn't the best of thoughts as regardless of how brilliant he was as a teacher and a mentor for me, he was dead. I remembered the last sight of him (well his coffin) as he was lowered into the cold December ground. I wondered how hard it must have been for the gravediggers to dig into the frozen ground for the grave. I imagined that they probably used mechanical diggers now instead of the old-fashioned shovels. Everything moves on and advances in life; accept for those who are left behind in the holes that remain.

It seemed so surreal seeing that coffin being lowered into the ground slowly whilst the priest muttered words that I was not paying attention to. I had never really been to a funeral before. Having not had the relatives around me when I was growing up I had not had the experience of grandparents and distant relatives dying. There was a distant interest in the procedures that were taking place. It was surreal because I couldn't quite get my head around the fact that there was a human being in the box being lowered in front of me. In that box there had once been a living human being, that I had known and spoken to. It didn't seem possible to me.

Not perhaps the best of things to be thinking about when you are laying in hospital whilst being scanned to see how serious your cancer was. Chances were it wasn't really going to be all that serious.

'It's quite serious,' said Doctor Moody whilst looking through his notes and the test results on the computer screen in front of him.

'How serious?'

It seemed like a rather daft question really when you think about it. Was there such a thing as non-serious cancer? Could you have cancer that no one was all that worried about? It all seemed a little daft to me. Doctor Moody was someone who obviously realised the daft nature of this question so he didn't seem to dignify it with an answer.

'The tests results have shown that the tumours have spread,' he swivelled the monitor around so that I could see a cross section of the scans that were on the screen. He used the tip of his fountain pen to indicate things on the display which frankly meant nothing to me whatsoever. 'You can see from this area on here the amount of growth that we have seen.' I couldn't see a thing, but I didn't really see the point in telling him that.

'What do you suggest we do about it then?'

He turned his monitor back towards him again.

'From what I have seen there is nothing that we can gain from an operation. An operation in these circumstances would achieve nothing, and if I am honest would be too difficult. The disease is too wide spread for an operation to be successful.'

I couldn't help but notice that we had moved away from using the C word once again. I am not sure if that meant that things were even more serious than I thought they were.

'Radiotherapy?'

He winched slightly as if he had caught a nail, or something like that. 'Radiotherapy might achieve partial results, but from what I am looking at here I think we will get the most benefit from chemotherapy.'

It was then that, regardless of all else, I suddenly realised just how serious matters were. Having cancer, in any form is serious, but I had always viewed chemotherapy as the last line of defence. The worrying thing was that beyond chemo, there was nothing.

'It is a game changer,' he continued. 'We are going to need you to take a course every day for six weeks. It will by necessity take over your life.'

It might take over my life, but I knew then and there that it wasn't going to be something that was going to define who I was. There are people out there who become defined by whatever illness it is that they have. The response to every question is about their illness. They don't mean it. It might not even be something that they intend to happen, but their illness, obviously cancer in my case, becomes the thing that guides their life and determines who they are. Every answer is framed around it.

I have seen them in hospital waiting areas. People ask how they are and they answer by saying how many days they have been cancer free; or they are asked about who they are and they answer by talking about their diagnosis as if they weren't a person before that date.

I had no intention of being reduced to just a disease.

***

The regularity with which I was required to take the chemotherapy meant that by necessity I would have to take time off work. I didn't like taking time off work. I grant you that I had never really considered my work as the key motivation in life and yes I liked to consider writing as my main work and being a librarian as something that I had to do in order to pay the bills until things got better, but nevertheless I was dedicated to being a librarian and I liked to do my work with professionalism, and that didn't mean taking days off 'sick' because of a hangover, or because you just fancied a day off lounging in bed.

Under the circumstances though I didn't see how they could really argue all that much if I took time off. Partially, because of the fact that I would need the time off for that amount of chemo and secondly because that amount of chemo was going to make me feel very ill indeed. I remembered the side effects that Doctor Moody had explained to me. I knew that the future was not looking brilliant, but it was a future. Nobody was telling me that I was on the path to following Mr Jones.

I have used a writer's trick here though to compress time. Mr Jones had died at the end of 2010, when Joseph was born. It was a year later that I had been having the discussion with Doctor Moody. It is amazing how you can do such a thing with a few taps of a keyboard and a whole year has passed in the blink of an eye.

I don't mean that to imply that the year was entirely unimportant that there was nothing that happened. It just means that there were other things that were taking up my time during that period, and that the things that were going on were perhaps not too much out of the ordinary.

Time is a funny old thing though. Have you noticed how time can change so much? I am not saying that there was nothing uninteresting that happened in that year since Mr Jones had died and Joseph came into our lives, but time has a habit of slipping away from you if you don't keep a firm grip on it. Seconds make up the minutes which move into hours, to days, to weeks, to months and then suddenly you look around and everything has changed.

There are some things that never change though, like Mrs Van Hopper for instance.

Twenty-Six

I was rather surprised, if not annoyed when I walked into my office a few days later and found the ample frame of Mrs Van Hopper who had somehow managed to squeeze herself into my desk chair.

I try to go through life with a live and let live attitude. I would hate to think that I have any prejudices against people, and I would not like to think that I have a habit of being nasty to anyone or causing pain. I may not be governed by any particular religion, or philosophical doctrine, but I simply try to go through life doing the best that I can and trying to make sure that I can be the best person that I possibly can be.

On saying that though, I took one look at the frumpy Mrs Van Hopper sitting in *my* chair and I wanted to rip the bitch's head off and use it to play football with.

'Oh, Mr McKenzie,' she stuttered whilst having the decency to try and stand up. I say try and stand up as she had managed to wedge herself into the chair in such a way that when she tried to stand up the chair tried to come with her. 'I wasn't expecting you.'

'Evidently. I am not dead yet, Mrs Van Hopper; no matter how much you may wish it were otherwise.'

'Head office said you had taken a period of sick leave.'

'I have. I've come to get a few things from my office. If that is alright with you, of course.'

'Of course.'

How gracious of the bitch.

'Head office have asked me to take over. Whilst you are away, of course.'

'How gratifying for you. You will be able to call the police for every misdemeanour that you come across now, as well as ensuring that the Bible is in the right place.'

'There is no need for that tone,' she sniffed and gave up all efforts to get out of her chair and sank back into the leather with a creak that was somewhat alarming.

'Mrs Van Hopper. You may be sitting in *my* chair, in *my* office, but regardless of all of that you are not, I would remind you, *my* boss.'

She gave me a look as if to say that this was only a matter of time and I inwardly cursed myself for losing my temper with her. She really wasn't worth it. I tried my best to ignore her, which was a little difficult to do and was like trying to ignore the Moon. Silence prevailed in the room for a little while before she decided to break it once again.

'I heard that you are ill.'

'That is why I am taking sick leave.'

'I don't hold with these new-fangled medicines. Putting your faith in all these doctors and hospitals and so on. It's a big mistake if you ask me.'

'It's fortunate that nobody did ask you then.'

'All these medicines and injections. It will kill you as good as anything.'

'I suppose you favour alternative medicine then, Mrs Van Hopper?' I was trying my best to ignore her and was collecting things from around the office, but she was really starting to irritate the living shit out of me. She had been doing that for some time if the truth were known, but it was now *really* starting to get to me.

'You could do a lot worse than to take the alternatives, as you call them, Mr McKenzie.'

'I think I would rather put my faith in modern techniques, thank you all the same. It is the twenty-first century after all, not the sixteenth.'

'You might as well be for the good that the so-called doctors will do you.'

'They are not "so called doctors", Mrs Van Hopper, they are doctors. They even have the certificates to prove it.'

'A piece of paper will not tell you anything. Using these harmful chemicals to cause you further ill if you ask me.' It would do no good to remind her once again that she hadn't been asked. 'Pumping your body with those harmful chemicals and then you wonder why you die.' I decided against pointing out to her that if you died from it you wouldn't have the time to be wondering why you had died.

'I suppose you would rather we all snorted crushed dandelion whilst dancing naked around the Maypole.'

'There is no need for that scoffing attitude, Mr McKenzie. And if I may be so bold as to say so, it is a mocking attitude like that which has made you the failure that you are.'

I was really doing a fantastic job of keeping my temper by this stage. I suppose part of the issue might have been that I was starting to feel so tired once again that all I wanted to do was to get my things and leave.

'It's a good job I don't have to answer to you then isn't it?'

'No, you don't have to answer to me. You have to answer to a much higher power than me, Mr McKenzie.'

This was something that I could really do without. Mrs Van Hopper and her holier than thou attitude.

'It is a judgement. You know that don't you?'

'What's a judgement?' I had a sneaking suspicion that I knew exactly what she was going to say.

'Your illness is a judgement. It is a judgement from God.'

Have you ever been in one of those situations where you are heading towards an argument and you can see all of the warning signals that you speed passed on your way to the argument? You know that you should stop before things get out of hand, but you know that you have no chance of stopping. The rational part of your brain (which is getting smaller by the minute) is telling you that this is not a good idea and that you should stop as you are likely to regret it, but the full momentum has picked up now and there is nothing you can do to stop yourself.

'God has nothing whatsoever to do with it, Mrs Van Hopper.'

'God has something to do with everything, I will have you know, Mr McKenzie. It is his judgement that marks us all, you mark my words.'

'Mrs Van Hopper, for once try and be rational. How the hell am I being judged?'

'God's judgement is on us all. We can hide as much as we like, but that is the way of things. Deny it as you will, but that will not prevent the truth from happening. You may be an unbeliever, Mr McKenzie, but that will not stop you from having to stand in front of your maker and justify yourself on the day of reckoning.'

'What is it that I have ever done to you, Mrs Van Hopper?'

She shook her head at this as if I was a naughty child that just couldn't understand the truth when it was presented to them. 'It is not me you have sinned against, Mr McKenzie. It is God.'

I had a feeling that it might have been. 'And how exactly have I sinned against God?'

'You are an unbeliever. A blasphemer. Remember when you mocked me for bringing that Bible to your attention that had been placed in the Children's Fiction section. Remember how you mocked me, and it?'

'Are you serious?'

'As you sow, so shall you reap, Mr McKenzie.'

'You are completely mad, aren't you?'

'Not me, Mr McKenzie. You have mocked the Lord, and now you are paying for it. It's judgement.'

'So you said.' I was trying my best to ignore her again. It was not as easy as I had hoped it would be.

'It stands to reason, Mr McKenzie.'

'I am sure you think so.'

'Our Lord is a kind and merciful Lord.'

'Doesn't sound it from what you are saying.'

'It is a just world, Mr McKenzie with a just God. A just Lord would not allow bad things to happen to good people. It stands to reason.'

'Does it now?'

'Indeed, it does, Mr McKenzie. God would not punish you with this illness were it not for the fact that you had done something to deserve it.'

'And you feel that I have done something to deserve it do you?'

'It is the only explanation, Mr McKenzie. There is no way that God would punish you if you had not brought it on yourself. It would be completely impossible for the world to exist if bad things happened to good people. You must have done something then. Perhaps it is because of your father.'

'My father?'

'Yes. I am led to believe that he is one of a perverted mind.'

'A perverted mind?'

'Deprived in body and in spirit, Mr McKenzie.'

'Do you mean because he is gay?'

'Gay! How dare they steal that word from us? Sin upon sin be on their heads. That is why they have the AIDS thing. It is God's punishment upon them for their unnatural acts.'

'And you feel that I am being punished because of my dad?'

'The sins of the father shall be visited upon the son. It states in the Bible that gayness is a sin, an abomination in the eyes of the Lord and they that indulge shall be punished.'

'You believe in the Bible do you, Mrs Van Hopper?'

'It is the word of the Lord and it is glorious.'

'And you follow the Bible and what it says?'

'It is the only way to a gracious life and to eventual salvation. One of these days I shall sit on the right hand of Jesus whilst your father burns in the fires of Hell.'

'Oh. Is that acceptable is it?'

'What?'

'To be sitting on the hand of Jesus? Having a fiddle, is he?'

'Outrageous. And you wonder why it is that you are being punished with the cancer of the Lord?'

'I only ask,' I said, ignoring her last comment, 'because you state that you follow the word of the Lord and that you abhor homosexuality because it is written in the Bible.'

'It is the word of the Lord.'

'And yet it also says in the Bible that you shouldn't eat pork, and yet I am sure I have seen you eating a bacon sandwich. It also says that if you work on the Sabbath then I have the right to stone you to death. Have you ever worked on a Sunday? I am sure you have in the past, and it certainly will be something that you will have to do if you want to sit in that chair.'

'Mr McKenzie –.'

'It also says in the Bible that I have the right to sell my daughter into slavery. Could you tell me how I should go about doing that?'

'You are being foolish -.'

'It also says if I remember correctly "thou shalt not make unto thee any graven image" and yet I see around your neck the crucifix, which unless I am very much mistaken is a graven image.'

'The devil speaks within you, Mr McKenzie.'

'Why? Because you feel you have the right to pick and choose what you want to follow and believe in from the Bible? Because you choose not to stick to the parts you don't like? Surely you believe in it all, or you believe in none of it? Either it is all the word of God or none of it is? What gives you the right to say which bit is the word of God and which is to be ignored?'

She looked at me with a degree of sadness upon her face that I found all the more irritating than any other look she could have given me.

'It would seem that you are further gone than I thought you were, Mr McKenzie. I shall pray for you.'

'I would rather you didn't.'

'The healing power of prayer is the only thing that will save you now, Mr McKenzie. You would do better to put your faith in that rather than putting it into doctors.'

'You are right about one thing.'

'And what might that be?'

'It is not a just world, Mrs Van Hopper.' I slammed shut one of the filing cabinet drawers that I had been looking in. 'If it were a just world, Mrs Van Hopper then they would have burnt you for being a witch years ago.'

***

'And then I walked out of my office.'

'Unbelievable,' Luke was sitting on the sofa in my living room whilst I filled him in on the latest developments. 'She actually said that?'

'Certainly did, and the sad thing, Luke is that there are more than enough people out there who are prepared to take that view.'

'It staggers belief in this day and age.'

The thing is that there was a lot of people out there who did take this view. I had done my research and I had learnt that there were a lot of people, like Mrs Van Hopper, who were of the opinion that the only way to justify the bad things that were happening in the world were to say that it was God's judgement on sinners. That is why people died from cancer and other illnesses. That is why they were punished. You could point out to them that this hardly justified the death or serious illnesses of young children who had surely done no wrong. The likes of Mrs Van Hopper would probably have stated that it was the sins of the father visited on the next generation. That was an easy way of proportioning blame. Go back far enough and you were sure to eventually find some kind of a sin that you could pin point to blame for something bad happening to someone otherwise innocent and blameless.

What's my point? I will tell you.

It was all a load of bollocks.

Bad things happen because that is the way that the world is. It is not the fault of anyone else. People get ill, they die. Bad things happen from genocides to natural disasters. Is it the will of God? Or is it simply that the world works on such a level that good things and bad things happen to people.

What you have to do is just try and get on with it the best that you can without feeling the need to blame it on someone else.

'Mrs Van Hopper no doubt thinks herself a good Christian,' I informed Luke.

'I thought that would involve comfort to the sick rather than telling them that they deserved what they got?'

'It would seem that this is not the case when it comes to Mrs Van Hopper.'

'All that natural alternative medicine malarkey. I bet if she were ever diagnosed with cancer she would go running to the doctors screaming her head off and demanding modern treatment and what science has to offer.'

'She is the kind of person that would accept what medical science has to offer whilst secretly taking the powdered testicles of newts on the side and when, if, she made a full recovery she would say it was thanks to the alternative medicine that she took rather than the efforts that medical science put into her.'

'Either that, or she is the kind of person who doesn't get sick at all.'

'No, you are probably right there.'

'God will probably get bored and just strike her down with a thunderbolt one day.

'I can't imagine that God is in any hurry to have her hanging around him for eternity, no doubt telling Him where He has got it all wrong. She will probably sleep easy tonight knowing that she has done her Christian duty in persecuting the unbeliever or whatever it is that she thinks I am.'

'Doesn't seem to me to be the kind of person that will be spending an awful lot of time in Heaven on the right hand of Jesus.'

'Well you'd better not tell her that.'

That was the thing though. I had met a number of religious people who thought that they were doing what was right by their God, when it really came down to the fact that they wanted to look in the community or amongst their peers, or whatever it was.

What is my point? I will tell you.

I have had many lessons in life and I have met many people of different religious and philosophical backgrounds as well as those who claim to have no beliefs at all. (No belief is, of course, in its own right, a belief). I have no problem with the likes of Mrs Van Hopper, or anyone else who firmly believes in something. Does it matter if some of the rest of us think that belief is wrong? No, not really. So long as you believe in it and are prepared to stand up and defend your belief if required, then that is fine by me.

I don't think that those of us who disagree with you have the right to try and stop you from believing whatever it is that you believe in. What right do we have to think that what we believe in is superior to what you believe in?

The flip side of that is that I do not believe that you have the right to force your beliefs on me, any more than I have the right to force mine on you. What a wonderful world it would be if we could just live in peace and harmony with each other.

The problem seems to be that there are too many out there who take the view that what they believe is right and there is no other way and if you aren't with them then you are against them. If you are against them then you need to be wiped off the face of the planet.

Doesn't give you a great deal of hope for the future really, all things considered.

Twenty-Seven

I tried my best not to be irritated by Mrs Van Hopper, but she is a difficult woman to be able to forget. I tried to put it to the back of my mind as I knew that I had other things to worry about at the moment, rather than what she was doing. There was a part of me though that couldn't get away from the fact that she was sitting in my chair in my office undoing what I had taken years to do; of that I had no doubt at all.

Even the most casual of reader would probably have worked out by now that Mrs Van Hopper and myself didn't see eye to eye about many things. She had resented the fact that I had been promoted above her and that I had made changes to the system to try and keep the library going into the twenty-first century when interests were elsewhere. I believed that without me there she would drag the library back into the Victorian age as quickly as she could. She would be too short –sighted to realise that this would mean job losses and possibly even closure of the library that I had spent so long in nurturing over the years.

It is difficult to sit passively back and see someone systematically destroy something that has taken you so long to create; particularly if it is something that you have lovingly laboured over for many years. Such is the nature of the way life is though.

Fortunately, I was not planning on staying away long enough to give her the opportunity to destroy everything that I had helped to create, but I knew that when I did return to my post after the chemotherapy I would have a long task ahead of me trying to correct the damage that she would almost certainly have done.

The therapy took a lot out of me and it made me feel very ill. Considering that I had not felt ill at all prior to being told that the cancer was back I found it ludicrous to find that now I was receiving therapy I was throwing up most of the time and the rest of the time feeling as if I had been run over by a very large truck. When I wasn't actually throwing up I spent a great deal of the rest of the time feeling as if I was about to throw up. I also felt so incredibly tired. I have felt tired before, but that was nothing to how I felt at the moment. I felt like punching the first person who complained of tiredness after one night's lack of sleep.

I also combated headaches that felt as if my brain was trying to knock through the bone and make its escape. It was terrible without a shadow of a doubt and it confused me greatly that the medicine felt worse than the actual illness had. My rational brain reasoned that if I had not undertaken this course of medication then it was likely that the eventual effects of the illness would have outstripped everything that I was going through now.

Many was the time that I, nevertheless, felt that it was severely unbalanced and I was prepared to chuck the entire thing in and go back to how I felt before, which was infinitely better than I felt now. At each turn though, there was Mary who stopped me and steadied my course, kept me on the straight and narrow. I freely admit that I couldn't have done any of it without Mary.

There are many things and times that I couldn't have done without Mary being in my life. She is my guide and shows me the way that I must go in all things. I can't imagine having been without her, and nor would I want to be.

It is true that I had gone sick from work, this was partly due to the fact that I was feeling so ill that there was no way on earth that I would have been able to have managed to get in each day and I would have found it impossible to have managed to get through the working day had I been able to, by some miracle, actually stagger into the office. The other reason being that I was required to go to hospital each day to receive my therapy.

It was impossible, therefore, that I should be able to work in any traditional sense of the word. I didn't want to lounge around the place feeling sorry for myself though, so I tried to write instead.

I couldn't do all that much at all. It is true that I was so weak and ill that I would write one word in the time it would have previously have taken me to write a sentence, one sentence for each previous paragraph and so forth. It was slow progress without a doubt, but it was progress none the less. I was actually doing something.

I cannot explain it, but I felt a drive to complete the novel and other work that I was in progress on. I felt I had to finish it. I suppose that there was something at the back of my head that was telling me that I should try and finish it all, just in case. Just in case it turned out that against my expectations I was not to have all that much time left.

Let me make it clear though that I was not a defeatist. I was not prepared to give things up, I have far too much to live for to be able to submit to the wretchedness of this contamination. Nevertheless, there was something at work within my soul that told me that I ought to get as much down on paper as I could. A precautionary measure really as none of us has any idea what the future may hold.

It might not make much sense to someone who is not a writer, but I was driven to try and continue with the creative process. To complete the work that I had started so long ago.

It was difficult getting through the chemo and took far too much out of me than I felt good it did in return. It probably is not the case, but that was how I felt at the time. I was able to make my way through it with the beloved support of my wonderful Mary, as well as my newly-found father and loyal friends like Luke. Then there was also Jessica and Joseph who spurred me on to get all of this behind me and not have to worry about it any longer.

In my darkest moments, and there were many of them around this time, I would think about my family, my children and my friends and all that I could end up leaving behind me should this cancer finally outstrip and get the better of me.

'When they tell you that you have cancer, or as they are reluctant to use the word, when they imply that you have cancer,' I told Luke, 'you immediately feel that you are under sentence of death.'

'I can't imagine what it must be like.'

'You're conditioned to believe that cancer means death and the moment you have it then you are surely going to die. It is possible to get away from this and realise that cancer doesn't necessarily mean that you are going to die.'

'Of course it doesn't. Lots of people survive cancer, especially these days.'

'You can't not think like it though. I don't feel it all the time, but in my darkest moments I can't keep the thoughts out of my head and I worry about Mary and the kids. Worry about what they will have to do without me.'

'You don't have to worry about it. It isn't going to happen.'

'I wish I had your faith.'

The great musical composer Stephen Sondheim said that the legacy that you could leave behind on this world when you left was either children or art. These are the two things that we can leave behind us as memories of us when we have gone. Most of us will leave children behind us as our legacies. We teach them as they grow and it is our hope that they will go out into the world and carry on what we have taught them and with any luck improve upon what we did on our own lives and then pass it on to their children. In many ways children are the greatest thing that we can leave behind us when we go.

Art is the other thing that Sondheim believes that we can leave behind us as a true legacy when we have finally gone. Whether it is music, art, writing, or what you will it is something that if done right will survive the test of time. If you have the right ability to create something that is worth leaving behind then it will survive generations, even beyond when your children have come and gone, perhaps even passed the end of your line and on into immortality.

I wonder how many of the writers today will still be read and available one hundred or two hundred years from now. Certainly, I have felt that when it comes to music there are some that will not be listened to twenty years from now, let alone two hundred years from now.

Any of us that like to consider ourselves as artists cannot truly say if our work will survive though. It is our hope, maybe. But we don't necessarily think about it when we are in the creative process, not unless we are supremely arrogant; in which case our art probably doesn't deserve to survive.

I often wonder what Shakespeare would feel if he were able to see the huge industry that had sprung up around his work. Work which he had probably created whilst slaving over parchment with a scratchy pen by candlelight and fuelled by ale. Thinking only that this work would provide him with the necessities of food, lodging and drink until the next creative process came along.

What would Van Gogh think if he could now see the huge amounts of money that his paintings are sold for now when he struggled to sell any in his own lifetime? Would he think it ludicrous? Would he be annoyed that the value was not recognised in his own life time?

And what would Thomas Tallis think when he learnt that you could buy a CD of his music that he had written whilst watching Henry VIII split from the Catholic Church?

Would Dickens be amazed that his books were not only still read, but were frequently republished and adapted for stage and screen; or would he think that it was only right? He had after all managed to experience some of the fame and celebrity that his writing had brought him in his own life time?

Would any of these think that the work is more important than their own name? Would it annoy them that there are those that might know a particular strain of music without knowing that it was Mozart? Or that they might have heard about Oliver Twist without knowing that it was Dickens that wrote the book? Is it better for them that their work goes on or that their name goes on?

What about all of those that have fallen by the wayside? All those musicians, artists and writers that were unable to survive their own lifetime and make it to immortality, even if they had been famous at the time that they had lived. The Elizabethan age was rife with playwrights and yet now the majority would only be able to name Shakespeare. Others, smaller in number, could name you Christopher Marlowe or Ben Jonson, but what has happened to all the others that have been forgotten about?

What's my point? I will tell you.

No matter how great we might think we are there is no certainty of immortality through our work. It could all be for nothing. We will never know. However, if we are writing because we want immortality then we are in the wrong game. It certainly was not the reason why I wrote. I wrote because it was something that I felt that I had to do; and it was something that was done with no thought to what the future might behold.

I have no idea if my work will survive me, I have no idea if I will even have any work to leave behind me, but I know I am fortunate enough that I have Jessica and Joseph who can go on after I have left this earth and carry on their own lives. I suppose that the only thing that I could really pass onto them is the desire that they make their lives extraordinary. Live without regret. Make the most of what comes your way.

***

My trips to the hospital were lengthy and caused me a great deal of frustration and annoyance. I know that this is not the way that anyone would imagine their life going, so it is probably stupid of me to say that I hadn't of imagined that I would be wasting what remained of my youth away in a manner such as this.

That is the wonderful thing about cancer though, it will not discriminate against anyone; young or old; rich or poor; you are all the same as far as it's concerned. It is the great leveller.

I do feel that so much of my youth was wasted away in hospitals rather than doing the things that I should have been doing at my age; but we have no right to pick our destiny. We must accept whatever it is that is thrown at us.

You know you are in trouble though when you start to know all the nurses and call them by their first names, and they all know you as well. That is the terrible sign that you have been spending too much time within the sickly walls. I am sure that I was far from being alone in hating the place. I had never liked hospitals all that much before I had been sick, I could hardly say that my opinion had changed for the better at all.

Mary came with me on the initial visits, to see me settled into the routine and to make sure that I knew what I was doing. As always, she was well aware of the fact that I simply couldn't do a thing without her. After the first week though I shooed her back to work. We couldn't really afford both of us to be off work for the time that the therapy took to run its course. I was also helped out a lot by the nurses and it wasn't impossible to get a lift to and from the hospital when needed. I hated it when I had a taxi though and the stranger of a driver would talk in their pleasant enough way and ask why it was that I was going to the hospital, was I visiting someone or was it for some other reason, and then I would find myself having to go into the entire 'cancer story' thing rather than just lying or telling them to shut up and drive the car, which is really what I always wanted to say, but never actually found the courage to form the words.

I would like to say that the treatment passed me by quickly and before I knew it we were at the end of the therapy and the weeks had flown passed without me knowing anything about it. I would like to say this, but I would be lying to you if I did say it because it was far from true. It felt to me as if time was dragging along as slowly as my own feet were. The heavy weight was carried around my neck and I felt each passing moment of it as we crawled towards the end of the treatment.

Whatever else might happen I would be pleased when the damn therapy stopped. I might then actually start to feel some of the benefits that it had brought with it rather than all the negative side which is all I seemed to get at the moment. Once the treatment was finished there would be a cooling off period and then a few tests before going back to see what exciting things Doctor Moody would have to tell us.

'I am afraid that it's not good news.'

I had half been expecting it, if I am totally honest. Mary gripped my hand as he continued.

'The chemo was really the last thing that we could throw at it, but looking through all your scans it just doesn't seem to have worked at all and in fact the entire thing has spread.'

'Where is it? Can't you operate again? Cut it out?' I could see that Mary was grasping at straws slightly. Bizarrely, my own thoughts were on the poor doctor sitting in front of me. How horrid for him, I thought. What kind of job is it where you have to go and tell someone, maybe each day, that there is nothing that you can do for them and they are going to die? For, I had no doubt now, that was what he was telling me.

'It's spread too far. It's almost everywhere. An operation would be entirely impossible.'

'How long?' I was surprisingly shocked at how calm I was taking the entire situation, but maybe the last few years had been building this way and I had been fooling myself to think otherwise.

'I think we are talking a matter of weeks rather than of months, but if it were to be in terms of months, I don't think it's likely to be many months.'

I nodded my head, thinking once again what a terrible job he had to tell people this. No wonder that I had met so many doctors that seemed aloof and detached. Would you really want to get to know your patients only to have them die on you? It must be very depressing for him.

Many of us who have more 'routine' occupations don't always think about those that have jobs that are out of the ordinary from what we deal with all the time. It can't be easy for them.

Twenty-Eight

The way that I ended things there probably makes me sound like I am such a noble person that when I am handed a death sentence I care more for others than I did myself. It is partially true and partially a falsehood.

I did think to myself what a terrible job Doctor Moody and the tens of thousands of people like him had having to tell people that they were going to die. I imagined it must be hard to tell someone that a relative of theirs, or a loved one has died. That is one thing. I have never had to do it, but I can't imagine that it is the easiest thing in the world. If that isn't the easiest of tasks to perform then how difficult would it be to actually look someone in the eye and tell them that they are the ones that are going to die? There can't be that many people that have to do that other than doctors, and murderers, I suppose, but that would be an entirely different problem.

You might be thinking that I was taking this all in a very philosophical nature. You might think that this makes me a very well-adjusted human being; or you might think that I was cold and heartless. Perhaps there is a little bit of truth in both of them.

There was a period of crying and trying to adjust to what we had been told whilst we each held each other and thought about the future; or rather the lack of it; for me at least. We then reached a point where we both felt that it was necessary to be practical about things and to make use of the time that we had left with each other rather than wasting what little was left to us.

Psychologists would no doubt shake their heads and tut when I say that I didn't go through the grieving stage where I stood out in the pouring rain and shook my fists at the heavens and demanded to know 'why me?' It may seem very strange, but as I have said before, what is the point of asking why me? At least a third of us will be treated for cancer at some point in our lives, so the question could just as easily be 'why not me?' Nothing was to be gained by bemoaning the fact that the lottery of life had selected you for this.

The way that I saw it you were faced with two choices. Either you could ask why it was you that had been chosen and then lock yourself away and die in a pit of misery and self-pity; or you could shrug your shoulders and take the attitude that it had to happen to someone and then try and get on with your life and make the most of the little of it that was left. After all people died all the time.

One of the things that I decided to be practical about was to plan my own funeral. You can visit many of these places on websites that will allow you a plan to put into place for your final act. I had looked a little about what was available and then decided that I would go and pay a visit to my local funeral home. This was something that I decided to do on my own. I was sure that Mary would have come with me if I had asked her to, but I didn't think it was fair enough to go that far to make her have to go through that as well as everything else that she was going through.

I suppose I had suspected something to be along the lines of *The Addams Family* and I was very disappointed when I walked in the door of the funeral parlour and was not met by a seven-foot-tall butler who groaned at me. Instead, what I was met with was a reception area that looked like it could have come out of any business. The only concession that there appeared to be was that I realised that there was no music being played. I suppose that choosing the music to play in a place like this could have been rather difficult. It would be so easy for someone at their most vulnerable to be offended by the smallest of choices.

Sitting behind the reception desk was an extremely bored looking girl that looked like she would rather have been anywhere else in the world rather than where she was right now.

'Can I help you?' she asked when she eventually did see me standing there.

'I would like to see someone about arranging a funeral.'

'Do you have an appointment?'

'I'm sorry, I didn't know I needed one.'

'If you wait a moment I will see if there is someone who is free to talk to you then.' She disappeared into a back room to leave me staring at the neutral paintings that were on the walls, which again seemed to have been designed to not illicit an opinion that might be considered offensive. Eventually she returned and informed me that Mr Embling was free to see me, and was said in such a way to seem to suggest that I should be honoured that I was allowed to see him.

When I was shown into his small office I was reassured to see that Mr Embling appeared to be more of the cliché that I was expecting from a funeral parlour. He was suited although had removed his jacket and was down to his waistcoat from which there hung a mighty gold chain which I assumed was attached to a pocket watch. It looked so massive that I was rather concerned that in the right hands it could easily have been used as an offensive weapon.

He rose from behind his desk to shake my hand as we introduced ourselves. His hand was clammy and from the look of his long, drawn face he certainly seemed to be the kind of person who really knew what the word 'insomnia' meant.

'I understand that you want to arrange a funeral?' It was a reasonable assumption, given where I was.

'Yes, I do.'

'A loved one?'

'You could say that. It's for me.'

Embling nodded his head and folded his fingers together. He didn't seem shocked by this piece of information so I assumed that it was not an unusual thing for the living to turn up to arrange their own funerals.

'It is a wise choice. Funeral costs go up every year. It makes sense to have some kind of plan in place to beat the rising costs of inflation. The average cost of a funeral is £3,500 these days, in a few years it could easily be double that.'

'I don't think I will have to worry about inflation all that much.'

'You seem a little young for a funeral plan though, if you don't mind me saying, Mr McKenzie.'

'I have terminal cancer.'

'I see.'

To his credit he didn't say he was sorry which was what most people did when you told them this as if it was in some way something that they were to blame for. Then again perhaps he wasn't sorry. After all his business did rather rely on people dying. Nor did he seem particular phased by the fact that he was talking to someone that he would soon have as a customer in every sense of the word. It struck me that Mr Embling was someone who was unlikely to be phased by anything. I imagined that this was something that probably brought comfort to some of the grieving family members that he usually had sitting where I was.

With a swift, well-practiced movement he fanned out three A4 sized pamphlets in front of me across his desk. He had clearly done this a lot before and as well as knowing his trade was good at the showmanship side of things.

'There are three basic packages that we do,' he said as he indicated each of the glossy pamphlets in front of me. 'The basic package through to the deluxe to the super deluxe package, each of which will cater to everything that you could possibly need.'

I should point out here that I did have something of an issue with undertakers and the general funeral business. First of all, it seemed to me that all 'you could possibly need' was to be stuck in a hole in the ground or a furnace. What I really didn't like about them was the parasitic way that they preyed on society when it was at its most vulnerable. When he had quoted £3,500 for the cost of a funeral I knew that he was talking a very basic end of the scale and you could end up spending a lot more money on them.

There were some who were of the opinion that you should shell out because it was the last thing that you could possibly do for your loved one, but I was of the opinion that you would be better off spending as little money as you could and then blowing it on something that you really wanted. I would rather Mary spent three and a half grand on taking herself and the kids somewhere hot for a holiday rather than pissing it up the wall.

'Perhaps we should start with coffins,' continued Mr Embling, which was ironic I suppose as that was what most people ended with rather than started with. 'There is the simple coffin, which is very basic,' he showed me a photograph. 'Then there is the next up which is the quality wood effect coffin.' Likewise, a photograph appeared. 'Finally, there is the high-quality veneer coffin, which I am sure you will agree looks marvellous.'

'Yes, it does.' I had to agree. It did look marvellous. 'Not much point in something that looks so nice that you are either going to bury and never see again, or set fire to though, is it?'

'Well, that is one way of looking at it, I suppose.' Mr Embling was nothing but charm, however I could see from the look on his face that he was disgusted that I was one of these cheapskates that wasn't prepared to spend out the cash,

'I don't suppose you have anything below the basic, simple coffin, do you?'

'Such as? A bin liner?'

'Perhaps.'

'Don't worry, sir. Just my dry sense of humour. If it is cheap you are looking for then I am afraid that they don't come much cheaper than this.'

'Well, I suppose I had better have it then, hadn't I?'

'Indeed. You mentioned burial. Is that what you had in mind, or were you preferring cremation?'

This was a very good point and something that I had discussed at length with Mary in the past, and not just when I knew that the decision to choose was more urgent than it was before. I think it is important to discuss these things. Many of us don't like talking about death as if not talking about it will somehow mean that it won't happen. The problem is that if we don't talk about it then it will mean that when we are taken by surprise in death we will leave behind a partner who hasn't got a clue about what we want done.

I had debated the merits of burial and cremation for some time. It was a surprisingly difficult decision. Initially I had been all for burial. It seemed to be the more natural way. I felt that until I watched a television programme where they documented the lack of space that there was for burials and how it was becoming a real problem which would only get worse in the future as more people were buried in a premium space.

You realised that the belief that you were being returned to the soil for eternity was not the case. The chances were that in a hundred or so years they were going to either dig you up and move you elsewhere; or something that I found even more worrying they would inter someone else with you. I grant you that you were dead so what would you care, but I didn't really fancy the idea of having some stranger stuck in there with me.

What I also didn't like was the fact that you might be buried alive. I suppose medical science had moved on rather a lot since the days of Edgar Allen Poe, but there was still the chance that you might wake up and find yourself buried alive. It was probably at that point that you would have wished that you had gone for the veneer coffin.

With cremation there was always the chance of being burned alive, I suppose, but at least it was something that would ultimately be quicker than being buried alive. As there didn't seem to be much chance that I would become such a famous writer in the short space of time that was left to me that Mary would be getting a call from Westminster Abbey saying that they had reserved a spot for me in Poet's Corner, I decided that I would opt for a basic cremation. Which seemed to me to be even more of a reason why I should have a basic coffin.

'Obviously there will be a hearse,' continued Mr Embling.

'Yes, I suppose so, but let's make it basic shall we, none of this horses, plumes and coaches stuff.'

'Of course, although we can do that for you if you would like.'

'No, I wouldn't, thank you.'

'What about other limousines for family and close friends.'

'No, I don't think so.'

'Very well. For the basic package we can provide one for your widow.'

I was still thinking of her as my wife, so to hear her described as my widow was something of a surprise, and strangely irritating.

'What about flowers?'

'Oh, something basic for the coffin, but nothing else, nothing elaborate. It is only a waste of money, they will die off eventually.'

'Perhaps you would like people to donate money to a charity instead?'

'Yes, perhaps that isn't a bad idea.'

'What about the service itself? Will it be religious?'

I had thought a lot about this and I will share my thought process on that later.

'Non-religious.'

'No hymns then. Perhaps songs?'

'Yes, not a bad idea.'

'Do you have any in mind?'

'Yes. How many should I have?'

'Well, you can have one for people to enter to, one for the main service, if you wish and an exit song.'

'Okay, I think I will have *Return to Sender* by Elvis Presley, *Light My Fire* by The Doors and *Another One Bites the Dust* by Queen.'

I had said that I didn't think that Mr Embling was the type to be phased, but he seemed to be totally phased by this.

'Are you certain?'

'Yes, I think so.'

It may sound like I was being frivolous, but I had discussed it with Mary and decided that I would rather people smiled and laughed at my funeral than sitting there looking sad and crying.

My planning with Mr Embling didn't last much longer after that as he had clearly decided that I was something of a lost cause and he just completed the package as best as he could.

Clearly as he ushered me out of his office he was hoping that his next customer would be more obliging.

***

'It isn't how I imagined I would go,' I told Luke when we chatted a few days after I had told him the news.

I have mentioned before that when you are told that you have cancer, the first thing that goes through your head is that you are going to die. Gradually though you allow yourself to have a degree of faith in the medical community and feel that you might actually get through this thing and come out the other side. It has always lurked in the back of my head though that this day would come when no matter what they had done to help me it would all come to nothing.

What's my point? I will tell you.

I had become somewhat conditioned to the inevitable in my own mind. It was the way that others reacted which was the most bizarre thing to watch. I ended up spending most of my time comforting them over the news when they should really have been comforting me. I didn't feel that I needed comforting though.

'No, I don't suppose it is.' Luke looked more miserable than I was.

'Do you remember me telling you about my old English teacher?'

'Yes. Mr Jones, wasn't it?'

'Yes. He died recently.'

'I'm sorry to hear that. What happened?'

'Alzheimer's.'

'Ah.'

'I got to know his wife a little bit during his final decline. Do you know what she told me?'

'No idea.'

'She said he never lost his sense of humour. He retained that for as long as he was possibly able. He treated his illness as a joke. She told me that when he was first diagnosed with Alzheimer's he told his wife to go out and buy him a complete Superman outfit.'

'Why?'

'He wanted to hang it in the wardrobe.'

'Why would he want to do that?'

'He said he wanted to fuck with his own mind later on when he started losing his memory. When he would open the wardrobe and not know why it was there and think that he really was Superman.'

I learnt a lot from Mr Jones, and it wasn't all about literature.

***

I have tried to develop a philosophy in my life that when it comes time to leave it I would have no regrets about anything. Granted I regretted that my time to leave had come a lot earlier than I thought it was going to be and I would have liked to have had a few more decades to spend with my family, but we don't get to choose these things in life.

I was very much aware of the fact that I was missing seeing my children grow up and finding out what kind of adults they would become, what dreams they would live to aspire to. I was missing the time that I would have to spend with Mary. We had married expecting to be together into our old age and I was leaving her to spend so much time on her own. She would probably live longer without me now than she had with me.

I also knew that all those ideas I had for novels and stories would remain unwritten now. There seemed to be so little time left and yet so much that I wanted to do.

I debated whether or not to tell work that I was diagnosed as terminal. I knew that a return to work was out of the question now. Even if I felt well enough to return to work I had no intention of doing so now as I would view it as a waste of the time that I had left. I thought that there was a possibility that they might decide to dismiss me on hearing that I was dying, but then I thought that if they did they would find themselves all over the front page of *The Daily Mail* and I think that they realised that dismissing someone for dying of cancer was tantamount to suicide.

It came as no real surprise to me that Mrs Van Hopper was made more permanent on a temporary basis. Presumably they were waiting for me to actually die before they replaced me completely. Mrs Van Hopper assumed that she would have it all sown up in the bag and would make her position permanent, but I had my doubts. She couldn't just walk into the job, she would have to apply for the position and be interviewed and I can't imagine that she would find it a walk over.

She had spent a lot of time complaining about the things that I was doing in the library and she had made it clear that she was more interested in going backwards than she was forwards. I found it rather amusing and thought it highly unlikely that she was likely to get the job. I wish that I could be around to see the look on her face when she was passed over again.

I had the unfortunate misfortune of meeting Mrs Van Hopper for what I assumed would be the last time when I returned to the library to clear out the last of my belongings.

'Mr McKenzie,' she always made it sound like she was sniffing a turd whenever she said my name.

'Mrs Van Hopper.'

'I hear that you are going to die.'

'Bluntly put, but accurate.'

'I told you that you would reap the fruits of what you sowed. How do you feel now that you are standing so close to your maker? It isn't too late to convert your ways and repent your lifestyle.'

I sighed deeply. She really was the most obnoxious woman that I could ever imagine being likely to meet in my entire life.

'I think you are the one who needs to worry about what will happen when you stand in front of your God. In the meantime, why don't you just fuck off?'

Okay, so I am a writer and I should have come up with something more cutting and barbed to hit her with as I walked out of the office, but I was so very tired. So very drugged up on all the pain killers and crap that they were feeding me with that I didn't have the energy to come up with anything at all.

As I walked out through the library for the very last time I plucked a copy of the Bible off the shelf and tossed it into the children's section as I passed. It is the small acts of rebellion that can count so much in life.

Twenty-Nine

The subject of religion has come up and it has appeared in a number of forms throughout this account, it is only fair that I give my attention to it now.

I know that there are many people who turn to religion when they know that their life is nearing its end. I suppose that this is because of the fact that there is nothing to lose at that point.

The philosopher Pascal tells us of what has become known as Pascal's Wager. Namely the decision on whether or not we should believe in God. In a nutshell it states that if we don't believe in God and when we die we find out that there is no God then we have lost nothing. However, if we don't believe in God and when we die we find out that there is a God then you might argue that we are going to be in big trouble. The wager is, therefore, that it is safer to believe in God as you have nothing to lose and everything to win by believing in Him.

The obvious problem with that is that you can't force yourself to believe in something. You either do or you don't and if you try and pretend that you believe in God when you don't, well that's fine unless it turns out that there is a God and He is going to see right through you.

Many will tell you, therefore, that you can't rationalise yourself into a belief in something like God, or a Supreme Being if you prefer. It is a matter for faith rather than intellect. The thing that I have always found about faith though is that you can shoot it down with all the intellectual arguments in the world that blow it rationally to pieces and all the other person has to say is that they have faith for none of it to have meant anything. Seems rather pointless if you ask me.

As the observant reader will remember I had talked about the possibility of a religious life when I had been younger, but it was something that I had grown out of. God was someone that was clumped together with other childhood myths such as Father Christmas, the Tooth Fairy and the Bogeyman.

Religion had previously made me feel that I could belong somewhere and be part of something, whereas as I became older I began to realise that being part of something was considerably less important than having your own individuality and independence.

I lost my interest in religion as I grew older. It no longer seemed to make sense to me any longer. It would do me no good to pretend to believe in God if I felt within myself that there really wasn't a God. I will be honest and say that I did think about religion a little more when I was told that I didn't have all that much longer to live, I would have been strange if I had not done so, I suppose.

I grew away from Christianity because it had become too unbelievable and fantastical for me. It just didn't make any sense when you got down to it. I suppose that a lot of faith in the Church had been rocked by their various attitudes to things as well.

What's my point? I will tell you.

I think the best thing that happened to this country was the formation of the Church of England. When Henry VIII split with Rome he did us all a favour. Steered us away from incredible bad judgements from the Catholic Church.

What bad judgements? I will tell you, but a few. How about the desire to make Sir Thomas More a martyr and a saint because he had stood against the split from Rome? All well and good if you take it to one side that More was also a murderer who tortured people who had turned against Rome and were preaching such things as allowing the Bible to be translated in English. Something that appeared sufficient for him to feel that you could be burnt alive for doing. Not very saintly was it?

More was also the man who was responsible for kick starting the tennis table game of burning. He burnt people because they refused to accept the might of Rome. Queen Mary came to the throne and decided that she would burn so many Protestants that she earned herself the nickname "bloody Mary". In her turn Elizabeth tried to bat it back to the Catholics by burning a few of them in her own turn. Yet it seemed to me that the Catholics tried to claim that they were the ones who were hard done by. I went to visit an old stately home once and got into an argument with one of the volunteers.

'Here we see a Priest Hole that was used for Catholic priests to hide in when the agents of the Queen came to arrest them and persecute them for practicing their religion.'

'This was a religion that also preached that it was acceptable, indeed a required and rewarding thing for Queen Elizabeth to be murdered for being a Protestant?'

'Everyone has the right to practice their own religion.'

'And yet, many of the Catholic priests that hid in holes like that one had come secretly into the country to ferment rebellion and see the murder of the monarch and to have their own religion forced back onto the country.'

The volunteer had sniffed deeply at me and given me a look of disgust that was clearly designed to make me feel like I was insignificant for daring to have an opinion against the one true religion.

It wasn't just the Tudors that had caused a problem. What about the silence over the Holocaust from the Pope? What about the almost daily reveal of Catholic priests that had turned out to be paedophiles or sex offenders in some way? I began to see it as virtually impossible to defend such a religion against anything.

It wasn't just Catholicism and Protestants. All religions seemed pitted against each other. Jew killing Muslim, Muslim killing Jew and so on. I rapidly came to the conclusion that none of it was really worth anything. God could exist. I don't think that there is anyone who can firmly state that God doesn't exist. We just don't know for certain. Whether God exists or doesn't exist is really immaterial though. Religion is the invention of Man. Most of the trappings that come with religion are things that you could cut away with and get rid of without losing a central belief in a God.

Nevertheless, whatever the arguments for and against I just didn't feel like I could believe in any form of organised religion. I did briefly toy with the idea of Buddhism. It seemed like a very respectable philosophy of a way to live your life. The problem that I immediately found was that I became angry far too quickly and was far too intolerant of others to be able to really be a successful Buddhist. The calmer life would have been great and would have appealed enormously, but it was never going to be the case for me.

The thing is that whether you believe in it or not you can't get away from the fact that religion is all around us. It is on television, it's in the architecture around us; most of us are probably brought up with a certain degree of it. We can't fully escape from it. But the real problem that I have with religion is all the bad things that are done in its name.

All the people that are killed because someone else believes something else. Religion is a free ticket to ethnic cleansing. It depresses me more than most other things in life. People fight wars over their religious beliefs. People take to the streets with machine guns to kill those who mock their religion or who are different from them. Religion breeds intolerance, and yet when you strip it down they are all basically saying the same thing and the undiluted, un-interpreted message is one of good and of peace.

Everyone has got it so wrong. I think there are times when we are too far down the road for people to put the brakes on and realise what the hell they are doing. The future doesn't involve flying planes into skyscrapers or blowing up Underground trains. That is no future for anyone. Least of all those who think that it is what their religion is telling them to do. It would better not to have a religious belief than to believe the preaching of hatred and intolerance.

***

A belief or non-belief in religion doesn't necessarily mean that you can believe or not believe in an afterlife. You can believe that there is a world that goes on after you die without believing necessarily that it involves big pearly gates and a man with a long white beard surrounded by people with wings and harps. I read a great deal about near death experiences, or NDEs as they were often referred as.

A lot of people will tell you straight off the bat that they don't believe in NDEs and that those that claim to have experienced one are just suffering from a delusion of the brain. It is an interesting subject worthy of exploration.

First of all, they do seem to follow the same pattern. People who have returned from an NDE state that they feel like they are travelling down a long tunnel. Sometimes the tunnel has light within its walls and at other times it is blank. They state that they move towards a light at the end of the tunnel which often involves a figure of light standing there. It is more than just an angel as some would have us believe it. It is a figure of pure light which brings with it feelings of peace, happiness and love.

In some cases, the reported figure of light is said to have been a deceased family member that meets the newly departed to comfort them with perhaps a feeling of familiarity. God alone knows who is going to be visiting me when I die then.

People return from the experience saying that they experienced these feelings very clearly and intently. The figure of light conducts the individual that has 'died' on a journey of their own life. I suppose this is where people recounting that their life has passed before their lives might come into it.

It is this account of life passing before your eyes that most interests me. From all of the accounts that I have read it is a judgement. The recently deceased, for want of a better word, is judged on their own life, but it is not the figure of light or anyone else that is judging them. You judge yourself. With no falsehood, pretence or ability to make excuses over the actions that have been taken, you view things exactly as they are, or were; and exactly as you were, or are.

How do your judge yourself? Well this is the bit that I really like the sound of. You watch all the events of your life over again, all the things that you did and didn't do, but you see and experience them through the eyes of all the people that you encountered. So, if you have hurt someone you will get to experience their pain and their suffering from the actions that you have taken.

You will get to experience the good things as well as the bad things, the love you have given as well as the pain that you have caused. You will experience it all again through the senses of those that you did it to.

Once you have viewed your judgement you will be led to what many describe as the 'point of no return'. Beyond that point you can no longer return to life. Beyond that stage is where the afterlife will truly start, where you have been purged from the mistakes and the pain of your life.

Nobody knows what lies beyond that stage, of course, on account of the fact that they have never been able to come back and talk about it.

It is at that stage that you have the last chance to return to the normal life or continue into the afterlife. At least I am assuming that you don't always have the choice at this stage, sometimes it might be possible to choose to return to finish your life, say for instance you have been in a coma and this is the point where you return to life and awaken from the coma. However, I am assuming that if, for instance, this is all taking place after you have just had your head cut off then you don't really have all that much choice when it comes to moving passed the point of no return or returning to your earthly body.

The most interesting thing about all of this though is those that have returned. Almost entirely without fail those who have returned no longer have an interest in material things. The pursuit of money that occupies so many of us suddenly becomes of far less importance than it was before you 'died'. These returned people also seem to go about their business with more of a concern about how they treat others. Perhaps after you have seen such a thing as your life through the eyes of others you will, upon your return, think more carefully about what you do and how you treat people.

Why wait though? Why does it take this experience to make you want to lead a less materialistic led world where you always try and do the right thing? Do we really have to die before we realise where we are going wrong? Why can't we make the change now?

What is doubly interesting to me is the fact that these NDEs are non-specific to religion or a belief. It doesn't seem to matter what you believe in while you are alive. When you die it is all as one. I suppose this reinforces my belief that religion is chiefly the invention of Man.

Numerous 'scientific' people have tried to explain away all of these experiences. It seems to me that the greatest problem that people of science have is that they just can't accept something as being real unless they can explain away how it works or why it is. Where is the mystery in life? What happened to the magic?

These scientific people just cannot believe that NDEs happen because they are impossible to explain. A collective hallucination is obviously rubbish as so many people from all over the world have experienced them. They then try and explain them away by saying that they are caused by a chemical reaction in the brain.

This raises some interesting questions. They say that as you 'die' the brain releases chemicals which allow for this illusion to take place and that it is not real. Not a shadow of proof to support this, of course. What is fascinating is that the doctors and scientists state that if NDEs are experienced because of chemical reactions in the brain then they are not real. They should be discounted then.

Depression is something that happens because of a chemical reaction in the brain. Does that mean it isn't real? How would you react if you went to see your GP and told them that you had depression and they replied that depression was just an illusion caused by a chemical reaction in the brain and that you were to pay it no mind and stop wasting their time?

I have no idea whether any of this is true or not. I know that there are many who cling to the idea of an afterlife out of desperation. They cannot accept that their life will come to an end and that there will be nothing but blackness afterwards. They cannot accept that there will be an end to it all and that this is all that there is. What is it all worth if one day it just all goes black and there is no explanation? They simply *have* to believe that it is all about something and will continue on with the fading of this world.

I can understand this view. What I cannot understand is those that actually believe this who then go about pissing their life away. If you really belief that this is all that there is then shouldn't you make more of it then you do?

These people will say that if you have an NDE it is because you desperately hope that there is an afterlife and so you imagine it for yourself. It is almost impossible to fight against these people because they have made their mind up and that is it.

Do I believe in an afterlife? I don't know. I wish I did, but I simply don't know. I would like to believe that there is a continuation after all of this that we experience now. I would like to think that there is some great purpose to it all. I would like to believe all of this, but I have no idea whether any of it is true or not. We won't know until such time as we stand on the threshold of the discovery ourselves. It would seem that

I am going to find out the answer a little earlier than I had expected to have.

***

I don't know whether there is an afterlife or whether there is a God, I do believe that the two don't have to rely on the other in order to exist. What I do know is that it shouldn't require an NDE to make you appreciate life, or to treat your fellow humans better.

You do get those who say that they don't believe in such a place as Hell, that when we die we all go to Heaven no matter how much of an evil sadistic arsehole we have been whilst on the planet.

'It doesn't matter,' one of these people who believe such stuff, once said to me, 'God forgives us all and makes us all equal when we die.'

'Well, that's rather disappointing.'

'Not disappointing at all. It's because God loves all of us you see. We are all children of God.'

'I would imagine it must be rather disappointing to have lived a life like Ghandi did or maybe Mother Teresa only to find out that when you die you are on the same level as Hitler.'

They didn't have an answer to this, but personally I wanted nothing to do with a Heaven where I was going to have to stand in line at the canteen next to Hitler and Margaret Thatcher. What I was personally hoping for was that when you died and arrived at the pearly gates, Hitler was strung up against the arches in an X shape and St Peter was there to welcome you all in saying 'Wanna free kick of him in the bollocks before you come in? Be my guest.'

The last thing I wanted was to turn up and have St Peter say: 'I'm ever so sorry, we are a bit short of room at the moment what with all the wars and so on. I hope you don't mind, but we've put you up with Mr Hitler. He's not all that bad really once you get to know him. Try and steer him away from politics if you can and don't mention the moustache and you will probably get along just fine.'

People like to go around saying that they don't believe in Hell because they want to appear nice as if to say 'look at me I am such a nice person that I don't even wish to have my enemies go to Hell.' These are the kind of people who usually stay like this until one day they flip and massacre everyone that they know.

It's a philosophical certainty, if you have one thing then you have to have the other in order to balance it out and bring order to the universe. You can't have a Heaven without a Hell. Back in the Middle Ages through the Tudor period priests would have to believe that you would go to Hell for just about anything from farting to self-pleasuring, as they would no doubt call it.

I don't think so. I don't believe that you are going to Hell just because you like to have a wank. If that were the case then there wouldn't be a lot of people in Heaven, would there? No, you can go to Hell for the big crimes, the murderers and the sex fiends. These are the ones that go to Hell, which ironically means that it must be full of a lot of Catholic priests rubbing shoulders with mass murderers.

That is what I find the most difficult about religion. How can you be a priest or someone like that and then go about absolving people when they confess murder to you and committing sex crimes against children *and* still stand there and preach to everyone that they are going to Hell if they break the Sabbath. I mean WTF?

***

What I really find annoying is those that are wasting life. There are so many of them about, I am sure that you must know one or two of them yourself. People that are wasting their days and throwing away their very existence. I know that I have so little time left to me and yet they go around wasting time, wasting love, doing all the things that mean so little and yet they will probably live long lives which will ultimately add up to nothing.

Make every day count. Treat every night as if it was your first and every day as if it were your last and I don't think that you can go too far wrong. There are just not enough people who choose to live by this philosophy though. You can't make people make the most of their lives. If people realised how precious each second of the day was though then they might decide to make the most of it. None of us know when the seconds will run out and we will be left with nothing of this existence left to us.

Make the most of it. I can't stress it enough. It is a time old saying that you never miss what you've got until it's gone. Well try it with life.

There is so much that I want to do, and there is so little time left now. I feel so tired for the greater part. It is hard when your mind wants to continue, but your body just can't cope with it. I suppose I was doing the opposite of what Mr Jones had experienced. A capable body that ended with a mind that had gone.

'How will it end?' I had asked Doctor Moody. I hadn't really wanted to put him on the spot, but I felt that I needed to know.

'It is difficult to say. The decline may be fast in which case you may succumb suddenly to cardiac arrest.'

'Or it might be slow?' asked Mary who I thought was putting on an amazing show of coping with all of this. Not for the first time I wondered how much of it was for my benefit.

'It might.'

'And how will that work?'

'The tumours within you will spread further and further until there is more tumour in you than there is anything else. You will be hospitalised, almost certainly, and it will probably be that you reach a stage where you are simply unable to breathe any longer.'

'He'll suffocate?'

'He will be medicated so much by then that he won't know anything about it or feel any pain.'

'Well, that's something, I suppose.'

I suppose it was.

Thirty

So, you may look over all of this, particular my sermonising of things and you may ask what's my point?

I will tell you.

I suppose that I have now realised that amongst some fragments of poems and a little bit left of a play this is the main body of my work that I have written. There is the bulk of an unfinished novel, which I know will never be finished and there is the bit of a short story here and there that can all be dug out from off my USB sticks, but this makes the most of what I have written.

In many regards it's my legacy. From the point of view of literature at least and I am stretching the point when I use the word literature. I have worked hard to create this because it is something that I will leave Jessica and Joseph. Something for them to remember their dad by, when I've long gone. They are my real legacy, of course, but this is also for them. Something for them to read and understand why things were the way that they were. With that in mind I have asked my dad to write a few words from his point of view so that I can include them within his pages. He hasn't done it yet, God knows when or if he will ever get them done.

'I'm not much of a writer,' he moaned at me when I put the task to him.

'Maybe not, but give it a go. It would be interesting to view things from your point of view.'

That was some time ago that I asked him to do that, and he hasn't done it yet. Maybe he is hoping that I will forget about it. I have also included the pages from my mother's journal so that we can see things from her side. I have deliberately not edited the passages from before I found out about my mother. Nor have I edited the events before I found out that my father was still alive. I thought it was best to have it raw and to share the opinions and thoughts that I had as I went along.

As I mentioned last time I have thought a lot about religion, but I have also thought a lot about the meaning of life. I suppose it matters to me more than it did that there is a meaning of life. I do like to think that there is some meaning behind it all.

As corny as it may sound one of the things that I really can't promote enough is love. I have loved many things in my life.

I love Mary. I can't do without her and I wouldn't want to do without her. She is my life. The first girl that I have ever loved and the only one that I have ever loved. You might think that is boring, but it is wonderful. She is my marvellous girl and the only thing that I regret about her is that I will be leaving her so soon. I can only imagine how she will feel. I know that I would find life very difficult without her and I regret the level of pain that she will be feeling when I am gone. I wish that there was something that I could do to make things easier for her.

I will not experience the grief of mourning a partner as she will. The cynical people will tell you that it is just part of life. Death is part of life and that is the way that things go. She may move on, of course, find someone else and marry again. I can't blame her if she were to do so, she has forty or more years ahead of her without me and that is a long time to be on your own. I wouldn't resent her if she did meet someone else, just so long as she was happy.

As I said before, I don't know if there is an afterlife, but if there is, and if there is any way that I can do it then I will look over her, look after her, until the day when we finally get back together again.

Then there is the love that I have for my children Jessica and Joseph. If I can watch over them then I will as well. I would love to watch them grow and to follow their dreams and make something of their lives. Jessica has grown into a fine young girl with a keen mind. She loves reading books and appears to have inherited the love of reading that her parents share. Joseph is still so young that I hardly know him and I know that when he grows he will probably not remember anything of me at all, accept for a vague distant memory, if I am lucky.

The last really big love affair that I have had in my life is that of reading and writing. When Doctor Moody told me that there was a possibility that I could die, medicated up to my eyeballs in a sterile hospital bed I cringed. The thought of dying is bad enough on its own. The thought of dying in such an environment was a terrible idea. I wanted to die amongst the books that I have collected all of my life in my own home.

That creates an issue. From a purely selfish point of view I want to die at home. I want to die surrounded by my books and my family and friends. Surrounded by the people and the things that I have loved. I don't want to die in the anonymous environment of a hospital with nothing familiar around me, where I might die with either nobody present or with some unknown nurse, that despite her best efforts to convince me otherwise, doesn't really care all that much that I am dying.

On the other side of the coin there is the fact that whilst dying at home might be more pleasing for me, it will be a burden for my family. Mary is the one who will have to provide my medication, feed me, clean me and do all the other things that a nurse would do for me. Do I have the right to impose that kind of life on her? That certainly can't be the best thing for her. Not only because of the pressure that it will place on her, but that her last memories of me will be cleaning up my own poo, which is not something that I would really like her to remember me by.

Chances are though that it will not be a choice that I will be able to make. The ultimate decision might very well be taken out of my hands entirely and I will end as I end. I probably won't even know that it is the end, either because it is so quick that I am gone with a snap of the fingers or because I am too medicated to know anything anyway.

I was talking about the meaning of life though. I have given it a lot of thought and I have realised that I do know what the meaning of life is. It isn't something that is Earth shatteringly brilliant that will change the world as you know it. It is the simplest of things that could ever be.

What's my point? I will tell you.